"PURE SUSPENSE."
Boston Globe

"SMART AND EXCITING."
Chicago Tribune

"[A] ROLLER COASTER RIDE."
Denver Post

"FIENDISHLY CLEVER."
Providence Journal

"MESMERIZING."
Albany Times-Union

"REED ARVIN IS THE REAL DEAL."
Harlan Coben

Books by Reed Arvin

BLOOD OF ANGELS
THE LAST GOODBYE
THE WILL

REED ARVIN

BLOOD OF ANGELS

HarperTorch

An Imprint of HarperCollinsPublishers

This is a work of fiction. Names, characters, places, and incidents are products of the author's imagination or are used fictitiously and are not to be construed as real. Any resemblance to actual events, locales, organizations, or persons, living or dead, is entirely coincidental.

HARPERTORCH
An Imprint of HarperCollins*Publishers*
10 East 53rd Street
New York, New York 10022-5299

Copyright © 2005 by Reed Arvin
ISBN-13: 978-0-06-059635-4
ISBN-10: 0-06-059635-X

First HarperTorch paperback printing: June 2006
First HarperCollins hardcover printing: July 2005

HarperCollins®, HarperTorch™, and ❦™ are trademarks of Harper-Collins Publishers Inc.

Printed in the United States of America

Visit HarperTorch on the World Wide Web at www.harpercollins.com

10 9 8 7 6 5 4 3 2 1

jɔŋdit dụnạrịr

your spirit is great

abiceŋ athɛɛr

it will live forever

ACKNOWLEDGMENTS

GRATEFUL THANKS ARE EXTENDED to Tom Thurmon, assistant district attorney of Davidson County; Laura Dykes, assistant public defender; Dr. Currie Myers, Ph.D; Jennifer Thomas; Dick Augustus; the entire staff at Brushy Mountain Prison; Randy Tatel with the Coalition to Abolish State Killing; and Dr. David Alfery, who assisted with many medical details. Also helpful were Bruce Benjamin and John Newton in the Material Science Division of EMSL Analytical. Thanks as well to the band Switchfoot, whose music inspired during the writing of this book. A line of homage is buried in these pages.

Thanks to the extraordinary Jane Dystel, Miriam Goderich, and Marjorie Braman. True professionals, all. Also, thanks to Mom and Dad, great supporters through thick and thin. And most of all, thanks to Dianne, the love of my life.

Much respect to the many lost boys of Sudan who honored me with their personal stories of courage. To sit in their living rooms and hear of their lives was an inestimable privilege. This book is dedicated to them. To learn more about their extraordinary story or to donate to their cause, go to http://www.crs.org/.

CHAPTER
ONE

I AM THE ASSISTANT district attorney of Davidson County, Tennessee, and on May 18, 2004, I killed Wilson Owens. He was determined, and I was willing. We were like lovers, in that way. Wilson pursued me with a string of petty thefts and miscellaneous criminal acts—working his way through his lesser loves—until he could wait for our union no longer. On that day—three years, two months, and eleven days before his own death—Owens killed Steven Davidson, the manager of the Sunshine Grocery Store in east Nashville. The moment Wilson's bullet entered Davidson's chest, the dance between us began.

I mention these names because it's important in my line of work that they are remembered. Both are dead, and both are lamented by their families. Ironically, both have gravestones in the same cemetery, Roselawn Memorial Gardens, in east Nashville; Wilson is buried underneath a flat, nondescript stone inscribed only with his name and the duration of his life. A hundred and fifty yards away, Davidson lies beneath an ornate, marble monument paid for by his numerous friends, fellow churchgoers, and family.

Wilson was what society calls a bad man. The truth, as usual, is more complex. What is certain is that his life went off the rails as a teenager, when his father—a man to whom the notion of family responsibility was as alien as a day without alcohol—took a final uppercut at his mother and walked out the door. From those sullen seeds Wilson grew, nurtured in the subculture of the Nashville projects, until he emerged, at eighteen years old, already twice a father, already once a felon. His destiny was sealed, as was mine.

I was born to kill Wilson Owens as surely as he was born to be my victim. This is clear only in retrospect, of course. When I was growing up in Wichita, Kansas, the son of a civilian airplane mechanic who worked at McConnell Air Force Base, the idea that I would one day kill a man was as distant from my mind as India. My father's world was full of wrenches, grease, and secondhand tales of pilot braggadocio. I loved that world nearly as much as I loved my father. In those days of blissfully low security, I would ride my bike from home to the base, wave at the bored guards, and screech to a halt outside hangar 3, where my father worked. I would watch him clamber inside one of the huge General Electric engines hanging under the wing of a tanker, or, perched on his shoulders, I would peer inside the still-warm tailpipe of an F-15 fighter. He and the other workers wore flattop haircuts, black shoes, and the gray coveralls of Faris Aircraft, the company that subcontracted the overflow aircraft maintenance work at the base. I wore my hair the same way, even though in the early eighties this had all the cachet of a funeral director. It didn't matter. To identify with my father and the easygoing men of his world was all that mattered.

My mother lived in an entirely different world, one which

I generally viewed with suspicion. A legal secretary, she worked in the grandly named but decrepit Century Plaza Building, an aging structure with noisy plumbing and elevators with doors that had to be manually pulled shut. The few times I went there—no more than five or six in my entire childhood—confirmed to me that the world of suits, ties, and paper-pushing was greatly inferior to the vibrant, masculine world of my father. My father's coworkers were muscular, told dirty jokes, and had eyes that sparkled when they roughhoused. The men of my mother's world all seemed slick, dark-haired, and smiling with secret agendas. That my mother seemed so completely at home in this world haunted me then, and now that I occupy the same world myself, haunts me still. To my surprise, I am more my mother's son than my father's, although physically I am his younger picture. I have his photograph before me now, as I sit at my desk at the DA's office on a gray, August afternoon. He is bare-chested, his wide-open smile pointed at the camera, a cigarette in his left hand, ready to fix any airplane that happens to roll by. Looking at his smile, I can almost believe he could fix the world.

On the day he died—having fallen thirty-eight feet from the wing of an AC-130 Hercules onto the griddle-hot asphalt beneath the plane, breaking his neck as cleanly as a chicken's wishbone—the world as I had known it ceased to exist. I spent the next year or so trying to bring him back, which my current profession has long since taught me is impossible. But at eighteen, the answer to my problems seemed to involve smoking a good deal of dope, drinking beer, and arguing with my mother over the direction of my life. Predictably, I wanted to join the military. She wanted me to go to college and become a lawyer. The compromise was inevitable: I agreed to go to college if I could be in ROTC, which paid my tuition in exchange for two years of active service. Since my father left us little, my mother could hardly refuse. I enrolled at Wichita State, and somewhere between marching for ROTC and an English class I found the part of my mother inside myself that I had denied. I was a hell of a student and a hell of a recruit. I put the two together, traded two more years of active duty with the Judge Advocate General's Corps for law school, and in 1992 walked out of Vanderbilt Law a second lieutenant ready to fulfill my commitment to the army.

My time in JAG's Corps offered definitive proof that of every ten people who join the military because they think it will keep them out of trouble, two are probably deluding themselves. There are thousands of admirable men and women in the army, but they don't interface with the JAG's Corps. My clientele bore a remarkable resemblance to the very people I would later prosecute when I returned to Nashville to take a job in the DA's office. I began with smaller cases, like insubordination, forgery, and failure to pay child support. Eventually, I was given more responsibility, taking on cases regarding drugs, rape, spousal abuse, and, on one occasion, even murder. Looking back on it, I can see that Wilson Owens and I were moving up the ladder of serious crimes together, although on different sides of the law. Destiny was pushing us toward each other and the moment of our consummation. By the time I met Owens, I felt I had known him all my life.

Moments of destiny rarely announce themselves. Even a few hours ago—just before all hell broke loose—I had no idea that the death of Wilson Owens was about to explode back into my life like a car wreck. I was back at my alma mater, Vanderbilt Law, pitching the DA's office as a career to the third-year students. This was a fool's errand, since the starting salary is thirty-nine thousand a year, with raises of two thousand for each year's service. After nine years, an impressive string of victories, and recently becoming lead prosecutor on capital crimes, I now am the proud possessor of a fifty-seven-thousand-dollar-a-year salary, about twenty thousand a year less than the students before me at Vanderbilt hoped to make their first year out. In other words, I might as well have been asking them to join the circus. But I was enjoying myself anyway. I wore my best suit—the light wool Joseph Abboud I save for closing arguments—and the black Magli shoes, for which I paid nearly a week's salary. The irony that I bought these clothes for the Wilson Owens closing argument—it was broadcast on Court TV, and I didn't want to look like a cliché of the old-fashioned southern lawyer—had not yet descended on me. The students who looked down at me from their plush theater seating had a lot to learn, too. They didn't yet know that they would eventually become as familiar with the case of *Tennessee vs. Owens* as their own names, as would the students of every major law school in the country. Destiny was marching toward us, and we didn't have a clue.

I made my points well, stressing that there was more to life than money. "Working for the DA's office is a passion, not just a career," I said. "The DA's office is a family, where people take care of each other. It's a great place to work, and I've never regretted my decision." The crowd looked bored, so I changed my approach. I turned off the lapel microphone and stuffed it in my coat pocket. I stepped off the podium and walked up to the front row of students, stopping in front of a cute brunette wearing thin, wire-rimmed glasses. "How much are you going to owe when you graduate?" I asked. Silence settled on the crowd as the topic turned to one they truly cared about: student loans.

"Eighty-one thousand dollars," the girl said.

Nervous laughter spread across the room. "Eighty-one

thousand," I repeated. "So why would somebody with that much debt want to work at the DA's office? You make a lot more in torts, helping people sue each other over their imagined slights. Maybe go for malpractice. You could make TV ads begging out-of-work women watching *Jerry Springer* to give you a call about the pain in their sciatica." More laughter now, and I could tell I was hitting home. "Or maybe you could get a little DUI work. I could read your ad in that little window above the urinal at my favorite bar. It's the Willie Sutton principle: *Why do lawyers advertise in bars? It's where the drunks are.*" I had them now; they were laughing, letting down their guard. "Look, if you want to be a hamster on a wheel, fine. I just don't see the point of getting a law degree to do it." I paused, letting my point sink in. "You want to know what I did last Friday? I sat in my office with a mother and a father whose son was murdered in a gang fight. The kid wasn't in the gang; he was just in the wrong place at the wrong time. There he was, walking down the street in the projects, and somebody says something, and the kid tries to defend himself, and things get out of hand. And now her son is dead. This kid's parents sat in my office wanting something so pure and beautiful that the word sits lovely in my mouth: *justice.*"

Every eye was locked on me now, soaking in my words. I loved this part of it, the drama, the wordplay, like an actor with a well-written script. "So they come to me to make their world right again," I said. "I imagine that while I was talking to that family, somewhere in the Seagram's building there was a lawyer making several times more money than I did that day. Maybe he was making sure that a big real estate deal had all its *i*'s dotted and its *t*'s crossed, so nobody got sued later over parking lot rights. He wants to make sure nobody gets a dent in their Mercedes. And you know what? *That lawyer can kiss my ass.*"

Sporadic applause broke out over the room, which was all the victory I would have, and all I needed. I had held them in my thrall for a while, like the experienced prosecutor I was, but I knew the spell would be broken as soon as the show was over. I was talking now for my own amusement, so I saw no reason not to enjoy myself. "Look," I said, "I know about the loans. You kidding me? I did it the hard way. I graduated from this auspicious institution courtesy of ROTC, baby, which meant I owed the U.S. Army four years in JAG Corps to pay my debt. And yeah, they make the lawyers go through basic training, just like everybody else. Compared to that, you guys are getting off cheap." I stuck my hand in my pocket, the trademark "aw shucks, Atticus Finch" move that worked so well at disarming juries. "Thing is," I said, "you can hunt clients—do the whole, join the country club, hand out business cards, kiss-ass rigamarole—or you can do something with your life that matters. You can put away the bad guys, and that still gets me up in the morning like the very first day I signed on with the DA. That's the kind of law I'm proud to practice. I get to set the balance of scales back to where they belong. That's *power.* If that sounds like something you want to try, I'm glad to hang around for a while and answer questions. Thanks for your time."

More applause broke out, but it was short-lived, and within a few seconds the students began gathering their belongings. *Thirty-nine thousand a year. Probably about the size of their first year's mortgage payments.* I watched the crowd file out, until the last student slung her book bag over her shoulder and left. I turned and shrugged at Louis Donahue, the instructor of Criminal Procedure II. "This time they stayed to the end," I said, smiling. "Last year a half dozen walked out halfway through."

Donahue laughed. "We had somebody from Baker and

Stewart in here last week. He was handing out business cards like candy. I had to escort him out of the room so he wouldn't get trampled."

"Yeah, well, the dark side is strong."

"Ever think about crossing over? A defense attorney armed with what you know could be a millionaire in five years."

"Do I think about it? Just every day, Louis. Just every damn day."

Donahue smiled. "See you next year, Thomas."

I picked up my jacket. "Thanks, Louis. See you then."

I left the Vanderbilt Law School Building and walked across the small parking lot to my pickup. Halfway across I reached in my pocket and turned on my cell phone, which I had switched off just before I began my speech. It rang five seconds later. "Dennehy," I said.

"Thomas?" It was the voice of Jeff Stillman, a young assistant who had just joined the office a few months earlier. "You got to come in, like now."

"Hold on to your pants, Stillman, I got to go by and pick up my daughter a birthday present."

"I think you're going to want to do that another time."

"You're probably wrong about that."

"Listen, Thomas, I'm serious. The DA wants you here ASAP."

"What's the big deal?"

Stillman's young, ambitious voice said eight words: "Have you ever heard of the Justice Project?"

There are four of us in the room. Along with myself, there is David Rayburn, the district attorney. Rayburn is fifty-two years old, wears his dark, gray-streaked hair combed back, and is a career politician. His wet dream is to shake the U.S.

attorney general's hand, a desire soon to be fulfilled since he just wrote a one-thousand-dollar check to the Committee to Reelect the President. He is not in any practical sense a lawyer, but he is a talented administrator, which is actually more his job. Also in the room is Carl Becker, my partner and a towering figure in Nashville legal circles. A prosecutor for thirty-one years, Carl has worked with me for the last seven. I learned the intricacies of criminal procedure at his feet, and he was an affable teacher. He is loved everywhere he goes, and hasn't paid for a drink for a decade. If I have a hero in my life, it is Carl. He is a little more than a week from a much-earned retirement, which he looks forward to with the same anticipation he would living in a dry county. He is wearing his trademark gray suit, of which he owns five identical copies. He accentuates this sameness with a spectacular collection of ties, my favorite of which is a Christmas version featuring a holiday pattern made up of—only upon the closest inspection—tiny reindeer caught in flagrante delicto. This bit of X-rated absurdity is typical of his sense of humor, which is prurient, utterly male, and one of the things I will miss most when he's gone. Two years ago every prosecutor in the office attended mandatory PC sensitivity training, after which, Carl stood up and said in a loud, clear voice, "Jesus Christ, I need a drink."

Standing next to Carl, vibrating slightly with excitement like a child eating his first Thanksgiving dinner at the grown-up's table, is Jeff Stillman, first-year prosecutor just out of the University of Georgia. Stillman is tall, good-looking, pledged Kappa Alpha, and still wears the fraternity ring. He's talking, and looking at him, I can't help thinking he would make an excellent newscaster. He's like a young Peter Jennings, only without the gravitas. Sort of a Jennings Lite. "I get this call from a Professor Philip Buchanan from

Georgetown University," he says. "He's the founder of the Justice Project. Their goal is to review every death penalty case for the last ten years where there's a chance DNA evidence can prove the convicted is not guilty."

Rayburn looks displeased. "God, not more of that. These clowns are just gaming the system, driving us nuts. We've got ninety-five people on death row in this state. What's he want to do, review every one of them?"

Stillman nods. "That's what he says. He's got funding from somewhere. It's a nonprofit foundation or something." *Not newscasting,* I think. *Maybe sports.*

Rayburn shakes his head. "They know we can't afford the time. You're talking about a crap load of paperwork."

Stillman waves him off. "Not all at once. It's going to take a long time. But he has a place to start. It's pretty interesting, too, considering the guy's already been executed."

Rayburn looks up warily. "If he's already been executed, I fail to see the point."

"Somebody else just confessed to the crime." For the first time, I start to seriously pay attention. The fact that my life is about to change is vaguely announcing itself now, a light humming in my synapses. I turn my head toward Stillman, and he's smiling, as though he's the bearer of good news. This impression, I'm pretty sure, couldn't be more wrong. "It's the Wilson Owens thing," he says. "The guy who got executed last year."

Rayburn looks at me, then bursts into relieved laughter. "I get it," he says. "It's the EMT thing. God, talk about beating a dead horse."

Stillman gives a confused look, and Rayburn points at me. "You're new here, Stillman. You don't know Dennehy is famous."

"For what?"

"For being the only man in history to get two different people convicted for killing the same man."

Stillman looks surprised. "You mean like a wheel man on a robbery? That happens all the time."

"No," Rayburn says, smiling indulgently. "Two people acting *independently,* who don't even know each other. It was one for the record books." He settles in to explain. "Wilson Owens, career criminal, calmly stands outside the Sunshine Grocery in east Nashville smoking cigarettes. He's working up his determination, because he's getting ready to go inside the store and exchange the life of the manager for—what was it?"

"Three hundred forty-six dollars and nineteen cents," I say. Rayburn's going to get it wrong, of course—he embellishes the story more every time he tells it—but I don't say anything. Once he starts in, there's no point in stopping him.

"So Owens walks into the store," Rayburn says, "he raises a Browning BPS pistol-gripped, sawed-off shotgun from inside his overcoat, and he empties it at point-blank range into Steven Davidson, the manager. Bad enough. But there's a woman unlucky enough to be in the store at the same time. She's in the back, and she takes off, moving pretty slow because she's old and overweight. Owens, the bastard, has emptied his gun. He didn't know she was in the store. So he calmly reloads from a TacStar side-saddle shell holder to take care of her. But by then, she's past him, see, almost to the front door. So he shoots her twice in the back—I told you, he's a bastard—and the shots splinter the lower vertebrae of her spine."

"God," Stillman says. "That's merciless."

"No shit, Sherlock," Rayburn says. He's enjoying himself now, not because of what happened to Lucinda Williams, the sixty-eight-year-old victim, but because of what happened to

Owens. "So picture the scene. We got the two victims down, and Owens loading up a bag with—damn it, Thomas, how much was it again?"

"Three hundred forty-six dollars and nineteen cents."

"Right. Owens thinks both victims are dead, so he takes his money and leaves. But the thing is, the woman isn't dead. She's alive, although just barely. She lies there, four, five minutes. Pretty soon, the EMTs arrive. The woman's got one hell of a will to live, because she's still hanging on, still breathing. At which point, an EMT three weeks into the job proceeds to . . . what was it he did, Thomas?"

"Performed an unrecognized esophageal intubation." Rayburn rolls his eyes, indicating he prefers English. "He stuck an air tube in the wrong hole."

Stillman's eyes widen. "You mean . . ."

"You got it," Rayburn says, nodding. "First, Dennehy gets Owens convicted for murdering the woman. Then he sticks the EMT with negligent homicide for killing the same woman." Rayburn bursts into laughter. "Damn, that took balls."

"The EMT was found to have methamphetamine in his bloodstream," I say quietly. "And a very troubled past he concealed on his job application. He had washed out of medic school once before, with the army. I couldn't let that slide." I hate this story for a variety of reasons: I don't like to relive what happened to Steven Davidson, the manager, or to Lucinda Williams, the innocent bystander; and even though I take pride in my work, I don't like boasting about sending somebody to the death chamber. To my mind, both are tragedies, although one is in the interest of justice. The EMT's lawyer had begged me to grant his client a pretrial diversion, which would have expunged his record after fulfilling some parole terms. But I wasn't going to sit across the table from Lucinda Williams's widower and tell him that what happened to his wife rated a slap on the wrist. The EMT had made a mistake that, under normal circumstances, could certainly happen. But there are standard tests to avoid it, and the EMT didn't perform them because he was six feet off the ground on meth.

"Come on, Dennehy," Rayburn says. "It was brilliant, and you know it. Two slam dunks."

"Didn't they appeal?" Stillman asks.

"Three times," Carl says. "It was inevitable, once the EMT got convicted. The defense wanted to know how they could *both* be guilty. Either one killed her, or the other did."

"Makes sense," Stillman says.

Rayburn smiles beneficently. "Which makes absolutely no difference to the law," he says. "You can't appeal merely on a logical basis. You got to have a *legal* basis. A misapplication of the law or inadequate representation. Something solid like that."

Stillman looks over at me again. "So what really killed her?" he asks. "The gunshot wounds or the screwed up medical procedure?"

Rayburn and Carl swivel their heads toward me. Even though Stillman's question is, as they say, the heart of the matter, I don't like this kind of talk. On a murder case I wall myself off, getting as far inside the head of the accused as humanly possible. I've been known to lose seven or eight pounds on a case, just from forgetting to eat. But when it's over, it's over. I never want to hear the accused's name again. "It was the usual dueling experts," I say. In the first case, "ours maintained the gunshot wounds were fatal, no matter what the EMT did. Theirs maintained if that EMT hadn't made the mistake, she'd be rolling herself around in a wheelchair today. In the absence of a consensus, it came down to the closing arguments."

"Which is where Thomas shines," Rayburn says. "He's like that guy for the Yankees—Mariano Rivera. He's a closer, God damn it."

Carl smiles. "The man can close, no question."

"Got covered on Court TV," Rayburn says.

Stillman raises an eyebrow. "No kidding. *Court TV.*" He says the words reverently, like they're holy.

"It was a long time ago," I say. "Seven years." *What was the EMT's name? Chuck. No, Charles. He was big on everybody using his full name. Charles Bridges.*

"And it's a dead dog," Rayburn says. "If this Justice Project or whoever wants to try to run this thing through the meat grinder again, fine by me. Let them make Wilson Owens their hero. Because at the end of the day, the EMT thing was just a sideshow. Nothing is ever going to change the fact that Wilson Owens is the man who pulled the trigger of that gun. And nothing is going to change the fact that he's the one who killed those people."

Stillman's relaxed smile doesn't waver. He looks like he's made of metal, he's so unchanging. "That's news to Kwame Jamal Hale," he says.

The humming inside me ratchets up a notch. The bad feeling is growing. "Who's Kwame Jamal Hale?"

"The man who swears he's the one who committed those crimes."

Carl, Rayburn, and I exchange glances. "You mean he made a confession?" Rayburn asks.

"Yeah," Stillman answers. "This guy Hale says it was him, not Owens. He says he framed Owens over some beef they had. He said he wanted to take Owens down, so he set him up."

"The hell he did," Rayburn grumbles. "Three women testified they saw Owens smoking outside the store just before the robbery. His DNA was found on the cigarette butts. Not this guy . . . what's his name again?"

"Hale," Stillman says. "Kwame Jamal."

"Yeah, not Hale's DNA. Wilson Owens's DNA. And not tested by the old system. Damn it, Thomas, what was that called?"

"RFLP."

"Yeah. *Not* that one. The new one." He looks at me helplessly.

"STR."

"Damn right. And the same women who said they saw Owens smoking cigarettes outside the store picked him out of a lineup. Twice."

Stillman opens a file, pulls out a photograph, and tosses it on Rayburn's desk. He's acting real casual, like we always discuss important cases together. This has never happened, except possibly in his mind. "Hale is already doing life without parole at Brushy Mountain," he says. "His crime of choice is framing people. He's done it his whole life. He looks a lot like Wilson Owens, too."

I look at the photograph, and Stillman is correct; I could swear Wilson Owens is staring back at me. "He's out of his mind," I say. "He's grandstanding, looking for attention."

"Kwame Jamal, my ass," Rayburn says. "His real name's probably Fred."

"It's Jerome," Stillman answers, as though he anticipated the comment. "He just became a member of the Nation of Islam. Kwame Jamal is the new version."

"What's Farrakhan's little army of hate got to do with this?" Carl asks.

"Before Jerome becomes a Muslim, he wants to make confession. So he's saying he's the guy who killed the people in the grocery store."

I look at the photograph. The two men could be brothers. "I thought this Justice Project uses DNA to get people's convictions overturned," I say. "The DNA evidence is what convicted Owens. His saliva was all over the cigarettes. That, and the eyewitnesses, sealed the deal."

"Which is my point," Carl says. "Just because Mr. Hale confesses to a crime doesn't make it so. We get confessions from wack jobs all day long. I once had a woman confess to killing JFK because their love affair went sour. She would have been fourteen years old at the time."

Rayburn nods hopefully. "Muslims can be wackos, too," he says. "Especially Nation of Islam. They're the kings of wackos."

"Buchanan and Hale want a meeting at Brushy Mountain State Penitentiary," Stillman says. "Hale says he's ready to tell us what really happened that day." He pauses. "He says he can prove it."

There's a moment of silence. "Well, God damn," Rayburn whispers. "How does he propose to do that?"

"He says he'll tell us when we get there." Another pause. "As long as we give him a guarantee."

"No death penalty," I say, quietly. "That's what he wants."

"Well he's not going to get it," Rayburn says. "If we sent Owens to the death chamber, what makes him think . . ." He almost finishes the thought before he realizes that we are completely screwed. "If we don't take the deal, they'll say we willingly suppressed the truth about an innocent man just because we insisted on putting somebody *else* to death. That would look like shit."

"Buchanan used words to that effect, yeah," Stillman said.

Carl, who has seen his share of brilliant legal maneuvering, whistles softly. "It's the smoking gun," he says. "The anti-death-penalty lobby's been looking for it for years. Positive proof the wrong guy went to the chamber. I never thought it would come on my watch."

I nod, because I don't know what else to do. Carl and Rayburn are right; we're over one hell of a barrel. If we don't sign the papers, this Professor Buchanan will probably have a press conference arranged within twenty-four hours telling the world we love executing people so much we'd actually rather suppress the truth about one of Nashville's most cold-blooded crimes than stop doing it. In the suddenly quiet office, it sinks in that we are inches away from being the unwanted focus of every major media outlet on Earth as the people who finally fucked up the big one. But as powerful as these thoughts are—and they are seismic, believe me—they slip through my mind at light speed, rapidly discarded. If I burn professionally for my mistake, so be it. Because right now, all I can see in my mind is Wilson Owens on the day of his sentencing. He's in his orange jumpsuit, his arms and legs shackled, tears streaming down his face. He's begging for his life. He's crying like a baby, something he probably had never done before in his adult life. As he's dragged out of the courtroom, he's staring me in the eyes, screaming my name, damning me to hell. *I'll get you, motherfucker,* are the last words that echo into the courtroom before he disappears behind a door.

I knew exactly what was going on in the minds of the jury during the sentencing phase of Owens's trial. The jury was wavering because of confusion about the EMT, and unless I lowered the hammer, they were going to let Owens off with his life. I know, because when he begged the court for mercy, his pleas were moving *me.* I thought he was guilty, no question. But I could also see how fucked his life was, how complicated his story was, and at that moment, as I watched him cry, it seemed like nothing but more of the same hell to put him to death. I remember the exact instant I said to myself, *No, this is my job, and I'm going to do it.* So I took Owens apart in the minds of the jury, dissecting his humanity bit by bit. I showed them pictures of Steven Davidson's disfigured body, even though Owens's lawyer tried to get them excluded as prejudicial. I paraded Lucinda Williams's family onto the stand—in the midst of their still-fresh misery—and let them cry tears equal to Owens's, canceling them out. I challenged the jury to do the right thing. Those were my very words: *do the right thing.*

Rayburn's voice breaks into my thoughts. Apparently, my internal dialogue has been playing out on my face, like a movie projected on a screen. "You OK?" he asks.

"Yeah," I lie. I'm so far from OK I need a map to get back. "So this Professor Buchanan wants a meeting."

"Right," Stillman says. He's still smiling, the bastard. I'm not saying he wished any of us harm. He was just exercising the luxury of knowing that he had come on board several years after the Owens case was history, so whatever stink landed on the rest of us was only going to be an interesting water cooler story for him. "Buchanan says no more than three people from the office. He doesn't want Hale overwhelmed by an army of lawyers. But one of them has to be Thomas."

Rayburn looks at me. "Think it's because you were lead prosecutor on Owens?"

"Yeah. Probably."

Rayburn turns back to Stillman. "Who knows about this?"

"On Buchanan's side, who knows? In this office, just the four of us."

"Let's keep it that way." Stillman looks like a crestfallen

puppy, and Rayburn points a finger at him. "Not a word, Stillman. When does Buchanan want to have this meeting?"

"He'll give us a few days to coordinate between him, the prison, and our office. He says he'll keep the lid on until then. Anything longer, he goes public."

"OK," Rayburn says. "Between now and then, I want business as usual. No continuances, no canceled meetings. If this thing breaks out, the whole office will go nuts."

The meeting breaks up, but Rayburn calls my name before I leave. "Hang on a sec, will you, Thomas?" he says. Stillman stops, too, and Rayburn waves him off. "Just Thomas, if you don't mind." Stillman slinks out, and I wait for the door to close behind him.

"Yeah?"

"Kind of lousy timing, don't you think?"

"What do you mean?"

"You have another death penalty case coming up. The thing with the immigrant from Sudan."

"His name is Moses Bol."

Rayburn nods. "We decided to go for the maximum. Everybody agreed."

"Bol raped and murdered a woman in her own apartment," I say. "It meets the standard." I watch the DA a second, trying to figure out what he's driving at, when it hits me. "You're wondering if I have the stones to prosecute a death penalty case while we're being hung out to dry on the Sunshine Grocery murders."

Rayburn leans his frame back in his chair. "I wouldn't blame you for sitting this one out, Thomas. If there's any Kryptonite in your superpowers, it's your conscience. You have one."

"I can do my job, David."

"Still, you see my point. Kwame Jamal Hale's confession is a hell of a distraction for somebody who needs maximum focus. Moses Bol is an immigrant, and the victim is white and female. People are pretty damn jumpy over this deal, already."

Rayburn's statement about nerves being frayed in Bol's neighborhood is a capsule of understatement. The demographics of the forty square blocks bordering Tennessee Village, the subsidized housing development in which the U.S. government saw fit to drop off its most recent crop of the world's castoffs, is as close to its conflagration point as any can remember. A turf war between the white, lower-middle-class in the area and any of at least twelve new nationalities a few blocks away is getting ugly. "I agree."

Rayburn watches me a moment, assessing me. "Capital crimes always require two lawyers in this office," he says. "You and Carl were a great team, but he's retiring."

"I'm going to ask Deborah Housel to act as cocounsel on the Bol case," I say. "She's young, but she shows a lot of promise."

"Yeah. I'm thinking Stillman, actually."

I stare. "If you don't mind, I'd rather you just fired me."

"He's smart, Thomas. He reminds me of you."

"I tender my resignation, as of this moment."

"Want me to tell you why you need him?"

"I'd be fascinated, yeah."

"Unlike you, he's merciless." He pauses. "Especially now."

"What do you mean, now?"

"Just look at your right leg."

I look, and my leg is bouncing up and down in tiny, nervous rotations. I put my hand on the leg, stopping it. "Stillman doesn't have the experience for a murder trial," I say. "He's a wet pup."

"He's also a pain in the ass. Yeah, I noticed. Thing is, I

don't hire people because they're nice. I hire them because they're smart, aggressive, and committed. And with this Hale thing, I can't afford to have you lose focus."

"I'm not going to lose focus."

"I know. Stillman is going to make sure." He stands up and starts walking me toward the door. "Incidentally, Carl said the same stuff about you when you came on."

"He did not."

"Sorry, he did."

That stops me. Maybe it's true; it's been nine years now—the last seven with Carl—and maybe I really was a snot-nosed, eager-beaver kid anxious to make a mark. *But I could never have been like Stillman,* I tell myself. *Stillman would prosecute his own mother, if he thought he could get a promotion doing it.* "If Stillman comes on, you have to promise me there are going to be ground rules."

"Such as?"

"Such as other than getting me coffee, he doesn't move without asking me first."

Rayburn watches me a second, then nods. "I'll explain things to him."

"You can do it now, since he's probably standing outside the door, trying to listen through the keyhole. Based on what he just heard, he'll probably have a little puddle around his shoes from excitement."

Rayburn nods, a tiny smile escaping his lips. "Send him in."

CHAPTER TWO

I LEAVE THE 222 West Building in downtown Nashville in something like a daze. I try to forget about Stillman for the time being—he'll remind me of himself often enough, anyway—and wonder if I've ever had a worse day as a lawyer. I walk onto the sidewalk, which is oddly empty for 3:30 p.m. I look up at the sky; it's a typical late August day, about a million degrees, with the haze that sits over Nashville most summer days. *It's going to get worse,* I think. I can remember Augusts so hot and humid, outdoors was someplace you had to be in-between buildings with air-conditioning. I wonder what I might do if I wasn't a prosecutor. *I could sell real estate,* I think. *Or maybe BMWs. I've always liked BMWs.*

I walk to my truck, which is parked in the employee lot on the side of 222 West. I sit in the truck—a Ford F-150, the same model my father drove—and let the engine run a few minutes, still shell-shocked. Apparently, I'm going to have to drive to Brushy Mountain prison in a few days to have a face-to-face with Kwame Jamal, née Jerome. Since he and his law-professor attorney have gone to the trouble of setting up the meeting, I have no doubt what Hale is going to say. He's going to tell me what really happened that day at the Sunshine Grocery, and we are going to have to deal with it. Carl's going to be all right, I realize. He's retiring, which will get him out of the limelight. He's indestructible, anyway. Rayburn, I'm not so sure about. He's ambitious, not in an ugly way, but he has plans. He's kept his nose clean, done a decent job, and carried the mail for the Republican party since he was in college. That means being staunchly, uncompromisingly, for the death penalty. He's about two elections away from collecting the rewards, and if Kwame Jamal Hale is the real killer of Steven Davidson and Lucinda Williams, David Rayburn can kiss the last ten years or so of bricklaying good-bye. Tennessee isn't very forgiving of politicians who fall from grace. We've got an ex-mayor in Nashville who currently sells aluminum siding.

I look up at the inside rearview mirror and scan my face. I'm thirty-six, but I've always looked younger than my age. I have my father's eyes—brown, wide-open. I'm less rugged, probably because for every hour he worked on jet engines at McConnell Air Force Base, I spent the same hour poring over legal briefs and drinking coffee with lawyers. But I can still feel him inside me, receding year by year. I don't like this gradual erosion of his clear-eyed optimism, and that, maybe, is why I catch my fingers strumming or a leg bouncing sometimes, as Rayburn did in the office.

The rush-hour traffic is picking up, and I need to get my daughter a birthday present. In a way, I'm relieved to have something to do other than think about what has just gone haywire. Jasmine lives with her mother and her stepfather, a Greek plastic surgeon named Michael Sarandokos. Although Michael is a doctor, the decisions he faces are a long ways from life and death. Mostly, he spends his days giving the wealthiest 10 percent of Nashville liposuction and implants and tucks and dermal abrasions and any of the other techniques he's mastered to help the affluent give nature and age the finger. The fact that my daughter lives with him in his six-thousand-square-foot house in a subdivision for rich people called President's Club makes buying her a birthday present a complicated process. Anxious to supplant my place in her life—even at the expense of ruining her character—he denies her nothing.

I pull out onto Second Avenue, a crowded street the town hoped would become a tourist mecca, but which ended up an iffy street bookended with a defunct Planet Hollywood and a dying Hard Rock Café. I lean back in my seat, unbuttoning my collar and loosening my tie while the truck cools.

Birthday present for the girl who has everything. Jasmine is ten years old. She's got an iPod and a computer in her room. Her clothes cost more than mine, and last time we were together I could have sworn she had a professional pedicure. She is also living proof that the genetic browning of the human race scientists are always braying about—the melting together of ethnic groups into one mocha milkshake—has at least as much upside as down. I'm watered-down Irish, with black hair, blue eyes, and the frame of a basketball player. Rebecca Obregon, the woman I married in San Antonio while stationed at Kelly Air Force Base, is mother-country Andalusian, with the kind of olive skin that doesn't get a tan line. The baby we made was so beautiful it made my eyes hurt. Jazz's eyes are brown, like her mother's, her skin is light olive, and she is probably going to be six feet tall. She is going to break hearts all over Nashville, at least until she leaves, which she'll start wanting to do about fifteen seconds after she realizes how beautiful she is. Then she'll go to New York or Los Angeles or somewhere to watch better-dressed men fall all over themselves opening doors for her.

I turn right on Broadway, heading to I-65 and the malls. I love that Jasmine is beautiful, and I even love that she reminds me of her mother. But I would love her just as much if she had a nose like a hockey player. She's my daughter, at least on weekends. She seems to enjoy our time together, and she understands that I'm her real father, not Dr. Knife. But this coming weekend she'll be at soccer camp, and the next, she's going to Orlando, for her birthday. Dr. Knife is attending a conference for doctors like him who have figured out how to make a handsome living mining people's vanity, and Jazz wants to go to Universal Studios. As much as I love spending time with her, I'm smart enough to know there's no percentage in saying no.

The traffic is still light, and I make good time going east the short drive to where I pick up I-65 south and head toward Franklin, an affluent and rapidly growing Nashville suburb where the smart money in Nashville is moving. I drive in silence, the radio off. Every half mile or so I force the picture of Wilson Owens begging for his life from my mind. I remember that as the bailiffs—it took two of them—removed Owens after sentencing, he stared at me the whole way out of the room. They were dragging him out, his shoes scraping the floor, and he was locked on my eyes like a missile. And I stared back, positive that hell was where he belonged, happy to be his sword of justice.

I look up and see the exit for Moore's Lane, where a collection of retail shops and car dealerships circle the mother ship of Cool Springs Mall. There's a Toys "R" Us in there, and I'm hoping something brilliant and affordable will explode off the shelves and into my shopping cart. Ideally, this item will costs less than seventy-five dollars. I pull into the parking lot and park, for a reason I don't yet understand, a good thirty yards away from any other cars. It's still hot and muggy out, and this makes the walk longer. I put the car in park and stare back at the toy store, wondering what the hell I'm doing. Then my hands, still clenched on the steering wheel, start shaking. I look up at the mirror, and I see that I'm crying. I'm shaking the steering wheel and crying, and I'm seeing Wilson Owens, that asshole, being injected with choline, a respiratory-suppressing drug which was recently outlawed for veterinarian use in putting down animals because it was deemed too cruel. *Jesus, maybe I do need Stillman.* I sit there and vibrate awhile, seeing my life and Carl's and Rayburn's and everybody else who's about to be fucked if Kwame Jamal Hale is the real killer of Steven Davidson and Lucinda Williams, and it takes me a good five minutes to come down enough to pull my hands off the steering wheel.

I last less than ten minutes in Toys "R" Us. It's the wrong place for me right now, this happiest store in the world, where the frozen, plastic faces of Barbies and American Girls stare down at me. If there's anything in this place Jazz wants, she probably already has it. I circle back out to the parking lot, ready to drive home. I walk up to my truck and I notice something stuck under the wiper, like a parking ticket. I look around; there's nobody near the Ford, which sits alone in the half-full lot. I pull out the paper, which is a pamphlet folded in half. I open it up and see an amateurish-looking leaflet from an organization calling itself Citizens for a Just America. I look up, trying to figure out from where it came; scanning the lot, I can see no other cars with anything on their windshields. The pamphlet has a picture of Leonard Peltier, an American Indian who was convicted of murdering two FBI agents. The pamphlet says Peltier has already spent more than twenty years in prison for a crime he didn't commit. Under Peltier's picture is a handwritten message in dark marker: *NO MISTAKES WILL BE TOLERATED.* I can't figure out why the pamphlet is there, and I definitely don't like the tagline, since it's more gung-ho than the tone of the anti-death-penalty faction.

I stand around for a minute or so, confused, wondering if some bogeyman is going to jump out and tell me he put the pamphlet on my car. The pamphlet is too weird to be a coincidence, but I only just found out about Hale myself, so I can't figure out how somebody could already be tailing me. Normally, I'm pretty good at ignoring the list of a hundred or so people who have a reason to be pissed off at me; I found out on my first day in the office that would be a part of the job, when I noticed the half-inch-thick bulletproof glass between the office receptionist and the waiting room. But if this is one of the usual wackos, it's pretty interesting timing. Maybe it's Professor Buchanan, softening me up for the kill before I meet him and his client at Brushy. If it is, it's a mistake, because it's pissing me off, which will definitely make me more difficult to deal with. I get in my car and pull out onto I-65 south for the three-mile drive from the mall to my house. At least as far as I can tell, nobody's tailing me. Unfortunately, my time in the army didn't include counterinsurgency or anything like it. I spent my time in a courtroom, when I wasn't playing racquetball or jogging with the other junior officers.

By the time I get home fifteen minutes later, I've decided to ignore the pamphlet, just like I ignore the three or four letters I get every month from prisoners describing, often in lurid detail, the various acts of revenge they contemplate against me, should the legal system ever be crazy enough to let them back onto the streets. I pull into my garage and walk into the house. My cat, Indianapolis, is waiting inside. He was a stray when I found him, about as lost as a cat can get. The tin ID tag on his collar was worn down, and the only thing legible on the street address was the city, Indianapolis. I don't like cats, something I impressed on this black-and-white fur ball the first ten times he came around by steadfastly ignoring him. But he took to me, or maybe the smell of my pine mulch. He ended up planting himself outside my door meowing his brains out until late one night I made the mistake of giving him a saucer of milk to shut him up. From that moment on, he regarded me as a tenant on his property, and I resigned myself to cans of cat food and bags of litter. Not that Indianapolis is in any way untidy. Compared to me, he's a monk. He looks at me steadily as I come in the door, inscrutable as a sphinx, and slinks his way through my legs, rubbing against me. I wonder sometimes why he picked me out of the hundred other houses he could have chosen in the middle-class suburban landscape. He must have known something about me I didn't know myself, because he was relentless. The damn cat would have starved himself before he left. I tell myself I keep him around because he's spectacular at hunting moles, which my yard attracts like frat boys to an open kegger. He makes gifts of their blind carcasses from time to time, dropping them off on my back deck like a sacrificial offering. But when he stares up at me with those pale, fathomless eyes, I keep thinking he's got something on his mind. Until I figure it out, it's *Mi casa es su casa, cat.*

The next morning, Thursday, I wake up and calm myself with my ritual two cups of coffee and a Zoloft. The Zoloft is courtesy of Dr. Tina Gessman, who convinced me that being an assistant district attorney is the kind of job that the human body isn't necessarily genetically prepared to do. She has a long list of clients, like social workers, third-grade teachers, and cops, who carry around what she likes to call "psychic weight." My father would have referred to the idea of psychic weight as psychic bullshit, but then, his world was a lot simpler than mine. I think about him a lot, making my morning coffee—I exclusively use Peet's—which, after I pay for shipping, costs me fourteen dollars a pound and is the single Sarandokos-level luxury I allow myself. My father fixed airplanes, and the idea of Zoloft and gourmet coffee making his day would have struck him as pretentious idiocy. I have his tools in my garage, and I tinker with things, little projects that bring me back to the days when he was alive. They're Sears tools, made in the sixties, and they'll be here when the earth is roamed by postnuclear holocaust cockroaches. I put on a back deck and later enclosed it; I swapped out older windows in the sunroom off the kitchen for newer, more efficient ones. Maybe the tools keep me centered, maybe the Zoloft, maybe it's the gourmet coffee. Zoloft wasn't my first try with mood-altering drugs. I went through a short list of pharmaceutical aids before finding the one least offensive. The first one, perversely, made me more combative; the second, foggy and sexually irrelevant; the third, Zoloft, had theoretically evened things out. Theoretically, because I've now taken it long enough to not clearly remember what things were like before. All I know is that spiked edges of nervous energy still run through my skin from time to time, clicking upward through my mood like electricity. Rayburn isn't the only one who catches me with a nervous leg twitch. I do it myself, all the time.

What I'm thinking while I wash the Zoloft down is that I've made it nine years in the DA's office, and I don't want Kwame Jamal Hale to be the reason I ship out. My talk at Vanderbilt yesterday wasn't just bullshit, after all. I do love what I do. I love it enough to endure the gradual grinding up of a lot of subtle distinctions in my personality, like the ability to be horrified by photographs of dead people.

Stillman is standing outside my office when I arrive, his ever-present grin pasted on his face. His arms are full of files, which I assume are from the Moses Bol case. *Until this plays out, it's business as usual,* Rayburn said. *No continuances, no delays.* How Stillman got the files out of my office to spend the night with, I have no idea. But I think again that maybe Rayburn is right; I probably would have spent the morning wondering what the hell I was doing getting ready to send somebody else to the death chamber while Kwame Jamal Hale was a few days away from giving his deposition. Stillman, however, is as untroubled as a puppy. I unlock my door, and he steps through in front of me, as though I were holding the door for him. He drops the files on my desk, plops down in a chair, and says, "Whaddaya think, partner?"

What I think isn't actually appropriate to share, so I walk past him and sit behind my desk. "David explained to you how I like to work, right?"

"He said to get you coffee. I assumed he was joking."

"Don't ever get me coffee, Stillman. You wouldn't make it right, anyway."

"Fine."

"Did he say anything else?"

"He said you're the boss, and I said I had no problem with that."

"So, if somebody wants to schedule a conference, what do you say?"

"Check with you?"

"Correct. And if you want to take somebody's deposition, what do you do first?"

"I think I got where you're headed here, Thomas."

"Say the words, Stillman."

"I check with you. Except I've already set one up. Should I cancel it?"

I look at my watch; it's 9:05. "Shit, Stillman, do you ever sleep?"

"Don't need it. Anyway, I made the call yesterday, while you were . . . where were you, anyway?"

"Shopping for my daughter." Stillman shrugs, because he doesn't have a daughter, or a son, or a girlfriend, or anything in his universe except achieving his goal of ruling the world. "So this meeting you set up. Who's it with?"

"With the victim's family. I've got the father, the mother, and the victim's boyfriend."

OK, probably not a waste of time. "And when is this auspicious meeting to take place?"

"Tuesday, three-thirty, Jackson conference room. If you approve."

If I don't watch this kid, he's going to run all over me. "OK, Stillman. We'll take the meeting."

"Thanks."

I point at the files. "I take it you've read this?"

"Yeah, last night." The smile thins into an ironic line. "Should I have checked with you?" I give Stillman a warning look, and he backs off. "Sorry."

"So tell me, Stillman. What do you make of our friend Moses Bol?"

"Mr. Bol's not from around here. Maybe he grew up somewhere where rape and murder are acceptable forms of behavior."

Stillman's description is understatement: Bol is from the horribly war-torn country of Sudan, and thanks to the vagaries of international politics, he and 150 or so of his countrymen are now attempting to scrape out their lives in the projects of the American South. This was a world I assumed was just as strange to him as his would be to me. "What's the victim's name, Stillman?"

Stillman shuffles through the papers a second. "Tamra Hartlett," he says.

"That's right. We claim Bol raped her and then murdered her. What's the basis for that assessment?"

"Phone records show a seven-minute call between Bol's apartment and the victim's less than two hours before the estimated time of death. Eyewitnesses claim to have seen Bol and Hartlett vehemently arguing on two occasions in the days before her death. Another witness places Bol's car in front of her apartment that night. Forensics claim that a bloody handprint on her body matches Bol perfectly. His DNA was found all over her apartment, and her blood was found in his car. His semen was found on the bedsheets and in her vagina."

"Why was she found in a bathtub?"

"Women often try to wash off what happened to them in a rape. Hartlett ran into her bathroom, locked the door, and got into the tub."

"And?"

"Bol broke the door down with a heavy pedestal, splintering it into pieces. Fragments of wood were found on the base of the pedestal, and paint from the pedestal was found on the door."

"Were Bol's prints found on the pedestal?"

"His, and only his. Bol and she struggled, and he beat her to death with the pedestal. Not before she got him once, though."

"Confirmed by?"

"Bol had a nice-sized knot on his own head consistent with a blow from the same pedestal he used to kill Hartlett."

"Let's see the photos, Stillman."

Stillman blithely pulls out a set of horror-show pictures, including the victim collapsed in a half-filled bathtub run red with human blood. Among them is a single picture of the victim while still alive and well. Tamra Hartlett, the picture shows, is a white woman, early twenties, with sexy eyes and breast implants that are definitely not the work of Dr. Michael Sarandokos. She's at least a EE, and her low-cut blouse leaves little to the imagination. I don't know what kind of skinny, half-starved women there were trying to stay alive in the refugee camp Bol lived in before he came to America, but it's a fair bet they were nothing like Tamra Hartlett. It didn't take a genius to imagine her effect on Bol.

"Tamra Hartlett," I say. "She's a part-time dancer, sometime waitress. No criminal record."

"Bol, meanwhile, is part of a group of recent Sudanese immigrants. His English is marginal. Work skills, apparently nil." I shrug. "Maybe in Sudan, he's a genius. He's probably the greatest cow herder in the history of the African continent."

"In Nashville, Tennessee, he herds carts at Wal-Mart."

I lean back in my chair, thinking that Rayburn has Stillman pegged about right. He's a courtroom machine, as merciless as the angel of death. "No murder case is perfect," I say. "What's wrong with this one?"

Stillman runs his hand through his perfectly coiffed hair. "There was no forcible entry," Stillman says. "Apparently, she let him in."

"We stipulate that the two knew each other. They had been publicly arguing. She called him that night, probably to settle things, have it out. She just didn't count on him killing her."

Stillman nods. "That works."

"Anything else?"

"Motive," he says. "We know they were arguing, but we don't know what about."

I smile. "Apparently, Stillman, you are not going to be a total loss on this case." He relaxes, and I realize that getting my approval is important to him. I hadn't actually considered that possibility, given his officious posing. "So here's how I work, Stillman. I only use investigators for surveillance, not to interview."

"What do you mean?"

"I mean I go to the locations. I talk to witnesses myself. I don't show up in court depending on a summary somebody wrote with a twenty-nine-cent Bic pen. I look the witnesses in the eyes and make up my own mind."

Stillman nods. "OK."

"That means you and I are going to track down everybody and anybody who can tell us why Bol and Hartlett hated each other."

Stillman flashes his TV smile. "Rayburn says we're going for the maximum."

"We all agreed."

"So you're OK with it?"

"Don't mess with me, Stillman," I say quietly.

"What do you mean?"

"I mean you're asking for David. He asked you to sound me out." Stillman smiles, knowing he's busted. "Listen to me, Stillman. Moses Bol sat in his apartment and premeditated the murder of an American citizen. He drove the ten blocks to her apartment, entered the premises, raped her, then brutally beat her to death by pounding her head with a weighted pedestal. It took six blows to finish the job, which, as far as I'm concerned, is like reloading a weapon. We are going to try him for murder in the first degree, and we are going to ask that the jury sentence him to death."

With those words, quiet settles on my office. After a while, Stillman nods. "So what about this new bail hearing? He's already been denied one, right?"

I shrug. "Rita West tries anything she can to get her clients out of jail, and I respect her for it. She's dreaming on this one, however. We'll be there fifteen minutes. The judge will reconfirm our trial date at that point, and we'll take it from there."

"Anything you want me to do in the meantime?"

I nod. "Yeah. Go get me a Coke."

I'm elbow-deep in Bol's files when Carl drifts by after lunch. He comes into my office, large and noisy, and sits down in a chair opposite my desk, spilling over the sides a little, like a friendly bear. "I just heard about Stillman. Sorry."

Every day Carl's retirement creeps closer, I realize more how much I'm going to miss him. "It's an improvement over you, Sasquatch."

"He's smart, Thomas. He'll be an asset on this kid from Sudan. Who I met, incidentally."

I look up, surprised. "You met him?"

"When they brought him in for questioning. The public defender wanted to make a deal, and they needed somebody from the office."

"That was you? For God's sake, it was two o'clock in the morning."

Carl smiles softly. "You know me, Thomas. Becker is always available."

This is true; other than work, it's hard to find any discernible thing in Carl's life. It's one reason he's so good at it. "So what happened?"

"They processed the kid, but I'm not sure he knew what the hell was going on. The PD's office assigned that cute brunette to sit with him. The one with the nice behind."

"Rita West."

Carl nods. "She was doing her best, but it wasn't the ideal situation. Bol jumped out of his chair every time the door opened. I think he must have been in jail before, only the kind where the jailers carry cattle prods."

"Back in the old country."

"All I know is something sure as hell happened to that kid. He was as jumpy as a poodle at a Vietnamese barbeque."

I smile; Carl is about as PC as a redneck Baptist preacher, which makes him invaluable over long, dreary cases. "So what happened?"

"Once they got him settled down, I had them bring in a translator. A Dr. Ahmed al-Hasheed, as I recall."

"Arabic?"

"Yeah. Bol might be from the jungle, but he speaks four languages."

I raise an eyebrow. "No kidding."

Carl nods. "Arabic, Swahili, Dinka, and English makes four. Because the kid's English wasn't that bad. I think he was understanding more than he let on. You could see it in his eyes, how he followed the conversation. Word to the wise, Thomas. The kid is smart."

"Noted."

"We got the translator anyway, just to avoid a basis of appeal later on. West would be all over that, saying he couldn't comprehend what he was agreeing to."

"Sure."

"Anyway, with the translator's help the kid makes a statement, and it doesn't hold up. He says he wasn't there at the time. He says he's got no idea how his car got to the victim's apartment." Carl pauses. "You know about the eyewitnesses, right? He had been seen arguing with Hartlett a couple of times, and it got pretty vehement." I nod. "Even that early on, they had his prints all over the place. So everybody in the room knows he's lying his ass off. I look over at Rita, and I can see it in her eyes. She knows the kid's toast."

"She wants to make a deal."

"Brilliant, Dr. Watson. I take Rita out of the room to talk things over. You know, leave the kid alone for a while, let him stew in his own juices. So I tell Rita, look, let's do everybody a favor here. We both know the kid's in over his head. He doesn't know where the hell he is, or what the consequences are of his actions. I'll drop the aggravated charge circumstances, which will save the kid's life. With a few breaks the kid could be out in twenty, twenty-five."

"What'd she say?"

"She put up a fight, but she was just going through the motions. The kid's a foreigner, and he's accused of raping and killing a citizen. That's a combination that's going to really piss a jury off. So she says, fine, let's go with it. But naturally, we got to sell it to Bol."

"Right."

"We all go back in, me, Rita, the translator, and a detective. I explain the concept to the kid, about how he's agreeing to the lesser charge in exchange for a lighter sentence. I could tell he didn't know what I was driving at for a while. He just kept shaking his head and asking questions. I'm going through everything slow, real patient. The thing's being videotaped, and I want to make sure everything is clear. Finally, it sinks in for him. Which is when all hell broke loose."

"What do you mean?"

Carl shrugs. "The kid looks over at me with an expression that would curdle milk, and he went *el loco*. The detective had to physically restrain him from ripping my head off. Rita's backing up to get clear of the chaos, and I'm trying to get the kid's hands unglued from my necktie. A couple more cops come in and settle the kid down, and everything gets under control again. The whole thing only lasted a few seconds, but it was definitely interesting."

"What set the kid off?"

"The translator said that in this kid's culture, he's like a prince or something."

"A prince?"

"Prince, shaman, witch doctor." He pauses. "*Benywal.* That's it."

"What the hell's a *Benywal*?"

"How do I know? Anyhow, I deeply insulted him with my offer of a plea deal. The kid said I was the devil, anyhow." He pauses. "Not *the* devil, now that I remember it. Just *a* devil."

"No kidding."

"I told the kid he had me all wrong. I was trying to help him. He looked like he was going to spit in my face." Carl shrugs. "It was pretty obvious we weren't going to get the deal, so I went home. I wasn't in the mood to be told I was a devil anymore, anyway. It was amusing for a few minutes, but it lost its appeal pretty fast."

I shake my head. "Looks like we might be in for quite a show."

Carl sighs. "You're in for the show," he says quietly. "They're leading me to pasture, Thomas. I've got good years left in me. Maybe not great, but good." He looks at me helplessly, which is a new expression for him. He is so good at what he does—so finely tuned, for such a precise purpose—that neither one of us can imagine his next act. He's only sixty-five, which means he could be looking at twenty-five years to fill.

"You think any more about that teaching job?" I ask. "Any law school in the country would be lucky to have you."

"I have a very serviceable revolver at home, Dennehy," he says. "If you ever see me sitting around a bunch of twenty-three-year-olds telling my old war stories, please use it on me."

He sounds tired, like he's already bored with doing the nothing he has staring at him for the next two or three decades. "I had to get out of my office for a while," he says. "It's like a parade in there. Everybody wants to say good-bye. It's all sad faces and moist eyes. Nightmare."

"I can't believe you have to come back next Monday for one last day."

"Yeah, and I have to wait until the next Friday for the party. The great state of Tennessee is forcing me to use four days vacation."

"Just as well. Knowing the group around here, nobody is going to be in shape to come into the office the next day."

"Speaking of the party, no speeches, Thomas. I'm serious."

"Fine by me, but Rayburn never met a microphone he didn't like."

Carl's eyes widen. "God, I hadn't thought of that. Look, want to meet me before at Seanachie's? I can't face David Rayburn with a microphone sober."

"Sure," I say, smiling. "And listen, Carl . . ."

I don't get the sentence finished before he's out of his chair and heading toward the door. "Like I said, no speeches."

CHAPTER THREE

IT'S FIFTEEN MINUTES BEFORE nine the next morning when I arrive at the New Justice Building for Bol's hearing. The old building, over on Union—a street conspicuously renamed by the conquering northern army shortly after the end of the Civil War—was an aging money pit of a structure, but it was a repository of extraordinary memories, both glorious and infamous. The new building, by contrast, is a high-tech paean to the power of the state. Architecture, I've found, often contains clues to the intentions of the people behind the structure. From the immaculate, unscalable walls of the exterior to the invisible, bomb-sniffing sensors in the entryway, this is a building bereft of history, thoroughly committed to the present and future. It sits a city block wide on the banks of the Cumberland River, testimony to the burgeoning prison population of metropolitan Davidson County. By the time I arrive, Stillman is already there—God, he's an eager beaver—and the two of us walk up the concrete stairs to the big, revolving doors of the main entrance.

Stillman and I clear security together. Stillman is looking nifty in a well-tailored, gray linen suit, white shirt, and bloodred tie. He jokes with the guards like an old hand, even though he's going to court for about the fifth time in his life. One of the guards, a huge black man everybody calls Hap, motions me over. "You going up to Ginder's courtroom?" he asks.

"Yeah," I say. "Another day in paradise."

"What's goin' on today?" he asks. "The United Nations is up there."

"What do you mean?"

Hap shrugs. "I haven't heard a word of English the last half hour, except a lot of brothers want to know the way to Ginder's room." I glance at Stillman, who gives me a blank look. We take the elevator to the second floor and Judge Joseph Ginder's courtroom. Ginder is a decent guy whom I know well, since I've spent about a thousand hours arguing cases before him. He's generally fair, although he has a temper. This doesn't usually present a problem, because most of the prosecutors know how to avoid his hot buttons. These mostly have to do with respect issues, along the lines of treating him like he's a god. He's got an election coming up in three months, and he's been on his best behavior, making sure he gets the endorsement of the trial lawyers' association.

Stillman and I come around the corner and see a crowd of about twenty white people standing around with pissed expressions on their faces. Most are male, under the age of twenty-five, and dressed in this summer's version of Caucasian street thug. Stillman pulls up short. "Is it just me, or did a trailer park just empty out around here?"

I smile. "Welcome to the Nation, Stillman," I say. "That's with a capital *N*." I point to the crowd. "I probably had five cases with this crowd my first year. They live in the whitest and poorest forty square blocks of Nashville. Their parents worked low-end manufacturing jobs, except there aren't any anymore. So now they have lots of time to decide whom to blame."

"Why do they call it the Nation?"

"All the cross streets are named after states. Indiana, Kentucky, Florida, that kind of thing. They don't look happy, do they?"

"No."

"What's bothering them, Stillman, is the fact that their little place in the world is now completely surrounded by Laotians, Ukrainians, Hispanics, Cambodians, and God knows what else. These are not the kind of people who like to hear Croatian at the corner grocery store. The city planning commission has been dumping immigrants on their borders, and they're freaked."

Stillman stares. "Somebody didn't think that through."

I nod. "And now, thanks to the United Nations of We-Bail-Everybody-Out, we can add Africans to their volatile little mix."

"So what are they doing here?"

"They're here, Stillman, because a member of yet another group of people they don't want to live next to raped and killed one of their own. Tamra Hartlett."

"She lived in the Nation?"

"Nationite, third generation," I say. "They want to get a look at the man who killed her."

Stillman finally proves he has something resembling an incisive mind by saying, "Damn, Thomas. We better not fuck this up."

I nod, and we push through the crowd of Nationites to the

door of Ginder's courtroom. I open the door, walk in, and pull up short. We have entered a sea of willowy, giraffelike young black men who, quiet and circumspect, are occupying almost every seat in the gallery. I look right and left; although it's hard to be sure with them sitting, it looks like the shortest of them is a good six foot three. The taller ones sprout from their benches like slender, ebony trees. Their clothing is a patchwork of cheap formal and hand-me-down casual, combined in startling ways: there are bright-colored T-shirts with rayon slacks, tennis shoes with sport coats, a mélange of Salvation Army and Dollar Store fashion. A few—I can't get an actual count, but it seems like no more than five or six—have ritual markings of some kind on their foreheads. Interspersed in the crowd—like white dots in a black puzzle—are three figures, stark and pale in their surroundings. One is Dan Wolfe, a raging conservative with an afternoon radio talk show who never misses a photo op; a few rows up is Linda Martin, a reporter at the local Fox affiliate; on the other side of the room, scrunched between two tall Africans who tower over him like black palms, is Gavin Davies, a reporter from the *Tennessean*. Stillman and I stand mesmerized a second, then push on through the swinging doors at the front of the courtroom to the lawyers' tables. We put our briefcases on the table and take our chairs. Stillman leans over and whispers, "What the hell is this?" The boys behind us are so quiet, it's like we've come upon them sleeping.

"Apparently, Mr. Bol has friends."

A minute later Rita West comes in, another woman trailing behind. West is in her usual lawyer's suit, but the other woman has a kind of Ben and Jerry's, retro-hippie look about her. She's taller than Rita, with black, shoulder-length hair pulled back behind her ears. She's slender, with a good fig-

ure, and immaculate, pale skin. There's no makeup discernible, except for surprisingly bright red lipstick on her full
lips. She wears a pair of proto-geek, black-rimmed glasses, a
man's dress shirt, fitted black pants, and heavy, black shoes.
Her left wrist is ringed by several bracelets, each a slender
circlet of a single color: one red, one blue, one yellow, and so
on. When she enters, the sea of blackness behind us comes
alive in a hum of languages. She stops and speaks quietly to
several of the boys, and I hear the word *mother* interspersed
in a lot of foreign words I can't understand.

Stillman shakes his head. "Shit, man, I thought this was
Nashville."

"Welcome to the new South, pal."

"Who's the woman?"

"Got me."

Rita tries to find the woman a seat in the gallery, which is
impossible since every square inch is occupied with silent
Africans. Apparently, giving up a seat to a woman isn't a
part of their culture, because nobody moves. The woman
doesn't seem bothered; she plops down next to Rita at the
lawyer's table. Rita looks exasperated; I look over to catch
her eye, but instead I get the full-on laser stare of the other
woman, who's glaring at me like I've just eaten her last
cookie.

I'll be damned if I'm going to sit there and not find out
what's going on, so I stand up and walk over to Rita's desk.
She stands, and we shake hands, as usual. I've been in court
with Rita seven or eight times, and we've always stayed
friendly. "Kind of an interesting crowd today," I say.

Rita has her game face on and ignores the comment. "I
hear Carl's retirement party is next Friday night," she says.
"Is that staff only? I'd like to come."

"Consider yourself invited. He wants a big enough crowd he can sneak out the back while nobody's looking."

Rita looks past me to Stillman. "This your new partner?"

"Could be," I say, and I nod toward the woman behind her. "This yours?"

"Could be." We're standing there talking in circles, ignoring the wall of still blackness behind us. I look toward the back of the courtroom; I can see curiosity seekers peering through the back window.

"Any idea why the media showed up?" I ask.

"Guess they like a good story," she says, and that's the first time I actually worry about what Rita West has up her sleeve. I don't worry long, because the side door opens, and Greg Seneff, the judge's amiable, 275-pound bailiff, steps into the room. I head back to my table. Behind Seneff, flanked by two corrections officers, comes my enemy, Moses Bol.

Bol is as tall as the others—around six foot six—and although he's heavier than most of the other Africans in the room, he still weighs no more than 190 pounds. Because this is a bond hearing and there's no jury to sway, Bol doesn't get to wear street clothes. He comes in the room wearing a Tennessee Department of Corrections orange jumpsuit, and his arms are shackled. He enters the room cautiously, looking tense and a little scared. The guards move him along, and he follows, walking woodenly. With Bol's entrance, the room comes alive again, this time with a lower, more guttural hum. I don't understand it, but forty young men a few feet away are saying *something* to each other, and they don't sound happy. The officers lead Bol toward the defense table, and for a moment he faces the gallery; a couple of voices call out to him, loud, clear, and alien. Bol looks back at them, eyes wide, and the guards get him seated between his lawyer and the other woman. The bailiff turns toward the crowd, calling firmly for quiet and threatening to clear the gallery. For a second, I wonder if all hell is going to break loose, but the black sea obeys and the humming descends back into the silence. The energy behind us is palpable, like a loaded gun set down but easily picked back up. Seneff stares out at them awhile, just to make sure the silence is going to take; when he's satisfied, the officers who brought in Bol take chairs near the witness box, against a wall to the right.

An awkward ninety seconds or so passes. Stillman looks over at me, his face a big question mark for which I don't have an answer. At the moment, I'm more interested in Bol: He's looking straight ahead, as nervous as a hunted deer. His hair is close-cropped, but his skin is surprisingly soft-looking, like a woman's. He has the ritual markings, however; his forehead is marked by three horizontal lines, scars of some tribal custom.

Finally, the door behind the judge's bench opens, and Ginder, resplendent in black robe, walks into the room. He knows about the packed gallery and the reporters; I can tell by how determined he is to act like it's just another day in Nashville. He sits down and flips open his laptop, ignoring the gallery just like Rita and I did. Somehow the Africans are invisible, even though they're filling the room. Seneff gives the "All rise," and the black sea is on its feet, its energy filling the air like electricity.

Ginder sits, and the crowd settles back down. Bond hearings are normally casual affairs, at least compared to actual trials. They usually take about five minutes—less, in some cases—and protocol is kept to a minimum. It's revolving-door justice at its most time-efficient. Ginder says hello to the attorneys, but his gaze stops on the woman beside the prisoner. "Ms. West, does your cocounsel need to have the dress code explained to her?"

Rita is on her feet in a nanosecond. "Judge, this is Fiona Towns, a friend of the defendant. She's here to speak on his behalf. There wasn't any other seating available."

Ginder gives his unhappy look. He has a repertoire of about five looks, and I've seen them all a hundred times. There's generic unhappy—he wears this 80 percent of the time—along with pleased, angry, bored, and above all, the one he gives when he thinks he's brilliant. "If she's at the lawyer's table," he says, "she'll have on suitable attire."

"Yes, Judge."

"Fine. We're here at the request of the defense counsel for a second bond hearing for Mr. Moses Bol," he says. "The charges are aggravated rape with special circumstances, use of a weapon with deadly intent, and one count of first-degree murder. Ms. West, you've asked for this hearing, and we'll get to you presently." He turns toward me. "Mr. Dennehy, how are you this morning?"

"Fine, Your Honor."

"Glad to hear it. Before we hear Ms. West, I assume your position on bail hasn't changed?"

I rise. Considering the seriousness of the crimes, having to say anything is probably unnecessary; I could just as easily read back the charges and sit down. The thing to do in circumstances like this is keep things simple: make the case, shut up, and sit down. Otherwise, you insult the intelligence of the judge. "The defendant is an obvious flight risk, Your Honor. He's an immigrant, with no ties to the community. He owns no property. He's not currently employed, having been recently fired from his job at Wal-Mart. As you know, the state has filed the paperwork with the court indicating we are pursuing the death penalty for Mr. Bol. Therefore, his motivation for flight would be substantial. Finally, the state believes that Mr. Bol is clearly a threat to this community and needs to remain incarcerated until such time as his future is determined."

Ginder nods soberly, like he's thinking things over, even though both Rita and I know that he's already made up his mind. Bol isn't getting out of jail, not on this day. "Ms. West?" he says.

Rita stands, all five foot three of her. What happens next is like a kind of dream. Rita gives a very nice speech about how the state may think it has a strong case against her client, but she thinks otherwise. Then she turns halfway round and makes real the invisible elephant in the room, namely, the packed gallery. She says Bol has the support of 100 boys just like the 40 who are in the room right now. She says that considering what these boys have been through together, he would no more abandon them than abandon his own mother, except that his mother was executed before Bol's eyes when he was eight years old by marauding Arabs, just like they executed his father and two brothers. His sister wasn't executed, Rita says, because the same Arabs dragged her off to be sold into sex slavery on the streets of Khartoum. She says that Bol was held captive by Islamic fundamentalists for four months, during which time he was routinely abused. She says Bol refused to convert to Islam, even under pain of torture and fear of death, and that he escaped the prison and led twenty other boys across two hundred miles of rugged terrain to a refugee camp in Ethiopia. She wants the court to consider how bad things have to be when your idea of improving your life is escaping to *Ethiopia*. She says that five minutes in jail for her client is horrifying psychological torture, because he has been punished on numerous occasions by some of the cruelest men on Earth, simply for being the wrong color in the wrong place at the wrong time. Rita spells out a story of unimaginable tragedy, which I badly want to stop, but doing so would make me look like an insensitive bastard, which is not in the interest of my case. None of this is going to be admissible in the actual trial, anyway, although the rules for hearings are considerably more lenient. After three or four minutes, however, Rita's story is drawn to an awkward halt by Judge Ginder, who holds up his hand for silence.

"This is a moving story, no doubt," Ginder says. I realize I haven't actually breathed in twenty or thirty seconds. Rita's litany of horror paralyzed everybody in the room, except, thank God, Ginder. "We are not presently on the streets of Khartoum, Ms. West," he says. "We are in the city of Nashville, Tennessee, where Mr. Bol is being held on very serious crimes. Is the court to understand that you have asked for this bail hearing because the internal psychology of the defendant is so tortured that conventional incarceration constitutes cruel and unusual punishment?"

"It's deeply traumatizing to him, Your Honor. I would recommend that Bol be remanded to house arrest, with electronic monitoring."

"I see. Well, I sympathize with the young man's story, but unless you have something more, I'm going to have to deny your client bail."

Rita takes this well, like the professional she is; she must have known that no matter how good she was on this day, she didn't have a chance. I sneak a look behind me, wondering how the wall of young men are going to take the news that Bol isn't getting out. But the woman beside Rita has not come to court this day to be a part of the furniture. She stands up, uninvited, and addresses the court. Under normal circumstances, this would have the bailiff escorting her out of the room before she had a chance to finish her first sentence. But it's a bond hearing, so Ginder merely looks at her like she's a kind of unwanted pest.

"Your Honor," she says, "I have something to say on this matter."

Rita looks pained; this isn't in her ideal script for the day.

"And who are you?" Ginder asks.

"I am Fiona Towns, the pastor of the Downtown Presbyterian Church."

I look up. The voice is lower than I expected, with a sexy rasp. *Pastor. Apparently, they're making them a lot more attractive than I remember.*

"Fine institution," Ginder says.

"Thank you, Your Honor. I'm here to speak on behalf of Moses Bol."

"In the future, I'd recommend you wait until called on to speak."

"You weren't going to call on me," she says.

Ginder gives his unpleasant look. "All right, Ms. Towns. Go ahead."

"January 7, 1994, Your Honor." This is followed by a long silence. Rita slumps down in her chair a little, like she wants to be somewhere else.

Ginder looks at her blankly. "That's it?"

"There's also April 23, 1998. And October 27, 2002. I could go on, but I think you see my point."

"I don't, as a matter of fact."

"Those were days when people accused of crimes similar to Mr. Bol were released on bail. By you."

Ginder's eyes narrow; he senses he's walking into a trap, but he doesn't see the teeth yet. "Every case is unique, Ms.

Towns. I'm sure that if those individuals were granted bail, it's because the circumstances warranted it."

He raises his gavel, and Towns says, "As far as I can tell, Your Honor, the only circumstances unique to those defendants were that they were white." The gavel stops in midair. I look up at the judge, as does every other head in the room, especially the media flacks. Ginder looks like he's been struck, then turns into stone. I see Gavin Davies physically lean forward, like he's a hungry dog and someone is unwrapping steak.

Ginder sets down his gavel and looks out into the black sea, weighing his next move. He's been a judge for almost twenty years, and he knows how things play in the media, how context is everything, how there isn't going to be a way to put into print how stilted and artificial things are in his courtroom right now. Ginder isn't a racist, not by a long shot. But whether or not Joseph Ginder is a racist isn't what's going to play in the newspaper tomorrow unless the next words out of his mouth are the right ones. All that's going to come across is that he lets white people out for the same crimes he keeps black people in for, and that is going to play like shit.

Ginder is very angry now, but not yet so angry he can't think. He locks onto Towns, eye-to-eye, knowing it's too late now to throw her out; he's entered the zone where appearance is everything. The standoff doesn't move for several seconds, until a barely perceptible smile creeps into his face. I recognize the "I'm brilliant" look; I've seen it a hundred times. He relaxes a little, leaning back in his chair. "October 27, that last date you mentioned," he says. "You say that was the same crime as Mr. Bol?"

Towns doesn't need to look at her notes. "The crime was

aggravated assault with intent to do bodily harm, and first-degree murder, Your Honor."

"What bail did I set on that occasion, Ms. Towns?"

"You set bail at seven hundred and fifty thousand dollars."

Ginder nods sagely. "How about the date before. What was that one?"

"April 23, 1998. The crime in that instance was rape with special circumstances."

"What was the bail in that instance, Ms. Towns?"

"Four hundred thousand dollars."

"All right, Ms. Towns. I'll tell you what I'll do. I'll set bail for Mr. Bol for one million, two hundred and fifty thousand dollars. Mr. Bol is facing both counts, and unless my math is rusty, that's the combination of the two."

"It is, Your Honor."

I look over at Stillman and smile; Bol couldn't raise fifteen hundred dollars' bail, much less nearly a thousand times as much. A million dollars to Moses Bol might as well be a billion. Ginder is smiling when he grants the bail and states court is adjourned. I'm impressed; it's a deft move that is scrupulously fair and deflates the racism charge without actually confronting it. Ginder stands—shit-eating grin on his face—and the gallery rises with him.

At which point, Fiona Towns asks, "Where do I pay?"

CHAPTER FOUR

"THAT DIDN'T GO WELL."

"No," I say, "it didn't." I stare at Stillman, who, along with David Rayburn, has gathered with me around the district attorney's conference table. It's two hours after Stillman and I left the courthouse. The last few moments there are a blur, but at least I managed to recommend to Ginder that he arrange for security to escort the Africans out of the building. The judge, still shell-shocked by the pastor's ploy, managed to pull himself together enough to get four officers to walk out the Sudanese in a long, protected line. The Nationites, angered that the man they considered Tamra Hartlett's killer would soon be walking the streets, hissed at them as they passed. The officers gave the Africans a fifteen-minute head start, but eventually, they had to let the lions loose. Bol was remanded to Towns's care, and his monitored house arrest will be at the church, not at Bol's apartment in Tennessee Village, which is right next door to the Nation.

"I did a Nexis search on Towns," I say. "I got six hits. It's definitely interesting reading."

"Who is she?" Rayburn asks.

"She took over the Downtown Presbyterian Church about eight months ago. The place has been on the verge of closing for years. Towns showed up, and it's become a hangout for the hard-core peace and justice types. She's got the eco-crowd, antiglobalization, the whole thing. It's more like a political party than a church. Apparently, she thinks a part of her calling is posting bail for murderers."

"But how did she come up with the million bucks? What is she, independently wealthy?"

"She got Bol out on a property bond. And you won't believe on what property."

"It must have been the fucking Taj Mahal," Rayburn says.

"It's the church's parsonage."

Rayburn stares in disbelief a second. "Are you shitting me? Can she even do that?"

"She had the power of attorney with her," I say. "The address is 625 Glendale Avenue, Belle Meade."

Rayburn whistles. "Belle Meade? The lots alone are worth a fortune over there."

"She had the last tax appraisal with her. A million-five. The original deed was dated 1956. Probably cost a tenth of that back then."

"OK, so the place is worth the money. How the hell does she sell this to the church?"

"Towns got a new church constitution passed giving her the right to dispose of church property however she sees fit. And she sees fit, apparently, to use it as collateral against the future court appearance of Moses Bol."

"The hell she does." Rayburn is fuming, feeling things

unravel with disturbing unpredictability. "Where did this woman come from, anyway? Does anybody know?"

"Basically, she's little Miss Protest. You remember when the state legislature tried to cut funding for low-income housing? That bunch of people who tried to storm the House chambers? She was a part of that crowd."

"And she's a preacher?" Rayburn asks. This offends his sense of order. In his thinking, preachers marry, bury, and stay the hell out of the way the rest of the time.

"Yeah," I say. "But the ultraliberal, radical-fringe stuff. Do you know she conducted a funeral in absentia for Bishop Romero?"

"Who's Bishop Romero?"

"Murdered in El Salvador by government death squads during the Reagan administration."

"Reagan? That's twenty years ago."

"Romero never got a proper funeral. Towns wanted to give him one. They had a casket, the whole thing. That was at her previous church."

"Where was this?"

"Muskeegee, Michigan."

"I bet that went over great in Muskeegee."

"They fired her for it."

"Good for them. How the hell did she end up in Nashville?"

"Far as I can tell, she worked for some homeless agencies in Michigan, did a lot of volunteer work. Ended up coming here to work for the Center for Peace and Justice over at Vanderbilt University. That lasted about a year, until the grant ran out—"

"Friggin' delusiacs," Rayburn interrupts. *Delusiac*—a combination of *delusional* and *maniacs*—is his favorite, made-up word for any over-the-top political movement he encounters. "All these friggin' delusiacs hate the government," he says, "but they don't have any problem taking money from it."

"Anyway," I say, "she quit when they ran out of money, and took the job at the DPC. She's been there ever since."

"She's a nut," Rayburn declares.

"Yeah, well, she's got a degree in public policy from Oberlin and a master's in theology from Harvard. So maybe it's better not to underestimate her."

Everybody looks at each other a second. Rayburn raises an eyebrow. "Shit."

"Care to know what her dissertation was about?" I ask.

"What?"

"The impact of the death penalty on race relations in the South."

A moment of silence, as pieces of a puzzle slide into place. "Son of a bitch," Carl says. "You think she's behind this thing with Buchanan?"

"Pretty interesting coincidence," I say. "There's only one way to find out for sure."

"It's not like you can just walk over and ask her," Stillman says. I swear to God, if he doesn't stop smiling, I'm going to deck him.

"Any reason why not?" Carl asks.

Rayburn sits thinking a moment, then nods. "Thomas," he says, "I'd say it's time to see if this preacher keeps office hours."

It's nearly three before I can leave for the Downtown Presbyterian Church, or DPC, as it's known locally. There's the usual pile of paperwork, and I need to make a dent in it now, before the Buchanan thing takes all my time. The church is only about eight blocks away from my office, and I decide to walk. My experience with preachers is next to nothing, having previously been limited to two: the first, who buried my father in a flat, dusty monotone, and the second, a flowery Episcopal priest who married me to my ex-wife. At least he looked like something, with robes as ornate as his speech. Since then, I haven't darkened a door to a church. Towns, to me, is still a mystery. Unlike Rayburn, I don't assume the worst about people without an actual reason. All I know about Towns right now is that we'd have a not particularly interesting argument about presidential politics and whether or not McDonald's or Disney or whatever other big corporation is the embodiment of evil. Why she's willing to risk her church on springing Moses Bol is still up in the air, as far as I'm concerned.

I make it to the church in about ten minutes. I stop at the bottom of the concrete steps, looking up at the structure. The building is framed by two brick, rectangular towers that rise sixty feet on either side of a surprisingly narrow main building. To reach the entryway you pass between two formidable pillars of white stone that rise almost to the roof. Above them is a portico covered in strange hieroglyphics. Behind the pillars are three substantial, aged wooden doors, the kind of doors it would take a battering ram to knock down. The whole is covered with decades of city pollution and grime. Apparently, the wealthy white southerners who once maintained the place have long since retreated to the safety of the gated suburbs. Making matters worse, what was once an imposing structure now crouches forlornly between skyscrapers of metal and glass, and in the face of so much progress, the church looks decidedly out of place.

There are about twenty steps, and I take them two at a time. I try the middle door, and I'm surprised to find it open.

This particular block is fairly well traveled by the city's homeless community, and I figure in a place like the DPC there are quite a few artifacts that aren't nailed down. I enter a wide inner chamber with walls of white rock. There's a bulletin board across the chamber, with a number of broadsheets tacked to it: *Inter-Asian Alliance for Justice; Lesbian Council on Reproductive Rights; Latinos Unidos.* A dozen or more groups have posted meeting times and agendas. Apparently, the Reverend Towns has put out an all-points bulletin for every victim group in the city, and the downtrodden are answering the call.

A second set of doors opens to the sanctuary. I pull one of them open, step in, and stare. For a moment, I wonder where I am. The room is dark and brooding—the only light streams in through stained-glass windows badly in need of cleaning—but it's not so dark that I can't make out great towers of what look like sandstone rising at the opposite end from the floor to ceiling. Egyptian writing and symbols are visible on the walls, and a substantial molding that rings the entire room is covered in depictions of palm trees. The stained-glass windows depict scenes from the Egyptian desert, rather than the acts of apostles. The ceiling is composed of interlocking panels, each painted as part of the sky. After a few moments, things fall into place: there is the sky above, sandstone pillars around me, scenes of palm trees and Egyptian writing everywhere I look. The sign may say the Downtown Presbyterian Church, but I feel very much as though I were outdoors, in some kind of Egyptian temple.

The sanctuary is large and tall, with the ceilings thirty feet above me. The front of the room, where the altar is located, is a good hundred feet away. I walk toward it, the ancient, wooden floor creaking under my steps. Over everything is the palpable sense of dust and abandonment. I can feel in the air that this is a place of the past. The days when this place was filled with the city's elite are long forgotten. *Now,* I think, *it's a haven for Fiona Towns and her band of delusiacs.*

I'm halfway to the front of the sanctuary when I hear a sound behind me. I turn, and a disheveled man is standing fifteen feet away, watching me calmly, as though he materialized out of thin air. "You're Thomas Dennehy," he says. He's five foot ten, with gray eyes, black hair, a heavy beard and mustache, inexpensively framed glasses, and a Ft. Lauderdale Beach ball cap pulled down over his eyes. He's practically invisible, enveloped in a too-large, well-worn trench coat, which makes no sense considering it's ninety degrees outside. *An addict,* I think. *Hard to tell his age, he's so weathered. Thirty? Forty-five?*

"You're Thomas Dennehy," he repeats. "Assistant district attorney of Davidson County." The man has the pungent odor of a man a long time between showers.

"Do I know you?"

He smiles. "No. I help out Fiona. Odd jobs. There's no staff anymore, you know."

"Big place," I say. "Must keep you busy."

He looks at me silently for a while. "I'm not the janitor," he says.

"Sorry."

"It's OK, Skippy. Sum me up by the clothes. Never mind." Behind the glasses his eyes are angry, glittery dots.

"Listen, can you tell me if Ms. Towns is around?" I ask. "I'd like to speak to her."

He points to a door behind the altar, his gray eyes not blinking. "There's a hallway to the pastor's study," he says. "Just knock."

"Thanks." He turns and glides away to the other side of the church, then passes through a doorway and vanishes.

The floor at the front of the church is covered with worn carpet the color of blood. At the altar, I pass a large Celtic cross sitting on an old wooden table. The cross is made of iron, and there are runes written on it in a language I don't recognize. I press open the door behind the altar, stepping through into a dingy but ordinary hallway beyond. The floor is industrial tile, and although it's clean, it's well worn. Only half the lights are illuminated. *Saving on electricity. Word is there's practically nobody left in this money pit.* I walk forward, not sure where I'm going. Along the wall there are pictures of previous congregations, dating all the way back to some monochrome pictures from the early nineteen hundreds. The early crowds are dour and grim, dressed in dark clothes and serious expressions. Things get better in the forties and fifties; the congregations look happier, and the flat-top haircuts in some remind me of my father. He would have looked at home in that crowd, except for the Bibles. In the late sixties the crowds become noticeably smaller, and by 1980 what was once a thriving enterprise is down to less than a hundred souls. They have a determined look, but there's no denying the grim realities of so few in such a large space. The last picture is in 1987. *Almost twenty years ago. Apparently, it got too bad to want to preserve in a photograph.*

I go up three short steps, turn left, and confront a large door made of dark, polished oak. I reach out and rap on the door, making a sharp echo in the empty hallway. I hear a female voice. "Come in."

I open the door, and Fiona Towns, who is balancing precariously on her tiptoes on a short stepladder, her right arm outstretched with a book not quite high enough to be replaced on its high shelf, her left arm straight out for balance, artlessly, noisily, and over several agonizing moments, loses her footing, and—frozen for a moment in midair, which gives her the chance to make angry, surprised eye contact—proceeds to tumble to the ground in a cacophony of books, arms, legs, and dust. She looks back up at me from the floor. "Ah. It's Mr. Dennehy, from the government."

Nice beginning. Very low-key. "I'm sorry. It happened so fast, and I just—"

"*Stood* there," she says, still on her butt.

She's right; for some reason, I was rooted to the floor, unable to move. "Sorry. Really, I'm sorry." I step forward reflexively and reach down to help her up. She ignores my hand and gets on her knees. "Do something useful for a change, Mr. Dennehy. Pick up books."

I crouch beside her, picking up volumes and stacking them on the desk beside her. I glance at a couple of titles: *Father Pio, Mystic, Confessor; Saint Anthony of Padua,* followed with something by the Society of Psychical Research in England. She has a light musk scent; it's subtle, but there's enough to convince me she wants it noticed. "A little light reading?" I ask.

She pulls the books out of my hand. "I had a feeling I'd see you, but not today. You really are Johnny-on-the-spot, aren't you?"

"Sorry I startled you."

"It's all right. I'm still moving in, really. I've only been here . . . God, it's been eight months. I'll have to come up with another excuse." We pick up books together, stacking them into precarious piles. The whole place looks like the overcrowded study of an Oxford don who hasn't had the room cleaned in years. It smells of dust and memories. At one end is a series of wooden carvings of African figures. We finish stacking and stand up. I stick out my hand. She stares at it a second, still not taking it. "I don't have to talk to you," she says.

"Correct."

"So tell me why I should."

"It might help."

"Who? You or Moses?"

"The options aren't necessarily mutually exclusive. I have nothing against the kid, personally."

"Except for thinking he's a murderer and a rapist. You're wrong about that, by the way." She pushes an errant strand of hair out of her face and tucks it behind her ear.

"All evidence to the contrary." She gets a tired look, as though things like evidence and testimony are somehow beside the point. "That was a bold move in court today," I say. "It wasn't very smart, but it was bold."

She raises an eyebrow. "Not smart?"

"You embarrassed the judge sitting on Bol's case. For somebody who wants to help the kid, it might not have been the smartest idea."

Her expression clouds briefly. "It's not as bad as leaving him in jail," she says. "The important thing is to get him away from you."

I laugh. "You mean, from me personally?"

"From the government. The people who want to kill him."

"Look . . . what should I call you? Pastor? Reverend?"

"Towns will do."

"Well, Towns, nobody in my office enjoys it when somebody dies. Personally, I hate the thought of it."

"Until you hate it enough to actually stop doing it, I don't see that it makes much difference."

I smile, in spite of myself. *She would have made a good lawyer.* "Place is a little empty," I say. "Not much staff around."

"There isn't any staff," she answers. "There were two, but they quit in protest when I took the job." She looks hurt, which surprises me; I had pictured her a Joan of Arc, impervious and warlike. "There's only me now. I stay busy, so maybe you should just come to the point."

"It doesn't look very good for Mr. Bol," I say. "The evidence against him is substantial."

"You mean the semen and blood evidence."

"If you're comfortable discussing that kind of detail, yes."

"Comfortable?" She gazes at me. "You don't know anything at all about my work here, do you, Mr. Dennehy?"

"I'm here to listen."

"Each one of these boys has seen more death than the most hardened criminal in this state. When they watched their families being slaughtered before their eyes, they were all less than twelve years old. A bloody handprint is of no more consequence to them than opening a window. And now death has followed them here."

"What do you mean?"

"The first was Peter Gurang, shot at the Sahara Club. Then Chege and Iniko Basel, two brothers who managed to survive five years of starvation, disease, and civil war, only to get killed in a gang battle in east Nashville." She pauses. "These boys come from a gracious and beautiful culture, Mr. Dennehy. They have no context for life here. They're drowning in our consumerism, defenseless against the crudeness of our society. One of them actually showed up the other day with a new car. Some unscrupulous salesman at a dealership got him qualified for a loan. The boy doesn't even have a driver's license."

"There are bad people around, Towns. That's what we have the justice system for."

"You're missing the point, Mr. Dennehy. In Sudan, these

boys had a context for living. They did noble work. Here, they sweep floors. They don't belong here, and they can't go home. It's no wonder some of them get lost all over again." She turns away, retreating behind her desk, and looks out the window onto the street. "I'm not going to lose Moses, Mr. Dennehy. Not him."

"I have the victim's blood in Bol's car," I say quietly. "I have a phone call from her apartment to his less than two hours before the murder. I have witnesses who claim Hartlett and Bol argued vehemently on at least two occasions, and evidence indicates they fought brutally with each other that night. Against which, he presents no credible alibi."

With one sentence, Towns turns the case upside down. "*I* am his alibi, Mr. Dennehy."

"Say again?"

"I was with Moses that night. We were here, five miles away from the crime. So it's impossible for him to have committed the murder. You have the wrong man."

I shake my head, not wanting to hear. *Don't do this,* I think. *Don't make me take you down with him.* "Someone with your education is obviously aware of the penalties for perjury," I say quietly. "This wouldn't be an overnight stay in the county lockup with your solidarity sisters. This is three to five in the state penitentiary. If the DA decided to go for obstruction of justice—and knowing Rayburn, he would—that's ten more."

"My statement stands."

"In that case, you might want to practice answering a few questions that are likely to come up," I say. "Like why you didn't mention this information at Bol's arraignment."

"I didn't know he had been arraigned until after it happened. I was out of town, in Washington, D.C." She gives me a caustic look. "Protesting."

"And at the grand jury?"

"Moses's lawyer seems to be under the impression that my testimony might be considered . . . unreliable." She pauses. "Rita West holds you in very high regard. She's convinced you would tear me to pieces on the witness stand because of my political activism."

"I have the feeling it might come up, yeah."

"Rita says my arrest record at previous executions would be . . . I believe the phrase was 'like bait to a hungry shark.' " She pauses. "Apparently, you are the shark, Mr. Dennehy."

I smile. "I accept the compliment."

"Rita is looking for corroboration before she brings me out, but she's not going to find any. Moses and I were alone, and no one saw us together."

"Then she's going to have to put you on the stand and let you sink or swim."

"That's right, Mr. Dennehy. She's going to have to let you at me."

"If you get on the stand and lie, you're going to leave me no choice. I can't have the system of justice compromised."

She gives me an unpleasantly knowing look. "It's a little late for that, isn't it?"

I step back. "So you're working with Buchanan." She says nothing, her face scrupulously neutral. *OK.* "You have to admit, though, it's a hell of an irony," I say.

"What's that?"

"The fact that you've tried to save the lives of all those criminals is the very reason why nobody is going to believe you now, when you try to save Bol's."

She stares at me, her face reddening. She brushes past me toward the door. "You should go," she says. "I have twenty homeless people showing up in an hour, and they're going to be hungry."

"Alone?"

"I have Robert."

"The addict?" She gives me a surprised look. "We met in the sanctuary. He didn't give me his name."

"Robert is cautious with strangers. He's had hard times, but he's found safety here."

"All the same, I'd be careful. Some of the homeless in this city aren't above taking advantage of a woman."

"I can take care of myself."

"Is Jimmy Roland in your group? Short guy, he'd be about fifty by now."

She thinks a moment, then nods. "Mr. Roland, that's right."

"He was my first case. He used a rock to beat in the head of another guy for stealing his coat. It was cold outside, but over at the DA's office we still look down on that kind of thing."

She watches me quietly for a moment, then shakes her head. "You're trying to rattle me, Mr. Dennehy. It won't work."

"I'm trying to warn you. But you're a grown-up. What you do with your time is your business."

"That's right. And my time with you is up." She opens the door, inviting me out.

I step through. "The twenty dinners. Who's paying for that?"

"We're selling the church's art, Mr. Dennehy. I can either welcome the hungry to my door, or I can turn them away and look at pretty pictures. Not a very complicated decision." The door closes, and I'm left in the hallway alone.

Outside, I decide to cut through the church's employee parking lot to Fifth Street, saving two long city blocks on my walk back to 222 Second Avenue. The tiny lot is behind the

church, twelve narrow spaces crammed between the back of
the church offices and a service alley that feeds the towering,
thirty-story bank behind it. The only car is parked in a space
marked *Pastor;* it's a white, midnineties Volvo sedan that
has definitely seen better days. *Perfect,* I think. *The classic
neohippie car.* As I walk past, I see a face looking down from
high above, in the church. The face is only visible for a moment; then it's gone. But I recognize the figure. It's Robert,
the addict.

Back in the office, I go by Gladys Morrisette's office.
Gladys, a career bureaucrat who must have been the perfect
hall monitor in high school, is the only query-certified member of our staff, which means she has access to MAGIC, the
national criminal database. Gladys has made it a life-and-
death principle that there will never be an unapproved
search while she lives and breathes. So I fill out the paperwork, declaring Towns an official witness on the Bol trial,
meticulously dealing with the minutiae of the form. She
scrutinizes it awhile, then nods. She then directs me to turn
around—she's that paranoid about anybody sneaking a look
at the codes—and punches "Fiona Towns" into the database.
After a minute or so, I hear her whistle.

I turn around. "What?"

"Girlfriend's been busy," Gladys says. "Four states and
the District." She points to the laser printer, which is spitting
out pages. After a few minutes, I hold Towns's FBI file, together with state arrest records of Washington, Florida, New
York, Texas, and the District of Columbia. I thank Gladys
and head to Rayburn's office, reading as I walk.

Dolores, Rayburn's secretary, nods me through. "He's
waiting for you," she says. "Carl's with him."

I push open Rayburn's office door and see Carl and the

DA standing beside Rayburn's coffee table. Rayburn gives me an expectant look. "So? What's up with the crazy woman?"

I shrug. "She's working with him."

"I knew it!" Rayburn explodes. "It's a friggin' delusiac conspiracy."

"She just told you?" Carl said. "Just like that?"

"Not exactly. It sort of came to light while she was telling me the other big news of the day." I pause. "Towns is going to testify that she was with Bol at the church at the time of the crime. She's going to be his alibi."

There is a moment of silence, which Rayburn shreds by saying, "Jesus Holy Christ! They're supposed to be fucking Presbyterians over there."

"There's more."

Rayburn looks up warily. "What?"

I spread the files across David's coffee table, and the three of us gather around. "Disturbing the peace, disorderly conduct, unlawful protest, and, most glamorously, incitement to riot."

Carl picks up the FBI report. "Arrested in Seattle, at a meeting of the IMF; again in Washington, making noise just outside Bush's second inauguration; and New York, at the World Economic Forum."

"Take a look at Texas," I say.

Carl pulls out the Texas file. "Arrested three times. Each one, outside a prison where an execution was scheduled."

I nod. "You know those nice people who just light candles and pray for the soon-to-be-departed? She's not one of them."

Rayburn reaches out and snatches the papers. He scans a few moments, then looks up. "She set fire to a police car outside a prison in Tarrant County. That's destruction of government property."

"It delayed the execution twenty-four hours," I say. "The police were afraid a full-scale riot would start if they went forward, so they had to clear the area and do the whole thing over again the next day."

Carl leans back in his chair with a thoughtful smile. "Moral chaos," he says, quietly.

I look up. "What do you mean?"

"A state of mind where the ends justify the means. Within the confines of the worldview, acts that would otherwise be repugnant make perfect sense. Think Greenpeace. Think Posse Comitatus. Hell, for that matter, think Al Qaeda."

"You're not seriously comparing a Presbyterian minister with Al Qaeda."

Carl shrugs. "Both may be equally committed to their cause."

"For God's sake, Carl, she spends her afternoons feeding the hungry."

"So does Hamas."

We sit in silence for a second, while a set of fairly extreme possibilities runs through our minds.

"Hang on, gentlemen," I say. "We're losing perspective here. Maybe this woman's a little hyped-up, but be serious. She's not a terrorist. It would go against her entire system of belief."

"I'm not accusing her of being a terrorist," Carl says, resolute. "I'm saying that given sufficient commitment to a higher calling, it's not the people *without* principles who do the damnedest things. It's the people *with* them."

"Like lie to protect someone from the death penalty?" I ask.

Carl stares down at the FBI report. "It's fair to say that

when Fiona Towns is motivated to raise a ruckus, she doesn't mind breaking a law or two to make her point. For her, this might be nothing more than jury nullification. A simple case of O. J."

"Carl's right," Rayburn says. "The evidence in this case speaks for itself. Against it, the defense has one thing." He points to Towns's picture. "Her." He looks up at me. "She's toast," he says. "As of this moment, this trial is no longer about Moses Bol. It's about *her*. "I want to know what she has for breakfast, lunch, and dinner. I want to know what kind of gas she puts in her car. I want to know *everything*."

I nod. "Anything else?"

"Yeah," he answers. "Watch that Sudanese kid, too. As far as this office is concerned, we've got a killer on the street."

CHAPTER
FIVE

THE WEEKEND COMES, and I miss Jazz like hell. This is her third year for soccer camp, a ritzy operation held down in Sewanee, on the campus of the University of the South. It costs a fortune, not that this bothers Sarandokos. But at fifteen hundred bucks, I hope they serve the kids shrimp cocktails before their filet mignon. At least soccer camp gives me an idea for Jazz's birthday present, and it's something Sarandokos can't buy at any price. Last year I was the coach for Jazz's soccer team, and Sarandokos had the grace not to come to a single game. There are a hundred good memories, even though the team only finished a little above five hundred. I want to freeze that last spring, the way she laughed and tried her hardest and forgot about the game fifteen minutes after it was over. She was still a little girl, and if she knew she was the best-dressed girl on the team off the field, she didn't show it. Her birthday present will be a scrapbook of photographs from the season. I put it together over the weekend, and Sunday evening I put the book in a box and wrap it with a note: *For you, Jazz. Mia Hamm better watch out.*

Father-daughter scrapbooks are not on the minds of people in the Nation over the weekend, however. Paul Landmeyer's assessment that things are getting tense there proves on the money. There are a couple of small incidents on Sunday, and by Monday morning, the Nation is alive. Well-used cars with dented fenders are circling Tennessee Village, hunting Bol, or if he's not handy, anyone else tall, black, and foreign. Always easy to rile, the Nationites have taken this one personally. Tamra Hartlett was raped and killed in her own home. There needs to be justice. This news comes to me courtesy of Josh Ritchie, one of six full-time investigators for the DA's office. Josh moved down from Wisconsin a few years ago, mostly to do more investigating and less freezing his ass off five months a year. He's got tousled, blond hair, a slim, athletic body, and although he's thirty-one years old, with the right clothes he can pass for anything from twenty to forty. He walks in first thing in the morning and plops in a chair, looking tired. He's wearing flared jeans, a red-and-black-striped dress shirt, untucked, and square-toe loafers without socks. He sets an opened can of Red Bull on my desk.

"What was it, business or pleasure?" I ask, smiling.

"Work, this time," he says. He turns his baseball cap around backward and leans back. "What you got for me?"

I push Towns's mug photograph and address across the table. "Fiona Towns," I say. "She's the pastor of Downtown Presbyterian Church. Let me know what she does with her life."

Josh picks up the photograph. "We're surveilling preachers now?"

"She's a material witness in a murder-rape," I say. "So, yeah. I want to be informed. Daily check-ins, at least."

"Nice eyes. I like green."

"Not to touch, Josh."

Josh laughs. "Haven't crossed that line yet, chief." He looks at the photograph. "What was the murder?"

I pull out photographs of Tamra Hartlett and Moses Bol. "The guy is African, named Bol. He killed the woman."

Josh looks up. "This is the guy everybody wants over at the Nation."

"You heard something?"

"There's already been a skirmish or two over this. Word is, if Bol walks, they'll take matters into their own hands."

Beautiful. Things aren't complicated enough, without a little vigilante justice on our hands. "Trust me, if Bol walks, it'll only be from the showers to his cell in Riverbend prison," I say. "Which is where you come in. Bol and Hartlett were seen arguing several times during the week before the murder. Problem is, we don't know what about. Your job is to answer that question."

Josh puts the pictures in his pocket. "You got it, chief."

With Josh dispatched, I dig into the paperwork to put a wire on the phone where Moses Bol's roommates are still living, which, thanks to the Supreme Court of the United States, is far from automatic, even when someone is accused of murder-rape. I run the paper by Rayburn before I send it over to Judge Ginder, just to get the DA's perspective on it. I've got an hour left before lunch, so I spend it preparing for the pretrial conference Stillman scheduled with Tamra Hartlett's father, mother, and boyfriend for tomorrow. Just before noon, I go by Carl's office, which Carl has spent the day emptying. It's Monday, which means a ritual lunch with Carl, me, and Paul Landmeyer, the chief of Police Forensics.

Carl has another week at work, but he's a lame duck, with no new cases. The more he gets his housekeeping taken care of, the cleaner his escape will be on the last day. He looks up when I enter, annoyed, then relaxes when he recognizes me. "I thought it was more good-byes," he says, grimacing. "It's been like a funeral in here today. Secretaries blubbering, lots of 'you lucky bastard' speeches. Makes me want to puke."

"It's only going to get worse," I say, grinning. I point to the few remaining boxes of books stacked on the floor. "What are you going to do with those?"

He picks up a thick crimson volume and reads the spine. "*Criminal Practice and Procedure*," he says. "I could bequeath it to a law library in Guam. Better yet, start fires with it. Seven hundred pages, say ten pages a fire. Ought to last me a couple of winters, easy."

I watch him replace the book, looking as bowed down as I've ever seen him. He's been like a father to me, only better, because he doesn't carry the psychological trauma of my real father's death. And as with a real father, watching him retire gives me a glimpse at my own ending: thirty-one years of hard work, packed up into boxes, then carried off as though they had never happened. I blink, then look out the window. Carl, as senior prosecutor, has a prime office overlooking the Cumberland. It's the de facto viewing location for the big fireworks displays over the water on Memorial Day, Fourth of July, and New Year's Eve. With Carl's retirement, the office is mine, if I want it, which I'm not sure I do. There's something eerie about displacing him physically, as well as in the hierarchy of the office. I only have a few more days to decide; other, less conflicted prosecutors are eager to take my place if I don't stake my claim. "So how does it feel?" I ask.

He stands and walks to the large picture window that makes up the back wall of the office. "It feels like I'll see this view a few more times," he answers, his voice quiet. "A few more walks through the front door. A few more trips to the courthouse."

"You going down there every day?"

He nods. "Call it habit. I just don't want to stop."

I smile. "You could always change sides," I say. "No age limit on that."

"Thirty-one years of putting them away, I'd feel like a traitor. Anyway, I'd just end up kicking your ass in court, and I don't think I could take that."

I laugh out loud. "You ready to head to the Saucer? We're a little early, but what the hell."

"Yeah. God knows, I've got nothing to do here."

"I'm going to invite Stillman."

Carl raises an eyebrow. "He's not as big a prick as you think, by the way."

"Glad to hear it, since he's my new partner. But I'm inviting him to spend time with you, not me."

"Because?"

"Because I've got a week left for you to rub off on him. You better work fast."

Finally, a real smile breaks out on Carl's face, which is when I realize that's all I wanted to see. He isn't kidding when he calls the DA's office his family; he never married, eventually outlived his parents, as well as one of two sisters. He knows how to do one thing in life—fight like hell to put away bad people—and it's hard to picture him in some retirement home making friends. He'd sit there at dinner listening to how somebody was the top salesman for the Aetna company or something, and he'd want to jump out a window. I'll be there for him then, if I'm still standing. But for now, I just want to see him smile. "Let's go, old man," I say. "We'll make Stillman buy."

We roll down the hall and pick up Stillman, who looks like he's just won the lottery when we invite him to lunch. Fifteen minutes later the three of us pile out of Carl's Buick and walk into the Saucer, a vast, informal club with tatty couches for seating, air the approximate color of cigarette smoke, and after 8:00, music provided by any one of the thousand desperate country music wannabes floating around Nashville. Stillman looks around like he doesn't want to sit his two-hundred-dollar slacks on any of the nappy couches, and Carl rolls his eyes. He points to the bar, which is fifty feet of polished hardwood. "You see that, son?" he says. Stillman nods. "Behind that bar is a row of eighty-three taps. *Eighty-three.* Each one pours a different kind of heaven into a glass. Ambers, ales, pilsners. Beer as dark and thick as sludge, as light and sweet as honey. Those taps are a ticket to the four corners of the world. Japan. Germany. And, thanks to the late, great Ronald Reagan and his victory over the evil empire, Russia, Poland, and the Czech Republic." He smiles reverently. "Not to forget the mother country."

"Ireland," I say. "I'm the Irish one, but Becker wants to convert."

"I'm a Miller Lite man," Stillman says, looking around the club.

Carl looks struck. "Good Christ, Stillman. We found you just in time." He puts his hand on Stillman's shoulder. "I trust your charge cards are all in working order." Stillman gives a worried look—the revolving bill for the CEO-level

clothes he's wearing is probably floating through his mind—
and mutters something unintelligible.

"Junior prosecutors always buy," I say. "It's how we keep
smart young guys like you from leaving. After you buy
drinks for a few years, it finally gets to be your turn. You
can't afford to leave all that money on the table."

"Precisely," Carl says. We sit on a couple of couches facing each other, Carl and me on one side, Stillman on the
other. A gorgeous waitress wearing a breast-defining T-shirt
walks up to take our order. I order a Paulaner Hefe-
Weizen—which gets Carl's approving nod—and Carl orders a little number called a Ratsherrn Trunk, a beer so
sharp and pungent just hearing him order it makes my eyes
water. Stillman flashes his TV smile at the waitress but
doesn't get to open his mouth. "Young Stillman will have a
Boundary Bay," Carl says. "We'll start him on the West
Coast, and work our way east." Carl smiles at the waitress.
"Three corned beef and ryes, please. And we'll be running a
bit of a tab today, dear," he says. "Stillman will give you his
card."

Stillman pulls out a Visa with as much aplomb as he can
manage, but he watches it disappear into the smoky distance
like a best friend marching off to war. As much as I enjoy
seeing him squirm, I put him out of his misery. "Don't panic,
Stillman," I say. "One beer's the limit at lunch. You'll get out
of here alive."

Stillman exhales slightly, and we settle in, Carl filling his
space on the sofa so comfortably it's hard to imagine him
more at home where he actually lives. The one-beer rule is
only a lunchtime thing; after hours he's always been a heavy
drinker, but at least he's positively religious about taking
taxis home. He's never been less than razor sharp the next
morning, either, which is testimony either to his constitution

or to his alcohol tolerance after thirty years' practice. I watch him quietly, wondering what he'll do other than drink when he retires in a few days. Drinking has been social for Carl, it's been a hobby, and, above all, it's been something he's done expertly, with élan and good humor. His love for the color and taste of fine beer has always had a powerful counterbalance in his life, namely, his even greater love for the law. With that removed, I wonder what will happen. He fits so comfortably in his seat now, I can imagine him receding farther and farther into the upholstery, until he vanishes completely, a perpetual buzz of forgetfulness flowing through his veins. God knows he hates to go home if there's friendly conversation and good beer to be found. To wit, he raises his pint and gives his usual toast: "Gentlemen, here's to men with nothing to do but save the world."

"Saving the world," I say, sipping my Paulaner. The gold slips down my throat, the perfect blend of bite and comfort.

Stillman tastes his beer, looks pleasantly surprised, and takes a bigger sip.

Carl leans back in the couch, the back of which comes up to the top of his shoulders. "Here's Paul," he says, nodding. "Late, as usual."

Paul Landmeyer, the third part of our usual threesome, is a brilliant, humorous man, with a Ph.D. in biochemistry, and has written papers for the *Journal of Police Forensics*. When he's not picking evidence apart for the police, he's grinding through the teenage years of his kid, a fourteen-year-old boy whose idea of accomplishment is mastering a new skateboard trick. Paul is thirty-eight, with a scholarly look: brown, thick hair, glasses, and deep, thoughtful eyes. He shakes hands with me and Carl, and I introduce him to Stillman. Paul looks at Stillman awhile, a thin smile on his lips.

He orders iced tea and a sandwich, sits back, and says, "Stillman. Yeah, that was the name I heard."

Stillman looks up, surprised. "You heard my name?"

Paul nods. "I just got back from a thing out at the Nation. You and your partner are a major topic of conversation out there."

He looks up. "Us?"

Paul smiles. "You're the two guys who let that Sudanese guy out on bail, aren't you?"

Stillman stares. "Yeah. I mean, Thomas . . . yeah."

"And he's accused of raping and murdering a white girl from the Nation, right?"

"Yeah."

"Well, there ya go."

Stillman's TV smile vanishes. "Am I supposed to be freaked out about this or what?"

I shrug. "You work for the Justice Department, so they hated you already, Stillman. They just didn't know your name yet."

"Tell us what you heard, Paul," Carl says. "It'll be good instruction for young Stillman."

Paul nods. "I was doing some fieldwork down there on a thing. There was a crowd of Nationites standing around, talking shit like they do. And I hear Thomas's name."

"Glad to be on their minds," I say, taking a bite of sandwich.

"Well, they seem to feel the two of you fucked up."

"We did," I say, washing the bite down with a sip of Paulaner. "Royally."

Paul smiles. "You might not want to have your car break down in that area for a while," he says.

Stillman looks like he's about to shit a kitten. "So what's

the story on these guys?" he asks. "What are they gonna do, slash our tires or something?"

Carl gets one of his sage looks. "You know what the problem is with criminal law, Stillman?"

"No."

"You're always dealing with criminals."

Paul and I laugh, and Stillman shuts his mouth, deciding he's had enough. I can see his mind working, though. I'll talk him down later, but for now, it's more important to let him suffer a little.

While Paul's talking, Rita West comes in with a couple of lawyers from the public defender's office. Rita looks good, as usual—for not being that tall, she's got great legs—but the two guys with her have on mediocre shirts, no ties, and slacks from another decade.

Stillman watches them take seats on the other side of the club, about forty feet away. "Public defenders make the same money prosecutors do, right?" he asks.

"To the penny," I say.

"Then why do they dress like that?"

Carl smiles. "Long tradition, Stillman. They say it's to relate to their clients, but it's actually just that they have no style."

"No shit," Stillman says, shaking his head. "They look like they work at Sears."

"The one on the right's no problem," I say. "He's a UT grad, just marking time. The good-looking kid with the brown hair is smart. Dukie named Kurt Mayer. You have to watch him."

Stillman glances over. "That guy went to Duke? What's he doing at the PD's office?"

"Defending democracy against the pernicious power of the state," Carl says, smiling. "Or, as Thomas prefers to put it, 'Learning the ropes until he goes private and gets rich.'"

I grin and say nothing. It's enough to watch Carl in his element: drinking excellent beer and holding forth on the law and lawyers.

"And I believe you've already met Ms. West," Carl says pointedly. He pulls out a cigar and begins unwrapping it. "Buy them a round, Stillman," he says, without looking at him.

Stillman stares. "Them? Why, for God's sake?"

"Because it's civilized," he says, getting out his lighter. "You had your ass kicked in that bail hearing, and you're letting them know it's not personal."

Stillman looks dubious. "Maybe if the cute one blew me," he says.

"I'm pretty sure Mr. Mayer is heterosexual," Carl says, lighting the cigar.

I burst out laughing, and Stillman's face turns red. "All right, damn it," he says. "But not this five-dollar-a-glass stuff." He motions the waitress over and sends over three domestics in bottles, which are going for two-fifty.

The drinks go to the other table, and Rita nods a thanks and waves.

"Nicely done, Stillman," Carl says. "You're doing fine."

So far, Stillman has had to pay for four lunches, bought drinks for a table of public defenders, and had the shit scared out of him.

I smile and finish my beer. After the last couple of days, I almost feel human.

Paul brings me down to Earth. "I'll tell you who needs to stay on his toes," he says. "That Sudanese kid. The Nationites just might finish your job for you."

CHAPTER
SIX

HOVERING OVER OUR HEADS like the angel of death is the name Kwame Jamal Hale, née Jerome Hale. His lawyer, Georgetown law professor Philip Buchanan, has arranged for us to drive to Brushy Mountain State Prison and interview his client. Kwame Jamal has it in his mind to confess to a crime we sincerely hope he did not commit. And since another man has already been executed for it, we had better be right. If we aren't, it's not hard to imagine a conflagration of epic proportions: the Nation calling for Bol's blood; the Africans defending themselves in whatever tribal way they brought back from their long-running civil war in Sudan; Fiona Towns and her peaceniks, caught in the middle.

The next morning, Tuesday, Carl, Rayburn, and I meet at Shoney's for the early-morning drive out to Brushy Mountain. We pile into Rayburn's Ford Crown Vic and pull out past the kitschy tourist traps selling country music memorabilia, heading east on I-40. We're nervous, except for Carl, who just looks annoyed. Kwame Jamal is taking a lot of the shine off Carl's last seventy-two hours as an employee of the state of Tennessee. Rayburn, who is holding a cup of black coffee from a fast-food joint in his left hand, doesn't look like he slept much. He probably spent most of the last few hours praying that Hale is certifiably insane.

Brushy Mountain is the prison James Earl Ray tried to escape from, and the one Hannibal Lechter tried to get sent to. Neither man got his wish, although Ray managed to spend four days on the run. Brushy prison rises, castlelike, from within the hollow of a mountain's hand, surrounded on three sides by sheer, white granite walls eighty feet high. Walking with a guard through Brushy at night—the steam curling up around the razor wire fence, the glare of spotlights illuminating the worn walkways, the clanking of keys at the guard's hip—is like stepping back in time. It's going to be torn down in a few years, and there are good economic reasons for that, I suppose. When it goes, it will take an era with it.

We ride in silence for a while, heading toward the mountains of east Tennessee. The poor South emerges, comfortable in its manufactured housing, wood-burning stoves, and junked cars parked up on blocks in yards.

Carl harrumphs from the backseat. I turn around, and he looks like he's smelled bad fish. "I bet this guy Buchanan is nothing special," he says. "He's probably just your ordinary, everyday-variety, bleeding-heart. The kind of guy who can't stand the thought of a mass murderer feeling a pinprick when the needle breaks the skin."

"*Prick*'s the word," Rayburn says, and he's off, thirty solid minutes of pure Republican propaganda on everything from legalizing drugs to teenage pregnancy to what the hell has happened to the school system. Being silent so long has topped up his fuel, and we glide on Rayburn's invective until we turn onto State Road 61.

"Maybe we should ask for a continuance on the Bol case," Carl says. "At least until we see where we are on this thing."

Rayburn looks stricken. "We are going to conduct business absolutely as usual," he says. "Nobody is even going to *flinch* around our office."

"Sure, boss," I say, but I can't help thinking that Moses Bol may end up the luckiest defendant in the history of the Tennessee court system. It's going to be pretty damn hard to convince a jury to send Bol to death if it turns out we fucked up the last time.

The car crests a final hill, and Brushy looms in the near distance. The road gently descends into the excavated pit that envelopes the main buildings, and Rayburn stops at the guardhouse. We're issued badges and drive slowly down the gravel road, passing outbuildings and the occasional trustee in his state blues. We park in front of the castle and walk up to the prison entrance, an electronically controlled gate topped with nasty-looking barbed wire. Our pockets are emptied, our briefcases searched. A guard stamps our hands with a number in invisible ink; the number shows only under black light and is our ticket out. It changes every day, so the inmates can't predict what it is. A voice calls out, "Free-world personnel coming inside." The door before us opens, and we walk past the blocks of medium-security cells. A few inmates are working in the main areas, scrubbing floors and walls. The inmates say hello with exaggerated politeness, anxious for conversation and brownie points. Hale waits in high security, a prison-within-a-prison where the worst-behaved prisoners are held.

We make our way through the building to the courtyard that leads to high security. We hear, "Free-world personnel coming across the yard," and we take the short walk to the concrete building where Hale is housed. Inside high security we're greeted by John Palecek, Brushy's warden. Palecek is the new face of criminal justice, which means he's an administrator who's comfortable with things like keeping the bill for cleaning supplies under control. He's also the man who physically gave the order to execute Wilson Owens. "So," he says, summing up how fucked we all are. He points to the shift manager's room. "Buchanan's in there."

"Is there anything to this?" Rayburn asks. "I mean, this guy Hale. He's a fruitcake, right?"

"He's got religion, David," Palacek says. "If he doesn't screw up pretty soon, I'm going to have to send him back to the general prison population."

A man walks out of the shift manager's room. He's smiling, which makes him a population of one in Brushy Mountain prison. *Buchanan,* I think. Buchanan dresses hip for a university type, with a pair of expensive-looking black pants, an open-collared shirt, and what look like—no shit—boat shoes. "Jesus," he says, "I knew I was going to the South, but nobody told me it'd be a million degrees out there." He sticks out his hand, and there's a nice, awkward moment before anybody takes it.

Rayburn, ever the politician, goes first, but he doesn't say "good to meet you" because it isn't good to meet Professor Buchanan. Maybe one day there will be five or ten people who are proved to have been wrongly executed, but there's only going to be one first time, and the people behind that will be the names who get remembered. They will be the Fuckups Royale, the ones who will be publicly skewered, left to wrestle with their consciences the rest of their lives.

"Are we clear on the ground rules here?" Buchanan asks.

He pulls out the original of the paperwork Stillman showed us in the office. "Kwame Jamal doesn't come in the room until we get some signatures."

"We came to hear what the man says," Rayburn mutters. He signs the papers, holding the pen like it's poison.

We file into the shift manager's office, which is square, about fifteen by fifteen. A metal desk has been put in the middle of the room, the parties situated around it. Two video cameras sit on stands, one for each side of the conversation. One chair remains empty for Hale.

Palecek nods to the guards, and a minute later we hear the massive cell-block door grind open. A few seconds later Hale enters, flanked on each arm by a burly guard. Hale wears the regulation white T-shirt and sweatpants of high security, with a pale green kufi skullcap. His arms are massive, the result of years of weight training. His left bicep is covered in an ornate tattoo, now stretched beyond recognition. He's growing a ragged and unkempt beard. He looks as evil and dangerous as any inmate in Brushy. He does not, however, look insane.

Hale sits beside Buchanan with a detached expression, as if this meeting is something he has to do, and when it's over, he's ready to go back to whatever it was he would have been doing. "*As salaam alaikum,*" he says, and it's clear he's speaking only to me.

Buchanan nods and repeats the phrase, with the goofy, eager look of a man who wants to be down with the brothers, especially when he's on the safe side of the bars. "Kwame Jamal asked for this meeting because he wants to set the record straight," he says. "He does this of his own free will."

Hale watches his lawyer with vaguely bored eyes. He knows that no matter what happens in this room, he isn't going to feel the free sun on his body again in his lifetime.

"Why are we here, Mr. Hale?" I ask.

"The Honorable Elijah Muhammad says he who blame another for his crime get the punishment multiplied to him tenfold. May Allah accept my good deeds."

"Did you blame someone for a crime you committed, Mr. Hale?" I ask.

"I killed that man at the Sunshine Grocery Store," he says. "The woman, too."

"Wilson Owens has already been tried and convicted of that crime, Mr. Hale."

"May Allah forgive me."

"Did you know Wilson Owens, Mr. Hale?"

He nods. "We was incarcerated together."

"Were you friends?"

Hale shakes his head. "Owens was a *shaiton*. A devil."

"Because?"

Hale shrugs. "He wanted what was not his."

"And what was that?"

Hale pauses a moment, drawn back in a memory. "She worked in food services. Real sweet face, like an angel. I went through the line, and she give me my first smile in a year."

Jesus, this is about a woman. "Who was this?"

"Damita D'Angelis. I just called her Angel. We was real."

"You developed a relationship?"

Hale nods. "I bought my way onto food services, and it was real good. I built my time, no problem."

"The guards tolerated this relationship?"

"You know how it is," Hale says, and I do.

"How long did your relationship last?"

Hale's answer is the mathematics of a man whose world is building time. "Four months, eleven days," he says. "Until Owens filed incompatibility on me."

Filing incompatibility is the neutron bomb of prison life;

a prisoner claims another will do him harm, and the institution is obligated by law to move one of them to another location. If they don't get moved and the violence goes down, the state can be sued for wrongful death. Like everything else in prison life, the inmates have learned how to use the filing of incompatibility for their own purposes.

"So who was moved?" I ask.

"Me."

"Once you were gone, did Mr. Owens start a relationship with Ms. D'Angelis?"

Hale's face proves that even the most godforsaken bastard on Earth feels his own loss, in spite of the fact he has exacted ten times as much misery on other people. "Yeah," he says, after a moment. "So we had business. I got out in October, Owens the month after."

"What did you do to him, Mr. Hale?"

He smiles. "I set his ass up. Owens hung out around Green's pawn, over near where he lived. Only took me a couple hours to get four butts. Once I had that, it was pretty much over. He's in the system, know what I'm sayin'? The DNA gonna nail his ass; case closed."

"So you stood outside the grocery store smoking, but dropping Owen's cigarette butts instead of your own."

"That's it."

"It seems to me this is a lot of trouble, Mr. Hale. Why not just confront him? Take him out?"

Hale smiles. "Because a niggah's got to have style."

"Style?"

"I got pride in my work. Everything I do, it got that mark of quality. Style."

"So now you're confessing," I say. "You don't want Allah to punish you for your crimes."

He nods. "I got to stand before Allah."

At this point, I let myself lose it a little, intentionally opening up to a slow, controlled burn. "So your idea of style is walking into a grocery store, pulling a sawed-off shotgun out of your coat, and blowing holes into Steven Davidson and Lucinda Williams? Is that what you're going to tell Allah, Kwame? That you killed those two people because it had more *style*?"

Hale's face flushes. "I don't need no lecture on the Koran from no white man."

"And I don't need a lecture about morality from a self-confessed murderer."

Hale moves up off his chair—getting him upset is child's play, really, considering his malevolent disposition—and the guards move to squash him back down into it. Hale is immensely strong, and for a moment, the three of them are locked in midair, Hale in a half squat, a motion he's probably done in the weight room carrying nearly the same weight he has on him now. Hale's fists are close together from the plastic cuffs, and he brings them down hard on the table, gaining leverage. Buchanan backs away like a scared cat, and the guard on Hale's left reaches for his nightstick. I do not move. What I want to do is to make Hale crack a little bit. I want to upset his game, play into his emotional makeup. I want him to end up saying more than he planned, and about two more incendiary comments ought to do it. Hale shrugs the guards' hands off his shoulders and sits back down, but he's still as tense as a spring.

I know this kind of baiting is going to make me look bad on the videotape, but I don't care, because compared to how bad I'm going to look if it turns out Hale is telling the truth, it hardly matters. "You're a liar, Kwame," I say, leaning forward until our faces are only about eighteen inches apart. "You've got a fifth-grade education, and you want to start talking shit about dropping DNA? You've been incarcerated six times, and you're in now because you were too stupid to wipe your fingerprints off a car you stole when committing a robbery. Oh yeah, you've got style, pal. You've got the style of a goddamn moron."

Hale loses it, and it's beautiful. He actually reaches for me, and the guards drop on him like a ton of bricks. Buchanan elevates once again out of his chair and away from the commotion, then starts screaming about prisoner abuse and the violation of his client's rights. I ignore him because he is now irrelevant. Kwame Jamal Hale is all that matters. The guards wrestle Hale back down into his chair, and he gives me a look that says if we were alone, he would end me. When the guards get him back under control, they chain his arms to his chair. Hale glowers at me, radiating hate.

"OK, Mr. Hale," I say. "Take me through the crime. Let's start with when you got up that morning. Where were you?"

Buchanan interrupts, as if on signal. "What happened was a long time ago. Trying to resurrect these details seven years after the fact is a stretch."

"Bullshit," I say. "I want him to tell me what he had on, and I'm talking down to boxers or briefs. I want to know whether or not he shaved that day. I want to know where he bought the shotgun shells and where he loaded the gun. I want *everything*."

"You want to catch some tiny detail that's not accurate, and use that as an excuse to call him a liar," Buchanan says.

"Are you telling me that your client is so blasé about killing two people that he can't even recall where he got up that morning?"

"I'm not saying anything of the kind," Buchanan says, flushing. "But after such—"

"After what, dammit?" Rayburn interrupts. He's been

quiet until now, but he can't take it anymore. "The whole thing's a load of shit. Somebody like Hale would have hunted Wilson down like a dog and blown him away. He tried to rip off Thomas's head thirty seconds ago, and everybody in this room saw it. This frame-up job is a crock."

"When it comes to that, there's more than one killer in the room," Buchanan spits. "How many have you sent down the river, Mr. District Attorney? You got ninety more waiting to die right now. Compared to you, my client is a choir boy."

"Goddamn it," Rayburn says, "if you think—"

We're seconds away from turning into a full-on circus, and I can't actually figure out if that's good or bad. Normal rules don't apply when there's so much at stake. But I don't have the chance to calculate, because Hale's voice enters the argument, as dark and quiet as spreading oil. "I can prove it," he says. "I can prove what I say." Rayburn freezes in midsentence. Hale has mastered himself again, and he's sitting with his shackled hands folded in front of him on the table. He is very still inside, his eyes focused straight ahead.

"Now would be the time," I say quietly.

"The gun," Hale says. "You never found the gun."

I look up warily. "That's right. There was an extensive search, but it had vanished."

"I know where it is," Hale whispers. "You can match it to the shells at the scene. Case closed."

I look at Buchanan. "You knew about this?" Buchanan smiles, which means he did. "OK, Mr. Hale. Where's the gun?"

Buchanan touches Hale's arm. "Not this way, Kwame. By tonight, it will be gone, like it never existed."

"Are you saying we would tamper with the evidence in this case?" Rayburn demands.

"Everybody in this room knows what's on the table here,"

Buchanan retorts. "If that gun disappears, it's like Kwame Jamal never happened."

Carl, until now, has said nothing. I've almost forgotten about him, this mountain of a man, wordlessly listening on my left. He clears his throat, and everybody shuts up and turns toward him. "We are men of integrity," he says, just those words. Carl Becker is the real deal, and accusations of illicit behavior bounce off him like pebbles off a boulder. He turns to Rayburn. "We can go together to the location, with a forensic team," he says. "It's not worth fighting with somebody like this."

Rayburn nods. "Today is Tuesday. Is there any reason we can't do this by Friday?" Buchanan shakes his head. "Good." Rayburn stands, and Carl and I rise with him. "Ten a.m. Friday, my office," he says. "Don't make my people wait."

Ten feet out of high security, I pull the escort aside. "Take me by Hale's cell," I say, under my breath. The guard nods, looks up at the officer in the control room, and points to the door. The door snaps open, and we walk across the polished floor to a cell on the opposite side. The guard points to a small window, and I peer in. The metal furnishings are standard prison issue. There are a few posters of girls in bikinis on the wall—apparently, Hale's Islamic convictions only go so far—and a small television set on a table. "When did he get the TV?" I ask.

"About four months ago, I think. The lawyer brought it."

Five minutes later, we've been released back out into the gravel parking lot in front of the prison castle. The white granite walls behind the prison shine in the sun. If it wasn't a seat of human misery, we would be in a beautiful place.

"He's lying," Rayburn says. "I didn't know what to think at first, but I swear to God, he's lying."

"Sure," I say, agreeing more out of loyalty than anything. "He's lying."

"Did you see that TV?" Rayburn asks. "There are two hundred guys in that building willing to lie to get something like that." Rayburn's right; I've had perps rat out their best friends just for the promise of a private cell.

Carl's eyes are locked on the windows of Brushy Mountain Prison. "If he is lying," he says quietly, "I'd like to know how he got that shotgun."

The miles reverse themselves as we head back in Rayburn's car, returning us to an office filled with workers who don't know anything about our visit to Brushy Mountain. Carl and I are ostensibly taking one of the fifty or so vacation days we have accumulated, and Rayburn is supposedly off raising money for his reelection campaign. About thirty miles from Brushy Mountain, I ask the obvious. "How long can we keep this quiet? If we find the gun, I mean."

"Nothing's conclusive until we run the ballistics," Rayburn says. "I can stretch that out at least a week. Maybe two."

"You know Buchanan's going to want his own lab to do the test," Carl says.

"Yeah, and he can kiss my ass. Anyway, if we get a positive, he's not gonna complain."

"You think Buchanan is going to keep his mouth shut until then?" I ask.

Rayburn stares ahead at the road. "It's like that Geraldo thing. The one with the vault. Remember that?"

"Al Capone's vault in Chicago," Carl says from the back. "Huge TV numbers, and there was nothing there. Geraldo looked like a moron."

"It's been more than seven years since the murders," I say. "A lot of things can happen to a gun in seven years. It can get found, or destroyed, or even paved over, depending on where it is."

Rayburn drives on silently for a second, then pulls off the road. He parks on the gravel and turns in his seat. "This guy Buchanan's got an ego. Think about it. Uncovering the murder weapon that proves, for the first time, the wrong person was executed in this country. It'd be on every news outlet on Earth."

"He's not going to risk a Geraldo," I say. "He wouldn't be doing this unless he knew the gun was there."

"That's my point. I'd bet my pension he's *been* to the site. He *knows* what's going to happen. And if he's been to the site, it's potential evidence tampering."

"Gentlemen," Carl says, "we might be into a full-blown Geraldo-type situation. He probably already has some choice media contacts in the loop, waiting to pounce."

"Jesus H. Christ," Rayburn whispers. He slips the car into gear and floors it.

CHAPTER
SEVEN

WE SHOW UP at the office about 3:30, half expecting to find an army of reporters waiting on us. Rayburn even makes us come up the elevators separately, to dispel the notion that we've been together. But it's wasted effort; we slip into the office without a blip, and nobody asks where we've been. "Calm before the storm," Carl says, when we meet in the hall a few minutes later. "Something's coming. I can feel it."

I head back to my office, and Stillman materializes beside me—he's developed the talent of appearing out of nowhere—and follows me inside. He's dressed immaculately, as usual, and he carries a Coach briefcase that costs 450 bucks. I know this because I priced it myself and decided it was too expensive. He flops into a chair and somehow manages to keep his clothes perfectly in place. *This guy is going to last six months*, I think. *Then it's Jeff Stillman, reporting from Hollywood on the latest washed-up actor accused of whacking his wife.*

"You look good, Stillman. Your parents rich or something?"

"Good clothes are an investment."

"For what? You already got the job."

"So," he says. "What happened up there?"

"Shut the door." He shrugs, closes the door, and turns back to me. "Nothing happened, Stillman. The professor told us what's on his mind, and we're going to check a few things out. Other than that, it was a big washout."

Stillman looks disappointed. "Really? That's great."

"Meanwhile, we're keeping our mouths shut. So unless there's something else, Stillman, I'll catch you tomorrow."

"You forgetting the pretrial conference?"

I exhale. "God, I forgot. With Tamra Hartlett's family."

"They're already here. They're waiting in the small conference room."

"Sure. Give me a second, OK?" Stillman doesn't move. "I mean alone."

"OK, but they're waiting." I motion for him to close the door behind him.

I spin my chair around to the window and look down on downtown Nashville. *I'm going to have to come to terms with Stillman,* I think. *I can't keep treating him like shit.* The traffic is light on Second Avenue; a handful of tourists are wandering around, probably wondering why Toby Keith or somebody isn't standing on a street corner playing guitar. What I have to do, I realize, is figure out where in my brain to put Kwame Jamal Hale for a few days. Problem is, the time I have to do it in is the thirty seconds it's going to take to walk between my office and the conference room. It seems about four hours short.

Hale didn't seem like a lunatic. That's what's pissing me

off, I realize. He just seemed your garden-variety evil lifer, a guy who's been in and out of jail a dozen times before he fell off the edge and got sent up for good. We had taken comfort from the TV in Hale's cell; the stuff about inmates selling out their mothers for favors wasn't just blowing smoke, after all. Once you're in for life, your personal economy boils down to what fits in a ten-by-ten concrete room. But the TV doesn't mean Hale was lying. Buchanan is exactly the kind of man who would think the whole idea of a jail cell is inhumane, and he probably knows enough people who think like he does to take up a "Buy poor Kwame a TV" collection. I swear to God, there are times when this job drives me crazy.

I stand. "So," I say out loud. "Let's go meet the bereaved."

Rhonda Hartlett, Tamra's mother, is forty years old. She has her daughter's pale skin, bleached hair, and depressing, overextended sexuality. Her lingering handshake isn't personal; it's like a nervous tic, something she doesn't think about anymore. I say hello, and she bats her eyes like a soap actress, then settles into a long stare at Stillman.

Tamra's father—never Mr. Hartlett—is a day laborer named Danny Trent. He lives in Chattanooga, hasn't seen his daughter in more than a year, and isn't a material witness. About fifty years old, he has moody eyes that stare at me from beneath a Titans ball cap. His teeth are stained with tobacco juice, and a pack of Skoal is visible in his shirt pocket. He nods wordlessly when I shake his hand.

Sitting to Trent's left is Jason Hodges, Tamra's boyfriend. Jason is a key witness, certain to come up on the stand. He's twenty-four, never been in trouble with the law, and has a nervous, eager expression on his face, like he knows this is serious and he doesn't want to screw up. He's about five foot ten, with short brown hair combed straight down over his forehead. He is a Nationite, down to his toes.

"It's your meeting, Stillman," I say, taking a seat. Stillman looks up, surprised. *Yep, I've declared pax, Stillman. Show me what you got.*

"OK," Stillman says, flipping open his notebook. "I've read your testimony, Rhonda," he says. "For today we'll just review a few things. You saw Tamra the day before the incident, about ten a.m. She loaned you fifty dollars. You talked about Jason, and she said everything was going fine. She was upbeat, happy."

"That's right," Rhonda says. She looks like she wants to eat Stillman between pieces of Wonder Bread. "That's just exactly right."

"OK. So, Jason, I think it's going to come down to you," Stillman says. "You're the closest to Tamra, and your testimony is going to have the most weight."

Hodges looks up, eyes wide. "OK."

"It says here you work at the Hiller Body Shop."

"That's right."

"When you ain't high," Rhonda says, under her breath.

Hello. I look over. "Is that right, Jason?" I ask. "Do you have a drug problem?"

"I ain't got no drug problem. I'm a skilled welder. That takes steady hands."

Rhonda rolls her eyes but says nothing.

"How about Tamra?" Stillman asks. "Did she do drugs?"

"I don't see what difference it makes now."

Stillman leans forward slightly. "It's important you answer the question, Jason."

"A little weed. Coke, when she could afford it. Big fuckin' deal."

"Did she owe anyone any money over drugs?"

Very good, Stillman. You're thinking like the defense, staying ahead. Hodges looks annoyed. "What's this have to do with anything? She's dead."

"We have a good case against Bol," Stillman says. "That means the defense will be grasping at straws. They'll try to create reasonable doubt. They'll want to find alternative reasons how she might have died."

"Bol killed her."

"If she owed money, the defense will say those people might be the ones who killed her, not Bol."

"She didn't owe no money."

Stillman nods. "Good. That's good, Jason."

"OK, then."

"I'm going to ask you another question now, Jason. You aren't going to like it."

"What?"

"Did you ever hit Tamra?"

"Anybody says that, I'll fuckin' kill him."

"Hang on, people," I say, quietly. "Let's just stay calm."

"But why's he got to say that? You got to hang that shit on me?"

"I think Mr. Stillman here was just giving you a little test."

"He can shove that test up his ass, too."

"He's just pointing out that you have to stay calm. *No matter what.* If you show anger, that sticks in the minds of the jury."

"That's a bunch of shit, too," Hodges says. "I never hit no girlfriend."

"The defense is fighting for Bol's life, Jason. In their minds, everything's fair. If they lose, Bol dies."

"He wins, I'll kill him myself."

I exhale. "It's very important you don't say anything like that on the stand, Jason. Do you understand what's happening here? If you let yourself look dangerous, you plant doubt in the minds of the jury."

Hodges stares. "Yeah. OK."

"Fine." We sit quietly a few seconds, but the air is malignant with Hodges's outburst. "There are witnesses that say they saw Tamra and Bol arguing in the week before the murder," I say. "Do you know what that was about?"

"For him to keep his damn distance," Hodges says. "Not to mack up on her."

"Was he macking up on her, Jason?"

"All the time," he says. "Made me sick. I told him to back the fuck off."

Stillman looks at me. "OK, then," he says. "It fits, too. Gives him motive." He turns back to Jason. "Did you confront him?"

"Damn right."

"What happened?"

"He backed off, but I couldn't be there all the time. And when I wasn't, he did his thing on her."

Stillman looks over at me. "You have anything?"

"No."

"OK," Stillman says. "I know this is all difficult for you. If there's any question you have about the process, now would be a good time to ask." The father shifts in his seat, like he wants to ask something. "Go ahead," Stillman says.

"I was just wonderin' if we can watch."

"Of course," I say. "There are seats saved for you every day."

The father shakes his head. "No. I mean when they kill him."

* * *

Stillman ushers Hartlett's family out of the room and comes back in, smiling. "Damn, Mr. Trent's pretty fucking gung-ho."

"Yeah."

"Of course, he's got a right to his anger."

"He hasn't seen his daughter in months, and all the sudden he wants to watch Bol fry?"

Stillman's quiet for a while. "So we ready to go on this thing? Ready to put the bad guy away?"

"Yeah, Stillman. We got what we needed. Bol and Hartlett were arguing because Bol wanted what she did not want to give. It's airtight."

"So we're gold."

"One problem. Jason Hodges has a hair-trigger temper."

"So?"

"So before I put that walking hand grenade on the stand, I'm going to find out everything I can about him."

Stillman stares at me. "This thing is on a silver platter, Thomas. We don't have time to go on a lot of snipe hunts."

"Rita West is a good lawyer, Stillman. It's going to take her about ten seconds to figure out that Jason Hodges is a nice, juicy alternative to her client. And she doesn't have to prove a thing. All she has to do is put a question in one juror's mind."

"Yeah."

"Not to mention the fact that you're one of four people in this office who knows that Kwame Jamal Hale is a few days away from possibly reopening every death-penalty case in this state. So there is no way that we are going to fuck this up."

There's a light drizzle on I-65, making traffic a bitch. I sit in the cocoon of the Ford, crawling home at twenty miles an hour, watching the wipers sweep warm rain off the glass before me. It's been a hell of a day, bookended on one side by Hale's confession and a victim's family on the other. *There it is*, I think. *The yin and yang of the job. Professor Buchanan trying to make Wilson Owens a martyr, and a father so bent on revenge he wants to watch Bol fry.* In between these two forces, I'm going to try to practice a little law.

I drive into the garage and park. Indy greets me with his swishing tail and mewing hunger, and halfway through feeding him I realize that it's the most satisfying thing I've done all day. *Feed the hungry cat. Now that's a simple, entirely positive thing to do. If I don't sell BMWs, I'll become a professional cat feeder. I'll just find hungry cats far and wide, and make their days wonderful with fucking Fancy Feast.*

Dinner is something overly salted and previously frozen. A cook, I'm not. Bec could cook. She made fabulous chorizo, and she hand-rubbed her roasted *pollo* with garlic and stuffed it with oranges. My daughter, I miss 24-7. Bec, I miss mornings and dinner. Dinner for the food, and mornings for her sweet, funky smell and the sight of her breathing peacefully beside me. A woman comfortable in a nightgown—it doesn't have to be something from Victoria's Secret, it can just be a big T-shirt—has always had power in my book. Tonight, I push a fork into some kind of brown mystery that Swanson's has the arrogance to call meatloaf.

The rain stops in a half hour, and I walk out to get my mail. I open the front door and practically trip over something as I walk out. A wreath of white flowers is at my feet. I reach down and pull off a note. There's a message: *Sorry for your loss.* I look around; there's nobody in sight. *What damn loss? I haven't lost anything.* I turn over the card, and see my name and address, and the name of the florist. I check my watch; it's nearly 7:00 p.m., probably too late to call the florist. I take the wreath inside and set it on the dining table. *White flowers and a note. This is a funeral wreath.* I stare at it awhile, thinking I've been pulled into some cheesy made-for-TV movie. *You gotta be kidding me. Are the fucking Nationites trying to send me a message?* I pick up the phone and call Paul Landmeyer, and his wife, Jenny, answers. Jenny puts Paul on the phone. "Hey. It's Thomas. You busy?"

"Nope. I'm watching *Millionaire* with my kid. Maybe he'll learn something, since he can't be bothered with school."

"Something weird happened tonight. I wanted to run it by you."

"Shoot."

"There was a funeral wreath left on my door."

A silent pause. "Hang on. I'm taking you into the study." He carries the phone away from his family. "OK. Talk to me."

"Not much else to tell. It's a local florist, with a note attached. *Sorry about your loss.*"

"Who do you think sent it?"

"Offhand, I'd say it's the same guy who left the note on my car."

"What note?"

"The freaky one about the death penalty."

"You keep it?"

"Yeah. I don't give a shit about the card, but I don't like this guy hanging around my house. That's a little too close."

"Or woman."

"What do you mean?"

"You said guy. It could be a woman."

"Yeah. Theoretically."

"You tell David?"

"He's got enough on his plate already. Look, I'm pretty

sure it's just some idiot from the Nation warning me not to fuck up."

"Makes sense."

"All the same, I was wondering if this thing was worth bringing in. It wouldn't break my heart to figure out who this moron is."

A pause. "You mean forensically? Since it comes from a florist, whoever sent it wouldn't have touched it. They'd call it in or, better yet, order it online."

"Right."

He pauses. "Your number's unlisted, right?"

"Of course."

"Well, I'd watch your back for the next few days, buddy. Looks like somebody knows where you live."

CHAPTER
EIGHT

DR. TINA GESSMAN, staff psychologist for the Metro Davidson County Justice Department, is smart and insightful. In the looks department, she has a Kathy Bates thing going on—minus the movie money and Hollywood sophistication—which obviates any potential for sexual tension. I've been seeing her once a month for what the DA calls "tune-ups," and which I call "a total bullshit experience that wastes both my and the good doctor's time." Except this time, I've seen Kwame Jamal Hale. His confession might actually have the psychic weight to tip me over on my side.

Tina's office is in a nine-story office building on West End Avenue, across from a Burger King and a Catholic bookstore. You park in the back—she doesn't validate—and ride up a small elevator to the fifth floor. Tina opens the door from her inner office, and I walk in. The box of Kleenex discreetly placed near the patient chair testifies to the kind of work she does. Another clue is the back door, which lets people escape with their crying jags without going through the reception area. The Justice Department is a tight little world, where everybody knows everybody, and walking out of the department psych's office in tatters wouldn't be well received.

"Come in, Thomas," she says. Her voice is soft, every time, no matter what. It's like her volume knob got locked on 3. "Have a seat."

I fall into one of the two patient chairs and stretch out my legs. "It's a million degrees out there."

She pulls out her notebook and flips to an empty page. I look around the office; same soothing pictures, same gentle hum out of the air-conditioning, same acrid smell of confession in the air. "So how are you?"

"Great."

"Glad to hear it. The Zoloft still working OK?"

"Sure."

"No sexual side effects?"

"You makin' a pass at me, Tina? I'm gonna have to report you to the authorities."

She smiles. "What's on your mind today, Thomas?"

"How do you know there's something on my mind?"

"You're on time."

I look at my watch; it's nine sharp. "You're right."

"Your habitual lateness is a way of communicating your disregard for our sessions," she says. "You've been on time exactly twice. The first session and today. So this is a special occasion."

"I went to Brushy Mountain yesterday," I say. "It wasn't a good trip."

"What happened?"

"I met a guy who claims I prosecuted the wrong guy in a death-penalty trial."

Her expression clouds. "I see."

"It was my first big case with Carl. We got the death penalty, and the guy was executed a few months ago. Everything seemed OK, until this guy from Brushy shows up. Carl, David, and I went out to see him."

"What does he say?"

"He says we killed the wrong guy. He says he's the one who committed the crime. He says we fucked up."

"Does he seem credible?"

I look out the window. "Yeah. Maybe. He's a crook, so it's hard to tell."

"What do Carl and David say?"

"Carl stays above it, somehow. Don't ask me how. David can't let the possibility enter his mind, so he's already decided the guy's lying."

"And how do you feel?"

The towers at Vanderbilt University are visible about five blocks away. Just beyond is the law school, where a fresh group of lawyers is being minted. "I think he's telling the truth. I think we got the wrong guy."

"So what are you going to do about it?"

"We've got some evidence to check. It might turn out OK. We might be able to prove the guy's full of shit."

"Then maybe it's not a good idea to carry that load until you have to."

"I've got a new murder trial in the meantime. We're going for the maximum."

Her expression darkens further. "Could you ask David to assign somebody else?"

I shake my head. "He feels like if I back out, it's a capitulation on the other thing. He's worried about a domino effect." I watch my leg, making sure it's obediently still. "There's a woman," I say, much to my surprise.

She looks up. "You're dating?"

I laugh. "No. In the case."

She gives me a curious look. "Oh. The case."

"Preacher over at Downtown Presbyterian. Her name's Fiona Towns."

"I see."

"She's going to give testimony that she was with the accused at the time of the murder. She's his alibi."

"Good for the kid."

I give a small smile. "She's lying. I mean, I'm pretty sure she is. Lately things are a little vague."

She watches me quietly for a while. "Do you hope she's not lying?"

A long pause. "Yeah."

"Do you like her?"

"She's this anti-death-penalty activist. I think she's lying as a protest over that."

"Is that a yes or a no?"

"I'm going to have to destroy her on the stand."

"Then maybe it's better if it's a no."

Silence, as I twist in her psychological wind. "She seems principled and not entirely out of her mind," I say after a while. "I can't put my finger on it. But she's decent."

Tina smiles. "So are you." She writes for a couple of minutes in her book. "Tell me more about the guy at Brushy Mountain."

I exhale. "The thing is, I had a little doubt at the time. The jury was wavering, and I had the feeling that I should let it be. Let them figure it out on their own."

"So what happened?"

I shrug. "It was a high-profile case. The community wanted it. It was there, and I knew I could get it." I rustle in my seat, wanting to change the subject. "Carl's retiring this week, you know."

"Is he? That's great."

"Yeah. I'm damned if I'm going to put a cloud on that. I don't want him thinking over what might have been for the next thirty years." She nods. "Anyway, you've met Carl. He's a rock."

She smiles. "I prefer you, actually."

"I'm half the lawyer he is."

"I doubt that." She leans forward. "It's not wrong to have doubts, Thomas. It's human. We've gone over this before."

"Yeah."

"My goal here isn't to make you a better lawyer. It's to let you be the lawyer you are and keep your humanity alive."

"How am I doing?"

"You're my star patient." She pulls out a card and writes a number on it. "This is my home telephone, Thomas. Let's keep track of where you are on this, OK?"

"Home number. I swear, Tina, I'm gonna slap you with sexual harassment."

We stand, and she puts her hand on my arm. "You're in a serious situation, Thomas. The jokes are fine. I understand that. But things are probably going to get a little hairy before this is over."

I push the card into my pocket. "Probably."

Josh Ritchie, the investigator I have working on Bol and Towns, is waiting for me in the small conference room when I show up at work. He's wearing blue jeans, a T-shirt, and a Daytona Beach ball cap. He radiates the kind of mellow calm that enables him to sit for hours on end in his van without going out of his mind. "Yo," he says. "I got news."

"What's up?"

"Bol's closest friends are a couple of guys named Luol

Chol and Matek Deng. Don't ask me where they get these names."

"Africa, Josh."

"Right. Anyway, the three of them are like brothers. They lived in the same village and escaped together. It's the hell-and-back thing, like brothers in arms. If anybody knows why Bol was arguing with Hartlett, it's them."

"Her boyfriend says Bol was hitting on her and she didn't like it."

He laughs. "Then he was the only one she didn't like it from. The lady got around, dude. Seriously."

"How do you know?"

"I sounded out the manager where she waitressed. He said she was taking home three hundred bucks a night in . . . um, 'tips,' if you know what I mean."

I nod. Wherever the money went, it wasn't her apartment. It was typical squalid, badly furnished Nation, right down to the pressed-board coffee table. "Have you managed to talk to Chol or Deng?" I ask.

Josh nods. "I shot the shit with Deng for a while out over at Tennessee Village." He pulls out a photograph. "I took this from the van. Deng's on the right; Chol's on the left. They're pretty much inseparable. They work the same shift at Wal-Mart."

"What did they say?"

"Nice guys, very talkative. Right up until I mentioned Bol, I mean. Then it was instant stonewall."

I nod. "You find out anything on the preacher?"

He smiles. "Florence Nightingale, dude. A real angel of mercy."

"How so?"

"When she's not feeding the homeless, she's holding

computer classes for the Africans. She uses one of their apartments."

"They've got computers?"

Josh nods. "A couple of tired-out laptops. The door was open, and I walked in and acted like I was in the wrong apartment."

I lean back in my chair. "What does she think they're going to do? Go work at Microsoft?"

"Got me. Oh, and one more thing. You don't want to go into the Nation anytime soon."

"So I've heard."

"It's gonna get worse. That dude on the radio is doing a thing today on the influx of third-world immigrants in town. He's gonna use Moses Bol as his feature. I heard an ad for it this morning."

"Dan Wolfe?"

"You know, the guy who says the best thing about a tree is what you can make out of it after you cut it down."

"That's him. His listeners call themselves the Wolfe Pack."

"Right. Anyway, I figure once the Nationites get a load of that, it's gonna be a party over in Tenn Village." He stands. "I got to run, dude. I'll call you when I get more."

Josh leaves, and I sit for a second, taking stock. Dan Wolfe is a moron, but he's our moron, which seriously complicates matters from time to time. He's resolutely pro–law and order, but whatever human gene that's supposed to keep him from saying every damn thing in his mind apparently got left out of his genetic soup. He is, in a phrase, the kind of friend your enemies love.

I walk toward my office, and Stillman silently materializes on my flank, falling into step as I round a corner. I pull up sharply. "Dammit, Stillman, how do you do that?"

"Do what?"

"Nothing. Come on in."

He walks in and drops a stack of files on my desk.

"What's all that?" I ask.

"Moses Bol," he says, stopping by my door. "His lawyer has just sent another truckload of evidentiary requests."

I unlock the door and walk in, Stillman following. "She's trying to delay. She's got her man out on bail, so she'd just as soon have this trial in the next century."

"She's asked for—"

"—every scrap of evidence we have, plus some she knows we *don't* have, because even those will take time to deny."

Stillman pulls out an official-looking paper from one of the folders. "I think you'll find this one pretty special," he says, a smile on his face.

I take the page and scan the first few lines. "An ex parte request for money to send psychiatrists to Sudan?"

Stillman nods. "The psychiatrists say they need a minimum of three weeks to bond with any remaining family members. There are cultural sensitivities that need to be understood."

I drop the page onto my desk. "Well, la-dee-frickin-da."

"Ginder already turned her down. He says the trial date stands."

"Good man."

"So I hope you got over your preoccupation with Hodges."

"Not exactly. I'm going over to Hiller's Body Shop in a few minutes."

"Then I'm going with you."

I look at my watch. It's 9:45. "Lemme ask you something, Stillman. What's the first thing you did when you came to work today?"

"I don't know. Why?"

"It's a simple question, Stillman."

He exhales. "I saw Rayburn."

"And the topic of conversation just happened to be?"

"You."

"Ah. So Rayburn agrees with you on this thing."

"He might have suggested I stick close to you today, yeah."

"Because he thinks I'm freaked out about the Hale thing."

"In so many words."

"Stay here." I walk out the door and head to Rayburn's office. I motor past Dolores, push open the door, and stand in front of the district attorney. "So I'm now assigned a babysitter?"

Rayburn looks up calmly. "Something on your mind, Thomas?"

"Lots. Right now, it's secret meetings between you and Stillman telling him to keep tabs on me."

Rayburn leans back in his chair. "Thomas, you're a superb lawyer who is under an incredible amount of pressure right now."

"I can handle it."

"Thing is, it's my job to keep this office running. That's what I do. If I'm a little merciless about it, you, of all people, ought to understand that."

I stare, deeply annoyed, because Rayburn has just made an unanswerable point: "a little merciless" is exactly what I have been in court. It is, in fact, the *ethos* of the office, and the fact that Rayburn does his job the same way I do mine gives me precious little room to complain. "Fuck," I say, putting things about as succinctly as possible.

"Exactly."

"OK, then." I walk back out, go to my office, and see Stillman sitting in one of my wing chairs, legs stretched out, toes pointed to the ceiling. "All right, dammit," I say. "You can come."

Hiller Body Shop is three miles out Charlotte Avenue, a ten-minute drive from the Nation. There are two garage bays, and the half-dozen wrecked cars scattered in its parking lot look permanent. Stillman whistles. "Looks more like the Hiller Wreck Shop."

"Not everybody's got platinum MasterCards, Stillman," I say. I pull the truck into a space, and we get out. There's not much work going on in the bays; a couple of beefy guys in their late twenties are poking around underneath a raised Oldsmobile, but that's about it. Angry rock music blares out of a tape player that sits on a fifty-gallon oil drum. One of the workers looks over at us—in our suits, we might as well have *Government Agent* painted on our backs—and whistles into the office. The door opens a few seconds later, and a fifty-year-old man with gray, thinning hair walks out in overalls. He's got a nice-sized chaw of tobacco in his lower lip, and he sends a brown stream onto the hot pavement as he stands outside the door, sizing us up. "You wanna talk, do it in the air-conditioning," he says, waving us over.

We walk into the office, where a manual cash register competes for space with what looks like a couple of years of paperwork on a large, metal desk. The man regards us levelly, waiting for a sign of which way things are going to go.

"Thomas Dennehy," I say. "This is my associate, Jeff Stillman. We're with the DA's office."

The man nods and sends a shot of tobacco juice into a wastebasket. "Randy Hiller."

"I understand Jason Hodges works here. I'd like to ask you a few question about him."

"Hodges in trouble? Bad enough his girlfriend got killed, you ask me."

"No. I'm just wondering what kind of employee he is."

"The ex-employee kind," Hiller says. "He hasn't worked here in more than three months."

I look at Stillman. "You don't say."

Hiller nods. "Up and quit. Not that he wasn't about to get fired, but that's not the question you asked me."

"Why was he going to get fired?"

"The same reason everybody else gets fired around here. Not showing up, and bein' two feet off the ground when they do."

"You mean high."

He nods. "Anyway, he quit, right after he got that new car."

"New car?"

"New to him, anyway—2002 Trans Am, last year they made 'em. Cherry. Screamin' eagle on the hood."

"What would a car like that cost?" Stillman asks.

Hiller squints. "Midtwenties, easy. I told him to put it up on blocks. Might be worth a pile in twenty years. He told me to put my advice the same place I could put my job."

I nod. "I appreciate it, Mr. Hiller. Thanks for your time."

"Watch out for that Hodges kid," Hiller says. "He's kind of a bastard."

Stillman and I walk out and head toward the truck. The workers have stopped, and they follow us with their eyes all the way across the parking lot.

"Don't say it," Stillman says, once we're in the truck. "There's no evidence Hodges had anything to do with Hartlett's death."

"I know that."

"Him being a bastard doesn't make him a killer, either."

"I know that, too."

"I mean, she's a part-time dancer. Of course her boyfriend's a bastard. It's like a law or something."

I nod and put the truck in gear. "Hodges lied to me, Stillman. I don't like that."

"He's a jerk. He doesn't want to admit he doesn't have a job."

I look at him. "Which he quits right after he buys a new car? Don't bullshit me, Stillman."

"So what do you propose to do about it?"

"Jason Hodges is a redneck, he's unemployed, and it's 10:30 in the morning. I'm pretty sure we'll find him in bed."

It's only a few minutes from Hiller's Body Shop to the edge of the Nation. We cross I-40 and head down Forty-sixth Avenue, and Stillman gives a satisfyingly worried look. "I thought you said we weren't too popular down here."

I smile and turn on the radio, tuning it to Dan Wolfe's show. Josh's prediction was right; Wolfe's in fine form today. I listen to him drone on a couple of minutes, ranting about a legal system so broken it lets killers like Moses Bol out on bail. I stop at a red light, and Wolfe actually names me and Stillman as the chief architects of the fiasco that got Bol bounced on bail. He calls for our heads, and it's not entirely clear he's speaking metaphorically.

Stillman turns pale. "Shit, Thomas. That was us."

"Yeah. Tell you what, Stillman. Let's not get a flat tire anytime soon."

Within blocks, the small houses, all built in the forties, begin their decline into disrepair. With every street the roofs sag more, the yards are more ill-kept, some actually looking condemnable. There's not much traffic, but Stillman still looks as nervous as a house cat with a dog around. Ten blocks later, we're in the heart of the Nation. I roll to a stop next to a particularly bad house: the yard is surrounded with chain-link fence, front and back; the blinds are drawn, and a large rottweiler dozes on a chain on the front porch.

"See this place, Stillman? What with the guard dog and the fence, you'd almost get the idea they don't like people casually stopping by."

Stillman looks past me out of the truck. "No shit. What's the story?"

I smile. *Time for Stillman's first lesson in Nationite mentality.* "You might be under the impression that these people are ignorant, backwoods peckerheads."

Stillman scans the neighborhood. "That about sums it up, yeah."

I point to the house. "This guy, a particularly malevolent bastard named Pickens, is fifty-three years old, and he has been selling one illegal substance or another for thirty-five years. He has only spent a total of eleven months in jail."

"How?"

"By knowing every trick in the book. Even the house is in his mother's name, because that way it can't be taken away under Rico statutes."

"You saying his mother's in on it?"

"Pickens is part of one of the Nation's dynasties, Stillman. His grandfather ran moonshine. His father sold pot. And he sells meth. He hates the IRS, government agents of all kinds, and, above all, foreigners." I hit the gas, driving on. "The point, Stillman, is not to underestimate these people. They were outsmarting revenuers a hundred miles east of here when your father was in diapers." I take a left on Indiana; two blocks later, the truck rolls to a stop in front of a one-story ranch badly in need of paint. Tall weeds ring the porch, and the mailbox is hanging by a thread. Jason Hodges's black Trans Am sits in the gravel driveway, polished to a high gloss. "Welcome to paradise, Stillman. We're home."

"What are you going to do?"

"I'm going to talk with our star witness, Jason Hodges. You coming?"

"Right behind you." I lock up the Ford and lead Stillman quietly up the steps to Jason's door. It's open, and I can hear voices inside. I put my finger on my lips, telling Stillman to stay quiet. One voice is Hodges, but there's a female voice I don't know. She's giggling something I can't make out, but whatever it is, she's being friendly as hell. I reach out and knock, and the giggling stops.

"I'll get it, J," the voice says, and a few seconds later a short-haired brunette in low-rise jean shorts and a white, bra-less T-shirt walks out of the darkness inside. She slows down at the door, looking us over. "Well, well," she says. "Must be hot in those suits."

"I'd like to speak with Jason," I say.

She smiles and calls back over her shoulder, not taking her eyes off us. "J, baby? It's for you."

A few seconds later Hodges walks to the door, bare-chested and in jeans. He sees us and stops dead in his tracks.

"Hey, Jason," I say. "We need to have a little chat."

"Go to the back," Hodges says to the girl.

"Come on, J." She giggles. "I want to meet your new friends."

"I said get on back, Tiffany."

The girl flinches, like she's learned the hard way not to cross Hodges. She vanishes back into the house, disappearing into the dark rooms.

Hodges opens the screen door, walks out onto the porch, and looks up into the hazy sky. "Motherfuckin' hot today," he says. "Melt your ass right on the street."

"I hate to see you grieving over Tamra like this, Jason," I say. "Who's your friend?"

"Her? She's just crazy."

"I was looking for a name."

"Tiffany. Tiffany Murphy."

"You two been friends long?"

Hodges leans back against a pillar that more or less holds up the awning over his porch. "We known each other awhile. She worked at the same bar as Tamra."

"Stillman and I had a chat with Mr. Hiller over at the body shop," I say. "According to him, you haven't worked there in months."

"Yeah. I quit that shit a while back. It was my last known job, so you know."

I look over at the car. "Nice Trans Am. You got the V-8 in that?"

"Hell, yeah. It's the same engine as the Vette."

"It looks lowered."

"It is. Put a shift kit in it, too."

"For a guy with no job, that's a pretty expensive car."

Hodges shrugs. "I got some things goin'. You know."

I step up to him, nose-to-nose. "I'm very, very pissed right now, Jason. Want to know why?"

He stands his ground, his mouth frowning. "I'm all fuckin' ears."

"I'm pissed because Rita West is a very smart woman. She's going to be looking for a patsy, and you're starting to look like a pretty damn tempting prospect."

"Ease off, man. I didn't do nothin'."

"If you fuck me over, Jason, I'm going to make you the pool boy in county jail."

Hodges stares at me silently a second, then steps back. "Look, man, I told you. I quit the job. Big deal."

"You quit your job. You've got a new car. You're screwing someone who knew your dead girlfriend. If I didn't have the evidence I do on Moses Bol, I'd arrest your ass where you stand."

"Yeah, well, you do have the evidence on Bol."

"And if you're lying to me about him, I'm going to throw you to the dogs."

He looks annoyed. "Shit, man, what flew up your skirt? Take a damn Valium."

I lose it, not gradually, but so completely and instantaneously that before either of us know what happened I have Jason Hodges pressed up against his screen porch, wriggling under my grip like a trapped bug. My right upper arm is pressed underneath his throat, snapping his head up and backward in a move I haven't practiced since basic training. "What flew up my skirt?" I say. "I'm going to ask the jury to kill Moses Bol, Jason. Do you read me, here? They're going to tie him down to a gurney and give him a lethal injection of drugs until his heart stops beating. Now you are going to tell me how you got the money for the car, or I'm going to take you downtown, and I am going to have you booked for murder."

"Jesus, Thomas," Stillman says, pulling me a step back. "Take it easy, man."

I release Hodges in disgust. "Yeah. I'll take it easy. Answer the question, Jason."

Tiffany appears behind Hodges, her form backlit from the windows behind her. "J, baby? You OK?"

Hodges is coughing, getting his breath back. "I told you, dammit. Stay in the back, Tiff." He pulls the door shut behind him. "OK. No more bullshit. We was runnin' those Sudanese guys. For money, you know?"

"What do you mean, running?" I say.

"They're *lonely,* man. They got no *women.* Black chicks from around here won't give them the time of day, and they got none from the old country. So Tamra and me started working them. She'd call 'em up. You know, be nice, talk shit to 'em."

"Go on."

"She'd tell 'em she needs somethin'. You know, money for this or that. They'd give her stuff. Stereos, money, whatever."

"You pimped her."

"Man, you got to understand the business opportunity," Hodges says, flushing angrily. "A hundred and fifty of these guys, fresh off the boat. No fuckin' *clue.* It was like shootin' fish in a barrel."

I swallow back my disgust. "How many boys were involved?"

Hodges shrugs. "Fifteen, maybe twenty."

"Did they know about each other?"

"Yeah. A few times that got a little ugly. But it wasn't our problem."

"Give me some names."

"How do I know, man? They're all a bunch of fucking Kunta Kintes."

I move back toward him, but this time Stillman grabs my arm. "Keep it together, Thomas."

I shake off his hand. "Don't play stupid with me, Jason."

Hodges pauses. "Deng. Matek Deng. He was one. That dude was a gold mine."

One of Bol's closest friends. "How much money did you make?"

"Good week, maybe a thousand. They're all pretty broke, but it added up. She had them coming over to her place all the time."

"How long did it go on?"

"Maybe three months."

I nod toward the Trans Am. "So you bought the car."

"Yeah."

"What did Tamra get out of it?"

"She did OK."

"Like how, exactly?"

"She didn't buy shit, OK? She was real generous."

"Yeah, I'm sure." I look at him. "Was Bol one of the boys she played?"

"Yeah. He got pissed off about the others, you know? He said he was the chief or whatever. I can't remember the word."

"Benywal."

"Yeah, that's it. He's the fuckin' *Benywal*. And the *Benywal* don't share his woman. Him and Tamra fought about it all the time. Finally, he just lost it."

"Shit," Stillman says. "You mean he killed her in a jealous rage?"

Hodges nods. "You got it, Ace." He spits off the porch into the weeds. "Look, I should've told you. But be reasonable, man. What me and Tamra was doing ain't exactly the kind of thing to bring up to the cops."

I watch Hodges awhile, thinking about how fucked Tamra Hartlett must have been to have turned to a guy like him. "It's sure as hell going to come up now," I say. "You're going to testify to every word of this in court. It's the real motive for murder. It has teeth. It's the first thing you've said that makes any sense."

Hodges looks up at me. "And then what, man? You gonna prosecute me for solicitation?"

"No," I say. "I'm going to give you immunity, Jason. It's a promise not to prosecute you in exchange for your testimony."

"Yeah, man. I know what it is. That's cool."

I stand very still, so I don't attack him again. "Listen, you little fuck. You pimped your girlfriend to get money from some of the most godforsaken and vulnerable people on the planet. You're banging her friend before her body's cold. You are the lowest slime on the face of the earth. I'm giving you immunity because I need your testimony to get Bol, and you're the kind of asshole who won't give it to me any other way. This ain't no friendship thing." I take one measured step toward him. "You got that, *Ace*?"

"Yeah. Shit, man."

I step back off the porch, taking Stillman with me. "You lied to me once, Jason. Don't do it again."

Hodges stares for a second, then turns back to the house, letting the screen door slam behind him.

Stillman and I stand alone in his yard. "Wow," Stillman says quietly. "That dude is cold."

I start walking to the truck. "Yeah. But if he's finally telling the truth, he just sealed Bol's fate."

The next morning, Thursday, Rayburn, Carl, Stillman, and I meet in the district attorney's office. Rayburn wants assurances about the case's progress, which isn't a surprise. Dan Wolfe's radio lambaste has made immigration and the murder of Tamra Hartlett the major topic of conversation from corporate water coolers to the projects. The DA eyes me levelly. "So," he says. "You're ready to take this kid Bol down, right?"

"Yeah," I say. "Hodges finally pulled the pieces together. We've got motive, means, and opportunity. We've got witnesses who place him on the scene, and we've got compelling blood evidence."

"And you've got Paul Landmeyer on the stand," the DA says. "He's a great witness."

Carl nods. "Against which, you've got the sworn testimony of one Fiona Towns."

Rayburn grins. "By the time Thomas gets done with her, there's gonna be nothing left but a Presbyterian stain. Ain't that right, Thomas?"

"The lady definitely has some credibility issues," I say.

"She's a preacher," Carl says, ever practical. "That has weight in a lot of people's minds."

"Which brings us to jury selection," Rayburn says. "You got voir dire next Monday at ten, right?"

"Yeah. Well, actually, it'll be at ten-fifteen. That's because Rita will spend fifteen minutes trying to convince Judge Ginder that it isn't possible to assemble a jury of Moses Bol's peers in Nashville, Tennessee, since he's so recently landed here from the moon."

Rayburn bursts out laughing. "Pretty fucking good point, too."

Stillman smiles. "That dude's peers are all back in the mother country, herding cattle."

"Bol's a resident now," Carl says. "Legally, his peers are the fine people of Davidson County."

Rayburn nods. "OK, then." We start to leave, but Rayburn softly coughs. I turn back, and he's inexplicably blushing. "Listen, before everybody goes, I just wanted to say a little something. It's not just Bol we've got Monday. It's Carl's last day, too."

Carl groans. "David, I'm begging you—"

"Shut up, Carl," Rayburn says, smiling. "Monday's gonna be crazy." He reaches into his desk and takes out a small box. "It's just something to remember this place by."

Carl takes the box. "What is it?"

"Open it."

Carl pulls plain white wrapping paper off the box. He lifts the lid and smiles. "Son of a bitch. And it's just my size."

"Seemed appropriate."

Carl lifts a tie out of the box and holds it up to me and Stillman. "It's Mr. and Mrs. Santa Claus. Naked, on a beach, drinking margaritas."

"Something to smile about during these dark days," Rayburn says, grinning. "You know, what with Hale and all that."

"Cancel the party, David," Carl says soberly. "It's the wrong time for it."

"The hell I will. You've been in this office for thirty-one years, Carl, and I'll be damned if some pipsqueak law professor is going to cheat you out of the send-off you deserve. The party is next Friday at seven, and you will not be late."

"How come you got to wait?" Stillman asks. "It's almost a week later."

Rayburn grins. "Because the state of Tennessee is forcing Carl to take four vacation days since they don't want to pay him everything they owe him. The beauties of government service."

"Well, hell, we can still have the party—"

"We will *not* have any retirement party until I am officially no longer an employee of this office," Carl says. "So it's Friday, or it isn't at all. Which begs the point, because there shouldn't be one in the first place. I should just be allowed to slink off with a little dignity."

"You realize there's no money in our budget for this kind of thing, right?" Rayburn says.

"Which is why—"

"Which is why we've been taking up collections for the last six months, just so we can have an open bar." He grins. "Well, for three hours, anyway."

Carl pushes out a barely perceptible smile. "I'm touched, David. Truly, I am."

"You're goddamn right, you're touched. You will also be front and center at seven on Friday night, and that's an order. Is that understood?"

Carl nods. "Yeah. I got it."

Rayburn looks at Stillman. "Remember this moment, Stillman. We take care of each other around here. This is family. Always will be."

Stillman is feeling, by all accounts, pleased. He's been invited into the inner sanctum of Rayburn's office, further evidence that he's handpicked for the fast track. Personally, I doubt Jeff Stillman is destined for Rayburn's definition of greatness. Stillman, in my opinion, is more likely destined for a shinier life, something that involves less legal legwork and more TV time. The DA is fifty-two years old, a world away from Jeff Stillman's eager, photogenic sensibilities. Carl is even farther removed; when Carl became a lawyer, there were four channels on TV, and none of them cared about local prosecutors. You came in, kicked ass, and raised a beer with your adversary at the local watering hole. It was an insular, and for him, satisfying, world.

I sit in my own chair after leaving Rayburn's office, and I watch Stillman smiling back at me in a wing chair. "So," I say. "We're ready to go to court."

"No doubt," Stillman answers. "Wired. Incidentally, I see what you mean about doing your own research. No way an investigator would have pried out of Hodges what you got today. That was deep." I write Matek Deng's name on a sheet of paper and hand it over. "Who's this?" I ask.

"Jason told us he pimped his girlfriend to this guy."

"Right. And Jason lies a lot, doesn't he?"

Stillman nods slowly. "Yeah."

"So maybe we ought to check Deng's bank statements."

Stillman's eyes widen. "Yeah. No shit. 'Cause otherwise—"

"Otherwise, Stillman, when Rita West puts Jason Hodges on the stand, there won't be any corroboration for his statements. And an uncorroborated Jason Hodges on the stand we do not need."

Stillman stares. "It's not like school, is it?"

"No, Stillman. Not so much." I lean back in my chair. "Start with Deng. His best friend is a guy named Luol Chol. Together with Bol, they're like the three musketeers. Inseparable. You can work outward from there. Run credit checks, bank statements, employment history."

"Got it. What are you going to do?"

"The money trail helps, but like too many things in this damn case, it's circumstantial. We need something concrete."

"Like what?"

"Hodges says a bunch of these guys were in Hartlett's apartment. Get physical evidence to confirm that fact, and we're done."

"How we gonna do that at this late date?"

"I could subpoena a hundred and fifty Africans, but I

don't think Ginder would think that's a very funny joke. Not three days before trial. Anyway, with this Hale thing hanging over our heads, a delay is the last thing we need."

"So what are you going to do?"

"I'm going to sit in my chair and think, Stillman. See you when you get back."

After a half hour, I start throwing wadded-up papers into my wastebasket. *Not good.* Tomorrow we go on Buchanan's wild-goose chase, and Monday we have court. Twenty minutes later, the basket's full. I look at the clock: it's nearly eleven. *I could take a walk. Walking helps people think. I read that, somewhere.* I stand up and sit back down. *It's a million degrees outside. The walk isn't such a good idea.* I stare at the wastebasket another few seconds, and it hits me. *It's a million degrees out there.* I pick up the phone and call Paul Landmeyer. "Listen," I say, "you took fingerprints all over Tamra Hartlett's apartment, right?"

"Sure."

"How many different people did you find?"

"Quite a few. Twelve or thirteen, I think."

"How many were you able to identify?"

"Just four or five. There was the victim, her mother, the boyfriend, Bol, and a female friend. The rest weren't in the database."

"Suppose I got you another five or six sets of prints to compare with what you found at the apartment. How long would it take you to tell me if there's a match?"

"Anybody else, two days. You, two hours."

I smile. "Thanks, Paul. Hang loose on this for a while. I'll be in touch." I hang up and call Josh Ritchie on his cell phone.

He answers in his easy, laid-back voice. "What's up, dude?"

"Where are you?"

"In my van, watching the Sudanese. They're milling around Bol's apartment, coming in and out."

"Good. How hot is it out there right now?"

"Philippines hot, dude. I'm frying my ass off."

"You know the grocery store just off Charlotte? Go buy a six-pack of the coldest Cokes you can find there, even if you have to get them out of a machine. Pack them in some ice and wait there for me."

"You buyin' me drinks now, counselor?"

"Nope. I'm buyin' the people you're watching drinks. I'll be there in twenty minutes."

I walk outside, and the still, airless heat of the day hits me like a blanket. I'm sweating by the time I get to the parking lot. I hop in for the drive to the Nation. I take the Forty-sixth Avenue exit, turning left for the four blocks to the grocery store. Josh is sitting in his van, the engine idling. We roll down windows. "You got 'em?"

He holds up a Styrofoam cooler. "Six, on ice."

"Lemme ride with you. I'll leave the truck here, and we can pick it up after." I hop out and get in Josh's van, the inside of which is trashed like a freshman's dorm room. "You ever clean this thing?"

"Home away from home," Josh says, smiling. "You wanna tell me what we're doing now?"

"Collecting fingerprints," I say, grinning. "Hot day, cold drink. Should be no problem."

"Shit man, that's not bad. You think the prints are gonna stick on the cans?"

"You got any better ideas?"

He shakes his head. "Nope."

"When we get there, dump the ice and wipe the cans so they're dry. Walk by and say the drinks are left over from a party and they look thirsty."

Josh nods. "Worth a shot." We drive back through the Nation, enter Tennessee Village, and park around the corner from Bol's apartment. A handful of Asians are hanging out under a tree, some with gang clothes and tats. Josh dumps the ice, wipes the cans dry, and opens his door.

"Try to keep Deng's and Luol's cans separate," I say. "You think this will work?"

Josh smiles a Dennis Quaid smile and pushes his hat back on his head. "No problem, pal. I'm just a friendly guy who likes to share." Josh disappears with the Cokes around the corner. I sit and wait in the idling van; the air-conditioning can barely keep up with the stifling heat and humidity. The life of the Village goes on around me: a group of Somali women walk by with their brilliantly colored clothing and scarves over their heads; more Asians, probably Laotian, by the tattoos. *Nashville, Tennessee, baby. The global village heads South.* After about ten minutes Josh rambles back, the Styrofoam cooler under his arm. He gets in the van and opens the lid. "Got to hand it to you, man. They drained them on the spot. Deng is front left; Luol is front right. I bent the pop-tops in different directions, to keep it clear."

"Beautiful."

"So where to now?"

"Just drop me back off at my truck. Stay here for now. If anything goes down tonight, I want you here to know about it."

Josh nods and drives me back over to Charlotte Avenue. He drops me off with the cooler.

The forensic lab of Davidson County is as glamorous as a run-down elementary school. The building is industrial and forlorn, and once inside, the floor is tiled with big squares of linoleum worn with decades of nightly cleaning and polishing. Enormous fluorescent lights in cheap plastic fixtures run the length of the hallways. I walk into the lobby, greet the receptionist, and ask for Paul.

Paul comes out to the lobby to meet me, and we walk together back to his lab. "Damn, that was fast," he says. "How'd you get the prints?"

"You aren't gonna like it, but I had to improvise." I open the cooler, and Paul raises an eyebrow. He slips on a latex glove and removes the cans by their upper aluminum ridges. "So this was your bright idea, I take it?"

"Yeah."

He looks at the cans dubiously. "You know how this stuff works, don't you? It's sweat. Preferably on a nice warm, dry surface."

"I know. Just tell me it'll work."

Paul places the cans on a tray and shines fluorescent light on them. There are a few print ridges visible, but not many. "In that heat, it's the cans that were sweating," he says, "not the people. Lots of condensation."

"So where are we?"

Paul raises an eyebrow. "How's your sense of irony these days?"

"Full-on."

"It's about to go up a notch. There's only one material in the world that can reliably retrieve fingerprints from a wet metal surface. Care to guess what it's called?"

"No idea."

"Sudan black."

I stare. "You gotta be kidding me."

"Nope. Fifteen grams of Sudan black powder, a thousand milliliters of ethanol, five hundred milliliters of distilled water. Immerse two minutes, then let dry. The prints show up blue. I'll photograph them with a digital camera, and then it's just a matter of letting the software find the match."

"If there is one."

He picks up the tray. "The process makes fumes, so I've got to wear a protective suit and hood for this. I need at least an hour. You want to wait here or head back to the office?"

"I'll wait."

"OK. Hang loose."

I walk back out into the reception area and wait. The minutes inch by until Paul comes back out in a white Tyvek suit. "I really ought to do this for a living," he says. "You got your match. Deng and Luol were definitely in Tamra Hartlett's apartment. It'll take more time for the others."

"How clean is it?"

"Sixteen ridge areas, four more than required. It's legal in court. I can let you know about the rest in a few hours."

Ok, Jason. Your story checks out so far. But I still don't trust you as far as I can throw you. It's almost five by the time I get back to 222 West, and the staff has nearly emptied out. Stillman, however, is waiting in my office. He's had nearly all day to hold up his end of the bargain, and from his expression, I'd say he has. He grins at me like he's just solved the Lindbergh kidnapping. "I've got 'em," he says. "Bank records, credit checks, and work schedules. Bol, Deng, and Chol."

I look at the papers. "Not bad. How'd you pull it off?"

He grins. "Ran the credit checks from my desk. Chol and Deng have checking accounts at AmSouth, and the downtown office is six blocks from here."

I raise an eyebrow. "You actually went there?"

"Hey, I've been paying attention. Face-to-face, right? Worked wonders."

"I take it she was good-looking?"

He grins wider. "She said she liked my tie."

"OK, Stillman. Break it down for me."

Stillman points to a set of bank statements on my desk. "Chol makes eleven-hundred forty-five dollars a month at Wal-Mart. He works forty hours a week. But he *was* making six hundred dollars more. I figure he was working about twenty hours a week overtime to pull it off."

"So what changed?"

"I drove out to see his shift manager. The guy was harried, man. I had to follow him around while I talked to him. But he said Chol used to beg for overtime, and he remembered when it stopped. Second week of February."

"The week after Hartlett's murder."

"Correct."

I nod. *OK, Jason. Maybe you're actually telling the truth.* "Did Chol have any debts he was paying off?"

"He owes seventeen hundred dollars to Tennessee State University for ESL classes, which he's paying off at eighty-five bucks a month. That's it."

"What does he have in the bank?"

"As of this morning, one hundred and sixty-five dollars."

I smile. "And Deng?"

"Same story, only bigger checks. Like Jason said, the guy was a cash cow."

"OK. So how about Bol?"

Stillman frowns. "Nothing."

"You mean he didn't make the same withdrawals?"

"I mean he doesn't even have a bank account."

"You're kidding."

"The manager at Wal-Mart says Bol cashed his checks at the store. And he didn't work overtime."

"Shit."

"Still, it confirms Jason's story, doesn't it?"

I exhale and look past him out my window. *Close. We're getting close.* "I'm really starting to hate this case, Stillman."

CHAPTER
NINE

I HAVE A SMASHED NOSE. Not bad smashed—not boxer caliber, for example—just slightly bent in a couple of places. My father, the airplane mechanic, imparted few direct lessons to me, preferring to lead by example—enjoy life, look but don't touch other women, treasure the company of men—but one thing he did drill in me was the necessity of learning how to defend oneself in a fight. I used this advice a few times in my life: twice in high school, once in college over a girl, and finally, in an idiotic bar fight during basic training that cost me the revised line in my profile. So that's what I learned from my old man: how to fight. The rest, like how to dress and act and attract a woman, I had to figure out myself.

In my second year of JAG, I met Rebecca Obregon, the woman I loved. She was standing in line in front of me at an outdoor restaurant on the River Walk in San Antonio. I asked her how her hair could smell so good on such a hot, muggy day. She looked at me a couple of seconds, making her mind

up about me, and answered, "Aveda Rosemary Mint Shampoo. Now tell me how a man with a nose that looks like
yours can have such beautiful eyes."

Being a twenty-six-year-old first lieutenant in the army, I
didn't know that a woman who can seduce you with an insult
is a woman who should be avoided like Odysseus's sirens. I
also had no idea that Aveda Rosemary Mint Shampoo is to
hair care as a Mercedes-Benz S500 is to automobiles. Rebecca Obregon was part exquisite pleasure, part stinging
pain, and all high-maintenance.

The honeymoon was heaven. There was the week in
Florida, paid for by me, followed by two weeks in Europe,
paid for by the Obregon fortune. The little condo on Long-
boat Key, just north of Sarasota, was private enough for romance but connected to the little Florida beach houses that
had not yet given way to the multistory towers. Our clock
was backward, so we were in and out of bed most of the day,
rising for good only for a late dinner. Nights we walked the
deserted beaches, the air still warm on our bare legs. Europe
was a whirlwind, less private but more exotic. I had never
been overseas, and I soaked up England and Spain. We wan-
dered the Alcazar in Seville, and took carriage rides through
the city's tree-lined parks.

We landed back in Nashville in a kind of romantic glow.
Rebecca settled in at Vanderbilt, working in the fund-raising
department. Her job consisted of throwing parties for rich
people and getting money from them without looking awkward, a task for which she was supremely well qualified. She
was born into money, was comfortable around it, and—
although neither of us realized it at the time we were
married—uncomfortable without it. Her father, a surgeon
from San Antonio, had smiled politely when meeting me,

but it had been obvious enough I wasn't his dream for his little girl. *No matter,* I thought. *I'm not marrying him; I'm marrying this gorgeous woman standing beside me. And anyway, he lives in San Antonio.* Which was only true in the most narrow, geographic sense; Dr. Raul Obregon lived in the hearts and minds of all three of his daughters, and his values permeated their thinking. I started in on the sixty-hour-week grinds at the DA's office, determined to make my mark professionally. Two years later, Jasmine came along, which pulled us together as a family, at least for a while. But the cracks were already in the foundation.

Maybe it was caring too much about work. Maybe it was coming home for a solid year with nothing but stories about the child support division—dragging creeps into court to force them to pay for the children they left behind—that drove her away. It had all been so unseemly for an Obregon, once the romance wore off and real life set in. I wouldn't let Rebecca's father pay for a country club membership, both on principle and because I didn't want to be known as a kept man among my peers, any one of which with a calculator would know it was beyond my means. When, in our fifth year of marriage, Rebecca showed up at home with a new BMW, courtesy of Daddy, and she had refused to take it back, the cracks had grown into chasms. Maybe—this is the theory I use to salve my wounded pride, anyway—maybe it was her lack of moral character that made her susceptible to what was about to happen. Whatever the reason, I ended up being the last to know.

His name was Michael Sarandokos, a Greek plastic surgeon seven years older and four hundred thousand a year richer than me. His workday ended at four—earlier, on surgery days, if everything went well—and he never came home with stories about welfare mothers and child support or, when I started getting promoted, capital murder cases. Dr. Sarandokos, it's safe to assume, comes home with stories about which of his clients' children are going to Auburn and who just gave her daughter the world's smallest cell phone.

It's now 7:30 p.m., and I stand in front of the door of their house. No one inside those doors knows what has happened to me the last couple of days, which is a good thing. My relationship with Jazz is already complicated enough, and I never mention work with her or her mother. She knows that I put away bad guys, and that's enough for now.

I push the doorbell, and in a few seconds I hear noise from inside. The door opens, and the maid, Maria, a fiftyish plump woman from El Salvador, sees me and smiles. She likes me, which helps. "*Señor Dennehy, bienvenidos*. Come inside. I go get Mrs. Sarandokos."

I step in and take off my coat. The entryway to the home is open to a height of fifteen feet, with marble floors and what looks like enough crown molding to build a separate structure. After a minute or so Sarandokos comes strolling around the corner. He's handsome, in a rich-guy kind of way, by which I mean his nose is not smashed, because he has never, ever been in a fistfight. He's simply great-looking, like he just walked off the island of Patmos, which, in fact, he did, in 1986. He rolls up, relaxed, like he just happened to be walking by his front door. I'm on his turf, and he instinctively feels the need to put in an appearance. I don't blame him for this, just like I don't blame him for wanting Rebecca. Any man in his right mind would want her, and since he can afford her, maybe they're actually happy. But I hate the idea of him being with Jazz, simply because she has the potential to be so much more.

"How are you, Dennehy?" he asks. He's wearing loose-fitting pants and a silk shirt. "Bec is somewhere, not sure where. Probably finding Jasmine."

I nod; Sarandokos's home is so large that it's possible to lose track of the people inside. We don't shake hands, thank God. "So you're off to Orlando," I say.

"Thanks for flexing on your days with Jasmine. She really wants to go to Universal Studios."

"Sure." That about wraps up the small talk, so he stands there a few seconds, until he's saved from having to produce an exit line by Rebecca's entrance. She is wearing low-rider jeans and a tan, sleeveless shirt. Her hair is pulled back into a ponytail, which makes her neck look long and elegant. She's in fairly tall shoes, which make her about five foot eight, and she hasn't gained a pound since the day I met her, snapping back like a rubber band after Jazz was born. She smiles—her teeth preposterously white—and I know I don't love her anymore. I feel something powerful, but it's mostly nostalgia. I want to go back in time to when we had nothing—not even Jazz, God help me—and we dreamed about our future together on a nearly deserted beach in Florida. I want her to be just like she is, only different, which is the short history of our love affair.

Sarandokos vanishes back into his study, leaving me alone with Rebecca. I never go into the house itself. I know that because we're adults I'm supposed to be able to sit and drink tea and act like the arrangement is fine. But it seems to me that it's because we're adults that we understand how fractured and painful it all is, not the other way around. It's children who trade in their best friends for new ones every few months. So I stay in the entryway. "We leave first thing in the morning," she says. She sees the package I hold. "Is that for Jazz? I'll hold it for you. I know you like presents opened on the day."

"Yeah," I say, but I keep the package. "I'm gonna give it to her myself, if that's OK."

"No. Sure. I mean, that's fine."

I hear Jazz running, a sound I love. She knows I'm in the house, and the steps are ridiculously fast, her ten-year-old legs churning along. She must be wearing clogs for all the racket she's making on Sarandokos's Brazilian hardwood floors. She comes around the corner like a puppy, skidding and sliding past the mark, recovering, and running straight up to me in an earthquake of energy. She grabs me, her arms around my stomach, her face in my chest. She looks up at me and says, "I'm going to Universal Studios."

"That's right," I say. "They've got Jimmy Neutron there."

"I know," she says. "And Shrek." She looks at my package. "Mine?" she asks.

"You bet," I say. "Happy birthday."

"Don't open it till the day," Rebecca says, and I shake my head no.

"Not this time," I say. "Come here, Jazzy. Let's open it now." I give Rebecca a nod, and she drifts back into the house, leaving us alone. She has tact, and I've learned to be grateful for small things like that. Jazz takes my hand and opens the front door. Somehow, in her ten-year-old head, she has already figured out a hell of a lot, like how Daddy doesn't like to be in the mansion.

We walk outside and sit on the steps in the warm air. In spite of the heat, she wraps my coat around herself like a poncho, her head sticking up out of the body. She is her mother and me, which is complicated and beautiful and a problem. Carl, who was only ever married to his work, once asked me how much more difficult divorce was when there are kids involved. I answered, "One million, million times."

"Let me see," she says, and I give her the package. She smiles, rips it open, and pulls out the photo album of soccer pictures I put together last weekend. She looks up at me, curious, and I say, "Look inside. That's the real present." She starts to flip through the pictures, obviously pleased. She goes through the whole book, page by page, until she finishes. She looks up and says, "I love it, Daddy."

"Good. Now go get ready for dinner. And have fun in Orlando."

She shimmies out of the coat and hugs me again. I lift her up and kiss her, but I let her go easily. I don't want drama attached to my visits. I open the door, and she runs in, holding her picture book. Rebecca appears again and sees it; she looks at the first few pages and glances up at me, smiling, and I know she understands. She steps outside with me, and for a moment we're alone in the warm air, standing close together in the twilight. "Thanks for letting her go, Thomas," she says.

"You said that already."

She gives me a look, and I catch my breath a second. Her expression is something like desire, but more distant. Then I recognize it; it's nostalgia, just like my own. *We understand each other perfectly,* I think. I kiss her cheek, chastely, and walk out of my memories back into the warm air of Nashville.

I drive almost two miles before I see the note on my windshield. It's small, and on the passenger's side this time, so I don't notice it until it starts to work its way loose enough to flap in the wind. I stare at it, wondering if I have driven all the way out to Bec's house that way—God knows, I was preoccupied enough to miss it—or if someone has followed me to the Sarandokos place and stuck it on the car while I was inside. Reflexively, I check my mirrors, but it's night now and one set of headlights looks like another. *Shit. This guy is really determined to fuck with me.* A couple of miles down I-65 I pull off—three exits before my usual one—and a car about a hundred yards behind takes the exit as well. We roll down the exit ramp to a stop sign, and the car sits behind me. There's a man in the car, although with his headlights glaring from behind, I can't make out any details. I sit for a few seconds, wondering if I should just open the door and march up to the door. I'm pondering this when he hits his horn, which jerks me back into the present. I turn right, and he turns the opposite way.

I pull over at a gas station a few blocks up, park, and retrieve the pamphlet. It's from the same group as the first, Citizens for a Just America. It's full of the same anti-capital punishment rhetoric as the other leaflet, but this time featuring the saga of Abdul Rahan, a name I knew well already. Rahan had a rap sheet as long as my arm, including three felony convictions. After doing seven years for an armed robbery charge, he wasn't on the street a month before he was accused of blowing away a couple of hitchhiking German girls naive enough to think it was still possible to travel America with backpacks, a few bus tickets, and goodwill. After sitting on death row for three years, he was exonerated when a new form of DNA testing proved he was innocent. The pamphlet has the same amateurish, homemade quality as the other, like it was cobbled together by somebody with a scanner and a cheap computer program. At the bottom is another blurry photograph, this time of a man in an electric chair, skull cap screwed on, restraints secure, his head slumped forward. The man's skin is blistered, split open at the arms, which are bare under a short-sleeve shirt. It looks like something out of the thirties or forties, judging by the equipment. The same words are at the bottom: *NO MIS-TAKES WILL BE TOLERATED.*

I stare at the grotesque picture a second, then punch in Sarandokos's number. He answers. "Yeah, Michael, it's Thomas. Can I speak to Bec?" The good doctor's tone is mildly annoyed, but I hear him call out to Rebecca. He puts his hand over the phone to tell her it's me—like it's a secret, for some reason—but he doesn't do a very good job of it because his muffled voice is still audible.

"Thomas?" It's Bec.

"Yeah. Listen, you guys have an alarm system, right?"

"Of course." A pause. "What are you—"

"Look, it's nothing. Just make sure you turn it on tonight, OK?"

"Is something wrong? What's this about?"

"Nothing's wrong. It's . . . look, it's no big deal. I'd just feel better if you had it on."

"We have it on every night."

"Wonderful. That's fine."

I know what she's thinking; even after three years of divorce, she's still the person I know most intimately on Earth. She's thinking about my job, and how glad she is her life and Jazz's don't have to be touched anymore by wackos and killers and all the rest. Five years married to an assistant DA have taught her the code words, the rules of understatement. And she's a little scared for me, because she still cares about me more than she admits. Maybe it's only emotional inertia, or maybe it's because I'm Jazz's father, but she definitely cares. She knows that something is bothering me, and that nothing bothers me unless it's significant.

I know these things because even though Sarandokos is standing right beside her, she says, "Be careful, Thomas."

CHAPTER
TEN

AS A SENIOR PROSECUTOR with Carl, I have enjoyed one surpassing privilege: I can handpick my cases, and I never work on more than one thing at a time. Carl and I have prosecuted more than thirty capital crimes together, taking the most complex, highest-profile cases that run through the district. Which means that if things were normal, I would spend the next day entirely focused on Moses Bol's case. But things are not normal. Professor Philip Buchanan waits to take us to a Browning BPS pump shotgun and Kwame Jamal Hale's version of the truth.

Coffee, Zoloft, the morning run—two shirtless miles on the hills around my house before the heat forces me back home—and a shower. In other words, I stay in my groove. Today is one of the biggest days of my professional life, but not because of Moses Bol. It's my past, exhumed by Professor Philip Buchanan to speak.

Carl, Rayburn, and I meet in the DA's office at 9:30, a half hour before Buchanan is due. Rayburn stands by his window, a place he's increasingly grown rooted to over the last few days. He's wearing one of his dark-blue suits, standard-issue politician garb. It's not hard to imagine him the state attorney general someday, or even governor. If the next few hours go the wrong way, it also isn't inconceivable that he would want to step through the window before him and into the void below.

Carl, on the other hand, is taking his next-to-last day as a prosecutor with classic stoicism. He just stands there, hands stuffed in his pockets, shirt slightly rumpled, suit needing a good pressing, his expression serious. "I just want this thing to be handled properly," he says. "Quiet, with a little dignity. What we find out, we find out."

"Lemme ask you guys something," Rayburn says. "What makes these guys hate us so much?"

"You mean Buchanan?" I ask.

"Him, and all the other bleeding-heart liberals. I mean, there's a million crimes in this country every year. We bust our asses trying to keep our cities safe enough to live in, and it's a hell of a job."

"Agreed," Carl says.

"And these guys come along and interfere every step of the way. If they're not screaming about police brutality, they're trying to get killers back on the street. They invest a thousand hours of legal research to prove a guy who's already been convicted of several other crimes is innocent of one." He closes his eyes, exhaling deeply. "Once in a blue fucking moon," he says quietly, "I'd like to have one of them just thank us for a job well done."

We sit silently awhile, the only sound the soft ticking of the clock on Rayburn's oak, three-drawer filing cabinet.

"David," I say, "this guy Buchanan isn't worthy to tie your shoes."

He opens his eyes and grins. "Damn right."

Dolores has been told to hold calls into the office except for Buchanan, so we sit in silence, insulated from the city below us. We make small talk for a while, until the phone rings. It's 9:50, ten minutes before Buchanan's due. Rayburn picks up the phone, listens a second, and hangs up. "Something's going on," he says. "There's a crowd gathering in front of the building." The DA's window is on the back side of the building, so we move in formation along the perimeter hallway to the side that looks down on the street. Rayburn opens a door, apologizes to the surprised staffer, and we clump around her window. There, nine stories below, two media trucks are jockeying for parking spots. About fifty people are standing around, as well. Several are holding placards, and though they're too far away to read, it doesn't take much imagination to fill in the blanks; Buchanan is bringing the full protest circus to the big day. Second Avenue is also a major tourist area, and we can already see a few people jaywalking across the street to check things out. Cameramen spill out of the media trucks and begin filming the protesters.

"Get the doors, David," Carl says, quietly.

Rayburn nods and picks up the telephone on the staffer's desk. "Have the guard secure the front door, will you, Dolores?" he says. "That's correct. Nobody in or out." We move back out into the hall, and heads snap up from desks as we pass; a few staff members drift out of offices to see what's going on. The pissed-off expression on Rayburn's face shuts down any questions. We get back to the DA's office, and Rayburn slams shut the door. "It's a Geraldo," he says. "The bastard leaked."

"That's disappointing," Carl says quietly. "One hopes for a little more honor."

"Can we possibly conduct this operation with a bunch of reporters tagging along?" Rayburn demands.

"Wrong question," I say. "Can we *refuse* to conduct it with reporters tagging along?"

Rayburn stares a second, as our situation sinks in. "No. We can't."

Dolores pokes her head in the door. "I've called the guards, but Buchanan's already in the reception area. There's five people with him, and the guard downstairs says both elevators are full."

"Holy shit. Excuse my French, Dolores."

"What do you want me to do?"

"Put one of the uniforms on the outer door. Call down and tell the guard that nobody gets on an elevator who doesn't work in the building. And try to get somebody outside, on the street. We don't want any rubber-necking goofballs getting hit by a car." He turns to us. "So what do we think, gentlemen? Any suggestions?"

Carl shrugs. I swear to God, the man is implacable. "The worse one's adversary behaves, the more important it is to behave impeccably oneself."

"What does that mean, dammit?"

"I think Carl's suggesting we turn up the dignity a notch," I say.

Rayburn stares, then nods. "Damn, that's not bad."

"Buchanan's got the usual hippie protest crowd," Carl says. "The more they rant and wave their signs, the calmer we become. People will know whom to believe."

Rayburn stands up straight and smooths his suit. He straightens his tie. "How do I look?"

"Like the district attorney," Carl says. "Which is who you are."

Rayburn smiles. "All right then. Let's go outdignify the fucker."

When Rayburn punches the code on the Simplex locks that open the door to the ninth-floor reception area, we're bathed in the cold, hard light of three video cameras. With one step out of the inner offices, we leave the real world and enter the weird zone, where appearance is everything. There, standing front and center, is Barry Dougherty, a reporter for the local CBS affiliate. Rayburn gets six inches into the room when Dougherty's accent-free, television voice rises above the din. "Mr. District Attorney! Was the wrong man executed in the Sunshine Grocery murders?"

Fresh from Carl's pep talk, Rayburn doesn't show a crease. "Hello, Barry. I appreciate the question. We have total confidence in the jury verdict that was handed down in that case. But in the interest of justice, we're here to follow up on Professor Buchanan's concerns."

Dougherty looks momentarily disappointed; today's film will not include the sight of a district attorney melting down. Not disappointed enough, however. He leans forward, grinning fiercely. "You mention the jury, Mr. District Attorney. Are you aware that two members of that jury have already stated they would not have voted to convict if they had known about Kwame Jamal Hale?"

I close my eyes. *Buchanan has been lining up the jury. This thing is choreographed, start to finish.*

Rayburn blanches slightly. "That's what makes this country great, Barry," he says. "People are free to speak their minds." He pushes past Dougherty to Buchanan. "So, Professor Buchanan. I thought we had a deal."

Buchanan stands, smiling and relaxed. With him are two

young women, college age, probably assistants. "People find things out," he says. "News travels on its own."

"Maybe it would be better if we just got on with this," Rayburn says.

"You have your crew ready?"

"In our lot, ready to roll."

The crowd moves into the hall, where a small but vocal crowd of protesters wait. They cheer Buchanan and his aides like rock stars. A second group, also early enough to make it upstairs before the cops sealed off the building, pile out of an arriving elevator, leaving Rayburn, Carl, and me surrounded by a group of twenty-somethings in blue jeans and tie-dyed T-shirts ranting in our faces against capital punishment. "No to state-sponsored killing! End the death machine!"

We're encircled by protesters, enduring a relentless barrage of camera flashes until an empty elevator arrives. The door opens, and the merry band piles in with us, chanting all the way down to street level. One of them, a mousy-looking girl about twenty, stands nose-to-nose with Carl; for nine floors we listen to her lecture one of the leading scholars on criminal law in America on how the justice system is a hive of racists who are used by a white hegemony to impose its control on a black underclass. Carl stands impassively, his eyes counting floors as we descend. When the door opens, the protesters bound out of the elevator like children on a field trip to the zoo.

By the time we hit the street there are at least seventy-five people milling around. The professor moves through the crowd, soaking up the love. There are more cameras waiting, and he starts giving interviews; this bit of theater reduces us to his wait staff, since without him, we don't know where we're going. Rayburn gives the expected no-comment—he looks good, not out of control—and we escape into his Crown Vic to wait. Eventually, Buchanan loads up his group. The professor gets in his rental car and pulls out on Second Avenue, followed by a line of a dozen or so cars. Rayburn pulls out after the last of Buchanan's crowd, and the police ID van follows us. Finally comes a row of five media vehicles, creating a motorcade of impressive length. We look like a funeral procession as we pull slowly out, Buchanan leading us back through downtown to I-40. We hit the four lights before the freeway, and the convoy is intact as it turns west, heading toward Memphis. Buchanan settles into a fifty-five-mile-per-hour cruise, running ten under the limit.

Now out of the camera's view, Rayburn grips the wheel like he wants to strangle it. He keeps looking in the rearview mirror at the vehicles stringing along behind us, cursing under his breath. After a few miles, the city begins its fade into semirural enclaves. The highway slices through heavily forested hills, the terrain on both sides of the highway scorched into a withering brown. The sky is hazy with humidity, muted into a nearly colorless gray.

After twelve miles, we turn south onto State Highway 70, a circuitous, two-lane road tightly bordered on one side by the Harpeth River. Buchanan slows for each switchback and S-corner, and the convoy bunches together behind his hyper-careful driving. The metaphor of following Buchanan to a place of unknown destiny is not lost on Rayburn. "God, he's loving this," he mutters. "He's like the Pied Piper of doom."

"Montgomery Bell State Park is out this way," I say. "You think he's heading there?"

"Three thousand acres of woodlands," Carl offers, from the backseat. "That gun would be a needle in a haystack." The road turns southeast now, and we click off twenty uneventful miles toward Montgomery Bell Park. We're nearly to the entrance when Buchanan slows to a crawl. The cars bunch up again, and Buchanan turns left onto a side road that's practically invisible in the trees. The road is ostensibly gravel, but nearly overgrown by grass. We move slowly, gradually climbing an incline through heavily forested acreage. We go this way about fifteen minutes, which in the difficult conditions feels like three times as long. We're several miles from Highway 70 now, seriously into *Deliverance* country. A meadow opens up before us, and Buchanan pulls off the road into the opening. The meadow is large, about twenty acres, and looks like it's been fallow for years. Tall brown grass blows in the hot air, and juniper and birch trees line the edges of the open space. In the distance, about seventy-five yards away, a dilapidated tobacco barn leans hard against the wind, its battered shape barely hanging together. It looks like a decent storm would send it splintering into pieces.

Buchanan steers his car through the rough pastureland toward the barn, and the convoy follows, the big vans hobbyhorsing up and down over the uneven earth, the protesters' cars following behind. Rayburn's Crown Vic is squeaking and protesting with the off-road treatment, its suspension barely up to the task. Buchanan eventually pulls up on the east side of the dilapidated structure. The vehicles in the convoy scatter across a thirty-yard area. Doors slam as the crowd of people pile out of cars and vans. "Everything about this is wrong," Carl mutters. "We're looking for a shotgun that killed three people in cold blood."

Everyone gathers around Buchanan, who's plainly aware of the cameras. We wait for the ID crew to get out of their van with their shovels and a metal detector. When everybody's ready, the moment of truth arrives.

"The weapon is inside the barn," Buchanan says. "Along the south wall."

Rayburn steps through the crowd to Buchanan. "How did you know this was the one?"

Buchanan pulls a Polaroid photograph out of his pocket. "Kwame Jamal told me the directions. I confirmed the location with him with this picture."

Rayburn plucks the photo from Buchanan's hand. "So you just went around looking for barns?"

"We've researched this whole area, and there are only three," Buchanan answers. "All long abandoned. I took photographs of each of them. Kwame recognized this one right away."

"Why inside a barn?" Rayburn asks. "Doesn't make sense. A structure draws people."

"He could dig without being seen. He also said the ground is softer."

People in the crowd start walking toward the building, and the ID squad moves quickly to cordon it off with yellow police tape. A couple of uniforms are posted, making sure bystanders don't interfere. The media photographers move toward the barrier to take their pictures. For a few seconds, Rayburn, Carl, and I are alone with Buchanan, out of media earshot. Rayburn leans over to the professor. "We're going to take this barn apart, stick by stick," he says. "If it turns out that anybody's tampered with any evidence, I'm going to take you apart next."

Buchanan turns with a sneer. "Is that a threat, Mr. District Attorney?"

"You're damn right, it is," he says. "And if there are footprints anywhere near this gun—assuming we find it—you better pray they're not your size."

Buchanan gives him a shit-eating smile of contempt. "Vietnam. North Korea. Iran. Your death-penalty compadres. How proud you must be to share a legal philosophy with these paragons of liberty."

Rayburn smiles back. "Obstruction of justice. Falsifying evidence. Perjury. If this is a scam, your compadres are going to be in Brushy Mountain prison. I'd suggest you try to shower alone the first year or two."

Buchanan recoils, finally giving Rayburn the response he wants. It's a small victory, but Rayburn seems satisfied. He shakes his head in disgust, then nods toward me and Carl. "Let's go," he says, leading us behind the barrier. Buchanan follows, and we move off in a group. The ID crew moves slowly, looking for signs of tampering. Rayburn looks at Buchanan and says, "It's not that we don't trust you, Professor. It's just that we don't trust you."

It takes twenty minutes to satisfy the ID crew that the entrance to the barn has been adequately examined. The barn door is ten feet tall and opens with a wooden bar-type handle. An officer dusts it for prints and takes a sample of the wood, meticulously tweezing off a splinter. He pushes open the door, which creaks like it hasn't moved in years. The photographer takes a series of flash pictures of the barn's interior from the doorway, and the floor is checked for footprints and debris.

After ten minutes of searching the floor, an officer walks in with his metal detector. He walks toward the south wall, and the thing squeaks a high-pitched signal. The officer slowly advances, and the signal gets stronger. By the time he reaches the wall, the signal meter is pegged at maximum. He sweeps back and forth a little, isolating the strongest spot. Satisfied, he hands off the metal detector and picks up a narrow spade. He starts moving earth carefully, digging under the bottom timber. The spade sinks easily into the soft, powdery dirt. About six inches under the timber, the spade stops. He nods at two other ID officers, who come over to help. They get on their knees and start pulling dirt out from under the timber with their gloved hands, making little piles as they go. Eventually, one of them manages to get his arm underneath, and he says, "I got something." They pull him out, and the first officer uses a crowbar to pull the bottom two timbers off the barn wall. The soft wood comes off easily, the boards splintering under the pressure. With the boards gone, the ID officer shines a flashlight into the hole. He reaches in and says, "I got it."

Carl and I stare like stone soldiers while we watch the officer struggle with something in the hole. Then, slowly, he carefully lifts out of the dirt a sawed-off, pistol-gripped, Browning BPS shotgun. Photographers shooting through the open door are jostling each other for the money shot, the picture they hope will give them the Pulitzer. I hear a voice from outside. "Yeah, we're on. We got it live."

I look at Carl, who is pale, washed out. Rayburn is staring silently, his face blank. *And so it begins,* I think. I don't know who's lying. But if it isn't Hale, we have killed the wrong man.

CHAPTER
ELEVEN

WE SIT INSIDE RAYBURN'S car back at 222 West, but nobody moves. The shotgun, along with extensive soil and paint samples from the location, are in the police ID van, on their way to Paul Landmeyer's forensic lab for examination. Upstairs in the office, we have the staff to face. Rayburn shakes his head. "It's the system," he says bleakly. "It's not perfect, which means somebody has to take the fall. And that somebody is us." He looks at me. "You OK?"

"Yeah." This is a lie.

"Look, we're going to stick together on this."

"Sure."

"I want everybody to get home as quickly as possible. When you're not here, they can't ask you questions."

"We're staying," I say.

"You're following orders," Rayburn says. "If reporters think they can get statements from prosecutors one at a time, it'll be open season. We have to coordinate through the office."

"He's right, Thomas," Carl says. "Let's get inside before reporters find us out here."

We slip through the back entrance into a tomblike office. It's late afternoon on Friday, which is slow anyway. But there's no denying that people have scattered. I don't blame them, nor do I interpret this as a lack of loyalty. It's just practical. I have no doubt that fifteen seconds after the live TV pictures of the shotgun were beamed onto Nashville TV screens, briefcases were being packed for the weekend. Dolores emerges from Rayburn's office, and hands Rayburn a note, which he reads stoically. He looks up. "The governor called."

Dolores coughs and hands him a second slip of paper. "Also the state attorney general," she says.

Rayburn nods. "You guys get outta here as soon as you can," he says. "And take your phones off the hooks."

I protest, knowing it's futile. "Listen . . ."

"That's an order, Thomas," Rayburn says. "Paul is going to do his thing at the lab. I'll stretch that out as long as I can. Meanwhile, I don't want one word out of this office except from me." He looks at Carl. "I'm sorry about this, Carl. It's a hell of a way to wrap up your career." He turns and vanishes behind his door.

Carl nods at me. "He's right, Thomas. We're a target as long as we're hanging out here."

"I need a few minutes."

"I'll wait and walk you down."

"Don't," I say. "I'm OK."

Carl gazes at me closely, but moves off. I walk down the hall and into my office. Stillman, for once, isn't anywhere around. I walk in, shut and lock the door. I lean back against it, trying to figure out what to do. *This is no academic exercise. This is a well-orchestrated attack by people who have figured this thing out from top to bottom.* The fact that

Buchanan—and Towns, apparently—have gone to extraordinary lengths to discredit the death penalty doesn't make them bad people, in my opinion, at least as long as Hale is telling the truth. But that doesn't change the fact that Carl and I are the symbols who stand in their way, and if they prevail, we go down the drain.

The phone on my desk rings, and I let it go to voice mail. I check and see how many messages have come in since we left with Buchanan: eleven. I push "play." First up is Dina Kennedy, anchor of the local NBC affiliate, followed by reps from all the other local networks. I punch through them without listening to the messages. The *Tennessean* has left three calls, each more urgent as the paper's deadline grows closer. There are two from fellow prosecutors; both are supportive, and one is an invitation to get pissed together. Then the one piece of good news for the day: I hear Jazz's voice, calling from Orlando. Of course. They left early this morning.

"Hi, Daddy," she says. She sounds happy, and eleven years old, and not a part of all the shit of the world, not yet, anyway. "I'm leaving you this message at work so you have something fun to listen to for a change. We're already in line for Revenge of the Mummy. It's supposed to be really scary, but I doubt it. Michael isn't here. He had to go to a meeting. It's just me and mommy. Wait, she wants to talk to you." There's a pause, and Rebecca comes on the line.

"Listen, I know this thing is gonna cut me off. Just wanted you to know we're fine. We'll be home on Sunday night. If you want to pick up an extra night with Jazz sometime, just let me know. Anyway, she'll see you soon."

I lean back in my chair. *God, I love it when Jazz calls him Michael. You bet your ass it's Michael. Buy her the damn world, pal, but I'll always be Daddy.* But I also know that when Bec and Jazz get home on Sunday, they're going to find out that Daddy is in the middle of a firestorm. She's eleven, and she won't understand it. But she'll see my face on TV, and she'll know people aren't happy. *Eleven years old.* I stand up, wondering how long before we have to have the talk about what I really do, about the kind of people with whom I interact. The bodies I've looked at. The coroner's reports I've read. The crime scenes I've visited. This year? Next? It's not that I'm not proud of what I do. It's just that I know that the moment she understands what my job is really all about, a part of her childhood is over.

I pack up and leave the office, taking the back exit to the employee parking lot; the lot's empty, with only a few cars left. The temperature is finally easing a little; heavy clouds are streaming across the sky from the north, bringing a cold front and rain. A few drops hit the windshield as I get in, and by the time I'm out of downtown and on the interstate, I'm driving through a steady drizzle.

The traffic is manageable, and I make it home in forty minutes or so. The weather front is solidifying quickly, with dark clouds coagulating above the city. I pull inside the garage and come in the house, looking for Indy: he's not around, which isn't a surprise. The cat hates water, and he's probably crouched under a neighbor's porch until the rain stops. My answering machine is blinking, which I ignore. I go through the house and take all the phones off the hook, per Rayburn's instructions. I make dinner—salad from a bag, topped with some precooked shrimp—open the first of what I plan to be several Killian's, and flip on the news. The CBS affiliate leads with the gun story, and a quick check of the others shows they do the same. I flip back to CBS and watch Barry Dougherty's videotape of the DA being questioned in the ninth-floor reception area of 222 West. Carl and I are visible in the background. The video cuts to the site where the gun was found. The picture shows the police ID officer holding up the Browning and pans to Rayburn's stoic face. Dougherty comes back on. "We're going to have more on this in our ten o'clock report, including exclusive interviews with two jury members on the original Sunshine Grocery case. Stay tuned for more." The show goes to commercial, and I flip the TV off. *The jurors.* I try not to think about them, because they're carrying their own truckload of weight at the moment, and carrying my own seems like a full-time job.

It gets dark about 8:30. I grab a couple of beers, open the sliding glass door that leads to the deck, and step outside underneath the protective overhang. I've put about a hundred man-hours into designing and building a pretty damn glorious, two-level deck with a covered spa. The backyard is fenced and there's nothing behind me but woods anyway, so the privacy is pretty close to total. Many is the night the spa and a couple of beers have leveled me out, and with the cool air finally giving the city a break, I decide to do the same tonight. I turn off the lights and pull off the heavy cover. The steam curls upward into the dark night. I strip naked, put the jets on low, and step into the warm water. The beers are lined up on the edge of the spa.

The water envelopes me, and I lean back, wanting a few minutes of freedom from the day. *My father fixed things.* I thought about him constantly while building the spa. It's when I'm making things or working on the truck that I feel closest to him. The house didn't really suit me at first—Bec picked it out, and it was always more her than me—but in the last eighteen months or so I've made it my own. My father would have loved this spa, and I imagined him swinging a hammer with me while I built it, telling me about a loose fitting on an F-18 Tomcat hydraulic line or what it was like to check an aileron the size of a man on a C5 Galaxy transport.

Looking west from underneath the protective overhang, I can see a smattering of stars where the clouds haven't filled in the sky. The rain is falling steadily now, and I let myself doze off.

Sometime later—I'm not sure how long—I become aware of a tapping on the door behind me. I listen a second to be sure, and the tapping happens again, harder. I turn to look; there, standing behind the glass, dressed in jeans and a black, tucked-in T-shirt, is Fiona Towns. I practically levitate out of the spa in surprise until I remember I'm naked. Towns isn't smiling, and she doesn't look particularly embarrassed. She slides the door open halfway and steps out of the house under the covering. "Your phone is off the hook."

I scrunch down into the water, grateful it's dark. "What are you doing here?"

"I just told you. You're not answering the phone."

"So you invited yourself in?"

She shrugs. "I knocked. Three times." She doesn't move, like she's willing to stand there all night.

"Look, if you'll go back outside a minute, I'll put some clothes on."

She looks at me like I'm nuts. "It's raining, Dennehy."

"Then go into another room, for God's sake. There's an office off to the right."

Her eyes briefly move down into the water. A smile flickers, and she walks back into the house, disappearing down a hallway. Cautiously, I climb out of the spa, making sure the coast is clear. *A towel would make a lot of sense right now.* I trot naked and dripping through the living room to my bedroom. I dry off and throw on some pants and a shirt. I walk back out, dressed but in bare feet. Towns is standing there, looking impatient. "You have a habit of walking into people's houses like this?" I say.

"When there's something more important than being polite, yes."

"So what is it, then?"

She looks at me calmly. "You had a bad day today, Dennehy."

"You could say that. I wonder if you had anything to do with it." She walks across the room and helps herself to a chair. "Have a seat, Ms. Towns. Seriously. You look tired."

She looks around, taking in my living room. "You've got taste, Dennehy. I wouldn't have figured on that."

"Thanks."

She smiles. "The pine armoire is nice. Kind of southwestern touch."

"It was my wife's. She's from San Antonio." I pause. "Ex-wife."

"Gone?"

"Not that it's any of your business."

"Well, she had good taste."

"Why are you here, Towns? Come to gloat over my office's embarrassment?"

She fixes me in her gaze. "I'm here about Moses Bol. I think you're going to win, Dennehy."

I shrug. "Rita West is a good lawyer."

"She's a marvelous lawyer, but she can't save Moses." She tilts her head. "I looked you up, Dennehy. You always win, even when you shouldn't."

"You mean the Sunshine Grocery murders. Wilson Owens."

She nods. "Like I said, you had a bad day."

"So you did come to gloat."

She shakes her head. "I came to invite you to church."

I look at her skeptically. "It's a little late for me to get religion, Towns. But the minute I decide to make confession, you'll be the first to know."

"It's ten o'clock at night, Dennehy. I'm not exactly inviting you to regular services."

"So what is it?"

"I drove all the way out here. It's the least you can do."

"Guilt," I say. "No wonder you're a preacher."

She smiles softly. "So how about it? Come to church, Dennehy."

"No thanks."

"Why not?"

"For starters, because you're a key witness for the opposition. And because I've got a fairly good idea you're behind everything shitty that's happened to me over the last week. But mostly because I'm pretty damn sure you're a few days away from obstructing justice and committing perjury. That being the case, I'd like to keep my distance."

She stares back at me quietly. "If you had any sense, you'd realize those are all excellent reasons to come."

"I don't follow."

"Come with me or stay, Dennehy. But I can promise you one thing. It won't be a waste of your time."

I still don't move. But then I think about the notes I've been finding on my car, and it hits me that somebody very smart and very determined is fucking around with me and my office lately, that I don't understand exactly who or what that thing is, and that the woman in front of me almost certainly does. "OK," I say flatly. "I'll come."

She looks up, a little surprised. "Why the sudden change of heart?"

"No questions, Towns, or I might change my mind." I

walk across the room and pick up some shoes near the door
that leads to the garage. "I'll drive," I say. "It's dangerous
around there at night."

She rolls her eyes but follows. We walk into the garage, and
she slows by the old Ford. "You have two trucks," she says.

I stop by the '82. "The new one's my daily driver, but
this older one is special; 1982 Ford F-150, belonged to my
father."

"So you own the same kind of truck?"

I shake my head. "This is actually his truck. I tracked it
down through the DMV nine years after he died. It had
changed hands a few times. Flew out to Kansas, gave the
guy who owned it four grand, and drove it home."

She looks at the pickup thoughtfully. "That's fairly human of you, Dennehy. Once again, I'm surprised."

"I don't even drink blood before midnight, Towns. Get
in." I step into my father's truck and reach across, opening
her door. She steps inside, and I turn the key, letting the V-8
rumble away in the night air. I open the garage door, and we
pull out into a dull rain.

Nobody speaks for a good five minutes, until she breaks
the silence. "How did your father die?" she asks.

"You don't beat around the bush, do you, Towns?"

"Not usually."

I stare ahead at the road. "An accident at work. He was an
aircraft mechanic. Civilian contractor with the air force."

Towns watches the last well-made houses and manicured
lawns pass by as we reach the commercial district. "My father died working, too."

I look over at her. "No kidding."

"Heart attack. Too much stress, too many martinis, too
many mistresses." She frowns. "He wore himself down to
nothing for the big house and a Mercedes."

"So you went the other way."

The smile flickers again. "Very good, Dennehy."

"Is your mother still alive?"

"Now there's a fascinating topic." She pushes back in the bucket seat. "My mother's God is Oprah. Not that she reads the books, of course. But she cries like clockwork when the celebrities come out and talk about their addictions."

"So the two of you are close."

She smiles and pushes a strand of hair behind her ears. "You know why I studied theology, Dennehy?"

"No idea."

"Because there had to be something more than my father working himself to death, and more than my mother numbing herself with pop psychology."

I stare out at the dark, wet highway. "And is there?"

The truck rumbles down the street for a good thirty seconds before she answers. "Took me a while to find out. A lot of unproductive roads. Boyfriends. Chemicals. I got lost for a while."

"So, what? You found yourself in church?"

"Not in most of them, I can tell you that." She smiles. "You know what my church is, Dennehy? It's the church of the losers, of the painfully uncool. It's the church of the dropouts and failures. Fools and sinners. It's the church of the second chance." She looks out the window. "Home, in other words."

"Don't be so self-deprecating. Not after what you did in court the other day, anyway. You took Judge Ginder to school."

"Yes, and you've already told me I may regret that. But I'm willing to take some risks at this point in my life." She lowers her voice. "Especially for Moses."

"What's the deal with him anyway? Carl says he's a *Benywal,* whatever that is."

"You'll see," she says. She falls silent, not speaking until we reach the church.

Fifteen miles down I-65, I take the ramp off the freeway to Church Street. We roll into downtown, the empty office buildings lining both sides of the street. I take the narrow alley behind the DPC and pull into the tiny empty lot behind the building. The rain is still coming down when we get out, and Towns and I jog up the grungy, concrete steps to the back door of the church. The alleyway and parking lot are both deserted; even through the rain, the smell of urine and homelessness pervades. Towns unlocks the large, metal door, and we step inside and out of the shower. She hits a switch and a set of fluorescent lights flickers on, but only half work. The light makes crazy patterns on the reflective floor. "Follow me."

We walk down the long hallway to the rear entrance to the sanctuary. She pushes open one of the ten-foot-tall wooden doors, and we step into the dim, cavernous room. The large stained-glass windows glow palely from the exterior streetlights. The Egyptian reliefs painted above us are shadowed, and the great sandstone pillars rise from the floor only to vanish into the dark heights forty feet above us. Towns walks to the first row of pews. "You know the history of this place, Dennehy?"

"No."

"You're standing in one of the most powerful pro-slavery symbols in the South. Before the civil war, this church preached against freedom so virulently that the Union army actually came for the preacher's head. He fled with his family to Mississippi, and he was never allowed back in the city. The government recognized that he had become a symbol himself, and kept him out in the interest of peace." She turns toward me. "When the city fell, the Union army turned this room into a military hospital. The pews were ripped out and cots were brought in. Even Negro soldiers were operated on here. It found its calling again, and became a place of healing."

I nod, looking around. "Why the Egyptian design?"

"That came later, after a fire gutted the original structure. The church rose out of its ashes, like the South itself. The building was once again the center of the city's wealth and power, and this extravagance is an expression of that. The symbols changed again."

"Somewhere along the way this place must have got lost. You're almost closed down."

She smiles. "On the contrary, Dennehy. It's finally found itself at last. We're a home for the wounded again, just as we should be. And nobody showed me that more than Moses Bol."

She leads me several rows down the center aisle, turning left into one of the pews toward the west wall. About twenty feet away from the wall, she stops. "You want me to tell you what *Benywal* means."

"That's right."

"It's impossible to translate. Something close would be 'One who draws strength from the ancestors.' But that doesn't do it justice." She leans on the pew behind her. "Once one of the boys wrote his name for me. It was ten lines long. He did this because his name is more than just *his* name. It's his father and father's father, back ten generations. He knew them all and could recite stories about each of them. They were real to him, Dennehy, as real as if he'd sat on their knees and touched their faces. Most Americans can't even name their own great-grandfathers." She looks out at the church's towering pillars. "The *Benywal* is the living connection with everything that comes before. Not merely the names, but the essence, the stories, the history itself. He heals their sickness. He finds their way forward in the darkness." She looks up at me. "He's priceless, in other words."

"Tell me you don't actually believe in all that. I'd prefer not to think of you as nuts."

She shakes her head. "If you're asking me if it meets a scientific standard of inquiry, I'd have to say no. But their stories are extraordinary."

"Meaning?"

"You know the boys marched hundreds of miles across Sudan to Ethiopia, and hundreds more to Kenya."

"Yes."

"Moses routinely went for days without sleep on those marches. He did this to drive away animals that would come in the night and drag away the sick or weak. The boys say he didn't eat or drink for days at a time. Two eyewitnesses claim to have seen him walk through walls."

I laugh darkly. "I'll be sure and let the guards in Riverbend know. 'Watch the African, gentlemen. He walks through walls.'"

"This isn't a joke, Dennehy. Moses and two friends were captured and put in an Arab jail. Their legs were shackled. The two friends claim he simply walked out, got the key, and released them."

"For God's sake, Towns, you went to Harvard."

She stands up off the pew. "I know how legends grow, Dennehy. I studied theology. Every generation embellishes the stories of the last, until they're deified."

"Exactly. Daniel Boone will probably be a religion some-day." I pause. "So tell me you didn't drag me down here to convince me to believe in Moses Bol."

She shakes her head. "I brought you here to show you of the power of a symbol. Look around, Dennehy. The hiero-glyphics. The cross at the front. A preacher, banished and never allowed to return. Wars are fought over symbols like that. A war was fought in this very city over them. They're immensely powerful."

"What does this have to do with Bol?"

"Moses is a symbol, too. He's the symbol of everything that makes these boys who they are. They love him, and if he dies, there's going to be a catastrophe."

"Which means?"

"These boys have been hunted since they were little chil-dren. They showed up here thinking America was heaven. They found a culture awash in commercialism and advertis-ing. They're doing their best to understand, but already they're growing disillusioned. I hold them together now by a thread. But I swear to you, Dennehy, if our system takes their *Benywal,* they will fall into despair." She closes her eyes, her breathing deep. "I love them. I love that they aren't full of our sickness. I love that they are still angels somehow."

"Angels."

"Somehow, they're still innocent, even after all the horror they've seen. They were children through all that, and mirac-ulously, some of that survived. But they're falling away, one by one. We offer them nothing but endless work for posses-sions they don't understand or want. Some are drifting into gangs, simply because they don't know what else to do. It's bad enough losing them one at a time. If Moses dies, I'll lose them all."

The storm outside is still growing; the wind and rain are

lashing against the building. "Tell me the truth," I say quietly. "Not as witness and prosecutor. Between you and me, right here, right now. No bullshit."

She stares right at me. "He didn't do it, Dennehy. Moses Bol was here that night with me."

The rain pelts against the roof and windows. "I don't like anything about this," I say. "I don't like the fact that there's a raped and murdered woman in my city. I don't like being hauled into a church in the middle of the night and told ghost stories about people walking through walls." I pause. "And I don't like the idea of sending you to jail."

"Then don't."

"I won't have any choice."

"Drop the death penalty, Thomas. Do what you must. But don't take his life."

She moves closer, and I can hear her breathing. A siren, distant but angry, cuts through the storm. We're less than a foot apart, and there's a moment when I know I should move back. We both know it, in fact, but she steps on a footing of one of the pews and balances herself against me, her fingers pressing into my chest. I realize I want to kiss her, which is wrong on a million levels. I know I'm not going to go for it, but I allow myself a moment to imagine it, to pull her into my arms in my mind, kissing her as hard as I can. Her mouth opens against my own, and her legs wrap around me, pressing her hips against me. I'm thinking about how soft her mouth looks, how her lips are slightly parted, and how the fact that I can see she wants the same thing I do is making me feel a little drunk. I'm thinking this right up until the moment one of the huge stained-glass windows above us explodes into a hundred thousand brilliantly colored shards of razor-sharp glass.

* * *

The explosion ricochets across the cavernous hall, brittle and angry. The glass showers down from the darkness like diamonds, beautiful as rain, dangerous as daggers, covering us like a wicked snow. I pull Fiona underneath me, covering her with my body. There's the ting of falling glass on the wooden floor and pews for what seems like minutes. I can feel the glass hitting us and see it gathering on the floor all around us. "Stay down! Stay down!"

We crouch between pews, waiting for the chaos to stop. Finally, there's an uneasy truce, as the sound of falling glass is replaced by cold wind and rain blowing through the hole where the window had been. "Be still," I say, my hand on her back. "We're covered in it." I stand up inch by inch, letting the glass fall to the pew and floor. "Stay there." Carefully, I pick glass out of Fiona's hair and from her back. I look up and see the gaping hole; remnants of glass cling to the window frame, ready to fall with a gust of wind. "We've got to get out of here." We make our way through the debris to the front of the sanctuary, glass crunching under our shoes. The force of the explosion has blown fragments in every direction. When we reach a safe place, I get a chance to look at Fiona. "You all right?"

She stares back at the sanctuary, eyes wide. "Uh huh."

A siren appears, distant but rapidly growing closer. "The police are coming," I say. "We'll be all right." I put my arm around her and help her through the big double doors into the dimly lit hall. "Where are the main lights in here?"

She gives me a blank look. *She's leaving me.* I lean her against the wall and go in search of the main light switch. I find it, and the hard, fluorescent lights flicker on. The siren is close now, and another is coming behind. I pull out my phone and call 911. "This is Thomas Dennehy, assistant district attorney," I say to the dispatch operator. "I'm inside the Downtown Presbyterian Church. I'm here with the pastor, Fiona Towns. You need to send the EMTs. I think the pastor is in shock."

"They're on their way."

"Listen, try to reach the officer before he arrives. We don't want to get shot by accident."

"Roger that."

I turn back to Fiona, who's slowly sliding down the wall. I get underneath her arms and lower her into a sitting position. She looks up, her eyes glassy. I try to get a pulse, can't find it, and try again, on her neck. It's slow, maybe twenty beats a minute, a sure sign her parasympathetic system is shutting down. I hear the police car pulling into the parking lot, its siren blaring. I sit down next to Fiona, my arm around her. A minute later, there's the sound of the back door opening. "In here!" I shout. The officer's wet shoes suck against the tile floor as he approaches, slowing as he reaches the entrance to the hallway.

"I'm inside," the officer says. "Yeah." A pause. "Roger that." The officer creeps warily around the corner, his weapon drawn.

I hold up my ID. "Assistant DA Thomas Dennehy," I say. "This is Fiona Towns, pastor of the church."

The officer walks to me cautiously, takes my ID, then holsters his gun. "What's an assistant DA doin' down here at this hour?"

"My job."

He peers at Fiona. "She OK?"

I stand. "She's not hurt physically. I think she's in shock. Dispatch says the EMTs are on their way."

He nods. "So what happened in here?"

"Something blew out one of the stained-glass windows. I was in the sanctuary with the pastor when it happened."

"Just the two of you?"

"Yeah."

He raises an eyebrow but nods. "Bomb squad got scrambled. The base is only ten blocks away, so they'll be here any second. Is there anybody else in the place?"

"I don't think so."

"Let's get her out of here," the cop says. "This whole place could go up in another blast." We each take a side and get Fiona out the door and down the steps to the parking lot behind the church. The EMTs are already pulling in, another cop car behind them. We hand Fiona over to the EMTs, who sit her down in the back of their vehicle. She's conscious but not responsive. One of the technicians gets a pulse and looks up at me. "It's thirty-five, but steady."

"It was slower before," I say.

He nods. "Yeah, a pulse that slow sounds scary, but we see it all the time when there's been a traumatic experience. Just gonna take her a while to come back around."

"I'm OK," Fiona says, slurring her speech a little. "Where's Thomas?"

"Right here," I say, taking her hand. "How are you?"

"I'm OK." She starts to get up off the back of the truck, but the EMT gently restrains her.

"Hang on a little while," he says. "You're not quite cleared for takeoff." He takes her pulse again and looks up, smiling. "Yeah, she's gonna be fine. She's already at forty-two. Give her twenty minutes."

The bomb squad truck arrives, shouldering its way past the cop cars, and parks, taking up a fourth of the small lot. Six officers spill out, three in dark blue search suits and helmets. Behind them come two yapping German shepherds.

Fiona looks at the dogs and turns pale. "Look, let's put her inside the truck for a while, let her get her bearings," the EMT says. He leans Fiona back into the vehicle and closes the doors, securing her from the growing crowd of officers.

One of the bomb squad officers, a burly-looking forty-year-old man with a flattop, introduces himself. "Victor Yenko," he says. "What happened?"

I replay the incident, and Yenko nods. "Nothing since then?"

"No."

"All right. There's probably nothing else to this, but we'll go through the building anyway, just to be safe." Yenko tells his team to enter the building, leading with the dogs. The officers in search suits snap down their ballistic face shields and walk up the steps through the doors. The building is so large—especially the labyrinth of rooms and storage areas on the upper floors—I figure it'll take at least twenty minutes to search, even with three men. Once the dogs are gone, the EMT opens the back of his truck. Fiona is sitting up, drinking water from a bottle. "She's doing good," the technician says. "Another few minutes, she'll be fine. Not to drive, though."

"That's not a problem."

We sit on the edge of the EMT truck for the next fifteen minutes while I give a statement to one of the officers. Eventually, Yenko comes out of the back door and walks across the parking lot toward us. He holds up a black piece of metal. "Rudimentary pipe bomb, very low tech," he says. "Not much to it, really. Just some metal, black powder, and pressed paper. You can find directions on how to make it on the Internet in about five minutes." He looks back at the building. "Figured out how they got it up there, too. There's a little doorway, leads right to a ledge that runs underneath the windows on the side. They probably used it when they were putting the glass in." He looks at Fiona. "The lady OK?"

"She's fine."

"Well, we're gonna be here half the night. Got to collect evidence, document everything. A bomb in a church automatically classifies as a hate crime."

Fiona gingerly steps out of the ambulance and looks up at the building. "Someone wanted to blow us up," she says quietly. "A house of God."

"That don't mean much to some people," Yenko says. "Look, why don't you take the reverend here home, if she can travel. Like I say, we'll be here most of the night. But you're gonna want to get that window boarded up, soon as you can. If it rains on you, there's gonna be an even bigger mess."

"I'm not leaving," Fiona says. "I need to be here." She starts toward the church, but a spate of dizziness leans her hard against me.

"Whoa, there," the EMT says. "What you need is some rest. A good night's sleep ought to be about right. And don't let her drive, not until midmorning, anyhow."

"We can't let you in the building until we're finished," Yenko says. "So all you could do is sit outside and do nothing."

"They're right," I say quietly. "Get some rest, and you can do some good tomorrow."

She looks up at me. "This is the Nation, isn't it? They hate me because of Moses."

"What about it, officer?" I ask. "Think this is Nation?"

He holds up a piece of the bomb. "Low brains, low yield. Right up their alley. And those folks can hold a grudge."

"Let's go," I say, putting my arm around Fiona. "We'll get you home and get you something to eat."

She relents, letting me guide her to the Ford. I fasten her seat belt, and she settles into the bucket seat. I come around and get in. "I'm sorry, Thomas," she says.

"What for?"

"For what happened. You could have been hurt."

I start the truck. "I will say this, Towns. You're a hell of a date."

I back the pickup past the official vehicles and pull back out onto Church Street, heading toward Belle Meade, the old-money neighborhood where the church's parsonage is located. Fiona leans back in her seat, her eyes closed. I drive a few blocks toward the freeway and hear her breathing steady as she drifts off. *Good. Let it go for a while.* I drive south down I-65, turn off on Harding, and wander through the ever-increasing property values toward the parsonage. It's hard to miss the irony of Fiona living in the bastion of a South that really doesn't exist anymore, a place where wealthy housewives chair brunches for charity and throw money-raisers for the symphony. I turn left onto Glendale and pull to a stop. "Towns? You got to wake up."

Her eyes flutter open, and she looks at me. "Where are we?"

"The parsonage, or nearly. I know it's on Glendale, but I can't recall the number."

"It's 625."

"Just a few blocks, then." Fiona pulls herself up in the seat and presses her hair back behind her ears. "You OK?" I ask.

"Yeah."

It's less than a minute before we pull into the parsonage's driveway. The house, an expansive, single-story, stone home on a large, level lot, is set back from the street by about forty yards. The driveway is circular, and I follow the curve halfway and stop by the front door. "Nice place for a radical like you," I say, putting the truck in park.

"It came in handy, getting Moses out."

"Yeah. Handy."

We sit in the silence of the truck for several seconds. I can't help thinking that I'm days away from taking her apart on the stand, and if I do my job well, I will probably send her to prison. It seems intolerable, but there's no way out. Recusing myself from a murder case now would send a message to every defense attorney in town that the department has lost its nerve, and worse, lost its faith in the very death penalty it has asked juries to invoke more than a hundred times in the last thirty years. And even though the woman sitting on the other side of the truck has moved me, I'm still not convinced she wouldn't lie to save Bol's life. "Well," I say, quietly. "Here we are."

She looks over at me a moment, then leans over and kisses my cheek. I feel her lips on my face, warm and soft. She opens the passenger side door of the truck. "You don't really believe in the death penalty, Dennehy. You can't and be the man you are."

I stare ahead without blinking. "If you take the stand for Bol, I'll do what I have to do."

I feel her watching me for a long time. "I know that," she says, at last. "And it breaks my heart." She steps out of the truck. "I'll get my car back from your place on my own," she says. "Don't worry about it." She shuts the door and walks away.

CHAPTER TWELVE

BY MORNING THE RAIN clears out, leaving behind a stifling, humid mist. One day's relief, and it's back to the sweatbox. I make a light breakfast and wash down the day's Zoloft with coffee. It's a weekend, so I would normally have Jazz with me. It turned out to be a blessing she went to Orlando with Dr. Knife; at least she wasn't here while her daddy was almost getting blown up. I check my watch; pretty soon she and her mother will be starting their second day of theme park attractions while the good doctor gets his lunch bought by the New and Improved Liposuction Company. I shake my head. Bec will be back tomorrow night, and she'll find out what's happened soon enough. I can picture her response: *See, Thomas? That's why I left you. Dr. Knife hardly ever gets blown up.*

Fiona's Volvo is no longer in my driveway; somehow, she's already retrieved it. At ten I call Rayburn and tell him what happened last night. He freaks, predictably, but I get him talked down. "It's just some Nationites pissed off about Bol," I tell him. "They want to make a statement."

"But I don't get why you agreed to go down there in the first place," he says.

"She asked me. I said yes."

"Why, for God's sake?"

"Because Buchanan's not smart enough to pull off the Hale thing on his own. He looks good, but he's kind of a lightweight."

"Yeah, I had the same impression."

"On the other hand, Towns has guts, brains, and principles. So I played along to get some answers about what's really going on."

"And?"

And I almost kissed her, I think. "All she wanted to do was beg me to drop the death penalty on Bol."

"I assume you made it clear that ship has sailed."

"Yeah. I made it clear."

Rayburn pauses. "All right, dammit. I'm not going to start second-guessing you now. But for God's sake, Thomas, watch your ass, OK? We don't want any more confusion than we already got."

I click off the phone and walk to the glass doors looking out on the backyard. I stare into the trees behind the house, thinking about what I would do if I quit the DA's office. I have thirty-eight thousand dollars in the bank. It would tide me over until I sorted things out. I run through the usual midlife crisis suspects: bone-fishing captain in the Keys, inner-city school teacher, back to college to study something else. None of them feel right, since I'm a prosecutor, expert at what I do, trained to point the state's finger in a court of law. "So," I say to the living room. "It's as clear as mud."

I get dressed, head to Dad's truck, and let its sweet V-8—

a well-tuned engine being the answer to most male conundrums—solve my problems, at least for a while. I hop in the truck, fire it up, and gently give it some throttle, just to listen to the engine respond. *Hell, yeah. Let's go, Pops. You and me. Lemme tell you how I ported the cylinder heads on this baby. And you can tell me what to do with the rest of my life. Deal?*

I back out of the garage and drive across suburban Williamson County, passing more or less identical subdivisions. Stones River. River Glen. River Farms. Each with a house stamped on its own quarter acre of land, a two-story box of furniture surrounded by a patch of grass. One thing I do know: a bigger box and more grass isn't the answer. Hell, my father had less box and grass than I do, and he was the happiest, most contented guy I ever knew. Dr. Knife seems happy, but he's Greek and rich and married to my beautiful ex-wife, so what the fuck else would he be? Maybe the guy actually enjoys carving excess skin off people's jowls. I turn the truck down the packed four-lane road that rolls through Franklin's busy shopping district. Williamson County's growing explosively, and it seems like every month the traffic doubles. *Bone fishing. I could live on the boat. No wasted space. Efficient.*

I decide to drive down to the DPC to see the hole that pipe bomb put in the building. It would be a hell of a mess, and with the rain continuing sporadically through the night, the interior would be pretty much a catastrophe. *Thirty bucks' worth of mischief, thirty thousand dollars' worth of repair. It's a hell of a lot more expensive to be on the right side of things, sometimes.* I pull out onto I-65 and head north, into town. There's no rush hour, so the Ford cruises at seventy-five miles per hour on a stretch of highway I normally pick my way through at one-fourth the speed. I take the Church Street exit into downtown, drive nine blocks, and turn right onto Fifth. I slow and see a medium-size ladder truck parked beside the church. A small group of people are gathered around, rubbernecking. Fiona is there, too; whatever the residual effects of last night might be, they're not slowing her down. She's arguing—it seems like every time I see her she's arguing about something—with a stocky man in dark blue coveralls. A group of workmen are hanging around near the truck, like they're waiting for orders. From their bored expressions, they've been there a while. I pull the truck behind the church and park in the small lot. Fiona's Volvo is there, but there aren't any other cars.

Fiona sees me come around the building and stops what she's saying, midsentence. She smiles, which turns on some pheromone-chemistry thing that I want to shut off, but can't, because there's no switch. You can intellectualize the shit out of the moment a woman's smile starts to matter to you, but it doesn't help much.

I walk up to her. "So you're OK." Her hair is pulled back into a ponytail, and she's wearing black jeans and a light T-shirt that says *Sprawl Mart.* Other than a small bandage on her bare arm, she's unscathed.

"You, too," she says.

"You came out and got your car pretty early."

"I got a little sleep and was fine. I took a taxi out and drove here." She looks up at the hole where the stained-glass window was before the explosion. "This can't wait."

The workman—his name is Ross, according to the tag stitched into his shirt—interrupts. "Look, while you two are having your little moment, I still got a crew of four sitting on their butts. So are we gonna work this out or not?"

"What's the problem?" I ask.

"The problem is the lack of forty-five hundred bucks, pal.

That's the charge for putting three people up on that roof, clearing the remaining glass, covering it with a temporary waterproof tarp, removing the other cracked windows, and coming back Wednesday with clear replacements."

"Other windows?"

Ross points up to the windows. "There's hairline fractures in the two adjacent to the one that fell in. They could go at any time. They got to come out, or you're gonna have lawsuits out the ying-yang."

"I don't have forty-five hundred dollars," Fiona says. "Or anything like it."

"Then we load up and go home, lady."

Fiona's face flushes. "This is a church, Mr. . . . what was your name again?"

"Moore. Ross Moore."

"This is a church, Mr. Moore. The interior of this building is of immense historical value. Surely we can work something out here."

"We sure can, for forty-five hundred bucks." Moore shakes his head. "Look, you're a nice lady. But I put somebody up on that roof, insurance, workman's comp got to be paid. I can't budge on this thing." He turns to his crew. "Load it up, fellas. We're heading out."

"I can't believe this," Fiona says quietly. "I absolutely cannot believe this is happening."

It's the middle of summer in Nashville, there's a gaping hole in the roof of the church, and it doesn't take a genius to figure out that air that humid will generate mold inside the sanctuary within days, even if Fiona manages to get everything covered inside. It's a disaster waiting to happen. I walk up behind Moore and put my arm around him as he walks. This is not a rational choice, but the smile matters now, so fuck it. "Forty-five hundred bucks is pretty steep," I say.

"So is the pitch of that roof, hombre. That's the price."

"I'd hate to think you were gouging this woman because of her desperate situation. Me being an assistant district attorney and all."

Moore's footsteps grind to a halt. He looks up at me warily. "You with the DA?"

I squint up at the roof, gripping his shoulder firmly. "Workmen's comp regulations are a pain in the ass, aren't they, Ross?"

"Yes, sir, that's a fact."

"And when I think about all the licenses and fees, and how easy it is to get hung up on a codes violation . . . I mean, a job can get shut down for days at a time." I shake my head, eyes on the roof. "You know, there's a door up there that opens up to the ledge. You really don't need the ladder truck."

Moore squints, too, making a pretty good show of it. "Yeah, I guess I see that. Still have to put tackle on the workmen, secure them to the building."

"Sure, no question. But I imagine the charge for the truck would be—what, about a grand?"

"A grand? Nope, not hardly, not for the truck."

I squeeze his shoulder, eyes still on the roof. "Yeah, I'd say it's about a grand."

"You would?"

"Yeah, I would."

Moore glances over at Fiona. "You reckon she's got the thirty-five hundred?"

I pull out my billfold and slip him my Visa card.

He looks at the card. "Yeah, that'll do."

"I had a feeling."

Moore heads off to his crew, and I walk back over to

Fiona. "Turns out Mr. Moore is a fan of architecture," I say. "Once he understood this place was on the National Registry of Historic Places, I couldn't talk him out of doing the job."

She looks at me skeptically. "What did you do, Dennehy? You realize I don't have the money."

"I told you. He considers it a contribution to the cityscape."

"*Cityscape*. He used that word."

"Yeah."

"My God, Dennehy, you're a bad liar."

She starts off toward Moore, and I grab her arm. "Everything doesn't have to be a battle, does it?" She stops and watches the workmen beginning to unload their ropes. A couple strap on safety belts and start toward the structure. "Just say thank you, Towns."

She looks at me. "Thank you. Now tell me why."

I smile. "Something somebody taught me. You go to battle, and you buy your adversary a drink when it's over. It's not personal."

"This was an expensive drink."

"Yeah, I guess so."

"So I owe you one. A drink, I mean." She pauses. "I suppose I should be glad it's not . . . personal."

There it is again; the surpassing desire, some kind of voodoo chemistry drawing me to her. *Last time I felt like this, a bomb exploded. Time to go now.* "I'll see you, Towns. I'm glad you're OK."

"You, too. You look . . . well."

I smile. "I look well."

"I mean you're OK."

"Yeah. I'm OK." I walk off, passing by Moore as I go.

"All set, Mr. Dennehy. We'll take care of it."

I take my Visa card from him and push it back in my bill-fold. "You need anything downtown, Ross, you just give me a call."

On the other side of the building, I stop and catch my breath. *I look* well. *What the hell is that?* She looked well, too. Way better than reverends have any right to look. I walk to the edge of the far side of the church and turn right again to complete the square. My car's up ahead, and there's somebody standing near it. I stop and watch; the guy is look-ing inside the driver's-side window, his face pressed against the glass. He steps back and gives the truck a once-over, like he's an aficionado. He stuffs his hands in his pockets and starts walking back toward the church. It's Robert, the so-called ex-addict who helps Fiona around the church.

"Robert!" I call his name, and he looks around, his dark, unblinking eyes staring out from the facial hair. He doesn't move as I approach. I smell him at ten yards; at five, it's a se-rious wall of scent, and I stop.

"Well," he says. "It's you, Skippy."

"That's right." Unlike the time before, he's definitely glazed. His pupils are a mile wide, and his eyes are glassy. "You like the truck, Robert?"

"It's nice. It's bitchin'. It's a completely bitchin' ride."

"I saw you checking it out."

He smiles, exposing a row of horrifying teeth, a telltale sign of time spent on the pipe. "And I saw you looking at Fiona."

I watch him, trying to read his face. "You ought to get a shave, Robert. It's too damn hot for a beard like that."

"Yeah. Maybe I'll do that."

"I understand from Fiona you've had a little drug prob-lem in the past."

His eyes darken. "Telling tales on me, the reverend. No matter, Skippy. All behind me now. I'm straight as a whistle. Clean as an arrow. And all because of her."

"Reverend Towns?"

He smiles and opens his arms wide. "Don't you know, Skippy? She's the patron saint of lost souls. She's my reason for being."

Sometimes, I have to admit, I get the whole totalitarian thing. It's so damn efficient. Somebody pisses you off, you haul them in, question them awhile—no witnesses, naturally—and you find out what the hell's going on in their weird little mind. I pull back out onto Fifth, turning away from the church toward the river. Totalitarianism may be an occasionally tempting prospect for a prosecutor, but here, in Nashville, Tennessee, people like Robert the ex-addict are free to annoy the hell out of whomever they please, as long as they don't break any laws when they do it. The little fucker's got things figured out pretty well, actually. He's a guest of Fiona, so he can't be arrested for vagrancy while he's near the church. It's sanctuary, in the old sense of the word.

I drive down Second Avenue, past 222 West. The tourist traps are all shuttered after a Friday night of draining money from country music fans. *Shee-it, we just missed Shania Twain. I hear she was in the Wild Horse Saloon, night before last.* I drive past the little park near Fort Nashboro, a reconstructed piece of history that harkens back to before the Civil War. The *General Jackson*, a dinner-cruise riverboat that inexplicably features a group of Chinese acrobats as its entertainment, sits peacefully at its docking, a slight wake lapping against its giant sides.

Thirty-five hundred bucks. That was an interesting choice.

Dr. Gessman will definitely have words of wisdom for that one. "Your attachment to your sworn enemy is a metaphor for your inner conflict. You don't know what side you're on, anymore. Check please."

I pull to a stop at a light. *Is that true? Is that why she gets to me? Because I actually want to switch sides?* I drive on, thinking I seriously need to get through this case. Nail Bol, take a vacation. Sort things out. Hell, the department owes me about twenty weeks. And the twenty weeks right after this case wouldn't be the worst twenty weeks to be somewhere else. I'll just let Rayburn handle the flack. That's what he's good at, and anyway, he's given everybody orders not to talk to the media. So good. Bol goes down, and a couple of days later I'm practicing my bone-fishing skills in Biscayne Bay.

CHAPTER THIRTEEN

BANANA. CUP OF PEET'S. Daily Zoloft. Breakfast, in other words. I stare at the blue pill, wondering if it makes sense to take it with coffee. *Sort of defeats the purpose.* Nevertheless, I'm amazed again at the *psychic weight*—Dr. Gessman's term—that one human being can carry while continuing to smile, crack wise, and otherwise appear to fully function. All it takes, apparently, is a blue pill and a Sunday to decompress. *Sunday, day of rest.* No local TV news. No talk radio, either, which means Dan Wolfe won't be fanning the anger of his hounds.

The reverend Fiona Towns will be preaching her proletariat-uprising message to a scattering of souls, no doubt, and thanks to a pretty hefty Visa bill I've incurred, she won't be doing it with the outside air pouring into the room. Other than that, everybody can just chill, even me. I do not, for the first time in my career, spend the day before a trial begins poring over every detail of the case. Bol's voir dire will kick off the festivities—and festivities they will certainly be, when the Wolfe Pack, the anti-death-penalty crowd, the Nationites, and the Sudanese all meet in one twenty-first-century, political cluster fuck in about a fifty-square-yard space outside the courthouse—and that conflagration is too much to take on in advance. What I need, I realize, is a fucking day off.

I spend two hours on the Internet, trolling through boat ads, picturing myself on one vessel after another, juggling numbers and interest rates. Apparently, offshore fishing is a rich-guy's sport, because two hundred grand buys thirty-six feet of used boat with mechanical issues, not the gleaming forty-five-footer I want.

The day looks up considerably when, to my shock and amazement, Indy shows up. He saunters through the animal flap in the back door casual as hell, like he's just stepped out for a drink, not disappeared for two days. He walks over, checks out the half-empty bowl—God knows what he's been eating while he's been gone—and looks up at me expectantly. I climb off the couch and size him up. "Well," I say. "Look what the cat drug in." He swishes his tail dismissively, then looks around, wondering where the good food is. "Listen, cat," I say, "even I eat leftovers." But Indy takes a hard line, so I open up a can of Fancy Feast, spoon it into the bowl, and set it down on the floor. The cat digs in, without so much as a by-your-leave.

I nap an hour in the afternoon, my body smart enough to know what's coming, storing a little energy in preparation. "Calm before the storm," as Carl said. Monday, the news organizations will be back on my ass in force. Monday, the trial begins. Monday, I realize with a shock, is Carl's last official day. Monday, it seems to me, can go to hell. I stay in for dinner, brew some more Peet's, and settle in on the couch with a book.

Maybe it's because of how Fiona showed up, but when the doorbell rings around 7:30 that evening, my first thought is that it's her. *Turn her around, send her home. Whatever it is on her mind, it's too late now.* I push a hand through my hair, unlock the door, and pull it open. There, looking concerned and beautiful, is Bec, just back from Orlando.

"Rebecca. What are you doing here?"

"Aren't you going to invite me in?"

"Yeah. Yeah, sure." She walks past me, her black hair in a ponytail, wearing Mr. Designer everything, looking like the doctor's million bucks. Her skin, fresh from a weekend baking under the Florida sun, is as dark and luscious as mocha ice cream. She hugs me, somehow distant and close at the same time, which is exactly what an ex-wife is.

"Is Jazz OK?"

"Of course." She looks around, taking in the living room like she hasn't seen the changes, even though she has, at least a dozen times. "Maria kept the papers while we were gone," she says. "I know about the gun at the barn, the explosion at the church, everything. I came as soon as I could get Jazz unpacked and answering her fifty e-mails." I breathe her in automatically—she smells good, like lavender—then step away. She walks past me, stopping in the middle of the living room. "So how are you? Are you hanging in there?"

"Yeah, I'm fine. Why are you here, Bec?"

She shrugs, her slender shoulders moving in a petite, dismissive arc. "I thought you could use some company." Her eyes run along the furniture, like she's looking for dust. "Everyone you know works at the DA's office," she says. "You're all in the same shape. You need someone from outside." She looks toward the kitchen. "I smell coffee," she says. "Pour me a cup?"

I follow her into the kitchen, and she sits, looking like she never left. I walk to the cupboard and take down a cup, filling it three-fourths with coffee. I add cream and sugar in the precise measurements that a thousand repetitions make automatic. Rebecca looks out to the deck off the back. "You've done a lot of work here." She leans back in her chair. "I always liked this place, you know."

I set the coffee down in front of her. "So Jazz had fun in Orlando."

"Um hmm. She's probably telling all her friends about it online."

"Watch who she talks to on that thing, Bec. There's bad people around."

She frowns, still beautiful, as though her mouth was made to frown, shaped perfectly for it. "I know what this gun situation must mean to you, Thomas. How's Carl taking it?"

"You know Carl. The man's a rock."

"Yes."

I can't figure out why she's here. Seeing her without Jazz hasn't happened since the divorce. "So you thought I could use some company," I say.

"Um hmm." She runs her finger along the rim of her cup thoughtfully. "Well, I had something I wanted to discuss."

"What is it?"

"I didn't come here to fight, if that's what you mean." She picks up the Zoloft prescription bottle and reads the label.

"Not that it's any of your business," I say.

"There's no shame in it," she said. "I'm glad you're taking something."

I close my eyes, knowing that she won't move until she's ready, and that she won't be ready until she says what's on her mind. I pour myself a cup of coffee and walk to the table. "So?" I ask.

"I think you should leave the DA's office, Thomas. It's no

good for you." I laugh out loud, and she interrupts before I can respond. "I know you're going to say it's terrible timing," she says. "But you're wrong. It's the only timing that has any chance of working."

"I think this is the point where I say something like, 'I like my work at the DA's office, Bec. We've got a whole script we could play out here, if you like. But since you left me for Michael, I don't really see the point.' "

"I didn't leave you for Michael," she says quietly.

"I think that would be a surprise to us both."

She shakes her head. "I mean, yes, Michael was a factor. But there was a reason I was so vulnerable."

And there it is, three years of polite conversation, up in smoke. "Was it my weakness or his millions? On second thought, I can't see what difference it makes."

"Weakness? Don't be ridiculous. You're the strongest man I've ever met."

"Fine. Then it was his millions."

She looks hurt. "What do you expect me to do, Thomas? Michael has money. It doesn't make me a hypocrite to enjoy it. It would make me a hypocrite not to."

"Then enjoy. It doesn't have anything to do with me."

"The plastic surgeon is stable, Thomas. And I'm not talking about money. I mean he goes to work and comes home the same man."

"Sounds perfect."

She smiles softly. "Perfect, Thomas, would have been you, if you had done something else with your life. But that wasn't one of my options." She watches me a moment, her eyes unblinking.

I set down the cup, ready to end the conversation. "Look, Bec, we're in different worlds now. You live your life. I live mine. If it weren't for Jazz, we'd never even see each other."

"Jazz adores you, and I adore her. So what kind of father she has makes a difference to me." She stands, frustrated the way only an old, badly ended love can frustrate. "You're not like Carl. If this thing about the executed man goes against you, you're going to unravel."

"If it goes against me, I'm quitting."

She looks up sharply. "Is that true?"

"Yes. I've already decided."

She walks to the windows and looks out over the woods. The tips of the trees are backlit with an early evening gold. "I want you to get police protection until this is over, Thomas."

"I'm fine, Bec."

She exhales. "I have a bad feeling."

I smile grimly. "More than the usual, you mean?"

She's quiet several seconds. "You've worked for so long with so many horrible people."

"And I've been fine."

"So far." She walks toward me, hugs me briefly. "Jazz needs a father, Thomas. Take care of yourself."

She lets herself out. I stand alone in my kitchen—*our* kitchen, the one she had painted the beautiful terra cotta, surprising me after work one day with the finished product. I stare out the small window above the sink, looking at the hazy, warm air of August sitting still and immobile on the Cumberland Valley. *She's got a bad feeling. Hell, she had a bad feeling the whole time we were married. And I'll be damned if I get police protection. Might as well paint a bull's-eye on my chest. And anyway, the protection goes home sooner or later, and you're right back where you started.*

I walk into my bedroom. I can still feel Bec's presence in the house, along with the vague agitation that being together always brings. *Jazz needs a father, Thomas. Take care of yourself.*

MONDAY. EGGS, BACON; coffee, immaculately prepared, then the blue pill. Indy fed, Fancy Feast again, and glad to be of service. Two-mile run, shower, dressed, the drive into town.

Court begins at nine, so I meet Stillman at the office before eight. Even at this hour, there are already four or five reporters hanging around the building, begging for scraps. I ignore a barrage of questions as I make my way through to the elevators: "Are we still going for the death penalty? Is Bol a sacrificial lamb? Was Wilson Owens innocent?"

The DA's office is eerily quiet; we are a fortress now, and the mood is battle-hardened, with one exception: the swirl of activity around Carl's office. It's his last day, and I want to see him early, since I'll be in court until late. I walk down the hall and see a sign posted on his office door: *YOU MAY ONLY SAY GOOD-BYE ONCE.* I stop and smile. He refuses to be sentimental, which only makes the office feel his leaving more acutely. The secretaries have brought so much cake and cookies that his retirement party this weekend is starting to look redundant. It's impossible to get any work done within fifty feet of his door, which is irritating him to the point of distraction. Not that he has anything to do; he's been packed for a week. It's watching other lawyers slack that's driving him nuts. By the time I walk in, he's as red-faced as an Eskimo. "Thomas!" he thunders. "For the love of God, tell these people to give me some peace and do something productive."

"Let them love you, old man," I say, smiling. "They only have a few more hours to do it."

He scowls and walks over to the windows that look down on Titans field. "David says you're not taking my office."

"That's right."

"You should. You earned it."

"Maybe in ten more years."

"Shut the door, Thomas." I shut the door, and we're alone. Carl is between the window and his desk, which is depressingly, finally, clean. "I've been thinking about this case you're starting. David's right. It's going to be about the preacher, not the kid."

"Looks that way."

"You want some parting advice?"

"I'd love it."

He nods. "You remember the story of Rahab? Book of Joshua, as I recall."

"No."

"Harlot. Beautiful woman, apparently. She lied her head off to save the lives of some Israelite spies. Hid them in her house when the soldiers came looking for them, then let 'em out of a side window to get away."

I smile. "So what's the point?"

"You'd think a liar and a prostitute wouldn't come out too well in the Good Book."

"Stands to reason."

He shakes his head. "Turns out, saving an innocent man's life trumps lying. Hell, it even trumps selling your body for money. Rahab is a hero of the faith. Gets listed as a direct descendant of Christ." He looks up at me. "You reckon Fiona Towns has read the story of Rahab? Her having a theology degree from Harvard and all?"

"Yeah, Carl, I reckon she has."

He nods. "Don't lose your focus, Thomas. If Towns has the right motivation, she won't have any problem putting her hand on a Bible and lying, just like Rahab." He stuffed his hands in his pockets. "Just thought you'd want to know."

I nod. "Thanks."

"You'll be OK. Don't give Stillman too much grief. He's a horse's ass, but he might do some good before it's all over."

"Listen, Carl—"

"Better go," he says, cutting me off. He's walking me toward the door, his hand on my back, and I realize this is it: Nine years come to an end in this moment. I turn to shake hands and end up bear-hugging him. We disengage, and I'm damned if there aren't tears in his eyes. He brushes them away, irritated, as usual. "Son of a bitch," he says, pulling out a handkerchief.

"Yeah."

"Get some cake on your way out."

"I will."

He turns and walks back to the windows and the view of the river he's stared at for twenty years. His view: nine floors up, 222 West. *I'm never taking his office, that's for sure.* I'd rather it stay a shrine to what we miss with Carl Becker not around anymore. I walk out, shutting the door behind me. Stillman is standing at the far end of the hallway, looking impatient to get to court.

"Yeah," I say, holding up my hand to him. "I'm coming."

The *delusiacs* have not been idle. Moses Bol might be from the completely fucked country of Sudan, he might speak only marginal English, and he might even be a cold-blooded murderer. But because his is the next capital murder case tried in Davidson County, he is also a human line drawn in the sand. So when Stillman and I cruise by the front entrance of the New Justice Building, there are already fifty protestors waiting. We stop at a red light, and Stillman looks past me and whistles. "Man, it's like the state fair over there."

He's right; between the placards and the balloons—no shit, Buchanan's troops have brought balloons—it's hard to tell a man's life is on the line. There are posters with the photographs of well-known criminals still on death row. And now, thanks to the efforts of Buchanan, we're treated to the first of what will certainly be many images of the face of Wilson Owens, the man already executed for the Sunshine Grocery murders. Representing the Confederate States, the south side of the lawn is covered by half the population of the Nation. They have come to demand justice for one of their own: Tamra Hartlett. On the north side, separated by a twenty-foot-wide strip of concrete stairs, about sixty Sudanese refugees stare at their adversaries. "Stillman," I say, "if this city gets through this alive, it'll be a fucking miracle."

We park underground, come up the stairs, and clear security. Stillman clears after I do, and I pull him aside to look him over before we hit the elevators. He looks like he just stepped out of a TV show, something called *Stillman to the Rescue.* "You look good, Stillman. Maybe I'll let you question the women."

"Fuck you, Senator," he says, smiling. "You ready for this?"

"Yeah."

We ride up to the third floor and head to Ginder's courtroom, which is guarded by Greg Seneff, Ginder's large, affable bailiff. "His Honor's waiting in chambers," he says, waving us in. "Rita's already there." Stillman and I walk through the empty courtroom and pass through the doors at the back. Ginder's clerk waves us in.

Ginder sits behind his huge walnut desk, not yet in his robes. Rita is there in a wing chair and looking vexed. "Good," Ginder says, waving us in. "We can start."

Everybody shakes hands, and Ginder sits us down. "Well, Mr. Dennehy," he says. "It seems you've made something of a spectacle of yourself over the weekend."

I nod. "Yes, sir. It does, indeed."

"Care to explain what you were doing talking to a key witness of the case without the presence of opposing counsel?"

"The witness invited me to church, Your Honor."

"To church."

"I believe the purpose of the visit was to elicit my sympathy for the accused, and to request the state drop the death penalty in this case."

"And was she successful?"

"No, Your Honor."

Rita grimaces. "I've discussed what happened with the witness, Judge. We have no complaint with the interaction between the two."

"Good. I don't need the extra grief before everything even gets off the ground. Just thinking about it gives me a headache." He leans back in his chair. "There's a lot of damned earnest people on the grounds today, and damned earnest people are my very least favorite kind."

"Yes, Your Honor," Rita says.

"Didn't ask your opinion. Point is, I've decided to sequester this jury for the duration of the trial. I don't like the idea of jurors having to maneuver through this crowd we've got outside every day. Agreed?" We shake our heads yes. "Good. Now, I've got the three seats for the Hartlett family you asked for, Thomas. I've got another ten for the media. But I'm not going to start counting chairs for Africans and white people. It's a slippery slope, and I'll never make anybody happy. So it's first come first served in the gallery, and if there's an empty chair, the bailiff is going to make sure the next person in takes it. Might do these people some good to sit among each other for a change." He smiles. "Now, Rita. Anything on your mind we haven't covered?"

"I'd like the courtroom cleared during voir dire," she says. "I don't want potential jurors answering questions while people hostile to my client stare them down."

Ginder nods. "Already seen to. Anything else?"

"Police protection for my client, Judge. I think it's pretty obvious the attack on the church three nights ago was aimed at him."

"It isn't obvious to me," Ginder says. "I'd say the Reverend Fiona Towns is none too popular among a certain portion of the population. But if you're worried about your client's safety, we've got a nice, secure jail where he's welcome to stay for the duration. How's that?"

"No, thank you, Your Honor."

Ginder smiles. "Wonderful. Now let's go get ourselves a jury, shall we?"

Once we're in the courtroom and on the record, Rita predictably and utterly ineffectually petitions the court that the odds of assembling a jury of Moses Bol's peers within the confines of Davidson County, Tennessee, are exactly zero. She asks the court to imagine the reverse: namely, that a bunch of suburban Nashvillians preside over legal proceedings in tribal Sudan. It's a hell of a good point, and, as I explained to Rayburn, it doesn't make a damn bit of difference. Further, since Ginder likes to keep his courtroom humming along, what with people's right to a speedy trial and all, he proclaims that if he's to remain in a good mood, in a day and a half twelve citizens of Davidson County will be impaneled to decide whether or not Moses Bol will live or die.

The morning goes well for Rita when she gets two she dearly wants: a retired political science professor from the University of North Texas who blames the United States for everything that's happened in Africa since the collapse of colonialism, and a house painter with a surly expression who says he thinks most people who work for the government are crooks, but he's pretty sure he can disregard those feelings when it comes time to deliberate. Balancing out these two prizes, Stillman and I land two women in the afternoon who have daughters of their own. Both blanch visibly when they're told they're sitting on a murder trial where a young woman has been raped and killed. It all goes to hell when another set comes up from the jury pool and gets disqualified for one technicality after another. At four o'clock, Ginder's had enough. He gavels things to a halt and sends the lawyers home until nine the next morning.

Stillman and I emerge from the bubble of court back into the circus outside the building, which has gone on more or less continuously during the day's proceedings. Now, however, the cameras are circling voraciously, looking for suitably amped-up subjects to deliver the perfect sound bite. I can see all the usual reporters, plus several from out of town. The antiwar, antiglobalization, anti-death-penalty crowds have merged, and they're chanting something at full volume. Dan Wolfe's Wolfe Pack is chanting back at them, trying to drown them out. The reporters look so happy they may break down and cry.

"You know something, Stillman?"

"What?"

"All we need is some Confederate reenactors, and we can have a dandy little war break out."

"Kind of makes you wonder how any justice is gonna get done," he says.

"No shit." I reach in my pocket and turn on my cell phone, which has been off during proceedings. Ten seconds later, it rings. "Dennehy."

"It's Josh Ritchie."

"Talk to me."

"You better get down here, pal. The party's started over at Tennessee Village."

"What's that supposed to mean?"

"It means one of the Sudanese kids got the shit beat out of him today."

I close my eyes. "Tell me it's not Bol."

"No, but he might be next."

"What happened?"

"Some Nationites picked one of the Sudanese up off the street. They dropped him back off about an hour later, much the worse for wear."

"How much worse?"

"He's at Vanderbilt Hospital."

"Shit. You there now?"

"Yeah, and so is your girl."

I freeze. "You mean Towns?"

"Yeah, and so is the Nationite army. This thing is about five minutes from a total meltdown."

"Stay there. We're on our way." I kill the call and dial 911. "Thomas Dennehy, DA's office. Something big is going down at Tennessee Village Apartments. It might be a riot. Get whoever you can over there ASAP." I flip shut the phone. "Stillman, by the time this is over, nobody's even going to care about Moses Bol. It's gonna blow up in our faces."

Stillman and I haul out of the courthouse and head down I-40 toward the Nation. The truck's V-8 punches us back in our seats as we accelerate through the on-ramp. We slip through the traffic and make it to the Forty-sixth Street exit in less than ten minutes. A right rolls us to Nebraska, the southern edge of the Nation. I slam on the brakes.

"What the hell is that?" Stillman asks.

The road's been barred by two vehicles parked head to head in the street. One of the vehicles is a pickup, like mine, and a couple of shotguns rest in a gun rack in the rear window. The other is a clapped-out, four-door Chevy. Two men in their early twenties sulk against the vehicles, wearing pissed-off expressions. But that isn't what we're staring at. What has us galvanized is a figure made of broomsticks hanging from a tree beside the road. The sticks are clothed with torn pants and a white T-shirt, upon which is written AFRICANS GO HOME. The head, which is a deflated volleyball, has been painted black. Sticking out of one side is a large, wicked-looking knife. I look behind us, scanning for cars. "People in the Village getting off work are going to head straight into this."

"Is there any other way through?"

"Two miles around, but you just end up on the other side of the Nation." Right away a couple of cars come up behind us; both are cheap Asian models, and neither driver is white. I pull my truck sideways in the street, blocking the cars behind me. "Stay in the truck, Stillman."

"Yeah, sure." Stillman steps out with me.

"Shit, Stillman, did you suddenly grow a spine?"

"I'm staying on your hip. Not that I don't think you're out of your mind."

I wave the cars behind us away. The drivers, who are Hispanic, are confused at first, but one of them sights the hanging effigy, waves to the other, and they start backing out.

"Listen to me, Stillman," I say. "Keep your mouth shut. I'm going to try this nice." Stillman and I turn around and walk toward the two men, who are sending us their full-on, "please-come-fuck-with-us" expressions. They lift up off their vehicles, loose-limbed, relaxed, and athletic. The one on my left is squat and powerful, like he spends his days in a gym; the other, on my right, is tall and lean, but no less intimidating. I hold up my Justice Department ID. "What's the plan here, fellas?"

"The plan is, we're takin' back our neighborhood," the tall one says. "We're the new neighborhood watch."

The short one laughs. "Yeah. We're watchin' for niggers, especially ones from the old country."

"Especially them motherfuckers," the tall one says.

I snap shut my ID. "New plan. You take down that offense to humanity, drive out of here with no trouble, and that way you won't spend the next six months in jail. How's that sound?"

The tall one eyes me warily. "You're not a cop. Cops don't wear suits." The short one hocks something up, spits, and drifts toward the passenger seat of the truck, eyeing the shotguns as he goes.

"*Don't*," I say, annoyed. "I don't have time for the full civics lesson, so I'll keep this short. My friend here and I are officers of the court, which means that even touching that gun is a class A felony. I figure about five years at Riverbend ought to do it."

"Bullshit," the short one says, but he looks at the other one doubtfully. "Is that shit right, Wayne?"

"What side you on, man?" the tall one says to me. "Don't it piss you off they let that African fucker off?"

"They didn't let anybody off," I snap. "His trial started today."

"Ain't what I heard. I heard he's *out*. Home free. Released on some legal mumbo-jumbo."

"You heard wrong. Now get this thing out of that tree and move these trucks."

The short one laughs. "Or what?"

I walk back to the truck, unlock the bolted-down tool box in the rear bed, and pull out the tire iron. I hold it in my right hand and walk toward the tall one.

"Shit, Thomas," Stillman says. "Take it easy, man."

"Shut up, Stillman." I walk past him, stopping three feet in front of the tall kid. He's tense and ready for a fight, but I can see doubt in his eyes. "Five years at Riverbend," I say. "You know, the place that's just full of the people you hate. Now move the car, Gomer, or I'm going to personally see that your cell mate is large, black, and very, very gay."

The tall guy stares at me a long, insolent second—he's angry but hasn't lost his mind—and caves. He walks to his car, fires it up, and backs into a driveway to turn around. "You too, move, Jethro," I say to the short one. "Get that piece of shit out of the road." He steps into the passenger seat, slides across, and backs out after his friend. They drive down the road, but I know they're not gone for long.

"Shit," Stillman says, "how'd you know they wouldn't beat our asses in?"

"The day guys like that start telling us what to do, Stillman, I'll quit the department." I swing the tire iron at the hanging effigy, and it splinters into pieces. I pull the remains down and throw it in the back of the truck. "Let's go."

It's fifteen blocks through the Nation to Tennessee Village, but five blocks away I see Josh Ritchie's van coming toward us, heading out. I wave him down, and we stop in the street. I roll down my window. "What's going on?"

"A few cops have arrived, but not near enough. They're sending everybody out that doesn't live in the area."

"OK."

"The Nationites are pissed, man. There's a rumor going around that Bol walked."

"We heard."

"The Africans are pretty jacked up about the kid in the hospital. Some of them are out hunting for the dudes that did it."

"They know who it is?"

"Not the name, but they recognized the car from the area. Black Trans Am, '02 model. But they just call it the car with the bird on the hood."

I look at Stillman. "Jason Hodges." I turn back to Josh. "Thanks for the heads-up."

"You got it." He rolls up his window and drives on.

"Stillman, if Jason Hodges has fucked up this trial, I will feed him to the sharks." I haul down to Indiana Street, where Hodges lives. We roll to a stop in front of the house. The carport is empty, and the Trans Am is nowhere to be seen. "He could be anywhere," I say. "Locked up tight in any of a hundred garages. These guys protect their own."

"You want to look around, or what?"

I smack the steering wheel. "Dammit, this thing is getting out of hand." I turn around and head back toward the Village. Along the way, we pass a car full of young Nationites, out looking for action. They glare at us when we pass, but leave us alone. Ten blocks later, we reach the entry to Tennessee Village and what amounts to a mob scene. About forty-five Nationites are milling around the entrance, talking shit, and looking ready for a fight. Two cop cars are parked in the entrance to the complex, barring entry. Behind them, congregated into an angry mass, are fifty Africans. The cops are seriously outmanned, basically hanging on until reinforcements arrive.

"What's the plan—"

"Listen," I interrupt. "Listen to that, will you?" The hair on the back of my neck stands up. The Africans are chanting. It doesn't make any difference that we can't understand the words. It's a war chant, and they are not fucking around. Some of the Africans are jumping together, pogo-ing in time to the chanting. High-pitched trills erupt out of the chants every few seconds, alien and angry.

"Jesus," Stillman whispers. "That is something to see."

The chant grows louder and louder, wave on wave rising from lungs and voices. The lost boys of Africa send out their warning to the city of Nashville, demanding some damn respect. It doesn't matter that they're dressed in Wal-Mart hand-me-downs in all the wrong colors or that their shoes come secondhand from some rich kids in the suburbs. The chant rises and falls like a thunderstorm on the move, and even the Nationites fall silent, watching something awesome to behold. The cops—overmatched in numbers and passion—look scared, and I see one of them keying his lapel mic, probably telling dispatch to get the damn help on the way. But all hell breaks loose before help arrives, courtesy of a nitwit Nationite who hurls a good-size brick out of the crowd into the mass of chanting Africans. One of the boys falls with a blow to the head, and the Africans break suddenly across the police, descending like a wave on the Nation. There's screaming as Nationites—unfortunately, there are about ten women in the crowd—scatter in every direction. Some of the toughest Nationites take up a position in the center of the melee and prove they know how to fight by decking the Sudanese around them. But they're badly outnumbered, and the riot rapidly starts to turn against them. The cops are on the backside of the fight, doing what they're supposed to do in that situation: not get themselves killed. Nationites are streaming past us in twos and threes as they retreat from the scene, but the Africans don't pursue them. Instead, they turn on the center group that's resisted them, and for the first time I wonder if somebody is going to get killed.

Finally—it only takes three or four minutes, but it feels like hours—sirens blare from the left. It won't be long before the police lower the hammer on what's happening, and the recriminations begin. In the meantime, a hard-core group of ten Nationites are trying to hold their own against twice as many Africans, and it's clear they'll only last another couple of minutes.

The crowd is thinning—at least half the Nationite mob has turned tail—and for the first time, I can clearly see through the crowd to the first row of apartments. A handful of Nationites have broken off and are headed toward the apartments, probably hunting for Bol. A half-dozen Africans pick them up and converge toward them, determined to head them off. They meet in a frenzy of malice I haven't seen outside a prison yard. They are hitting each other with unspeakable anger, both sides utterly releasing themselves to their frustration.

Meanwhile, a board flies up out of the main crowd and lands near the truck. "We gotta get outta here," Stillman says. "This shit is out of hand."

"Where the hell is Fiona?" I inch forward, scanning the crowd, and freeze. Fiona has come flying out of one of the apartments and is clinging to any African she can reach, trying to keep him out of the fight. The knot of battling Sudanese and Nationites is converging toward her. Africans near her are heading over to help, and she's screaming for people to stop. In another few seconds, she'll be in the middle of the battle.

I slam the truck into park, open the door, and sprint through the crowd toward her. I dodge a random fist and jump over two boys locked in each other's grip like wrestlers. Fiona is gesturing wildly, trying to get people to stop hammering on each other. The African she's pulling on takes a blow to the face, and he drops to his knees. Fiona shrieks at the kid who hit him, who stares at her, face screwed up in anger, trying to figure out whether or not it matters to him that the person in front of him is a woman. I don't give him or his anger the chance to decide. I put my shoulder into his back, and he goes flying, sprawled out a good ten yards from where I hit him. He rolls over on his side, writhing in pain. I grab Fiona's arm and start dragging her back to the apartment she came out of, but she's fighting me, clawing at my hands to let her go. "You're gonna get killed in there, dammit!" I yell, pulling her back. "Let the cops handle this. It's out of control."

At that moment, a cop car and a SWAT truck converge simultaneously on the scene. Within seconds, what looks like ten police with batons raised are spreading out, barking orders and moving people apart.

"Stay here," I say, holding her fast. "Let them do this."

She stops struggling and stares, breathing heavily, tears streaming down her face. "My God, what are people doing?" She falls back against me, and I relax my grip. The police wade through the Nationites, who start disappearing back into houses and alleys.

"It'll all be over in a few seconds," I say, letting her go. "Just stay calm."

A few of the cops are taking over the Africans, who are now far more numerous than the Nationites. They're still amped, not falling back. The cops bark for people to freeze where they stand. The few Nationites remaining ignore this command and run hard in the opposite direction, knowing the cops won't follow until the scene of the riot is secure. Most of the Africans obey, but a few ignore the cops, some running after any Nationite still in sight. About fifteen yards away from us one of the Sudanese walks rapidly away from the scene, and a cop yells at his back to stop. The African keeps going, and the cop starts to jog after him. When he's about seven feet away he yells again. "Stop! I'm telling you, stop where you are." The cop raises his baton.

The African looks back a second, sees the cop almost on him, and takes off running. The cop sprints forward, but only manages to get a hand on his arm. "Damn it, I told you stop. Now stop!" The boy struggles to get free, and the cop lowers his baton on the kid's shoulder, crumpling him to the ground. He raises the baton again for another blow; there's a high-pitched wail beside me, and Fiona is out of my grasp and heading headlong for the policeman. The baton starts to come down, but Fiona gets there first and lands on the cop, sending the baton flying. Fiona and the policeman fall to a heap on the concrete. The Sudanese kid scrambles to his feet and takes off, disappearing behind a row of buildings.

Before I can get there, the cop has Fiona's face pressed down into the asphalt. He wrenches her hands behind her and secures her hands in plastic cuffs like a cowboy on a calf.

"Hang on!" I yell, running up. "Hang on, take it easy."

"Back the fuck up!" the officer screams, standing up, defiant and angry. "Not one fucking word, unless you wanna get cuffed, too." He pulls Fiona up to her feet and starts marching her off. She's bleeding on her temple and lip from the gravel.

Fiona's hair is flying, and she's giving the cop hell. "He doesn't speak English! He didn't stop because he doesn't speak English!"

"You sure as hell do," the cop retorts, pushing her forward. "Son of a *bitch*!"

Fiona turns her head back to me. "You saw what happened, Thomas! He was beating him!"

Within another minute, the police have the scene secure. They wade into the crowd, cuffing people. Eleven Sudanese and five Nationites end up restrained and lined up on their knees beside the SWAT truck. The Nationite side of the entrance is almost abandoned, but there's still a crowd of Africans watching from a distance.

I try to figure out who's in charge, spot a sergeant, and head over. He looks up and nods. "I know you," he says. "You're Dennehy, over at the DA's office. What the fuck happened here?"

"It was full-on by the time I got here."

He nods. "Well, this is a son-of-a-bitch situation, I can tell ya that. Somebody started a rumor that this African kid you're prosecuting got off. Any truth to that?"

"None."

"Figures. Things have a life of their own."

An out-of-breath cop appears around the corner with the African Fiona was protecting in cuffs. "I got him, Sergeant. If he hadn't stumbled, I'd never have caught him." He forces the Sudanese boy down to his knees in the line of the arrested. "Now stay there, dammit."

The sergeant looks over at Fiona. "Tell me who in the holy hell that is."

I'm about to answer when Stillman appears, a relaxed smile on his face. "Afternoon, officers. Jeff Stillman, DA's office."

The cop looks at him. "What's your story?"

He points at Fiona. "Assault and battery on a police officer and resisting arrest, for starters. I saw the whole thing. The officer was attempting to execute his duty and Towns physically assaulted him."

"Don't worry, she'll get her turn." The sergeant yells over at an officer. "Bring the woman over, will ya?"

"You took your time showing up, Stillman," I say quietly.

"I guess I didn't feel the need to interfere with the police," Stillman says, looking at me. He pulls me aside. "Look, this is *beautiful,* Thomas. She just hit a *cop.*"

The officer Fiona fought with marches her over to us. "Here she is, Sergeant," he says, shoving her in front of him. "And you can throw the book at her, far as I'm concerned."

The sergeant looks her over. "Let's start with your name."

Fiona, hands bound, bleeding in two places, shirt torn, and pants dirty, is a blaze of righteous indignation. "I am the Reverend Fiona Towns. Your goons were manhandling my boys." She looks at the cop with her. "Him, in particular."

The sergeant looks up. "Reverend? I bet that's some kind of church."

"It's the kind that doesn't sit idly by while people are brutalized by the police," Fiona snaps.

The sergeant rolls his eyes. "Frank, what the hell happened on this deal?"

"I gave one of the Africans a direct order to stop," the officer says. "He refused, and I repeated myself. He refused again, and I put a baton on him. I was in the process of subduing him when this woman attacked me."

"The boy doesn't speak English, you imbecile," Fiona retorts. "For all he knew, he thought you were ordering pizza."

"That's his problem," the officer grumbles. "Your problem is assaulting a police officer."

"I didn't *assault* you, as you so colorfully put it," she says. "I was keeping you from beating the life out of someone who doesn't *speak English.* If anybody was going to get hit, I wanted it to be me."

"God help your boyfriend, if you have one," the cop says, under his breath, but not far enough under. Fiona revs up for a verbal barrage, and the cop steps away, waving his hand. "I'm done, lady. Tell it to a judge."

"That true, Frank?" the sergeant asks. "Did she hit you?"

"More like she jumped on me."

"Oh, poor baby," Fiona mocks.

"Well, did she hurt you, or what?" the sergeant asks.

"'Course she didn't hurt me, but that ain't the point, Sergeant. I'm trying to subdue a prisoner."

The sergeant nods. "It's gonna look a little shitty, Frank. Her being a woman preacher and all. Still, we can't have people interfering with a policeman doing his duty." He points to the African. "Bring him over." One of the officers hauls the African to his feet and pushes him toward the police. There's a disquieting murmur from the remaining refugees, who watch from stoops and doorways. The sergeant taps the boy on the shoulder. "What about it, *amigo?* You speak English or what?"

The boy recoils in fear. "No English."

The sergeant shakes his head. "This'll make a hell of a headline in tomorrow's paper. We got a woman and some kid who doesn't speak the lingo." The sergeant spits. "Damn mess, is what it is." He looks back at the Africans watching from their apartment doorways. "How'd this thing get started, anyway?"

"Some Nationites picked up one of the Africans to send a message," I say. "He's in Vanderbilt Hospital."

He shakes his head. "We didn't even get called. These refugees don't trust us." He looks back at the officer. "And now they've seen Frank use a baton on one of them." He spits again. "Dammit, when did this town turn into this?"

"One day at a time," I say. "One damn day at a time."

The sergeant nods. "I can't let this kinda thing go down without consequences, but I wouldn't mind reaching out to these African kids. I'm gonna have to take 'em downtown and hold 'em for a while, but if you think it's okay, we can let 'em go after a few hours."

"Fine by me."

He nods. "How about the woman?"

"She goes downtown," Stillman retorts.

The sergeant raises an eyebrow. "Your pal here's pretty gung-ho, ain't he?"

"Yeah," I say, quietly.

The sergeant pulls me aside. Stillman follows, leaning in. "Thing is, that officer who hit the African kid is a bit of a hothead. It ain't the first time somebody's had to calm him down."

I look over at the officer; he's glaring back at the three of us with a surly expression. "Yeah."

"I can smell bad PR when I run into it, and this whole thing stinks of it. So I'm not hauling that preacher down there if the DA's office won't press charges. Puts my department in a bad light for no reason. So I'd say this is your call, Counselor. Do I bring her in or not? Yes or no."

I look over at Fiona, who is standing with her hands bound behind her back. She's staring straight back at me, her eyes blazing. "Book her," I say flatly. "Take her in."

The sergeant nods and turns back to the others. "Roll 'em up!" he bellows. "Africans in the truck, Nationites in cars. Put the woman in mine."

Stillman and I follow, walking within five feet of Fiona. The officer she jumped on is turning her around and moving her toward the sergeant's car. "Let's go, sweetheart," he growls.

Fiona looks back over her shoulder at me. "Don't," she pleads. "Don't do this, Thomas." The officer opens the back door of the car and pushes Fiona's head down, forcing her into the car. I turn my back and walk away, heading to my truck.

Stillman shuts the passenger door of the Ford and smiles at me. "You know, man, I had you wrong."

I stare out the windshield. The officers are loading the Africans into the truck, one by one. "How's that?" I ask quietly.

"I thought you had a thing for the girl. You know, you were going soft."

"I see."

"I would have sworn you would have told the sergeant to

let her off. You know, keep her out of trouble." He pauses. "I even thought you had second thoughts about Bol, what with Hodges being such an asshole and everything. The move on the kid he put in the hospital doesn't look so hot."

I watch the last of the watching Africans slowly disappear back into their homes. "If Towns doesn't testify, she doesn't go to prison for obstruction."

Stillman stares, working out what I saw from the first moment. "Shit, man. This had nothing to do with Bol. You did it to protect her. She's useless as a witness now. 'So, Reverend Towns, I understand you were arrested three days ago for incitement to riot and assaulting a policeman. Now what was it you had to say again?' " He smacks his hand down on the side of his door. "Fucking brilliant, man. You're gonna plead her shit down, and she'll be out in thirty-six hours. But that's the thirty-six hours that keeps her out of prison for three to five. Meanwhile, Bol's one chance for an acquittal is officially history."

I start the engine. "Let's go home, Stillman."

CHAPTER FIFTEEN

RITA WEST AND I are seated in the hallway outside the revolving door of justice known as Night Court. She stares across an empty bench at me. "So," she says.

"Um hmm."

"You vex me, Thomas. You really do."

"Something to live for."

"You've got incitement to riot on here, Thomas. *Incitement to riot.*"

"The police were attempting to quell the disturbance. At which point, the accused assaults an officer."

"Thomas . . ."

"I'm a reasonable man, Rita. We can work something out. I'm thinking simple assault, resisting arrest."

"Very magnanimous of you, considering the original charge is complete crap."

"That's not what the cop says."

Rita curls her lip. "Frank Bratton's a macho idiot who's probably just embarrassed a woman flattened him."

"He's also a police officer, and between him and Towns, I'm pretty sure which one the judge is going to believe."

"You know something, Thomas? You can be a real jerk sometimes."

"Probably, but this isn't one of them."

"What would you call it? This is nothing but a nail in Moses Bol's coffin. How am I supposed to call a witness right after she gets convicted for assaulting a policeman?"

"There is a solution."

"I'd be pretty interested to know what it is."

"Get Bol to plea."

She looks up. "You said there weren't going to be any more deals."

I nod. "Lemme ask you something, Rita. You ever feel like we're just pawns in some big game we don't control?"

"In this job? Every day of my life."

"Yeah, well, I know the feeling. You, me, Bol, we're all nothing but chess pieces on the board. You've got people on your side right now who don't give a damn about you or Bol. They're just using him for their own agenda."

"Agreed."

"Same thing for me. There's going to be three hundred idiots from the Wolfe Pack showing up for court tomorrow, and friends like that I don't need."

She pauses. "So what are you saying?"

"I'm saying that David Rayburn's not an idiot, Rita. This city is on the verge of chaos. Right now he can't afford to look like he's caving, but a guilty plea would be just what the doctor ordered. Justice served. Towns is off the stand. Bol does time, but he lives. Everybody goes home alive."

She nods thoughtfully. "Bol's a hard case, Thomas. I'm not sure I can get him to go for it."

"He's going to lose, Rita. And if he loses without a plea, he's going to die."

"Bol's already seen a lot of death," she says, shaking her head. "I don't think he's afraid of it."

This is not in my calculations. The whole *idea* of the death penalty is that people are afraid of dying. Take that out of the equation, and you don't have shit. "Seriously?"

"Thomas, if you knew the half of what this kid's been through, it would break your heart."

"At this point, I'd just prefer his kept beating. But that's up to you. I've done what I can. Get the deal, and I'll handle Rayburn."

"You give me your word?"

"Get the deal." I push paperwork across to her. "This is for Towns. It's already signed by me. It pleas her down with time served. She walks out tonight."

She stares at the paper. "You were pretty confident."

"Talk to Bol, Rita. This is the only way he's going to survive. If this comes to trial, he's done." I pause. "And talk to Towns. She's got to let this go, now. I'm trying to keep her out of prison. You know that."

She stands. "Yeah. Tomorrow morning?"

"I'll be there."

Outside the New Justice Building, I look up at the night sky. *BMWs,* I think. *I could always sell BMWs.*

CHAPTER SIXTEEN

SIX O'CLOCK THE NEXT MORNING, Tuesday. The *Tennessean,* open to the front page. "AFRICAN REFUGEES RIOT AT TENNESSEE VILLAGE." I scan down the text: "More than fifty Sudanese refugees confronted police and area residents yesterday at Tennessee Village . . . high immigrant population . . . nearby residents express fear and concern . . . quoted as saying it was 'like something out of *National Geographic*' . . . outspoken pastor of the Downtown Presbyterian Church was arrested for incitement to riot . . . police spokesman Donald Marsh asks for calm . . ."

Coffee. Zoloft. Cat, vanished again. *Where the hell is that damn animal this time?* I peer out at the woods behind my house. Something bigger and meaner could have got ahold of him; there's some pretty ugly-looking possums in the woods behind the house. The food and water still sit in their bowls, untouched. *I take it all back. Fancy Feast morning and night. Come on back, buddy.* I walk back through the kitchen but decide against breakfast today. But I need the run. I put on shorts, tennis shoes, don't bother with a shirt. I pound out a couple of miles, letting the sweat roll down my body. I push up the final hill like somebody's chasing me.

Shower, shave, dress. I pull out the light gray Ferragamo two-button suit, white Zegna shirt and bloodred tie, black Bally shoes. Three weeks' salary. One of the few lessons I took from the military: if you're going to face the fire, look good. Had a drill sergeant—drunk on his ass at the time—put it this way: *Know the real reason we lost Vietnam, son? By the second year, our soldiers looked like surfers. Walking around with no uniforms, smoking dope. Other side stopped taking us seriously. I mean, who can't kick a bunch of surfers' asses?* It was dubious history, but I took his point.

I drive into town, the traffic its usual pitch of molasses. I switch on the radio and hear Dan Wolfe's morning drive-time show. He's extolling his troops, telling the Wolfe Pack to show up and demand justice for Tamra Hartlett. He's read the day's paper, including a description of the Africans doing their war dance. He is as happy as a little boy locked in a room with ten kinds of ice cream. He can barely contain his self-satisfied rage as he gives his trademark yelp. "Howwwwwlllll," he says, the microphone crackling with distortion. "I wanna see my Pack on the courthouse steps today! I wanna hear some howwwwwllllling! Can you feel me? Tell me, Pack, can you feeeeeeeel me?"

Yeah, moron. I feel you. I can also feel the fact that it was Fiona Towns who got arrested for incitement to riot, when Wolfe is far more guilty. But Wolfe has the very expensive lawyers of Wide Channel Communications on his side, ready to wrap him in the protective shield of the First Amendment at the first hint of complaint. And anyway, the only thing between him and a nationally syndicated show is a little free publicity, which a lawsuit would deliver on a silver platter. *So howl on, moron. Wrap yourself up in the flag and give yourself a raise.*

Ten blocks from the New Justice Building, I meet the other side of David Rayburn's delusiac equation: this time, the anti-death-penalty forces have come in on three buses. I figure by this point, we've got them from several states away. The vehicles are plastered with banners and— horrifyingly—enormous, blown-up photographs of Wilson Owens, the man executed for the Sunshine Grocery murders. I actually get caught at a red light beside one of the buses, and Owens's face stares at me, eye level, like a condemning angel. I look up cautiously; the bus is filled with Buchanan's merry revelers, ready to spill out onto the courtyard steps and come face-to-face with the Wolfe Pack. *Talk about a global village. Arabs kill a bunch of Africans ten thousand miles away, and it's high times in Nashville, Tennessee.*

I drive past the front of the NJB and see that after yesterday's disturbance, the police have finally got the picture: there's a substantial cop force deployed around the building, including a large van parked up on grass beyond the steps to the front doors. It's still early, but Dan Wolfe proves his pull with his demographic; there's already a good hundred members of the Pack ensconced on the grounds. They're wearing their Wolfe Pack T-shirts, which say *Howl at a Liberal* on the back and *Wolfe Pack* on the front. Judging by their availability, the Pack doesn't hold down much in the way of jobs, but they don't waste any time doing the bidding of their radio master.

The Africans are back, as well. They're forming en masse on the other side of the stairs leading to the building's main entrance. They number only about thirty, but more are walking across the grounds to join the group. I watch them arrive, remembering the raw, electric energy coming from them at the Village. *If that gets unleashed around the Pack, God help us. And that doesn't even factor in Buchanan's clowns.*

I head around to the rear of the building, wave my mag card at the employee entrance, and park. Stillman's arrived ahead of me; his used but freshly waxed BMW is parked at the far end of a row, the better to protect its immaculate paint job. I get out of the Ford, clear through security, and head straight to Ginder's chambers.

I come out of the elevators and feel Stillman on my left, materializing, as usual, from out of nowhere. I pull up. "Damn it, Stillman, you got to stop that."

"What?"

I stare at him. "Let's go. We've got to see Ginder."

"So Rita can throw in the towel."

"We'll see what we see."

He stops. "What, you don't think she'll do it?"

"It depends on Bol. On the other hand, she might use what happened yesterday to ask for a continuance."

"Forget that, man. Rayburn says we got to roll."

"If she asks for one, I'll support her motion," I say quietly.

Stillman looks shocked. "Are you nuts, man? The kid's goose is cooked. All we got to do is turn on the heat."

"We know whose car it was that picked up that kid who got beat up, don't we, Stillman?"

"News flash, Thomas. Jason Hodges is an asshole."

"Lemme ask you something, Stillman. Has it actually never occurred to you that just maybe Jason Hodges is also a big enough asshole to have killed his girlfriend?"

Stillman stares at me. "What's your point? You didn't tell Rita about Hodges last night, did you?"

"No. But I'm telling Ginder this morning. I want his opinion on whether or not it's exculpatory."

"Exculpatory, my ass. It's everything defense attorneys use to confuse a jury. We got the blood evidence. We've got Bol's semen in her vagina. We got her bludgeoned to death. We got Bol's handprint on her naked body. We got her blood in his car. Against which, Jason Hodges proves he doesn't like black people and there's a hung jury, minimum. Maybe even an acquittal."

"Maybe. And maybe the rule of law actually means something around here."

"What the hell does that mean?"

"It means that if Ginder rules it's exculpatory, Rita is going to want time to determine if Hodges has a pattern of violent behavior. She'll want to subpoena his medical records. She'll want to interview the other girls he worked, see if he was ever violent with them. You saw how he treated that brunette at his house."

"I saw shit, man. David was right. You're losing your nerve."

"Whatever."

"You were a great prosecutor, man. You were ice."

"So I hear. But this is how it's going to be."

Stillman frowns disdainfully. "Jason Hodges is nothing but a fucking O. J. glove, man. Smoke and mirrors. If Rita West is as talented as you say she is, she'll turn Jason Hodges into a monster before our eyes."

"C'est la vie."

"I'm going to Rayburn with this. I'm not a part of it."

"See ya, Stillman."

I watch Stillman walk back to the elevator, then turn back to Ginder's courtroom. The hallway is nearly empty today; the action's outside, and anybody with a stake in the case is lining up out there. I head through the courtroom into Ginder's chambers. Rita isn't there yet. Ginder is standing by his window, which looks down over the front of the building and the hordes of protestors massing on the grounds. He glances up as I come in.

"Well, that's a hell of a thing," he says. "Haven't seen that since the sixties."

I smile. "Were you a radical, sir?"

Ginder shrugs. "You know how it is. Start out communist, end up subscribing to the *Wall Street Journal*."

"Yes, sir."

He turns and walks to his desk. "Let's get this jury empaneled, Thomas. The sooner this case is behind us, the better."

"There's a little business to attend to first, Judge. I've got some evidence that might be exculpatory."

Ginder looks up. "That so?"

"You know about what happened at Tennessee Village yesterday," I say. "One of the African refugees was abducted and beat up by some Nationites."

"Yeah. Damn shame."

I exhale. "I have reason to believe it might have involved Jason Hodges."

"The boyfriend?"

"Yes, sir."

Ginder nods. "You're thinking the defense is going to want to fly him as an alternative to Bol."

"What she does with this information is her business, Your Honor."

Ginder leans back in his chair thoughtfully. "She'd need a week, anyway. Try to establish a pattern of violent behavior. Hell, it might take two weeks."

"At which point, we'd petition you to rule it inadmissable anyway, Your Honor."

Ginder nods. "I know." He points toward the window.

"The city's in a bad place, Thomas. I don't like the idea of two weeks' delay."

"Neither does the state. But I felt I had to bring this to you."

"A lot of people wouldn't. You did the right thing."

"Thank you, sir."

There's a soft knock on the door, and Rita enters. She's uncharacteristically disheveled; her hair is out of place, and she's flushed. She walks to the center of the room and drops her briefcase on the floor.

"Hello, Your Honor."

"You OK, Ms. West?"

"Yes."

"Those guys outside didn't give you any trouble, did they?"

"No."

"Fine. Mr. Dennehy and I were just having a very interesting conversation."

Here we go. Two weeks of chaos. It'll be a miracle if we make it through this.

"Bol confessed." I open my eyes to see Rita staring at me blankly. "An hour ago, in my office."

"What did you say?" I ask.

She shakes her head, dumbfounded. "Right out of the blue. 'Excuse me, ma'am. I wish to confess.'" She looks confused, like she's not sure where she is. "He did it. He killed her."

Ginder looks like a man who just popped up after a blow, right as rain. "Excellent news," he says. "This solves everything."

"Everything?"

"Never mind, Ms. West. Let the young man know I'm happy to accept his change of plea."

"Hang on a second," I say. "You told him about the deal first, right? Then he confessed."

"I never had the chance. 'I wish to confess,' he said. That's it. He wouldn't take no for an answer."

"And he's serious? He knows what he's doing?"

"I made him stay put and ran down the translator, just to be sure. I explained all the implications to him. He won't be dissuaded."

Ginder picks up the phone and calls his clerk. "Have them put the jurors back into the pool, will you, dear? That's right. We just got a guilty plea." He looks up at us. "All right, Ms. West. Have your client in court tomorrow morning, ready to plead."

Rita looks at me. "I didn't get the deal, Thomas. What are you going to do about the death penalty?"

I stand outside Ginder's courtroom, stunned. *He did it.* For some reason, I'm actually surprised. *The evidence is overwhelming. Like Stillman said: the semen, the blood, the handprint. It's all there. Hell, maybe it's like Kwame Jamal Hale. Maybe he just wants to get right with his Maker.* I lean back against the hallway wall, feeling weight fall off me. *There was no coercion. He didn't even know about the deal. It's a free confession, freer than 99 percent of capital cases.*

I stand up and breathe deeply, letting the air go with a sigh. "I did my job," I say out loud. "It's not my responsibility how he pleads." I walk back out through the hallway and stop at the windows looking down on the grounds. A hundred protestors have already gathered, and it's only 9:15. They don't know it yet, but Moses Bol, their ticket to fifteen minutes of fame, has just made them irrelevant. "Pack up and go home," I say to the window. "Party's over."

* * *

"Congratulate me." I am holding a four-and-one-half-inch-long Cuesta Rey Robusto, having retrieved it from the lower drawer of my desk. I plop down into one of the district attorney's wing chairs, casually snip off the end of the cigar, and pocket the end. I roll the finished product between my fingers and set my size-eleven shoes on the edge of his desk. Rayburn and Stillman are giving me incredulous looks—in Stillman's case, mixed with a hefty dose of malevolence—but I studiously ignore them. I pass the cigar under my nose, left to right, inhaling its deep, musky scent. "Congratulate me," I repeat.

Rayburn stares at me. "I'm trying to decide why I shouldn't fire you," he grinds through his teeth. "We went over this stuff again and again. We were on the same page. And from out of the blue you go and fuck everything up."

"The blood evidence," Stillman says. He's loving being on the same side as Rayburn, especially lined up against me. "The arguments between Bol and the victim. The phone call the night of the murder. It's overwhelming. You got distracted, man. You lost your focus, and now, God knows what's going to happen."

"Pandora's box," Rayburn agrees. "You went and opened it." He looks at my shoes. "And get your shoes off my desk."

I smile. "It's over. Bol confessed."

Stillman's mouth snaps shut. Rayburn stares a second, then leaps to his feet. "Damn you, Stillman, I told you Thomas wouldn't do anything as idiotic as you said!" He walks over to me and pounds me on the back. "This right here is the *man,* Stillman. You, on the other hand, are a sniveling pup who's still wet behind the ears." Rayburn is beaming. "The man can close, Stillman. Like I always said."

Stillman's TV face is flushed a beautiful shade of rose.

"What happened?" he demands. "You were going in to support a motion for a continuance."

"Bol confessed. He's giving his statement at one o'clock today. I told Rita we would drop the death penalty." I look at Rayburn. "We do, right?"

Rayburn exhales. "Yeah. OK. The confession covers our asses."

"We're not caving; he did."

Rayburn looks happy for the first time in a week. "God, we needed that. It gets nine pounds of shit off our backs." He looks at the cigar. "You got another one of those?"

Oh yeah, pal. I got another one. I reach in my coat pocket and pull out another Robusto. Rayburn looks like he's going to cry with pleasure. Strictly speaking, smoking is against regulations in any government building. And strictly speaking, we are sitting in the building that most has to do with the enforcement of laws and regulations. On the other hand, a closed door is a happy door. Rayburn nods at me like he's reading my mind. "Stillman," he says, "get the fuck out of my office."

The District Attorney of Davidson County, Tennessee, sits behind his desk, happily ensconced in a haze of cigar smoke. His coat is off, his tie loosened. Beside him is a bottle of Tennessee sipping whiskey and three shot glasses. I have removed the battery from the room's smoke detector and now sit in one of two wing chairs, my own coat and tie having likewise decamped. Rayburn pours one glass, another, and is on the verge of tipping the bottle into the third glass when he catches himself and stops. "Shit," he says, setting down the bottle. "The third one's Carl's."

"Force of habit," I say, nodding. "We've been through this ritual how many times?"

Rayburn picks up one of the glasses and hands it across the desk to me. "Twenty-five? Thirty?"

I hold the glass in my left hand, cigar in my right. "Every one of them with Carl in that chair."

"To Carl," Rayburn says, lifting his glass. "He was the best."

"Still is." We drain our glasses, and I set mine down for a refill. Rayburn pours whiskey, and I wave him off at halfway. "I gotta take Bol's statement in a couple of hours."

He nods, fills his own, and leans back. "Damn fine cigar," he says. "Nicaraguan?"

"Honduran. Doesn't matter. All your third-world dictatorships knew how to make cigars."

Rayburn pulls on the cigar, closes his eyes, and sends a thin stream of smoke up toward the ceiling. "Guy goes into a bank to pull a job."

"Is this a joke?"

Rayburn shakes his head. "Object lesson."

I nod. "I'm listening."

"It's a bank job. The guy freaks out and kills a teller. He makes a break for it, five grand in hundreds, teller on the floor in a pool of blood. Cop catches up to him a few blocks later. He tells the guy to stop, but the guy keeps on running. What happens?"

"Teller's down?"

"Yeah."

"Guy is still armed, right?" Rayburn nods. I shrug. "Cop takes him out."

Rayburn smacks his desk. "Right, dammit! No jury, no judge, no legal representation. Just instant justice. But say the cop's bullet hits four inches to the right. *Four inches.* So the guy's not dead, see? His shoulder's hit, he goes down and gets arrested. He gets tried and convicted. Jury of his peers. He appeals and loses. Appeals again—his counsel didn't use the right kind of aftershave or something—and he loses again."

"OK."

"Finally, after seven or eight years of legal process, all of which is provided to this cold-blooded bastard free of charge, it's time to do what the cop would have done if he had *just been a better shot*."

"Damn good point."

He looks at me through the cigar haze. "At which point, Professor Philip Buchanan and his friends set up a candlelight vigil at the prison. They hold hands. They sing hymns. They raise money so Alan fucking Dershowitz or somebody can file motions to stay the execution. And then they all start crying when the clock strikes twelve, like it's Bobby Kennedy's funeral. And nobody—this is the fucking salient point—nobody can even remember the *name* of the teller who got iced." He leans forward. "The bastard who shot her's got Web sites dedicated to him, and his victim's just a forgotten spot in a cemetery. Can somebody please explain that shit to me?"

"Wouldn't want to try."

"No, you wouldn't. You're a reasonable fucking man, that's why." He looks over at the empty chair. "I miss Carl at a time like this, you know?"

"Yeah."

"Call me crazy, but sometimes I wish I practiced law fifty years ago. I would have liked that. The old boy's club. Nothing against the women, but you know."

"They're fine lawyers."

"Sure. But you, me, Carl, lighting up another victory. You can't touch that."

I smile at Rayburn. I've always liked making him happy.

He's kind of a puppy dog, and getting his tail to wag is satisfying somehow.

"So now all we got to do is get through the Buchanan mess," he says, his expression clouding. "But you know what? Right now, I can even believe that's gonna turn out OK. I mean, who would have thought Bol would confess? Talk about out of the blue."

"Not the first time somebody got the message at the last minute."

Rayburn exhales another stream of smoke. "True, my friend."

I stand, down the rest of my drink, and set the empty glass on Rayburn's desk. "To family."

Rayburn downs his own, smacking the glass hard on the polished surface. He stands and shakes my hand. "Damn right."

I am home. *Home.* The shower runs over my naked body, washing me clean. Clean of office politics, of Stillman, of Moses Bol and his godforsaken story, of Tamra Hartlett and the Wolfe Pack and angry Nationites patrolling their neighborhood. Clean of everything but a Browning pump shotgun pulled out of the ground forty miles west of here; in a few more days, I'll have the answers to that, too. If it goes against us, there's no shower hot and strong enough to wipe that away.

So it's official. You said get Bol out of the way, and you're on vacation. And if the Hale thing goes the wrong way, you just make it permanent: I'm bone fishing in the Keys. The secret of that gig is the ability to hang with men. And that, I got. Me, a boat full of pasty midlevel execs running away from a Chicago winter, and some fish on the line. Somebody else can try to figure out what justice means in the New South of the twenty-first century.

I wrap up in a towel after the shower and pull my first Killian's out of the fridge. In Carl's day, this ritual would have been continued from Rayburn's office, straight to Seanachie's. I'm drinking alone tonight. Stillman, it's safe to say, is not celebrating. He's licking his wounds, caught out being disloyal, which is the first deadly sin with Rayburn. I twist open the Killian's. *Here's to you, Stillman. Here's to the three hundred grand a year you'll make at MSNBC. Of course, you'll have to live in New York, and you'll want to do it in style. So I figure you're fifty grand in the hole, first year.* I take a long, satisfying pull on the beer and set it down on the counter.

Dinner. As a concept, desirable. As a reality, more complicated. I pull out a pan and stare at it awhile, when it hits me. *Omelet. Bachelor's special.* I scavenge some eggs, milk, bacon, a green onion, and some Edam cheese. Fifteen minutes later I'm pulled up in front of the TV, telling myself that beer with eggs isn't that much of a stretch, since restaurants serve the same thing with a glass of champagne and call it brunch.

The Fox affiliate runs its news early, at five. The first feature is, without doubt, the most satisfying three and a half minutes of television I've ever seen. The reporter is shown on the courthouse steps, which are nearly empty. Denied the object of their hatred, the Wolfe Pack has dispersed like a popped balloon. Even Buchanan's troops are down by two-thirds. Without a current case bringing the cameras, only the die-hard protestors have stuck out the rest of the day.

After dinner I walk to the back sliding-glass door, wondering where the hell is Indy. I put my hand on the glass and say out loud, "I take it all back, pal. The Fancy Feast is waiting." I turn around and look at the kitchen, facing an empty evening, and smile. "And fuck you, too, Carl," I say to the walls. "Retiring and leaving me with Stillman took some kinda nerve."

I wait until dark and strip naked for the back half of the soak outside that Fiona interrupted. I'm almost glad I didn't get to finish it; free of Bol's case, the relaxation will be deeper, more satisfying. *And if I'm lucky, she'll show up again, just like last time.* I drop my clothes on the bed and head out to the back deck. It's not a bad night; clear, with a sprinkle of stars overhead, and late enough to be cool. I walk over and hit the button that turns on the jets, even before I lift the top off the spa. It rumbles to life, shooting water through the tub. *Fatal error. Forgot the beer.* Leaving the door open, I walk back to the kitchen and grab two bottles. The pump on the spa sounds funny; it's straining, the pitch changing up and down for no reason. I grab a towel and listen; the pump is definitely working harder than it should. There's a grinding sound—I can't help thinking it's going to turn out to be expensive—and the jets shudder to a stop. I walk out to the deck and sniff the air. There's a burning, horrid smell in the air. *The motor's gone. That's going to cost.* I reach down and pull back the cover, exposing the spa. Immediately, I'm overwhelmed with a horrible stench. I retch involuntarily, but force myself to look down. There are dark pieces of something visible, and the water is discolored. Just then, something furry floats to the surface, in a shape I don't like. *Jesus. It's a head.* Holding back vomit, I force myself to look again. There, in my spa, is what remains of Indianapolis. I fall back, horrified. I right myself, swallow, lean over, and throw up off the side of the deck. The smell coming out of the spa is overpowering, like a suffocating blanket. I step off the deck, hands on hips, bent over, trying to pull myself together. After stewing in eighty-five-degree water for what must have been a couple of days, Indianapolis is badly de-

composed. The hair and body parts quickly clogged the spa
jets when I turned them on, although not before being
strained and cut up through the plastic blades for twenty or
thirty gruesome seconds. Heart pounding, I stumble back
into the house and slam shut the sliding-glass door. I drop to
a knee, holding my stomach together with an act of will. I
try to figure out some way he could have gotten in the spa on
his own, but realize it's impossible. The cover is far too
heavy, and anyway, he hated water. He'd sprint out of a
shower.

Ten minutes later, I've managed to pull on some pants,
but my skin hasn't stopped crawling. Indianapolis's water
and food bowls are on the floor near the refrigerator, where
they've sat undisturbed. I pick them up and set them on the
kitchen counter. There's a handful of food left in one, irrelevant now. I stare at the bowls for a while, numb. Eventually,
I empty the food into the trash, empty the water, and stack
one bowl on top of the other. I pick them up, place them
carefully under the sink, and close the door.

At some point—I'm not sure how long—I realize I'm sitting in a chair, holding an empty beer bottle. I look at my
watch; it's 10:30. I pick up the phone and call Paul Landmeyer. He answers, and I can hear the TV in the background. "Paul? It's Thomas. You up?"

"Yeah. You get more flowers?"

"Look, you got any equipment at home?"

"Some in the trunk. What's going on, Thomas?"

"Somebody drowned Indy in the spa out back."

"Your cat?"

"Yeah."

"What the hell happened?"

"I couldn't find Indianapolis the last few days. Tonight, I
went out to the spa. He was floating in it."

"Shit, Thomas. You figure it's the same person who sent you the funeral wreath?"

"I don't know. Listen, the flowers were one thing, but this is too far in my business, too close."

"Especially with animal cruelty in the mix. It's a certain kind of mentality."

"That's what I was thinking."

He pauses. "Listen, I'm coming over. If it's Nationite, it'll be sloppy. Maybe I can find something."

"I'd appreciate it. It wouldn't break my heart to find out who's behind this."

"Gimme twenty minutes."

It's only fifteen before I hear Paul pull up into the driveway, and I go out to meet him. He pops the trunk of his car, gets out, and grabs two aluminum-sided cases from his trunk. He looks up at the house. "You got lights back there?"

"Yeah. I'll turn 'em on for you."

"Leave them off for now," Paul answers. "I got a new toy I wanna play with." We walk around the house and enter the backyard through a side gate. Paul stops about thirty feet away from the spa and pulls out a couple of masks from his pocket. "Put one on," he says. "It'll help with the stench." He opens one of the cases and removes what looks like a large handheld spotlight. The light, which is encased in black hard plastic, is connected by a cord to a separate, lunch box–sized device. He switches the light on, and it casts a pale, blue light onto the ground. "Swiss energy light," he says, smiling grimly. "There's eight in the country. One's in your backyard."

"What's it do?"

"Picks up debris invisible to the naked eye. We'll start by looking for footprints. Stay behind me, OK?"

"Yeah." The air is foul with death, and only the thought that we might be able to nail the bastard who did this to Indy keeps my thoughts focused. Paul starts toward the spa, sweeping the light in large arcs. He shines the light at the grass, peering intently. After five minutes or so, we've covered half the way to the spa. "Must have come the other way," he says. We make a wide berth behind the deck to approach the spa from the opposite direction. Paul shines the light all the way around but sees nothing. "Weird," he says. "I ought to at least see tracks for your cat." He pauses, thinking. "Stay here, OK? I'm going to go up to the spa."

Paul walks to the spa, the blue light arcing back and forth in the moonless darkness. He shines the light on the spa cover, inch by inch. "I see your prints, where you pulled the cover off. That's it. It doesn't help that the thing is dripping with warm, condensed steam." He switches off the light and walks back to me. "No prints. No debris. No footprints in the grass."

"The odds of that happening?"

He shakes his head. "Pretty much zero," he says. "Maybe your cat just got in there on his own, Thomas. It might seem like a stretch, but it's easier to buy than this place being clean."

I nod. "Yeah," I say.

But neither of us is buying it; we both feel the violation in the place in our bones. Something malicious is in the air, something willing and able to commit a violent act. We walk back around the corner to the front of the house, when Paul gets a funny look on his face. "When did the cat disappear again?"

"I'm not sure. Two, maybe three days ago."

He squints a second, then points. "What's that?" he asks.

I follow his gaze. "Control box for the sprinkler system. Runs every Thursday."

"Five days ago." I can see the wheels turning in Paul's mind; he switches the energy light back on and points it on the ground. Our footprints show up clearly under the pale glow. There are no visible prints around the box, however. Paul stands up and switches off the light. He pulls out his keys, reaches across the space between himself and the box, and using a key as a lever, carefully pulls the front face open. "What do you usually have this thing set on?"

"Forty minutes a zone. It runs at night automatically."

Paul smiles grimly. "It's on manual now. Eighty minutes a zone." Using the key, Paul gently closes the box door. "So this guy walks into a fenced-in backyard. Once inside, he can do what he wants without being observed. He picks up the cat, dunks him in, and closes the lid over him." A mental image of Indianapolis struggling to live jerks through my brain, and I wince. "Sorry," Paul says. "I'm just thinking out loud."

I look away. "Yeah."

"The aggregate outside is a potential problem, but he could have walked back on the grass. The grass would leave footprints for a while, but it's been three days. The sprinkler system puts out a nice blanket of water on the entire yard, washing off any debris and making the grass stand up." We stand in silence awhile, the energy light casting an evanescent blue into the darkness. "I can come back tomorrow with a crew. We might find something."

I shake my head. "It's OK. The case is over. So is this, probably."

"You mean Bol."

"Yeah."

"But not the other thing."

"No."

"Look, I gotta be honest with you. This doesn't look like the Nation. Somebody thought this out."

I exhale. "Yeah."

Paul looks at me. "You own a gun?"

"I still have my officer's pistol from the army."

"I'd make sure it's operational."

I stuff my hands in my pockets. "Listen, thanks for coming out here at this hour. Tell Jenny I appreciate it."

"No problem." He reaches in his pocket and pulls out a card. "The clean-up service we use," he says. "They do all the crime scene stuff for us, blood on walls, floors, you know what I mean."

"Yeah."

"Call them, Thomas. You don't want to do this yourself. They'll give you a rate, since you're law enforcement."

"Every cloud has a silver lining."

"Be somewhere else when the service comes, Thomas. It won't be pretty."

CHAPTER SEVENTEEN

RHONDA HARTLETT, Tamra's mother, wears a blue, knee-length dress, high heels, and fake pearls. The dress shows her ample cleavage, and the dress clings to her still-trim body. Danny Trent, the father, wears black pants and a white dress shirt. A pack of Salems is visible in the front pocket. Jason Hodges, not surprisingly, is nowhere to be found. Hartlett and Trent have taken seats behind the prosecution's table in Ginder's courtroom, waiting for Bol's appearance. Rita is at the defense table, and beside her is Dr. al-Hasheed, the Arabic translator. Between them is Moses Bol, the man who confessed to raping and killing Tamra Hartlett. Behind him sits Fiona, who is as still and grim as death.

Every other seat in the courtroom is filled with a silent African. I don't have to turn around to feel them. They are a physical presence in the room as palpable as the furniture. In two minutes, Moses Bol will petition the court to change his plea, and the court will accept. And Moses Bol will surrender the rest of his life to the penal system of Tennessee.

The seconds creep by. Fiona begins weeping openly now. Rita has her hand on Bol's shoulder, steadying him. But it doesn't look to me like Bol needs steadying. Bol stares straight ahead impassively, as though this is something he has to do, and having made his decision, he is unable to be further moved.

The door from the judge's chambers opens, and Ginder, in robes, steps through. He takes his seat, and the bailiff calls for the gallery to rise. Forty Africans stand, silent as graves. Ginder takes his place and says, "Be seated." He opens a sheaf of papers. "Mr. Dennehy and Mr. Stillman. Good to see you today."

"Your Honor," I say.

"Good afternoon, Ms. West."

"Judge."

"I understand Mr. Bol wishes to change his plea."

"Yes, Your Honor."

"Fine. Mr. Bol, please rise." Bol stands, Rita rising with him. "If you'll translate, Dr. al-Hasheed." The translator stands and leans in to speak quietly in Bol's ear. "Mr. Bol, I want you to understand the penalty provided by law for aggravated rape in this state is not less than fifteen nor more than twenty-five years. In the matter of murder in the first degree, the minimum penalty is life with the possibility of parole, and the maximum penalty is death by lethal injection. Do you understand these facts?" Bol listens and nods. "Speak up, son."

"I confess, please."

Ginder shakes his head. "Do you understand the penalties, Mr. Bol?"

"Yes."

"Mr. Bol, you are entitled by law to a trial by jury and also entitled to the legal representation you now have. If you change your plea to guilty, you will forfeit these rights, and there will be no trial. Do you understand this?"

Bol listens. "Yes, please."

"All right, Mr. Bol. Regarding the matter of first-degree rape with aggravating circumstances, how do you now wish to plead?"

"I confess to guilty."

"Let the record show the defendant responds with a guilty plea. Now, Mr. Bol, regarding the matter of first-degree murder with aggravating circumstances, how do you now wish to plead?"

"I confess to guilty."

"I have here the statement that you made yesterday in the presence of both Mr. Dennehy and Ms. West regarding the circumstances of these crimes. In this statement you describe the manner and fashion in which you entered the victim's home, committed rape upon her person, and murdered her. Is the statement you made to Ms. West and Mr. Dennehy correct, Mr. Bol?"

"I confess to guilty."

"Is that a yes, Mr. Bol?"

"Yes."

Ginder nods. "The court accepts your verdict in both instances, Mr. Bol. Take your seat." Bol and Rita sit down. Fiona sits weeping behind them, her head up, tears streaming down her face.

Ginder shuffles through some paperwork. "Since we have guilty pleas, I see no reason why we shouldn't proceed directly to the penalty phase of these proceedings. Mr. Dennehy?"

"Yes, Your Honor."

"I have here a plea agreement between the district attorney and the defendant, which says the state wishes to rescind its initial intention to pursue the death penalty in this case."

"Yes, Judge."

"What is the state's recommendation for sentence regarding the charge of aggravated rape, Mr. Dennehy?"

"The state recommends the maximum penalty of twenty-five years, Your Honor."

"And regarding the murder charge?"

"The state recommends life without possibility of parole."

"I see. Ms. West?"

Rita stands. "Yes, Your Honor."

"No doubt you have some views on this matter."

"Yes, Judge. Mr. Bol, as you know, is a Sudanese refugee. He has endured a great deal of suffering in his life already, through which Mr. Bol has been deeply traumatized. I believe that at the time of the crime, Mr. Bol lacked the cultural context to understand the implications of his actions."

Ginder interrupts. "Are you saying he didn't know raping and killing a woman was wrong, Ms. West?"

"No, Your Honor. But Mr. Bol, since he was eight years old, has himself been the victim of a series of violent crimes. I believe that locking up Mr. Bol for the rest of his life would simply compound one more tragedy in an already tragic life. I believe that given the right counsel and education and opportunity to understand the place where he now resides, he could one day become a productive citizen. I do not wish to diminish the brutality of Mr. Bol's actions. But I ask the court to consider all the factors as it makes its decision."

Ginder nods. "Thank you, Ms. West. I appreciate your

comments." He looks at me. "I understand there are some family members present, Mr. Dennehy?"

"The father and mother, Your Honor."

"All right. If either of them would like to be heard, the court is willing." They both shake their heads. The judge nods. "In that case, I'm ready to pronounce sentence. Mr. Bol, please rise."

Bol comes slowly to his feet. With him rises every African in the room. The Africans stand in their crazy, inappropriate, hand-me-down clothes, faces set forward as sternly as Bol's, as unmovable as granite. Ginder looks up, annoyed. "Just the accused, please," he says. Nobody moves. Ginder looks at the translator. "Is there a language problem? You speak their language, correct?"

The translator stands. "I speak Arabic, Your Honor. The majority of these Africans do, also."

"Please instruct the people in the gallery to have a seat." The translator turns and speaks to the crowd. No one moves. Their expressions are implacable, almost blank. Ginder's expression turns surly. "I'm happy to clear this courtroom, if that's what it takes," he snarls. "Now take your seats."

Not a muscle moves. The bailiff steps off his chair and looks to Ginder for instructions. But the fact is, one bailiff can neither clear forty determined people nor make them sit. It's a standoff, and Ginder is smart enough to realize that it's better to end the proceedings in the next minute rather than risk a confrontation. He turns his face toward Bol. "Mr. Bol, have you anything to say before the court passes sentence on you?"

"I confess to guilty."

"Very well. Dr. al-Hasheed, see that you translate what I say to Mr. Bol precisely." He leans forward. "Mr. Bol, your counsel has made a plea for leniency on your behalf. I am not persuaded. You have committed an unconscionable act of violence upon another human being. It makes no difference to me from where you come or what happened to you before you got here. What matters to me is the extraordinary violence of these crimes, and the fact that you have expressed absolutely no remorse for committing them. Mr. Bol, regarding the charge of aggravated rape, I sentence you to the maximum penalty of twenty-five years. Regarding the charge of first-degree murder, I likewise sentence you to the maximum of life without possibility of parole. These sentences are to be served consecutively. I have no idea what kind of life you will have in prison, Mr. Bol. I don't care, either. What matters to me is that you are kept locked away from the people of this state for the rest of your life. It's my sincere hope that you never take another breath of free air as long as you live. I direct that this sentence is to begin immediately, and order that you surrender here and now. Bailiff, remove the prisoner."

The translator finishes, his own face ashen. Bol stands perfectly straight, eyes ahead, unrepentant. Two officers accompany the bailiff to Bol, who doesn't flinch while they shackle and cuff him. They lead him from behind the lawyer's table, and he calmly walks toward the exit.

A single, plaintive wail comes from the back of the courtroom. The voice is joined by another, and another, until the room vibrates with sound. But this is not a war chant. The Africans are singing. Ginder stares, nonplussed, overmatched in his own courtroom. The exit door opens, and Bol turns briefly, looking back at the Africans. The sound surges upward, the melody deep and full of loss. Bol calls out something in Dinka, his voice strong and clear. The officers push him through the door, and it closes behind him.

The singing goes on, growing even louder. The lost boys of Africa stamp their feet in time to their song, adding thunder to the singing that has broken out in the New Justice Building of Nashville, Tennessee. The song is repeating, and although I can't understand the meaning, one word occurs again and again. *Benywal.*

The sign on the side of the truck is discreet: *Tennessee Environmental Systems.* It could be anything from an air-conditioning service to asbestos removal. What the people loading up their equipment into the truck do, however, is decidedly more grotesque: they clean up a city's horror. On this day, they removed the contents of my spa and disassembled it, so that nothing remains but the concrete surface upon which it sat. The concrete was bleached, and it's as spotless as if the spa never existed. To look at my back deck, whatever freak perpetrated his abominable act against Indy never existed, either. Only the pungent smell of the powerful solvents the company used remains, and one of the workmen tells me that within a few days, that will be gone, too.

The crew started while I was in court, and I stayed gone until they were nearly finished. Now, at 5:30 p.m., I hand over a check to the crew foreman and watch the truck drive away. I turn and head back into the house. *Damn cat. Never would stay inside, where he was safe.* I walk inside, sprawl out on the couch, and think about Paul's words: *This doesn't look like the Nation. Somebody thought this out.* I grimace. *To which he added, "You own a gun?"* After a few minutes I rise, walk to the spare bedroom, and open the closet door. In the left corner is a small personal safe, used as much for its fireproof qualities as theft prevention. I drop to my haunches, spin the combination, and pull open the door. *House title. Some bonds, due God knows when. My father's*

*ID from McConnell Air Force Base. My marriage license to
Bec, for some reason never thrown away. Birth certificate.
Passport. And wrapped in a white cloth, a Rock Island .45-
caliber officer's sidearm.* I reach in, grab the weapon, and
unwrap it; the barrel gleams black, impersonal and lethal. I
close the safe and stand, feeling the heft of the weapon in my
hand. It's heavier than I remember it, but perfectly balanced.
*So it's come to this. Loading a gun in my bedroom is now the
price of doing the state's business.* I reach up to the top shelf
in the closet, feeling around for the box of cartridges I left
there years ago. I pull the box down and let a half-dozen bullets roll out into my hand. I load the weapon, slip on the
safety, and put the gun in my nightstand.

The gun and Indy make what should have been a night of
victory loom bleakly before me. Of course, it's nothing
compared to Moses Bol's. *Night number one of the rest of
his life.* Somewhere along the fifth year, the hopelessness
will be official, and he'll make some kind of peace with it.
*The lost boy of Sudan. Lost in Africa, lost in America, lost
for good in the U.S. penal system.*

I grab a Killian's and flip on the TV, hoping to blank out
on something mindless. A third of the way through something about a girl who finds herself having swapped bodies
with her mother, the phone rings. I glance at the caller ID,
drain the last of the Killian's, and answer. "Miss Towns."

She doesn't speak. For a second, I think she's going to
hang up in my ear. Finally, she says, "So I owe you that
drink. Because of what you said. That it's not personal."

That voice. It's always just a little lower than I expect,
with a trace of rasp. "That's right," I say. "When it's over,
you buy your adversary a drink." I glance at my watch.
"Nine-thirty, Arthur's. OK?"

More silence. Then, "OK."

She hangs up, leaving me holding the phone. *Son of a bitch. Didn't see that coming.* I flip off the TV and look at a second, unopened beer. "Well, Mr. Killian. It appears you'll have to wait."

Charcoal-striped two-button blazer, tan slacks. Off-white shirt, open collar. Ferragamo shoes. Then to the garage, where I don't even think of taking the new truck. I crank the '82, open the garage, and head into town.

Arthur's is located in the old Union Station, a ritzy hotel converted from a closed-down railway terminal. The area around the hotel is still spotty, including some notorious stairs that lead down to the old railroad tracks, some of which are still in use. It's a favorite hangout of prostitutes and homeless types, especially when there are open railroad cars parked there overnight. But Union Station was gutted and renovated from the ground up, and it's the closest thing Nashville has to grand style. The appeal tonight, however, is its strictly enforced dress code: men in jackets, women dressed accordingly. One way or another, I'm going to see Fiona Towns in something other than that day's version of the worker's-uprising shirt.

I drop off the Ford at the valet stand—I give the kid who's parking it a stern look, so he understands this isn't just any truck—and drift into the bar. It's an intimate place, with seating for maybe twenty at tables, another ten or twelve at the bar. The weekday business is light, and I grab a table to wait on Fiona. A well-dressed guy stands at the bar chatting up a blonde. The guy reminds me of Stillman; he's got TV looks, and he's definitely a player. He's working on the blonde, who has definitely received the full Dr. Sarandokos treatment. She stands smiling at the guy, her round butt planted on a bar stool, cleavage emphatically calling for at-

tention. I absently watch the guy soak up her parade of
charms until the waiter comes. I tell him to give me a
minute, that somebody's coming. The guy at the bar is leaning toward the blonde, ready to close, when I see him move
his eyes off her and plant them on the door. He locks there,
five . . . six . . . seven seconds. The blonde, getting curious,
turns to see what the hell is more fascinating than the doctor-
enhanced symmetry in front of him. I turn, too, and see
Fiona standing in the doorway.

Chocolate brown, fitted dress—V-neck—with a jagged
edge along the bottom. Not too expensive but beautifully
proportioned. Slingback shoes, black. Her hair down, curled
seductively behind her ears. The usual multicolored circlets
on her left wrist, a splash of funky color that says there's
something interesting going on here. Small catch-purse, also
black. She walks to the table, and I stand and pull out a chair.
She moves past me, and I get the scent again, that gentle,
earthy musk.

"Dennehy."

"Towns. You look . . ." I stop, because the only correct
word is *fabulous,* and offhand, I don't know if that kind of
thing is going to generate a smile, an irritated roll of the
eyes, or a slap. "Nice," I say.

"Thanks."

She nods and sits, legs crossed demurely. The waiter appears. "Bushmills, please," she says. "Just ice."

I nod. "The same."

She looks around, taking in the bar. "Rita says I should be
grateful to you," she says. "She says you saved Moses's life."

"The drink will do."

"The drink is for the church windows." She exhales
deeply. "Moses wouldn't have confessed unless he was
guilty. So I'm saying it. I was wrong."

"Then he wasn't with you that night. You were willing to lie on the stand for him."

She smiles softly, a mysterious flicker in her eyes. "I'm against the death penalty, Dennehy. And I believed he was innocent." She shakes her head. "I still do, somehow. It doesn't seem possible."

"Moses is a long ways from home," I say. "After everything he's seen . . . maybe violence isn't the stretch for him you think it is."

She looks down at the table. "Maybe." But I can see she doesn't believe it. *Faith dies hard,* I think. *No wonder she's a preacher.*

"Still," I say, "he's alive, and he's going to stay that way."

"Yes. There's that."

The drinks come, and she holds her whiskey between two fingers. "To life," she says, staring me in the eyes.

"To life."

We tip back the glasses. She sets hers down, half empty. "I was still willing to testify, even after what happened. Just so you know. A slim chance is better than none."

"Then I would have had to discredit you and impeach your testimony. I decided to do it at Tennessee Village, rather than on the witness stand. A few hours in county lockup, rather than a few years in prison."

She finishes her drink, the glass resting on her bottom lip. She holds the whiskey in her mouth a moment, swallows, and sets the glass back on the table. *Jesus, she drinks like a man.* "How do you do it?" she asks, suddenly looking up at me.

"Do what?"

"Live by calculations like that. Instead of by your heart."

I laugh quietly. "Thanks."

"I'm serious, Dennehy. I want to know. Because there are times you almost seem human. And then you say something that reminds me you're a guy who can walk into a courtroom and tell the jury that the absolute right thing to do is kill the person sitting fifteen feet to your right."

"Justice. You take a life. You give one back."

"More calculations."

"Can't we agree to disagree?"

"No. Not on this."

I push back from the table. "Look, I came to this job like every young prosecutor, naive as hell and wanting to make a difference. Then reality sets in. My first year in the office I watched Carl Becker prosecute Paul Dennis Reid. And Reid was quite a piece of work, because he loved cops. He'd see one in a restaurant, he'd buy the cop dinner. Christ, he gave money to the benevolence fund. Bunch of cops standing around, he'd ask to have his picture taken with them. You know, kind of goofy, a little too eager."

"So?"

"So then he'd go to a fast-food place and blow the heads off everybody in the place. When he wasn't buying cops lunch, he was the city's worst serial killer."

She turns her head, repulsed. "He was obviously insane."

I shrug. "That's what three expert witnesses for the defense said. The guy actually waived his right to appeal, on the grounds that God told him that the death penalty was His idea, so who was he to disagree with God? Of course, he also said God told him to kill those people, so that's pretty insane, wouldn't you say?"

"It's classic psychosis."

"A month before Paul Dennis Reid was supposed to pay the ultimate price, he said God had changed His mind about the death penalty. He said that God had thought it over, and all of a sudden He had some new information on the subject. So Paul Reid told his lawyer, who was provided free of charge to him, and that lawyer started filing motions like crazy for a stay of execution. And now Paul Reid has a Web site, a letter-writing campaign, and a bunch of people who are making it their life's work to keep him alive." I lean forward. "So now how crazy does he sound?"

She turns away. "Look . . ."

"Paul Dennis Reid killed seven people in cold blood, and the idea that the state of Tennessee is going to be buying that man three squares a day for the rest of his natural life makes the families of his victims sick to their stomachs." She turns away, and a part of me regrets the heat I sent in her direction. "Look, it's complicated, OK? But I get a little tired of this idea that yours is the only position that can be held with a little fervor."

She nods. "OK."

"*OK*. God, I need another drink." *Great. This is going really well.* I wave the waiter over and order two more Bushmills. He brings them, and I pay him in cash. Fiona reaches into her handbag, and I wave her off. "Don't worry about it. I've got nobody to spend money on."

"No family?"

I shrug. "A daughter, but her stepfather could buy this restaurant."

"What does he do for a living?"

I nod toward the blonde at the bar. "He's in the physical enhancement business."

She gives a barely perceptible smile. "You're immune from charms like that?"

"Not my cup of tea."

"And what is your cup of tea, Dennehy?"

"At the moment, I'd say, smart, brave, and beautiful. But maybe that's the Bushmills talking."

"At least you're not naked this time. I tend to disregard the statements of men in that condition."

"That reminds me, Towns. Just how much did you see?"

"Are you putting me on the witness stand, after all?"

"That's right. And you're sworn to tell the truth."

She raises her glass and sips, leaving a drop on her lip. She sucks it gently into her mouth and sets the glass back down. She gazes at me a second, then picks up her purse. "I should get going, Dennehy. It's late."

I watch her a second, knowing I could talk her into staying, but also knowing it's a bad idea. "I'll walk you out." I throw a few bucks on the table and walk Fiona to the front entrance.

"I parked on the street," she says. I give the valet a five to bring around my truck, and tell him I'll be back in a minute. I walk Fiona along the sidewalk to the street, and down a half block to her Volvo. She fishes out her keys, unlocks the door, and stands beside it. "So," she says. "We're even."

I can't help thinking that we'll be even when I've seen her naked in a hot tub, but some things you keep to yourself. "Yeah," I say. "Even."

"Good-bye, Dennehy."

I step toward her, and in one fluid motion, she tips up her head, parts her lips slightly, and kisses me on the mouth. Her lips are soft and warm, and I press mine against hers, not hard, but enough to let her know this is no schoolboy kiss. I press my hands gently down her arms until our hands are locked together. It's a single kiss, but it's enough to wake me up inside, to remind me how substantial this woman is, how her combination of intellect, soulfulness, and beauty are enough to knock me off my balance if I don't watch myself. The kiss lasts ten seconds or so, and we pull apart. I can feel her breathing more deeply, and I know the warm fire inside me is mutual. "It would never work," she says quietly, looking away.

"Yeah. I know." I put my hand under her chin, pull her toward me gently, and kiss her again, more softly. "See you, Towns."

She turns and gets in the Volvo. The motor cranks over laboriously, and she drives slowly away. I turn and see the valet pull up in the Ford at the hotel. I walk over to the truck, put my right foot inside, and notice movement out of the corner of my eye. I stare out into the dim end of the lot and see a figure; there's something familiar about it, but I can't get a clear look. I fire up the truck and drive to the far side of the hotel. The figure is about to slip away into an alley that leads to the old stairs that descend to the maze of railroad tracks and cars beneath the hotel. I can't catch him; he's too far away. But as I swing the truck to turn around, the headlights illuminate a face in the distance. It's Robert, Fiona's addict.

I floor the truck. *Damn it. Am I in this guy's world, or is he in mine?* I reach the stairs in about five seconds, screech to a halt, and bail out. I can hear the metal stairs rattling as Robert jumps off the end of them. I can make out a shadow moving across the first row of tracks, diving between cars. Industrious drug dealers hang out down there all the time to pick up a little business, especially the two or three days after SSI and disability checks get issued. The tracks are where most of the desperate, downtown users make their connections. It's exactly the kind of place where I would feel a lot more comfortable with a gun, only mine is in my nightstand, at home.

I grab the rusty rail of the stairs and head downward, taking steps three at a time. The stairs rumble with every footfall, the sound echoing across the rail yard. *Might as well carry a sign.* The lights from the hotel fade as I descend, and within twenty steps—about halfway to the rail yard—I'm in a deep gloom. The moon is the only light above, and it's half covered by clouds.

I reach the bottom of the steps and peer into the darkness, looking for movement. The first tracks start twenty yards away, then stretch forty more beyond. A half-dozen railcars sit empty, singly and in twos. I hear a metal scrape about thirty yards off at ten o'clock, behind a couple of cars. I take off in a run, trying not to stumble over the minefield of abandoned parts and the jetsam of the homeless. There's a louder clunk, and I see Robert bolt out from behind the cars, heading up the track toward the station, about two hundred yards away.

I shift up a gear, turning it on. I catch up to him in ten seconds or so, just as he dodges behind a railcar. He tries to scramble up into the car, but I grab his ankle and yank him back to the ground. He bangs against the edge of the car as he falls, crumpling to the gravel and gripping his shoulder in pain. He collapses into the gravel dust and stares up at me like a trapped rat.

"Look who it is," he says, crouching down. "It's the great Thomas Dennehy. His Royal Highness, come to see the lost."

I stare down at him. "Who are you?" I demand.

He looks up. "The fucked, Skippy. The fucked."

I reach down for his arm, and he flinches back. "Get up," I say. "I'm not going to hurt you."

"Too late for that, Skippy."

I take his arm and firmly lift him to his feet. He leans back against the railcar, wincing. "What are you doing here?" I demand.

He squints at me, surprised. The glasses, apparently, have

flown off his face in the chase. But in the dark, I can't make out his eyes any clearer than before. "You know what goes on down here," he grumbles.

"You're here on a buy."

"Tell the man what he's won, Skippy."

"Fiona thinks you're clean."

"Some things I keep to myself."

I stare at him, trying to see his face through the gloom and the thick facial hair. "I know you, dammit. Who are you?"

"You ruin my life, and you don't even remember." He shakes his head. "Yes, it's the brilliant prosecutor Mr. Thomas Dennehy. The merciless bastard himself, ladies and gentlemen." He stands, unsteady on his feet. "I use my middle name now. That was my parole officer's idea. He said it might help me find work, since I'm a convicted felon." He looks up at me. "Thanks to you."

I lean forward, staring at him in the dim light. "Jesus. You're . . ."

"The woman was on her back on the floor of the Sunshine Grocery Store. She's been fucking shot, her whole lower back's torn open, right behind the liver. She's dead already, only she doesn't know it. I try to intubate her trachea, but I can't get her mouth open. She's struggling with me, using her energy to fight me instead of stay alive. So I give her twenty ccs succinyl choline to paralyze her, so she won't fight me."

I stare. The facial hair and glasses would have been enough to hide his identity, but they're not the most dramatic change. In the seven years since I last saw Charles Bridges, he has become a wrecked human being. Counting years, he should be in his early thirties by now, but drugs, prison, and a life on the street have aged him to look at least fifteen years older. "You put the tube in her esophagus, not her trachea. That's what killed her."

"Do you even know how often that happens in hospitals?" he snarls. "Every damn *day.* And I'm supposed to get it right in the middle of a crime scene? It was bullshit."

"She couldn't breathe. You were supposed to listen to her ventilate."

"She was fat, dammit," he growls. "I couldn't hear shit in there. People running all over the place, I'm trying to hear her breathe through fifty pounds of tissue. Impossible."

"She was fibrillating, and you weren't even watching. You were high on methamphetamine."

"Half the docs in this city are on something. They pay their malpractice bill and have another martini." He steps toward me menacingly. "Do you know what you did? *You stole my life.*"

"You went to work impaired, and you fucked up. A mistake like that . . ." I grind to a halt. "A mistake like that can't be tolerated."

His face twists in hatred. "That's right. It's all coming back now, isn't it? *A mistake like that can't be tolerated.* Your last words to the jury. And they sent me away."

"You deserved what you got."

Bridges begins pacing back and forth, lecturing me. The stench off him is palpable. "So I guess you'll be checking into Brushy for your five years too, asshole. Because the only difference between you and me is that you kill for the state."

"This is how the system works."

"*Fuck* the system. You sent the wrong man to die, and you know it. You did it for the state, so you get to walk. I can't help that. But one thing I can do, and that's make sure everybody on this fucking planet knows that the great Thomas Dennehy is no better than me."

"You're the source behind the whole thing with Hale."

"That's not a crime. It's a fucking public service. Check the dates, Dennehy. I was in Brushy with Hale. He told me what happened. I found out Fiona was the one to tell, and I told. She got Buchanan involved, and now your ass is about to be served."

"Fiona. She's why you hang out around the church."

"Just until your career is dead and buried. Not that I can't use the free food." He smirks and turns away again, heading toward the grim darkness near the empty station.

"Where do you think you're going?"

"Arrest me," he says, over his back. "I haven't done anything against the law, and I got nothing left to lose. Unlike you."

I watch him recede into the blackness under the train station. *Charles Bridges. Back from the dead for his taste of revenge.*

CHAPTER EIGHTEEN

COFFEE AND ZOLOFT, but no run. There are two days left before we get the ballistics report back on the Browning. I intend to use the time discovering every rat hole Charles Bridges has stuck his nose into since the day he walked out of Brushy Mountain. I pull on blue jeans and a shirt and drive into town, but not toward 222 West. Instead, I go to the state parole offices, down at the New Justice Building. I park out back and take the elevator to the fourth floor. I step into the offices, which are a revolving door for the city's human flotsam. Everything about the place is depressing, from the worn, industrial furnishings to the line of released convicts waiting for appointments with their parole officer. I step up to the front desk, identify myself, and ask for the officer assigned to Bridges. The receptionist asks for his Social Security number, which I don't have.

"Bridges. Charles Robert Bridges. There's probably only one."

She gives me a pained expression, searches on her computer, and looks up. "Brushy?"

"That's right."

"You want Ronnie Tate."

"Can I see him?" She picks up a phone in slow motion and punches a button. "Mr. Tate? Someone here to see you. No, not one of those. From the DA. Uh-huh." She points down a hall. "You can go on back."

Charles Bridges's parole officer is in his mid-thirties, with the indifferent dress of a GS8-grade government employee. Ronnie Tate looks like a community college professor: the khakis are worn, the shirt is not entirely tucked, the hair, longish, is indifferently styled. Judging by the smell hanging around his clothes, he's also a heavy smoker. His office in the New Justice Building is less than a year old, but it already seems as depressing and aged as the forty-year-old one it replaced.

"Bridges?" he says. "His resentment is poetic, man. It's like the haiku of pissed-off-ness. It's fairly entertaining, actually."

"Does he ever mention a woman named Fiona Towns?"

"Sure. She's his contact number."

"How would you describe their relationship?"

"Don't know. Never talks about her, and I've never called."

"You think he's dangerous?"

Tate shrugs. "I'm not a trained psychologist," he says. "I wouldn't want to say."

"Off the record. Just give me your best shot."

"Bridges hates jail, man. Unless that changes, I don't see him doing anything that sends him back." He pauses. "On the other hand, life after jail hasn't been a picnic, either."

"What's happened?"

"Your basic post-incarceration spiral. Can't find work because nobody will hire him. Also, he's an asshole. He imagines himself something of a doctor, so he won't do anything menial." He smiles. "One of my predecessors tried to get him a job as an orderly in a hospital. Bridges didn't appreciate that."

"When was this?"

"Pretty soon after Bridges got out of the joint. It was the guy before me."

"You remember the guy's name?"

He shakes his head. "It's been a couple of years."

"So you aren't aware of Bridges's long-term history."

"No, but I've got the files. It's all pretty straightforward, at least on paper. Like I say, he's reliable, never breaks the rules. With the overcrowding, you have to screw up pretty bad. But Bridges is a very good boy. He doesn't risk anything."

"Does he ever leave you notes?"

"Notes?"

"On cars. Or at your house."

He shakes his head. "I wish I had more for ya, but I got thirty-nine guys on my plate right now. If somebody doesn't make noise, he's fine by me."

"You know he's going by Robert now?"

He nods. "That was my idea. I thought it might help him find work, but it didn't."

"You mind looking through the file for the officer who worked with him before you?"

Tate walks to a filing cabinet and pulls out the center drawer. He fingers his way through several files and pulls out Bridges's. "Yeah, it's Kavner. Abe Kavner."

"What happened to him?"

"Off the radar. Retired, I think."

"You got an address?"

"Nope." He reaches under his desk, pulls out a phone book, and hands it to me. "Be my guest."

I hand him my card. "Don't tell Bridges we talked."

"You got it."

Back in the Ford, I call information and ask for Abraham Kavner. There's no such number, but there's a Mrs. A. Kavner out in Rayon City, a lower-middle-class neighborhood on the outskirts of the city. I drive out north on I-65 to Old Hickory, head west, and soon see the huge DuPont chemical factory looming on my left. The houses are working-class, inexpensive squares put up for workers at the plant. I take Mrs. Kavner's street and park in front of her house. It's modest but well kept, with a green yard and impatiens and begonias planted around the mailbox. I walk up the entry to the porch; a trowel sticks out of a bucket half filled with topsoil that sits by the door. The entrance is barred by a substantial, black, cast-iron storm door. I ring the doorbell, and a dark-haired woman in her sixties opens the inner door, leaving the storm door locked. The living room behind is well lit, and more flowers are visible in pots and hanging from the ceiling. "Can I help you?"

"Mrs. Kavner?"

"That's right."

I show her my Justice Department ID. "Thomas Dennehy. I'm with the DA's office. I was wondering if your husband was around."

She looks at me blankly a moment. "Abe's not here."

"Can you tell me where I could locate him? It's important."

She shakes her head. "You don't know?"

"No."

"My husband is dead."

Dread begins crawling up my spine. "I'm terribly sorry." She nods and begins to shut the door. "Mrs. Kavner? Could you tell me how he died?"

She stops the door half-shut. "He was murdered. He was out walking. It was after dark."

"Around here?"

"The park, over by Dupont. They took his wallet."

"They?"

"Whoever it was. The police never found out. They think maybe it was a junkie."

"I'm really very sorry."

She looks at me. "He'd been with the county for thirty-six years. Abe had just bought an RV. We were going to go out West."

I nod. "I'm sorry to have bothered you." The door closes, and I'm standing alone on her porch. Tate's words come back to me: *One of my predecessors tried to get him a job as an orderly in a hospital. Bridges didn't appreciate that.*

CHAPTER NINETEEN

I HEAD TO PAUL LANDMEYER'S office, hoping to get a few minutes of his time to go over Abe Kavner's autopsy report. Paul comes out of his office and meets me in the lobby with a worried expression. *Something's happened.* "Talk to me," I say quietly.

"I just got off the phone with Rayburn," Paul answers. "Buchanan's people won't be stalled any longer. We're going to have to do the ballistics test on the shotgun today." He glances back into the restricted area. "It's just as well. His guys have been sitting on their hands so long they're becoming a problem."

I nod. "When will we have results?"

"I'll get a preliminary tonight. If it goes against us, they won't ask for a second test to confirm, obviously. But our people are good. The results won't change." He looks at me. "What are you doing here?"

"I need fifteen minutes."

Paul grimaces. "It's not a good time."

"I know that. I need it anyway."

Paul regards me a second, then nods. "Okay. Fifteen minutes. What are we looking at?"

"An autopsy report. The name is Abe Kavner. He was murdered two years ago in Old Hickory."

Paul starts toward the door leading to the inner offices, then stops and turns back to me. "Kavner?"

"Yeah."

"I remember that one. I didn't work it, but it got talked about. Everybody said the guy was really unlucky."

"Unlucky? He got murdered."

"Yeah. It was *how* that got people's attention." He starts back toward the doorway. "Follow me."

Paul drops me off at his office and returns shortly thereafter with a large file. He spreads the papers onto his desk and runs his thumb down the documents, scanning for salient information. He pulls out some photographs and maneuvers his movable desk light to shine light directly on them. "Yeah," he says. "This is it." He pulls out a gruesome autopsy photograph that shows Kavner's body lying on its stomach. The skin is purple-pale, and layers of flesh have been pulled back for examination, revealing the organs beneath. "The victim died of cardiac arrest stemming from a knife wound from behind that punctured the heart. But since the ribs are only about a half-inch apart, the blade had to come in horizontally, sliding exactly between them. That was where he was unlucky. If the knife had been positioned vertically—blade up, instead of sideways—it would have hit bone and he would have had a superficial wound." He flips to another photograph. "The blade punctured the dermis and the subcutaneous tissues, here. It then went through the parietal and visceral pleuras and entered the lung, here."

"I thought you said he died of a puncture of the heart."

"The knife had to go through the lung first. The blade penetrates the alveoli, severs these blood vessels, then enters the left ventricle of the heart, here." He looks up. "That was another interesting thing."

"How so?"

"The left ventricle is the high-pressure side of the heart. You die quicker if you get it on that side." He shakes his head. "Help got there pretty quick, but it was too late. If the wound had been on the right, he might have made it."

"Unlucky."

He nods. "First thing that happened, he got a collapsed lung, and he started coughing up blood." He pulls another picture under the light. "See? Blood on the chin, on the clothing in front. Meanwhile, his heart's bleeding into the pericardial sac, creating pressure, so it can't function properly. He feels more and more pressure, like somebody's sitting on him. He's freaking out now, becoming aware that he's going to die. His heart rate starts rising to compensate for the pressure, up to maybe two hundred before the end. A guy that age, he can't last long at that speed. He fibrillates, and a couple of minutes later, the brain dies. His heart follows soon after." He closes the file. "It would take a hell of a knife, I will say that."

"How long?"

He shrugs. "At least nine inches, maybe more. But slender, more like a filleting knife than the typical weapon." He looks down at the picture. "We all talked about it. The wound was so perfectly placed, it's almost like whoever did this had some kind of medical training."

"He did."

Paul looks up. "You got something on this?"

I'm already moving for the door. "Thanks, Paul."

* * *

David Rayburn looks like something foul just climbed out of a half-eaten sandwich. "What did you say?"

"Charles Bridges, the EMT from the Sunshine Grocery murders. The guy we went after for negligent homicide, remember?"

"Of course I remember."

"He's the source on Kwame Jamal Hale."

"How the hell did you find that out?"

"Bridges was at Brushy at the same time as Hale. He says Hale told him what really happened at the Sunshine Grocery."

"He says?"

"I spoke to him. I've been speaking to him, actually, only I didn't know it. The point is, he goes to Towns, who is the highest-profile anti-death-penalty activist in the city. He spills his story, Towns contacts Buchanan, and the rest is history."

"Shit, Thomas. Are you saying this is all an attempt to even the score against you?"

"Yeah, well, evening the score is a big deal to Bridges. The word is, his first parole officer insulted him right before he retired. He was found murdered shortly afterward."

Rayburn stares. "Do we have enough to pick him up?"

"Not even close. But at least we can call Homicide, reopen the murder, and start building a case."

Rayburn's expression darkens. "Listen, if you're right about this guy Bridges killing his parole officer, you need to watch your ass. I mean, he killed a guy just for pissing him off. He's had seven years to think about how he feels about you."

"Yeah. I know."

Rayburn nods. "I'm having him picked up, Thomas. We need this guy off the streets."

"We haven't got enough to make it stick, David."

"I don't care. If we have to let him go later, we'll do it. But I want him out of commission until this thing is finished."

I catch Josh Ritchie walking down the hall on the way back to my office. I pull him into a small conference room. "Anything new?" I ask.

He shakes his head. "It's quiet," he says. "Bol's confession took the air out of a lot of sails."

"Good, then you're free. I want you to find out everything you can about Charles Robert Bridges."

"Who's that?"

"About thirty-four years old, looks older. Dark hair, heavy beard and moustache. He goes by Robert."

"And?"

"He's a guy the cops are looking for but won't be able to find."

"Then how am I going to do it?"

"You don't have to find him. I just want you to dig up information. He's currently on the streets and spends a lot of time at the Downtown Presbyterian Church. When he's not there, he's buying meth down on the tracks underneath Union Station."

Josh frowns. "Dude, I don't go down there."

"Just ask around the usuals. Find out who his dealer is. Find out where he sleeps. Anything."

Josh nods. "What's he done?"

Brought down the entire DA's office? Eliminated the death penalty in the state of Tennessee, and possibly in the whole country? Killed a parole officer in cold blood? In that moment, I realize how seriously I have underestimated Charles Robert Bridges. "Just do it, Josh. And be careful."

My office table is covered with the paperwork of death. It's 4:30 now, and I've spent the last few hours poring over the negligent homicide case of Charles Bridges. What I want to know, above all else, is this: what is the depth of his anger, and what are his skills to execute revenge?

I start over once more through Bridge's history, provided from the ETNAC military database for the original trial: Bridges took the ASVAB armed services aptitude test to enter the army and scored off the charts for the medical corps. So high, in fact, that he was given a separate IQ test— probably by the National Security Agency, although the file doesn't say—and scored 151. He was probably due to head into intelligence work, but something went off the rails, because his psych profile got flagged. Bridges grudgingly accepted an offer for the medic program and entered the service via the processing station at Nashville. Then came the standard nine weeks of basic training, during which he incurred two negative notations: a late to report, and an incidence of wearing the wrong uniform for an occasion. He survived—barely—and went through the sixteen-week crash medic training. Academically he was brilliant, scoring in the 99 percent range.

Bridges's monthly counseling reports after graduation started poor and went downhill, including a drunken fistfight on leave that resulted in another man's broken jaw. The comments in his fourth month were typical: "Specialist Bridges interacts poorly with other personnel. He is not particularly well liked and has distinguished himself primarily by his intelligence, arrogance, and condescension." Predictably, there were two failure to salutes, and a few months later, he got an Article 15 for being thirty minutes late for staff duty. He was docked half a month's pay and reduced in rank from E4 specialist to E3. But the end came when he was caught with his hand in the controlled-substances cookie jar. The last line of his file is a masterpiece of classic army understatement: "Specialist Bridges is involuntarily separated from the service, due to failure to adapt to a military lifestyle."

Back in Nashville, Bridges concealed his army history and enrolled in the Nashville Technical College EMT program. He sailed through—having already completed the army medic program—and quickly landed a job with a local company doing contract emergency response work for the county. Six weeks into the job, he and a partner answered a call to the Sunshine Grocery in east Nashville. The partner tried unsuccessfully to resuscitate the first victim, while Bridges made a mess of an esophageal intubation on Lucinda Williams. The cops on the scene, recognizing Bridges was impaired, arrested him on the spot. When he tested positive for a truckload of methamphetamine, his fate was sealed.

So Bridges sits in Brushy Mountain for a few years, figuring out how to pay me back. Time enough for his hate to burn bright. I glance up at the clock; it's getting close to five, which means the ballistics team has probably already fired the Browning shotgun. *We'll know something soon.* I watch the second hand on the clock tick off seconds for as long as I can stand it. I snap shut the file and head for the door.

I walk back to Rayburn's office, thinking that it's important to be together when we hear the news. *Family. We sink or swim together.* Dolores nods me through, and I head inside. Halfway through the doorway, I pull up. Carl is standing by the window, his hands stuffed into his pockets. "What are you doing here?" I ask.

He shrugs. "I'm damned if I let you guys face this music alone," he says. "Paul called me earlier today, right after you left his office. He thought I'd want to know things were going down today."

"It was a hell of a gesture, you coming," Rayburn says, coming around from behind his desk. "Pure class." He walks to me and shakes my hand. "We should hear anytime, Thomas. They've already fired the gun."

"Paul called?"

Rayburn nods. "He's our eyes and ears. He said stay by the phone." Rayburn hands me a fax. "Buchanan is pretty confident. He's already called a press conference for two p.m. tomorrow afternoon, over at the Regal Maxwell House."

We look at each other in silence. This is not good news. Buchanan, if nothing else, would never do anything to embarrass himself. I can see it in Rayburn's eyes: he goes into damage control as the last bit of hope drains away.

"So we hold our own press conference," Carl says sternly. "Except we do it earlier, in the morning. If we're going to crash and burn, at least we can drive the car."

Rayburn nods. "Good. Either way, we announce it, not him. We turn his conference into an anti-climax." He walks over to his desk. "Look, we've got some time to kill. I say we draft two statements, one for each way it goes." He picks up the phone. "Dolores? Hold all my calls, unless it's Paul. And bring in some coffee, will you? We're gonna be busy a while."

Over the next hour, Rayburn, Carl, and I pound out the statements. The one where we win takes little time; we settle on a magnanimous, mostly humble tone, and keep it simple.

The one where we lose—where the ballistics match— quickly reveals itself to be a grind the equal of any closing argument I've ever prepared. It's obvious we could spend hours parsing words and sliding through excuses. After half an hour, Rayburn's had enough. "We tell them this is the system," he says, walking to his window. "If people don't like it, there are ways to change it. We regret Owens's death. Just like we regret the two victims at the Sunshine Grocery, and the other three hundred and fifty people who got murdered in this city in the last year."

Carl nods. "Well done, David."

Rayburn looks at his watch. "Any minute, now."

Nobody speaks when the phone finally rings. David walks calmly to his desk, picks up the phone, and listens. He asks no questions, but when he looks up at us, we know the worst has happened. Rayburn hangs up the phone and says, "It's a match. Paul says nothing's going to change. We're done."

So. This is how it ends. I'm in the old truck, and the blocks pass under its tires as I drive out of downtown. My career, it seems obvious, is over. The rest of my life—the things other than work that make me who I am—suddenly seem frighteningly inconsequential. I realize that if I add everything together other than work in my life, there's precious little other than Jazz. *And she's old enough now to understand some things. She's old enough to figure out her father's done something terrible. She'll watch the TV and see the news clips.*

I wrench the truck suddenly down Union, cutting into the alley behind the DPC. Towns's Volvo sits with a couple of other cars in the little lot. I pull into a spot, scanning for Bridges, but he's nowhere to be seen.

I go up the steps and down the poorly lit hall, to the pastor's study at the end. I try the door; it swings open, but the study is empty. I jog back toward the sanctuary and push open the large, wooden door. Above me are the stark, transparent windows that replace the three stained-glass ones that were lost in the explosion. I don't see anyone in the sanctuary at first, but as I turn to go, I see a shadowed figure three-quarters of the way in the back. "Who's there?" I call out. Nothing. I walk down the center aisle, and as I approach, the figure raises her head. It's Fiona.

She looks at me a moment, then stares back down into her hands. "I went to see Moses this morning," she says quietly. "They're moving him this afternoon to Brushy Mountain."

I slip into the pew beside her. She looks worn and washed out. "Everybody goes there first. It's the clearinghouse."

"It was horrible seeing him behind bars, in the orange uniform." She stares up at the sacristy in the front of the church. "I was here praying for his strength and his safety. For his spirit to somehow survive. It would take a miracle." She looks over at me. "The rest of his life. It's unthinkable."

"So was the crime."

She looks back down. "Why are you here, Thomas?"

"I know about Charles Bridges. The man you call Robert."

"So you found out. Are you here to berate me? Or to accuse me of dishonesty?"

"I'm here to warn you. You think Charles Bridges brought Hale to you. You're wrong."

Finally, she looks up. "I don't understand. Of course he brought Hale to me."

I shake my head. "He was bringing you to me, Fiona. He's using you. You, Buchanan, and the whole anti-death-penalty movement. He's hiding behind you to get what he really wants."

"And what does he want, Thomas?"

"To hurt me, because I sent him to jail. Bridges was the EMT at the Sunshine Grocery . . ."

"I know," she says, her voice barely audible.

I stare, momentarily stunned. "You know?"

"Charles Bridges is a wreck of a human being, drifting on his own hate. But he paid his debt to society and came here for refuge. I offered it to him." She turns toward me, her eyes like steel. "Maybe you're right about him using me. But he's also telling the truth. His story checks out, Thomas. And if that means nobody else will be killed by the state in a prison again, then I'm happy to be used."

"The evil inside Bridges isn't something you can harness for your own purposes, Fiona. He's already murdered another person."

She looks up, doubt in her eyes. "Murdered?"

"Just ask yourself one question, Fiona. Didn't you ever stop and wonder why Bridges only came forward now? He's been out of jail for more than two years."

"He said he was working up his courage."

"He was waiting for Owens to be executed. He could have saved his life by coming forward earlier, but he willingly sacrificed Owens on the altar of his hatred for me." I stand. "You want to believe that even the worst of us can be redeemed. But Charles Bridges is a machine bent on revenge, and he'll kill anyone who gets in his way."

I don't know if it will make any difference that I warned Fiona about Bridges. I assume she's out of my life now, and maybe, since Bridges made his point, I'm out of his, too. Rayburn will reopen the Abe Kavner murder, and maybe something will turn out with that. But as I get back in the Ford, I feel in my gut that Bridges has done his homework too well. I see him in my mind, slipping the blade precisely between Kavner's ribs, the knife perfectly positioned to puncture the lung and heart of the victim. Kavner probably never had a chance to turn around and see his assailant. I step into the truck and fire it up; it starts on the first turn, settling into its familiar, masculine *thrum*. I pull out into traffic and make my way to I-65 for the drive south to Franklin.

Five miles out of downtown, I pull out to pass a slower car. The engine seems a little weak; I can feel a misfire. I have to gun it to merge back into traffic, but the truck responds lazily. The engine straightens out again for a while, and I think it might just be some bad gasoline. A couple of exits from my house, however, the truck begins losing power. It crosses my mind I might not make it home. *Shit.* I'm surrounded by rush-hour traffic, and pulling across four lanes of traffic without power would be dangerous. *Dammit. What is this?* I watch my mirrors, calculating my move, the truck slowing all the time. I push my way across traffic into the right lane, the truck struggling to run thirty-five miles per hour. At the Franklin exit, I pick up the smell of something burning. I consider shutting off the ignition, but I'm less than two miles from my house, and I want to get the truck home. I limp on, but as I turn on my street a tongue of flame shoots out from underneath the hood. *Fuck this.* I switch off the ignition, shove in the clutch, and let the car glide downhill. The flames grow under the hood, and smoke starts pouring into the interior. It's risky staying with the truck, but my only chance to get a fire extinguisher on it is to get home. I roll into the driveway, slam the brakes, and hit the garage door opener. The engine compartment is burning fiercely now, flames pouring around the hood opening. I run into the house, grab the CO_2 extinguisher from under the sink—it's pitifully small for the job, I instantly realize—and run back to the driveway. There's a loud whoosh of air, and the Ford is engulfed in flames. The metal creaks and buzzes as it contracts, and sparks fly from the interior and engine compartment. I empty the extinguisher, but it's too little too late. The truck is a total loss. Eventually, even the tires ignite and melt onto the driveway, sending an acrid, black smoke into the sky.

When the engine compartment cools enough, I wrench open the hood and see a blackened heap: everything that isn't metal has melted into a sickening, foul-smelling mess. I start working my way through it, looking for a reason for the fire. Wearing heavy gloves to protect myself from the melted chemicals, I spend two hours going through every fitting and component. Eventually, I pull up half of a steel fuel line; it's been severed. There's residue visible at the cut, and though I can't be sure, it looks like epoxy. Finally, a simple straight pin has been driven into a spark plug wire, which would cause it to arc across to the engine block. I lower the hood and stare at the truck's remains. *I started the truck, and the gasoline began dissolving the epoxy. Fifteen miles later the epoxy gave out, and the fuel began spraying all over the engine compartment. The truck is running badly, but the fire starts when the pin arcs a spark across the fuel vapor, and the truck goes up in flames. Tools required: small hacksaw, straight pin, tube of epoxy. Total time: less than five minutes.*

I am more angry than I can ever remember. More angry than I was over what happened to Indy; angrier, even, than when I first heard Rebecca say the name Michael Sarandokos. I have no doubt that Bridges is behind what happened, and I realize that he isn't going to be satisfied merely with destroying my reputation as a lawyer. He wants to destroy everything that matters to me, and he has now proven he knows enough about me that he knows my points of maximum pain. Bridges and I are not finished, which means I have to call Bec.

Bec answers my call warily. "What's going on, Thomas? It's getting late."

"Listen, Bec, I need you to keep Jazz this weekend."

"Thomas, we've got . . ."

"She can't stay here," I say, and that's all that's required. She *knows*.

"Are you OK? I thought the big case was over."

"Yeah. It's just . . . things need to settle down a little bit."

Her voice turns petulant. "Things are never going to settle down, Thomas. Not as long as you take those kinds of cases."

"Look, Michael will love it. It's more time for him to take my place."

She ignores the jab. "She's eleven, Thomas. She's getting too old to lie to. What am I supposed to tell her?"

"I don't know, Bec. I'm out of town. Something." I close my eyes. I can't tell her more, not without making things worse. "Listen, Bec, I've got to run."

"It sounds like it."

"I'll make it up to her."

"Good-bye, Thomas."

I hang up and look out at my deck. I've prosecuted more than a hundred defendants. Ninety-eight were convicted or took pleas. I have received more than a dozen death threats, mostly mailed from prison, a few left on my phone machine, two in person while the defendant was dragged from court. But it has taken a pissant army dropout with delusions of grandeur to finally get inside my life.

It's after eleven before the wrecker arrives. The driver

steps out of the truck and stares. "Shit, man, when you said, 'burned,' I didn't know you meant *burned.*"

"Just get it out, please."

"You got it, boss." The driver hooks up chains to the underside of what's left of the truck and prepares to pull it up onto the inclined ramp of his wrecker. "This is probably gonna leave some marks on your driveway, boss," he says.

"Get it out."

He yanks down the lever, and the chains start grinding forward. The truck rolls uncertainly on its molten tires, scraping its rear bumper as it begins its ascent onto the wrecker. Once it's up, the driver secures it to the flatbed for the trip to the scrapyard. "I'm all set," he says, nodding. "Appreciate the business." The wrecker's diesel engine clatters to life. The driver pulls out, and I watch the remains of my father's truck disappear into the night.

CHAPTER TWENTY

THAT NIGHT, I DON'T SLEEP WELL. I wake in the night several times, the last time in a dream about Rebecca. We are back in Florida, on the beach where we honeymooned. But she's too far out in the surf and can't get back to the beach. She's calling to me, but my feet won't move. It's the classic, my limbs like lead, shoes rooted to the ground. The surf carries her out to sea, and the last thing I see is her hands flailing wildly on a sheet of foam before she disappears. Then I wake up, heart pounding.

I rise, make coffee, and wash down the day's Zoloft. *The thing they don't tell you is that you need to be a robot to do this damn job.* For a while, I don't move. I just stand there, thinking that today is going to be my last day as a prosecutor, and I wonder once again what I'll do with the rest of my life. There aren't any easy answers, and they all lead through coming to terms with the fact that I sent the wrong man to the death chamber.

I drive into town like I'm going to a funeral, which is an

apt analogy. It is the funeral for the Davidson County DA's office, and for the careers of many fine men and women who, rightly or wrongly, will have the stink of this debacle attached to them for years to come. I give the office until closing time before it shreds apart in a blaze of recriminations and regrets. And at the center, I will stand and take my medicine. Halfway to town I've almost completed my resignation letter in my mind. By the time I walk into David Rayburn's office, I have determined to personally apologize to every jury member and to the family members of Wilson Owens. This will be a grinding, humiliating experience, but if it can take a measure of guilt off the jurors and remove an ounce of pain from Owens's family, I have no choice.

I park and take the elevator up to Rayburn's office alone. When I get there, Dolores has, for the first time in my memory, an absolutely defeated expression on her face. She nods me in, and I walk through without speaking. When I open the door, I see Carl and the DA, and also, surprisingly, Paul Landmeyer. Paul is in the middle of a sentence when I come in, and Rayburn waves for silence. "Keep going, Paul. So you were up all night."

Paul nods. "Right. Buchanan's people went home after we got the result. They were good, by the way. Very professional."

Rayburn nods. "Go on."

"Well, like I said, there's no doubt about the gun being the one used in the murders. But I didn't want to leave anything on the table, so I stayed around, trying to break things down another level."

"Good man," Carl says quietly.

"The barrel was wiped clean, so there wasn't any human evidence there. And the ballistics were conclusive. What's left?"

"No fucking idea," Rayburn says.

"The gunstock," Paul says. Everybody's always focused on the barrel, which is understandable. But I got to thinking. You bury wood seven years, it gets porous. The one on the Browning was so soft I could just pick off splinters. So about ten o'clock last night I take a few off and examine them under a polarized light microscope. And what do you think I find?"

"What?" Rayburn demands.

"Organochloride crystals."

"For God's sake, Paul, speak English."

"It's pesticide," Paul says. "At some point the gun was exposed to the chemical, and it dried, leaving the crystals behind. At first, I didn't think much about it. I mean, the gun's been buried in the ground. There are residual pesticides in a lot of the farmland around here, and if you want to test hard enough, you can come up with a few parts per million most anywhere."

"Cut to the chase, Paul," Carl says. "What are you driving at?"

"Well, about five this morning, it hit me. That gun was found at a state park. The ground there has been fallow since the fifties."

Carl nods. "Makes sense."

"I tested the ground samples we took from around the gun for the same chemical. It wasn't there. It's *only* in the gunstock."

"Which means it couldn't have been absorbed from the ground around it," I say.

Paul nods. "There's no doubt that gun was used to commit those murders. But there's also no doubt that it was buried somewhere else first. It was moved to the park later."

"Owens lived in Sumner County," I say. "That's one of the biggest tobacco-producing areas in the state."

"There you go, then," Paul says. "He probably buried the gun a few miles from his house, like most criminals would do. Somebody moved it to Montgomery Bell to give Kwame Jamal Hale's story credibility." He looks at Rayburn. "He's lying, David."

Rayburn looks hopeful, but cautious. "Is this enough to stick, Paul? Pesticide in the gunstock?"

"The chemicals were deep in the wood. It's not incidental contact. It would have taken a long time to absorb to that extent. Years, probably. I've wracked my brain, but I honestly can't think of any other explanation than that the gun was buried somewhere for a long time, and only recently moved to where it was found. And if that's true, Hale's story falls apart."

Rayburn sits thinking a moment, like he's almost afraid to believe what he's hearing, then exclaims, "Holy Jesus, Paul, you saved our asses!"

"You might want to check around Owens's residence at the time. See if he lived near an agricultural area. Knowing Sumner County, it's pretty likely."

"Look, do Buchanan's guys know about this?" I ask.

Paul grins. "They were asleep in their hotel rooms, dreaming about their consulting fees."

I look up at Rayburn. "Better and better."

Paul lays a sheet of paper down on the DA's desk. "I've put together a page of details so you can go over them before your press conference. I'll be there to make a statement too, if you want."

Rayburn collapses back in his chair. "God damn," he says, looking at us. "God damn."

Carl reaches over to me and shakes my hand. "You OK now?"

I'm strangely numb. It's like we just missed a horrible car wreck by an inch, and the adrenaline is still coursing through our bodies. "I don't know. I still can't believe it."

Carl looks at Rayburn. "What do you say we put our heads together and write up a new statement?"

Rayburn nods. "You know something, gentlemen?" he says. "When this is all over, I'm going to have Professor Philip Buchanan's ass."

Having so recently come within a gnat's ass of losing nearly everything important to him—position, career, purpose—and, equally important, because he despises Philip Buchanan so utterly—David Rayburn is determined to orchestrate the professor's reversal of fortune down to the smallest details. Written statements, featuring Paul's findings about the pesticide, will not be made available before the DA appears before the cameras. Popping the professor's bubble is something Rayburn reserves for himself, not a curious reporter flipping through the written materials before the press conference begins. The statement will be brief, and there will be only ten minutes of questions. The plan is to attack, destroy, and leave as quickly as we came. "Then let Buchanan have his damn press conference," Rayburn says. "That ought to be fun."

We drive together over to the New Justice Building at 10:45. We carry with us one hundred copies of a tidied-up version of Paul's findings, including graphics of the actual crystals under a polarized light microscope, and the count spectrum from his X-ray diffractometer. The Justice Building is ringed by news vans, including Court TV, Fox, CNN, and all the local affiliates. From here they'll travel the five miles to Buchanan's conference at the Maxwell House. We park underground, come up the back side, and move together down a private hallway that leads to the press room. Rayburn walks like Patton arriving in Sicily, ready to kick ass. We stop just outside the side entry to the front of the press room, watching the crowd cram in on a closed-circuit monitor.

It's standing room only for what the press assumes will be the worst day in the history of Tennessee law enforcement. All sixty chairs in the press room are filled, and another twenty or so people are standing around the edge of the room, jostling for position. "You guys hear Wilson Owens's mother has already filed a civil suit against us?" Rayburn asks, watching the monitor. "She's got Ronnie Durban representing her." Durban is high-profile, high-dollar, and has a high win rate. For a fuckup like the one we're accused of, it's not out of the question he would be looking at eight figures. Rayburn smiles. "The next few minutes are really gonna piss him and his accountant off."

"Just as well," Carl says. "He would have bankrupted this county."

"I don't think that would have bothered him much," I say. "Durban's more of a me-and-mine kind of guy." We fall silent, waiting for the last minute to tick away.

At the stroke of 11:00, Rayburn puts his hand on the door. "Gentlemen?"

"Absolutely," Carl says.

The DA pushes open the door, and the three of us walk into a barrage of camera flashes. Rayburn moves steadily to the podium, his expression serious but calm. The rest of us take places behind him. He clears his throat. "I have a brief statement, and then I'll introduce you to Paul Landmeyer, the county's chief forensics officer. We will take a few minutes of questions, and there will be a written statement available as you leave."

Rayburn's voice is sober, clear, and unrepentant. "Seven years ago, two innocent citizens of our city were brutally gunned down in an east Nashville grocery store. These crimes, which came to be known as the Sunshine Grocery murders, achieved a high degree of notoriety in our community. Wilson Owens, a career criminal with seven prior convictions, was arrested, tried, and found guilty by a jury of his peers for these murders. These convictions were twice upheld on appeal. Having exhausted his due process, Mr. Owens was executed at Brushy Mountain Prison on May 18, 2003." He pauses. "Two weeks ago, my office was contacted by Professor Philip Buchanan, lead counsel for an organization called the Justice Project. Mr. Buchanan stated that a Mr. Jerome Hale, now known as Kwame Jamal Hale, claimed responsibility for the Sunshine Grocery murders. The DA's office met with Mr. Hale, who is currently serving life without parole in Brushy Mountain State Penitentiary. Mr. Hale is a career criminal and has spent thirteen of his thirty-four years incarcerated. Mr. Hale stated that he had framed Mr. Owens because of an argument the two had incurred while serving time together at Brushy Mountain. In support of this assertion, Mr. Hale stated he knew the exact location of the weapon used in the Sunshine Grocery murders, information only reasonably known by the murderer himself. Following his instructions, a Browning pump shotgun matching the description of the weapon used in the murders was located within the confines of Montgomery Bell State Park." Rayburn looks out into the crowded room. "Last night ballistic tests were conducted by our office to determine if, in fact, this gun is the same weapon used in the Sunshine Grocery murders. I can now confirm for you that it is, indeed, the same weapon."

The reporters scribble away, soaking up what they are certain is history unfolding before their eyes. "However," Rayburn says, "this office is more convinced than ever that the original verdict in this case was correct and just." Heads pop up, eyes fixed on the DA. A few of the reporters glance at each other, question marks in their expressions. "Central to Mr. Hale's claim is his statement that he buried the weapon where it was found. But evidence proves that this is not the case. In fact, evidence proves that the weapon was only recently buried there. That gun was, in fact, *moved* by someone to make it appear that Mr. Hale had intimate knowledge of the crime, when, in fact, he did not. This is a clear attempt to discredit this office, the prosecutors in the case, and the jury's original verdict. It is nothing less than obstruction of justice, and this office is immediately instigating a full investigation to determine the parties responsible." He pauses. "I would now like to introduce you to Paul Landmeyer, the county's chief forensic officer."

Paul takes his place at the podium and demonstrates why he is such a powerful witness in court with his professional, unemotional statement. "As the district attorney stated, ballistics tests confirmed that the weapon unearthed at Montgomery Bell was used in the Sunshine Grocery murders. However, upon testing the gunstock of the weapon, I was able to identify the presence of an agricultural pesticide commonly used in the farming of tobacco. This would not be unusual for an object buried in the surface soil in many parts of Tennessee. However, the gun was located within the environs of Montgomery Bell State Park. The park was incorporated in 1954, and since that date, no agricultural activities have taken place within its borders. A call this morning to the Park Service confirmed that the field where the gun was located has been fallow for the entire history of the park. Further, the soil immediately surrounding the gun was also tested and found not to contain this chemical. Therefore, my reasonable conclusion is that the weapon was previously buried somewhere else where it absorbed this chemical, was later unearthed, and was buried again at the Montgomery Bell location. It's my expert opinion that there is no other rational explanation."

Paul steps back, and Rayburn takes his place at the podium. "Questions."

Voices explode toward the stage as reporters demand to know more about Paul's findings. Rayburn lets Paul handle most of them, and he once again proves unflappable. "That's correct. . . . The chemical is an active ingredient in many agricultural pesticides. . . . No, the ground surrounding the weapon did not contain this chemical. . . . Yes, the entire procedure was videotaped, and I'm happy to make copies available to the media."

After fifteen minutes—five more than he intended— Rayburn cuts off the questions. "I wish to commend Dr. Landmeyer for his professionalism and dedication in this project," he says. "I especially wish to commend the gentlemen standing behind me, Carl Becker and Thomas Dennehy. They prosecuted the original case, and they have behaved impeccably during this entire proceeding." He looks out at the crowd. "I can assure you of one thing, ladies and gentlemen. The next project this office will undertake is to determine who is responsible for moving this weapon. The families of the victims and the jury members—and indeed, these fine prosecutors standing with me—deserve no less. This has been a difficult time. But we consider the question of whether or not Wilson Owens was guilty of the Sunshine

Grocery murders closed. Our focus is now on finding the people responsible for tampering with this vital evidence." He looks out into the audience. "I now direct your attention to the young lady at the back. She has the complete documentation for the tests performed by Dr. Landmeyer. Thank you very much."

We stand in the private hallway, outside the press room, the stunned reporters scrambling for the paperwork being handed out. Rayburn shakes Paul's hand. "You realize you're never going to have to buy another beer in your life, don't you?"

Paul grins. "I can live with that."

I look back up at the monitor; most of the reporters are milling around, flipping through Paul's documentation. A few are already heading for the rear doors. Rayburn starts to lead us back to the underground parking, but a figure on the monitor catches my eye, and I stop. A man in a well-tailored suit is pressing against the flow of people, coming into the room as others exit. I can't see his face clearly, but he's definitely agitated. He rips a press release off the table and stands reading it, his head down. The farther he goes, the more upset he becomes; by the bottom of the first page, his hands are trembling.

My colleagues are already at the door at the other end of the hall. "Thomas!" Paul calls out. "You coming?"

"I'll catch up."

"You sure?"

"Yeah. I'm right behind you." Paul shrugs and steps through the door. I stare back up at the monitor, trying to see the man's face. He's about five-foot ten, and his black hair is cut well but fairly long, down over his ears. He's angrily flipping through the press release, manhandling the pages. I squint at the monitor. *His arms. Are those welts?* The image of Indy clawing for his life while someone presses him underwater flashes through my mind. The man lifts his head, unaware he is staring directly into the camera. It takes me a second to recognize him; the street clothes are gone, replaced by a properly cut suit; the hair is well trimmed, and the beard and mustache have vanished. There's a two count, and by the time I realize I'm looking straight at Charles Bridges, he's dropped the papers onto the floor and is striding back out into the hall.

I pull open the door and head toward Bridges. The second I appear, a dozen reporters who are still in the hall converge on me and start hurling questions. I try to push through them, but it's hard going. The closer I get to the front, the bigger the crowd becomes, and there's already a crush of people filling up the exit. I finally break out of the front of the hall and see Bridges is about thirty-five yards away, halfway down the concrete steps to the street. If I can get a clear shot, I can reach him in less than ten seconds. Suddenly, I feel a large hand on my shoulder, spinning me around in the opposite direction. It's a reporter, and standing next to him are Wilson Owens's brother, mother, and half sister. The mother hurls herself on me, her big, sloppy tears in the air and on my face, her hands pummeling my chest. "You're a liar!" she howls. "You lied about my boy! Wilson didn't hurt nobody, and you tellin' lies about him!" The reporter stands a couple of feet away, grinning fiercely. I try to restrain the woman, but within seconds I'm encircled by reporters and cameramen. The mother of the man I sent to the death chamber hammers away on my body for twenty agonizing seconds, until at last she grinds to a halt, her fists pressed into my chest. She collapses against me and grips me, holding me so tight I can barely breathe. The crowd around us falls silent, the only sound the merciless singing of camera shutters.

Gently, I disengage from the woman. She looks up into my face with regret as deep as an ocean, a regret that goes back to her own childhood and the freight-train path of her life. Her boy was lost; for a brief, shining moment, he had come back to her. And now I have stolen him from her again.

Bridges has finally become aware of the commotion behind him. Fifty yards off he turns back and looks; our eyes meet, and he spins away and starts off in a run. Beyond him are a maze of alleys and buildings, each of which he knows like the back of his hand. I don't bother calling 911. Somewhere deep in my gut, I know that Charles Bridges will never be caught hiding in a stairwell by some patrolman. Until he chooses to show himself again, Charles Bridges is gone.

CHAPTER TWENTY-ONE

THE *UNOFFICIAL* "Paul Landmeyer Saved Our Asses" party—precursor by only a few hours to the *official* Carl Becker retirement party—has already started by the time I arrive back at 222 West. Rayburn insisted that Paul go back to the office and even dragged Carl back with him. In the main conference room there is now an informal receiving line as the staff heaps affirmation on Paul, mixed with undisguised disdain for Buchanan and his crowd. The rest of the day is going to be spectacularly unproductive, followed tonight by what promises to be an equally spectacular debauch.

In the midst of a chorus of backslapping and "hell-yeahs," I manage to get Rayburn back in his office for a talk. He follows me in, grinning like a kid at Christmas. "Good people in this office, Thomas. They stuck together through this."

"Charles Bridges was at the press conference, David."

He looks at me skeptically. "The hell he was. The cops

are out looking for him, and he walks right into the New Justice Building?"

"The cops are looking for a homeless guy with beard, mustache, and a smell that knocks you down. Bridges looked like a banker. Shaved, nice haircut, suit, and tie."

"You're serious."

I nod. "I should have figured it. Watching us go down would be important to him. It's everything he's worked for. The point is, I don't think anything about Charles Bridges is what it seems. And as of now, there's no current description of him. It even took me a while to recognize him, and I sent him to jail."

Rayburn grimaces. "He's going to be pissed about what happened."

"Bridges killed his parole officer over an inadvertent insult, David. And Paul just seriously ruined his day."

Rayburn nods thoughtfully. "I'll ask the sheriff's department to put a plainclothes officer on Paul, another on his house."

I nod. "We have to tell him about it, David. He's got a family."

I watch Philip Buchanan's press conference alone, in the small conference room. The professor looks satisfyingly rattled, a brave face in shit circumstances. His position undermined, he dissolves into a standard, antiprosecutor rant. Buchanan demands that his experts have the chance to examine the evidence, which Paul will scrupulously provide. And knowing Paul, that work will be found to be impeccable. In the end, Buchanan will claim that pesticide in the gunstock of the murder weapon isn't ironclad proof one way or another. Paul's opinion is good enough for me, and more important, it will be good enough for the people of Tennessee. The truth of this case will, for people like Buchanan, always be in doubt. But it is certain that the people of Tennessee don't want to believe that their representatives in the justice system have killed the wrong man. In the face of such dubious testimony, to accuse them, they will dismiss the claims of Kwame Jamal Hale. This is not the case that brings down a DA's office. We will not carry that cross.

I flip off the TV and call Josh Ritchie, who answers on the second ring. "It's Thomas, Josh. I haven't heard back from you on Bridges."

"Yeah, well, that's its own story. I got nothin' against street work, but shit, dude."

"What do you mean?"

"It means your boy's social circle ain't exactly at the governor's mansion. But I got a line on him. You were wrong about him going down to the tracks to buy dope, by the way."

"I saw him head down there with my own eyes."

"He goes down there, all right. To sell, not to buy."

"Are you sure?"

"Yeah, and it was like pulling teeth. Nobody wants to say shit about your boy Bridges. But he's got a nice little business going on downtown."

"Who's his supplier?"

"That's where I hit a wall. I've pretty much decided he must be doing his own cooking."

"Then he has to have space somewhere," I say. "He'd need a house, an apartment, something. A place for a stove, some storage, and doors that lock."

"Yeah, but nobody has a clue where he lives. Don't even ask me where I went trying to find out."

"Thanks, Josh. I owe you."

"That you do, amigo."

* * *

The rest of the staff, untroubled by concerns about the plans of Charles Bridges, convene early and enthusiastically that evening at the Saucer for Carl's official retirement party. And although the Department of Homeland Security has specifically requested that the personnel of the Justice Department maintain constant vigilance, many of them are on their way to a night they won't remember very clearly. This is not merely a party to send off Carl. This is an exorcism of the demons Philip Buchanan and Kwame Jamal Hale. The staff drinks like people who, on the eve of their own executions, received a last-minute reprieve.

Nevertheless, Carl remains the titular star of the evening, and the law enforcement community has come out in force to honor him. The entire bar has been reserved, and the place is crammed with at least two hundred well-wishers, ranging from police detectives to defense lawyers to Justice Building staffers. Carl stands smiling thoughtfully at the front of the crowd, his shirt disheveled, his tie seriously askew. Cigar smoke wafts above his head, the liquor is flowing freely, and for now, all is well.

Someone calls Carl's name, and he breaks from his reverie. The DA hands him something—it's yet another plaque—and he smiles, tolerating it all under the salutary influence of several fine Pilsners. There is muted applause, and he looks down and reads out loud the inscription of the plaque: *In Gratitude for Meritorious Government Service.* There are the obligatory calls for a speech, little yips like the barking of dogs. Carl bows with the cautious, overstated grace of the inebriated. "What to say, on the occasion of my sudden irrelevance?" he asks. There are boos and catcalls, and Carl states in a loud voice that he is proud to have served with such a goddamn fine bunch of lawyers. There's a satisfying round of applause, but I can see something's still bothering him. His face clears suddenly, and he turns to Rayburn and says, "Except for you, obviously. But it's not your fault you have to get elected every two years."

Rayburn flushes bright red, which brightens Carl's expression considerably. Carl peers out at the crowd, and he finds me standing several rows back. "I would also like to say that the best thing about retiring is that I will no longer have to carry on my back the highly overrated Mr. Thomas Dennehy. If not for him, I would be a Supreme Court justice. At least." There's genuine laughter at that, including from me.

"Thank you, Carl, thank you very much," Rayburn says, moving Carl firmly back toward his seat. Carl starts to protest, but the DA's hand is in his back, and between that and the alcohol, he finds himself trickling toward a waiting, enveloping crowd of well-wishers. I walk up to my friend and put my arm around him.

"That was beautiful," I say, smiling. "Pure poetry. The crack about Rayburn was fatally true."

"Yeah, and the one about you was pure bullshit," Carl says, smiling unsteadily but sincerely. "Thank God you'll still be here after I'm gone, so the place doesn't fall apart."

"I take it you'll be slipping away as inconspicuously as possible?"

Carl presses his finger to his nose. "A disappearing act," he says, smiling. "Look for me, and I won't be there."

Something in his expression gives me pause. *Good Lord. He means permanently.* "You mean you're not coming back?"

Carl looks wistfully around. "This is it, Thomas. The last night."

"You can't give up the Saucer, Carl. It's un-American."

"And run into you, and Rayburn, and everybody else? Have you all look over at me with pity? No, thanks."

"Admiration, you mean."

He smiles. "I'm moving to Seanachie's for the duration. Only Irish beer. Less complicated. In fact, I think I'll start tonight."

"Want some company?"

He shakes his head. "God, no. I'm not ready for that talk."

Right. The talk about how the hell this friendship is going to work, now that only one of us is left in the fight. "I'll call you," I say.

"Sure." He turns away, and I watch him enveloped by a crowd of backslappers. Carl soaks it all in; then he melts away down a hall, turning back at the doorway. He looks at the crowd a long moment, and he's gone. The party continues at full speed without the guest of honor, people anxious to let off steam. I stay for twenty minutes or so, but my heart's not in it. By the time there are rumblings about moving the party to another club, I slip silently away. I walk out of the party and into the warm air of a late August night.

Seanachie's is four blocks away and the opposite direction from my car. I head toward it anyway. I don't want the night to end, because it means Carl is really gone. I get to the pub and look in the street-side window; Carl is there, at the bar, a drink before him. He's alone, staring straight ahead. I don't go inside, because I don't have the right. Carl isn't just saying good-bye to me and the staff; he's saying good-bye to his life. Over the next few hours and beers he's going to take leave of his knight's roundtable, the place where his victories were celebrated and his defeats lamented. After tonight, he will have no reason to return.

I circle back to the parking lot and head toward the truck. I put my hand on the truck, turn, and call out into the dark.

"Come on out, dammit." Silence. "Come on, I know you're back there. I'm not in the mood to play any games." There's a rustle of movement, and a man steps out from behind a nearby car. "Who the hell are you, and where on earth did you learn to tail a person so badly?"

The man walks out under a streetlight. "Officer Nielsen, sir," he says. "The police academy on Lebanon Road."

I sigh. "Rayburn sent you, didn't he?"

"Yes, sir."

"Go home, Nielsen. I'm fine."

"I can't actually do that, sir."

"So you propose to follow me all the way home to Franklin?"

"Those are my orders, sir."

"And then?"

"I work third shift, sir. I'll be outside in the car until seven this morning."

I shake my head. *Rayburn and his family.* I unlock the truck, get in, and pull out toward home. The cop jogs to an unmarked Crown Vic and fires it up. I drive home, the officer fifty yards behind the entire way. I pull into the garage, and the officer stops at the end of the block and parks. I strip off my clothes, climb in bed, and fall asleep the second my head hits the pillow.

The dream begins like before. It's of Rebecca and water, and the beach in Florida. But this time, Jazz is with us, and we're a family again. Jazz looks about four, and she's riding on Bec's shoulders. She's laughing, her hair dripping with salt water. Bec splashes water up onto her, and she whoops and waves her arms in the sun. But this time, it's not the sea that carries them away from me. Instead, Bec simply turns her back to the shore and walks toward the horizon. I scream my lungs out, but they keep getting smaller and smaller. I call out a final time, but the small point they have become vanishes into the glare of the water.

Sometime deep in the night—when dreams are black nothingness—I hear what I think is the alarm, ringing harsh and close to my ear. It stops and starts again, and I realize it's the phone. I reach groggily over and knock the receiver out of its cradle, fumbling for it in the dark. I pull the phone to my mouth and mumble, "Dennehy."

"It's David."

I sit up; my bedside clock shows 4:05 a.m. "Yeah, I'm here. Talk to me." There's no answer; I hear noise in the background, like Rayburn is in a crowd.

"It's Carl. Something happened to him."

I jerk awake. "What about him?"

"We don't know what happened exactly."

"What are you talking about, David? What's happened to Carl?"

"He's gone, Thomas. He's dead." He chokes back a sob. "Somebody stuck a knife into him. You got to get down here, Thomas."

My chest constricts. "Where are you?"

"Broadway and Sixth, downtown. Paul Landmeyer has a small army down here, taking it apart, brick by brick." He chokes back another sob. "It's my fault. I put protection on Paul and you. I didn't even think about Carl."

"Hang on, David. I'll be there in twenty minutes."

I pull on jeans and a shirt, push my feet into shoes, feeling a horrible buzzing in my ears. I go to the bathroom, thinking I'll throw up. I don't, but I'm unsteady for a while, my balance just out of reach. I fall back down onto the bed, holding my sides, feeling like I can't breathe. I stand back up and force myself to walk toward the bedroom door. Halfway out of the bedroom, I stop. I walk to the nightstand, pull out the Rock Island .45, and hold it quietly in my hand. I take a breath and move toward the garage.

I hit the garage door opener, and the cop car pulls up beside the driveway, his window down. "I heard on the radio. You rolling?"

"Yeah." I shove the gun into the glove box. I pull out and drive through empty streets, the cop tailing me. When I turn onto Broadway, I see a police barricade blocking the street.

An officer walks over hurriedly, then recognizes me. "Sorry," he says, giving way. "Go on in."

Powerful portable lights are set up on stands, their electrical lines trailing to a van. Yellow police tape secures a large area. Two men in white Tyvek suits are bent over at the waist, examining something on the sidewalk.

Rayburn picks me out. "Jesus, Thomas," he says, walking toward me. He opens his arms, and we embrace. "I've got twenty cops looking for Bridges."

"Where's Carl, David?"

"In the alley, around the corner. A patrol officer found him. His billfold and watch are missing." I start toward the location, and Rayburn grabs my arm. "Not yet. Let Paul do his job."

"Then take me to the cop who found him."

Rayburn nods and leads me toward a patrolman about twenty yards away. "This is Glen Maxwell," he says. "He found the body."

The officer nods. "I got a call about an open 911. You know, no voice on the other end."

"No voice?" I ask.

"Just an open line."

"Any sound of struggle?"

"No. The operator recognized the name on the caller ID and called her supervisor. They traced the cell tower, which put the call in a sixteen-block area downtown. They called me, and I searched the area until I found the vagrants."

"Four homeless people," Rayburn says. "Maxwell found them arguing over Carl's coat."

"They're regulars, usually too drunk and too much trouble to be admitted to the mission," Maxwell says. "I searched the coat for ID, and there wasn't any. That's when I felt the blood on the inside."

"Blood," I repeat, feeling sick.

"When I found the body in the alley, I figured the vagrants rolled him. But then I saw what happened. . . . Look, I wouldn't trust those guys around a ten-dollar bill. But I don't see them taking it to that level."

I look up warily. "What do you mean, 'that level'?"

"Serrated knife, right through the ribs. Punctured the heart."

Exactly how Bridges's parole officer died. A wave of nausea rolls through me. "I'm going to need a minute." I walk away and retch into some shrubs planted around a streetlight. I support myself on the post, heart pounding, gasping for breath. It takes a good minute and a half to pull myself together. Rayburn and Maxwell walk over, letting me get my breath.

"You OK?" Rayburn asks.

"Go on. I want to hear everything."

Maxwell nods. "There wasn't anything on the vagrants, so what I figure is, the murder was earlier. These four came on the body later and started arguing over the coat. But you can ask them yourself. They're right over there."

I turn and see Paul Landmeyer talking to four people by the forensic van. The vagrants look jacked up, like they had big plans for the night and Carl's death is a major inconvenience to them. Paul looks over, and our eyes meet. For once, his professional demeanor is rattled. He's keeping himself together by a thread. I walk up to Paul and embrace him. "You OK?" I ask quietly.

"No. I saw you talking to the officer. Did he tell you about the wound?"

"Yeah. Just like Kavner's."

Paul nods. "It's Bridges." He looks at the vagrants. "But if I'm going to have a shot at nailing him, I need these idiots to start cooperating."

"Talk to me."

"I need their clothes, mouth swabs, and hair samples. They're taking it personally."

I start toward the group. "Give me five seconds . . ."

"No, not that way. They need to give it voluntarily, so nothing gets contaminated in a struggle."

"You got something for them to put on?"

"Orange jumpsuits from correctional."

"Give me one of them." I pick up a jumpsuit and walk over to the little crowd. One of the men looks to be in charge, and I walk up to him, feeling a ringing in my ears. I start hoping he doesn't do anything stupid, because I am one wrong gesture away from beating the shit out of him where he stands. I hold up the jumpsuit. "Get behind the van and take your clothes off," I say. "Officers will create a blind for you. Once the clothes are off, you can put one of these on."

"Anybody tries to take my pants, he's gonna get a boot up his ass," the man in front of me says.

"You don't want to piss me off right now," I say. My voice cracks a little, betraying the ragged edge on which I dance.

"You can't take a man's pants," another man snarls. "This is about dignity."

I take a deep breath, which buys me a few moments of rationality, but not more. "You have ten seconds," I say. "If you don't comply, I'm going to have each one of you booked for obstruction, resisting arrest, disturbing a crime scene, public drunkenness, failure to comply, and vagrancy. Then I'm going to put you on the shortlist of suspects for the murder of my best friend."

"We're already suspects," the first man says under his breath. But he heads toward the van, the others following.

I turn back to Paul. "They're going. Now tell me what you have so far."

Paul shakes his head. "Here's the thing, Thomas. Even if we find this guy, I'm not sure we can make it stick."

"What the hell do you mean?"

"The alley has immense debris. We've got fecal material, urine. The footprints of hundreds of people. It's not a crime scene; it's a chemistry lab. But that's not the worst of it." He looks at me. "It's the *party*, Thomas. Carl's clothing is virtually opaque with debris. He came in contact with a couple of hundred people tonight. There was hugging, backslapping. I don't think there's a square inch of his clothing that doesn't have something on it."

"How bad is it?"

Paul stares back at the alley. "To have a shot? I'll have to get DNA and clothing samples from every person at the party, same as the four on the street," he says. "Then each one of them will have to be scientifically excluded. *Then* I can start."

"He went to Seanachie's after," I say. "Knowing Carl, he closed the place down."

Paul grimaces. "Which introduces the random factor. Unless they were regulars, they could be hard to track down."

"So how screwed are we?" I ask quietly.

Paul looks at me, and I know it's bad. "If I were going to plan the one scenario to get away with murder, I couldn't do better than this. A decent defense lawyer would have a field day." He shakes his head and walks off. For the next hour or more, Carl is going to be pored over by Paul's forensic squad, reduced to nothing more than evidence, his humanity stripped. He will be measured, sampled, have swabs of chemicals placed on him, and generally treated like a piece of meat. I walk away from the scene, forcing myself to stay removed from a process I understand well enough to be repulsed by the thought of it being applied to someone I love.

I turn away, feeling sick again. *Two hundred people to exclude. It would take weeks, and that's without the cross-contamination. It's a nightmare.* I look up and see headlights appear on the edge of the crime scene; predictably, media vans are arriving. It's getting light, and within another hour cars will start streaming into downtown as the early birds arrive for work. But even though Paul's team will be working the location for hours, I overhear on a nearby radio that Paul wants to get Carl's body out sooner rather than later. A few minutes later, a gurney slowly rolls out of the alley toward the coroner's van. By now a few photographers have unloaded their equipment, and Carl's long trip along the crime scene to the van is lit up with the merciless glare of cameras. Carl is zippered in a body bag, the universal symbol of the victim. Two Tyvek-clad coroner's officers load the body into the vehicle; a door slams, and the van pulls out, taking Carl to the horrors of the autopsy tools. The lights suddenly vanish, signaling that the show is over.

Paul's words come back to me. *Even if we find this guy, I'm not sure we can make it stick.* I walk to my truck and see the officer tailing me pop up, ready to follow. *I've got to track Bridges on my own, and I'll never get anything done with this guy on my hip.* I go over to him. "Look, I'm headed to the office, and I'll be there all morning. Just have the next shift guy pick me up there."

"That's not my orders," the officer says doubtfully.

"There's thirty cops here, Nielsen. I'm driving six blocks. Give yourself a break."

The officer looks around a second, then smiles. "Yeah. Listen, you'll probably have a guy named Barrickman this morning."

"I'll look for him." I nod, get into my truck, and drive out. To the left is 222 West. I turn right and head for the railroad tracks. Charles Bridges might be wearing a suit now, but his customers aren't. And one of them must know something.

It's less than ten blocks to Union Station, which is completely still at this hour. I pull into the lot and drive to the metal stairs that lead to the railroad tracks. The hardest-core derelicts in Nashville are down there sleeping it off, and they are about to be rudely awakened. I park, push the Rock Island .45 into my belt behind my back, and descend into Nashville's most dangerous square mile, looking for addicts.

The sun is inching higher, splitting light across the railcars. I step over bottles and trash, threading my way toward the empty, decrepit cars. Ninety feet into the yard I pass two figures huddled together in sleeping bags, but the empty bottles tell me they're not the target. *Your drinking problem doesn't interest me, pals. I'm looking for the ice addicts.* The smell of urine is powerful, even in the outdoor space. A shadowed figure picks me up as I pass my first railcar, cir-

cling behind. I keep walking, ignoring him, knowing he'll
show up when he's ready. Thirty yards farther on I hear him
on the other side of a railroad car, making a hell of a racket
as he goes. I reach behind my back and pull out the .45, not
breaking stride. When I reach the end of the car he appears
in front of me, holding a nasty-looking, homemade shiv.
He's blind drunk, which means he's of no use to me. I shake
my head and show him the gun; he stares a second, then vanishes back behind the railroad car, gone as quickly as he
came. Alone again, I look in several open cars before I find a
man lying on his side in one, asleep. I step up into the car,
slide through the narrow opening, and stand over the figure,
straddling him in the near darkness. There are no bottles,
and a lighter is on the floor beside him. The man, who
weighs almost nothing, sleeps on, oblivious, his autonomic
system crashed after the previous night's whack. I push him
over onto his back with my foot. Nothing. I nudge his side,
which gets little more than a "mnff." I cock the hammer of
the gun with a metallic click, reverberant in the railroad car;
like magic, one eye slides upward, then the other. The man
stares up at me, crust in his eyes, snot in his nose. I bend
down until the gun is a foot away from his face. "Don't
move. You understand?" The man's head moves gently up
and down. "Good. Now tell me where you buy your ice." The
junkie's eyes widen, but he doesn't speak. I push the barrel
of the gun into his right nostril, forcing it upward. "Three
seconds. One. Two. Thr—"

"Dude with a beard," the man croaks. "Wears glasses."

"Tell me everything you know about him."

"Crystals. Good quality. Clear, no orange or brown."

"He makes his own?"

"I don't ask."

"What kind of quantities does he move?"

"Quarters, mostly. More when the state checks come in."

"Where does he live?"

"I don't know."

I press the gun harder up his nose, until he winces. "Don't fuck with me," I growl. "I'm having a bad week."

"I don't know, man. You think he invites me over for dinner?"

"Is he ever with anybody?"

"No. He works alone."

"You ever see a car?" His eyes shift left slightly. "One. Two. Thre—"

"*Fuck,* man. Yeah. Once I seen him downtown. He drove by me, didn't see me."

"What kind of car?"

"Four-door. A little shitty. Ugly tan thing. Maybe seven or eight years old."

"What make?"

"You know, shitty. I ain't no car dealer, man."

I stare at him a second, then slowly lower the trigger on the gun. "When are you due to see him again?"

The man stares up at me, his eyes hungry for more of what's killing him. "I was due yesterday, man. He's late already."

I step over him, put my foot on the metal step, and turn my face back into the car. "Don't count on him coming back."

I step into my truck, and the phone goes off. The number coming in is unlisted, but I figure it's Rayburn, wanting to know where I am. It's not a voice call, however; instead, someone is sending me a picture. I start the truck and put it in reverse, ready to pull out. The picture scrolls down on my screen. Before it's halfway down, I stop and put the truck back into park. The photograph, taken from above and at close range, shows Carl, lying on his back, his face contorted in agony. I hold the phone, trembling, barely believing my eyes. I set the phone on the seat beside me and grip the steering wheel, trying to contain my grief and anger. I look out the window, wildly hoping to see Bridges standing there so I can empty my gun into his self-satisfied brain. I get back out of the truck and stand a few feet away, rage coursing through me. I walk into the shadows of a nearby building, pull out the gun, and fire off all six rounds into the ground, imagining each of them cutting through the body of Charles Bridges. I feel cold inside, but there is something deeply satisfying about each round as it shreds through the soft dirt. I push the gun into my belt and walk back toward the truck. Ten feet away, I can hear the phone ringing again through the closed door. I sprint forward and press "talk," gripping the phone. This time, it's not a picture; instead, a text message crawls across my screen: *THIS ISN'T FINISHED.*

CHAPTER
TWENTY-TWO

I MAKE IT BACK to 222 West just before 7:00 a.m., but it's ten minutes after before I trust myself to walk into the office. I'm barely hanging together, ricocheting between scarcely controlled rage and crippling grief, and neither will help me find Bridges. Using every ounce of discipline, I settle myself, doing my best to clear my mind. I enter the office and see the news about Carl has already spread through the staff; half the department is already here, gathering to commiserate. Each has his or her clothes from the night before in a bag, per Paul's instructions. Several are in tears, but most look numb, like they're in shock. After three decades of service, the city has repaid Carl Becker with his death. That violence has now come home to everybody in the office.

Paul already has an evidence ID team set up in the conference room. He looks exhausted—thanks to his work on the Browning shotgun, he's only slept about four hours in the last forty-eight—but he's quietly getting things organized. I catch his eye, and he walks over. I show him my phone; Paul stares at it silently a moment, then looks up at me. "When did you get this?"

"Just a few minutes ago."

Paul nods. "So that's the kind of bastard we're dealing with."

"Yeah."

Paul looks at the picture again, this time clinically. I see the change in his face, emotion replaced with scientific acumen. "This is evidence, Thomas. The angle of the body, the details of the concrete around him."

"That's why I'm here. There's a text message, too." I scroll down and show Paul. He nods, his expression grim.

Paul motions over a member of his staff and hands him the phone. "Get everything on this downloaded onto a disk," he says. "And do it now." He turns back to me. "You did the right thing bringing it in so quickly. We'll analyze the picture and try to catch a break."

"Is David around?"

"He's in his office with the ones who are the most broken up."

I nod. "Tell him I need a trap-and-trace on this line, will you? All incoming calls for the last twenty-four hours. The provider's Sprint."

"Knowing the way this guy works, the phone will just be stolen."

"At least it's doing something." I look over at the workers setting up their collecting equipment. "Last night you said it looked bad."

Paul shakes his head. "You have Carl, already hammered. His responses are going to be slow. The killer comes up from behind. He runs the blade into Carl, steps back, possibly never even touching him. Now factor in where Carl was found, which was basically a petri dish of foreign material, throw in the massive human contact from the party, and top it off with the random factor at Seanachie's."

An evidence ID technician walks up. "We're ready to set up the video equipment," he says. "Which way is the line going to move?"

Paul nods. "Left to right, and get at least two views." He looks back to me. "We've set up an assembly line. Clothes, hair, saliva, tagged and bagged. With so many people, the pressure will be to go too fast. We've got to be methodical, not make any mistakes." Paul walks off, leaving me alone in the center of the room.

The office is winding up, beginning its morbid, wounded day. More than two hundred people will file through Paul's evidence line over the next several hours, yielding six hundred bags of evidence, each of which will have to be meticulously analyzed. More staffers arrive in twos and threes, each needing and receiving comfort from the group who's already here. After I see my third breakdown in as many minutes, I recognize the obvious: *This place isn't healthy for me right now.* If I stay in the office much longer, I won't be able to avoid falling apart like everybody else. I find the evidence ID officer and retrieve my phone; then I slide out of the room as inconspicuously as possible, retreating to the exit.

At the door, I look back and see the first staffers are starting through the assembly line; an ID officer with rubber gloves swabs the mouth of a woman, then stores it in a clear plastic bag. She bends down to write, and a flash from a camera goes off. The line of people behind her is swelling. Watching this, I'm sure of one thing: by the time Paul has cross-analyzed the DNA and fiber evidence of more than two hundred people, conducted Carl's autopsy, and examined the evidence from the crime scene, whatever it is

Charles Bridges wants finished will be over and done. If I'm going to survive this, I have to find Bridges myself.

My truck rolls down Church Street, heading toward the DPC. I pull into the small lot behind the building, hoping to find Fiona's Volvo. *Not there.* I punch her number into my cell phone, and she answers. I skip the pleasantries. "Carl Becker is dead. Your friend Bridges killed him."

After a shocked silence, she answers in a whisper, "My God, Thomas. How do you know?"

"Because he killed his parole officer the same way. And because he knew it would kill a part of me when he did it."

"Where are you?"

"In the church parking lot."

"I can be there in twenty minutes."

"To do what?"

"Stay there, Thomas. I think I can help you find him."

I hang up and get out of the truck, too wound up to sit. I push the .45 into my belt behind my back and pace the parking lot, waiting for Fiona to arrive. Finally, her Volvo pulls up the alley. She gets out and stands by her car, pale and washed out. "Are you sure it's him?" she asks. "Is there any doubt?"

"No. And he's not finished." I walk up to her and show her the photograph on my phone. She covers her mouth and stifles a moan. "I'm so sorry," she says, her voice a whisper. "So, so sorry."

"Psychopaths like to take photographs of their atrocities. It plays into their sense of heroic self-importance."

"I think I can take you to him."

"Tell me."

"I followed him once. It was right after he showed up at the church. We actually did some due diligence, you know."

"We're past that now, Fiona. Just tell me what you know."

"It will be hard to find the exact house. It's been a few months."

I'm walking to the truck before she finishes the sentence. She follows, but the footsteps suddenly stop. "What's wrong?" I ask, turning around.

She points at my belt. "You have a gun."

"That's right."

"I won't help you kill him, Thomas."

I walk up to her and push the photograph on the phone in her face. "You have to choose sides now, Fiona. This isn't some academic conference. You've got principles. Great. I applaud you. I just don't feel like dying for them."

"And then what? Another killing? And another? Maybe after you and Bridges kill each other your families can fight each other. Maybe it can just be the Palestinians and the Israelis. That's worked out so well for them."

"You don't mind if I defend myself, do you?"

She looks at me, her expression doubtful. "I know how anger takes people over."

"Help me find him before he does something even worse, Fiona."

"How can it be worse?"

"He's increasing terror, which is the classic tactic of the psychopath. He started small, by murdering my cat." She screws up her face in disgust. "That's right, Fiona. He ran him through the water pump of my spa. Then he destroyed my father's truck." I hold out the phone. "Now this. Do you see a pattern here? Somewhere in this city Charles Bridges is getting ready to take his final revenge on me, and if he's allowed to follow through on it, maybe I'll just *wish* I was dead. So this is it. You either help me find him, or what happens next is on your conscience."

She stares at me a long moment, locked in indecision. "All right." She walks to the truck, opens the door, and gets in. I jog to the driver's seat and start the truck. "So where are we going?"

"The Nation."

I catch glimpses of Fiona as I drive; she's grim, like she's on the way to a funeral. A part of me hopes she is: the funeral of Charles Bridges. I turn down Forty-sixth, pass the Harley-Davidson dealership, and pull to a stop. "So?"

"Four, maybe five streets ahead. I'm not sure." I roll forward slowly, letting her get her bearings. I slow on the fourth street, and she nods. "Take this one, and look for a fire hydrant." I drive down the street, rolling past the decrepit houses. We drive nearly ten blocks, near to where the street ends. "It wasn't this far," she says. "Try the next street over."

I go a street farther into the Nation, and head back toward Forty-sixth. Four blocks up, she points at a beige house with a sagging roof. "That might be it."

"Might?"

"It was several months ago. Anyway, I didn't see him actually go in the house. He turned in, but I was a couple of blocks behind. I just remember it was near a fire hydrant." She looks out of the window. "I'm pretty sure this is it. It's one of these three or four houses."

I nod. "OK. Stay in the car." I walk behind the truck and pull out a crowbar. When I come back around, Fiona's standing on the sidewalk looking at me. "You did good," I say. "Now get out of the way." I start off, but I feel her following behind. I spin around. "You know who always ends up getting killed in deals like this? The innocent bystander. Now get back in the truck."

"Are you going to shoot me, Thomas?"

"No."

"Neither is he." She marches off toward the first house. There's nothing I can do, since standing on the street arguing with a woman while I hold a tire iron is pretty likely to attract a crowd. I start after her, when I catch a vague scent in the air. I move farther down the street, sniffing. I walk to the side of the next house over; it's not any stronger. I jog down the yard across the front of the building to the third house, testing the air as I go. There's a breeze, and I pick up something acrid, like cat urine. I look up at a nondescript brick ranch with a sagging roof and a sign for an alarm in the yard. The blinds are all closed, and there's a metal storm door on the front entrance. I hear Fiona tramping up behind me.

"What are you doing?"

"You smell that?" I ask, quietly.

She sniffs. "No. Wait, yes, I . . . that's foul."

"Ammonia." I turn around. "Look," I say quietly, "just going in this place could be dangerous. Meth fumes can kill." She starts toward the front door, and I grab her by the arm. "What the hell do you think you're doing?"

She wrenches her arm free. "I don't believe in violence, Thomas. That doesn't mean I won't stand up to what's wrong in my own way."

Fuck, she has guts. I grab her arm again. "If you're going to go in, at least go in behind me. I don't want you getting shot by accident."

"Thomas . . ."

"I swear to God, Fiona, I'll put you over my shoulder if I have to. Now *get behind me.*"

She stares at me a second, then nods.

I lead her quietly around the house to the rear. There's a chain-link fence around the small backyard; I get a running start and climb, dropping down on the other side. Fiona follows. Keeping her behind me, I advance onto the back porch. The porch creaks as I walk, its timbers dry-rotted. *If there was any doubt, he knows we're here now.* There's another metal storm door; I reach out and jiggle it, but it's locked. *So. Here's where I officially step over the line.* I take the crowbar and force it into the lock of the storm door. Working the bar back and forth, the bar takes a good set; bracing myself, I jerk back on the bar and feel the lock mechanism explode outward. The door swings violently back, then flaps loosely on one hinge. I glance over at the windows, but there's no movement. *Whoever lives here, they're either not home, or they're on the side of this door with a gun.* The wooden door remains; there's a dead bolt, and it takes a solid minute to get the end of the crowbar between the metal plate and the wooden frame. Finally, I get a set between the metal plate of the lock and the wood of the door frame. The door is substantial, and it takes all my strength to raise the door a half inch against the frame and pull apart the lock. There's the sound of splintering wood, and the door swings open. I stand outside a moment, sniffing the air. The smell is pungent but not overpowering. I pull out the gun, take off the safety, and step into a narrow kitchen and a breakfast table.

"Is it safe?" Fiona asks.

"Yeah, since we're not dead." On the table are three cans of Drano and several boxes of wooden matches. "Dishes in the sink," I say. "He was here recently."

I lead Fiona into the living room, which is furnished with a brown, sagging couch and a single folding chair. A small television sits on a card table, its rabbit ears sticking out at a crazy angle. The living room leads to a hallway with two closed doors, one on the right, one on the left. I start down the hallway, and the source of the smell is unmistakable now; every step nearer the last door increases the intensity. I open the door on the left, which leads to a bathroom. I step in and pull back the shower curtain; the bathtub is filled with containers of lantern fuel, paint thinner, muriatic acid, along with some funnels and several lengths of rubber tubing. "He's set up for a pretty good operation," I say. "Profitable, but small enough to stay under the radar." I walk back to the hall and try the door across the hall; it swings open, and I walk into a twelve-by-ten-foot bedroom. A single bed hugs the wall to the right; on the bed is a pile of old clothes. "Recognize those?"

Fiona nods. "His street clothes."

I open the closet; four empty, wire hangers are on a rod. "It's almost like he's already moved on." Straight ahead is a desk, which has a cheap-looking printer but no computer. Three cell phones—each a different brand—are stacked next to the printer. *Stolen, like Paul thought.* I start through the drawers, but they're mostly empty.

"You find anything?"

I pull out the keys to the truck and hand them to Fiona. "Take the truck out of here."

"Why?"

"Maybe he'll come home. If the truck's not here, he won't know until it's too late."

"And you can have the gunfight at the OK Corral."

I shake my head. "I'm trying to stay alive here, Fiona. At least you can not get in the way."

"You can call the police right now. They can wait for him."

"All of a sudden you trust the police?"

She starts to answer, but my cell phone rings. I flip it open. "Dennehy."

"So, Skippy. You're inside." I freeze; the voice is

Bridges's. I walk to the front window and jerk back the blinds. The street is empty. "No, Skippy, I'm not out there. The silent alarm calls my phone. Well, today's phone, anyway."

"Where are you?"

He laughs. "God, you must be desperate, Skippy. Everything you touch becomes inadmissible as evidence."

"Yeah, well, I don't have busting you for meth in mind. Anyway, I've decided to work outside the system for a while."

He chuckles. "Doesn't matter. I won't be coming back there. The phones are already dead. I usually get two or three days out of one. I used one to take the picture. I hope you liked it. He looked so peaceful, lying there. I told him to smile, but he didn't."

Nausea floods through me. "Tell me where you are, you miserable fuck of a human being."

"Now, now, Skippy. Be nice. That way, I'll make what's coming next more merciful." He pauses. "It really is spectacular. Truly my finest work."

"You're a fucking coward, Bridges. You hide behind stolen phones and phony identities. Be a man. Come out and face me."

Bridges explodes with laughter. "Jesus, Skippy, is that right out of a police manual? Or maybe Psych 101?" His voice drops. "I make the rules. Not you. And I say we have unfinished business."

Suddenly, Fiona rips the phone out of my hand. "Robert. It's Fiona. What you're doing is terribly wrong. It's shameful. You have to turn yourself in."

I stare, stunned, and pull the phone back from her. "Bridges? It's Dennehy. Forget her. Tell me what you're going to do." I can hear Bridges breathe, but he doesn't speak. "Talk to me, Bridges."

"She's with you." His voice is petulant, annoyed. "She shouldn't do that."

Shit. He's got a thing for her. "Forget her, Bridges. This is about you and me."

"I've humiliated the great Thomas Dennehy. I was smarter than her precious Professor Buchanan. And she's with *you*." Bridges is losing it, talking to himself on the other end of the line. "Every single person in this thing has done exactly what *I've* decided. I'm in control."

"Leave her out of it, Bridges. This is about you and me."

Bridges pulls the phone up to his mouth, making his voice a breathy rasp. "It's already over; you just don't know it. You're in the wrong place, Dennehy. You've been in the wrong place since the beginning. You've been chasing ghosts. Now you will pay for the life you stole from me."

"Tell me what you're going to do, you coward."

"This is my schedule, do you hear me!" he screams. "You just stay by the phone, Skippy. You'll find out." The line goes dead.

I turn to Fiona. "Are you *trying* to get killed?"

"I'm not afraid of him, Thomas."

"You don't get this, do you? You were safe when he was using you. Now you're on my side." I start toward the back door. "Come on. We're leaving."

"To where?"

"I'm taking you someplace safe until this is over. I won't have your head on my conscience."

"No."

I whirl around. "Excuse me?"

"You gave the lecture that Bridges used me. You were right. I didn't understand how far hate could take him. And maybe you could cart me off now, except for one thing. I don't walk away from my responsibilities."

"What the hell does that mean?"

"You say you won't have my head on your conscience? Join the club, because I won't have yours on mine."

"You're not helping, Fiona. You're in the way."

"He loves me, Thomas. He won't hurt me."

I look at her cautiously. "You know how he feels about you?"

"Of course. Being a preacher doesn't make me dead, Thomas."

I watch her, considering. "What are you saying? That you'll act as bait?"

"If it has a chance of bringing him in, yes."

"He's a dangerous man, Fiona. You don't know what you're saying."

"You have no other choice."

"So you figure I'll let you put yourself at risk to save my ass. Not hardly." I exhale. "Look, I appreciate the offer. It's admirable. Every time I'm around you, you do some damn thing I don't expect. But on this, you're dreaming."

I take her to my home. There's nothing else I can do, because she's in this thing now. *She shouldn't do that,* Bridges had said, and that can't be good. He killed his parole officer for suggesting he work as an orderly in a hospital. The penalty for siding with the man he hates above all others, I can't imagine. We pull into my subdivision about noon. I make Fiona stay in the truck until I go through the house, room by room. The house is clear, and I lock it down once we're inside.

I set the .45 on a table in the front hallway, pick up a phone, and call Sarandokos's number. "Maria, please get me Rebecca."

"Si, Señor Dennehy. I get her."

A few seconds later, Rebecca answers in an icy tone. "Hello, Thomas."

"Is Jazz okay?"

"Of course she's okay. What's this about?"

"Where is she, right now?"

"Fifteen feet away from me."

"Good. Keep her at home, and turn on the alarm."

The silence that follows contains a truckload of recriminations, disappointments, and frustrations. Finally, she says, "How bad is it?"

"I'm going to send over a uniform tonight."

"A uniform."

"Yeah. Just for tonight."

Her voice is pure metal. "And what do I tell Jazz when she asks me why there's a man out front with a gun?"

I close my eyes. "Keep her away from the windows. Play games or something. Is Michael home today?"

"He's going to play golf."

"Tell him to cancel it."

Another pause. "You're scaring me, Thomas. What's going on?"

"Nothing's going to happen. Just keep her in sight today, and everything's going to be fine. It'll be over soon." *Sarandokos's alarm is state of the art. A mouse couldn't get through that thing.*

"It's never over, Thomas. That's the problem." She hangs up.

Three adults, perimeter security, a gated community, and tonight, an armed guard. One thing I know. I'll never let him get his hands on Jazz. Let him come after me, and we'll finish this once and for all. I hand Fiona my cell phone. "I'm taking a shower. Come get me if it rings."

I go to the bedroom and strip. The shower water's as hot

as I can stand, but it doesn't soothe. I'm inside Charles Bridges's clock now, forced to wait. I don't call the police, since there's nothing to tell them. *The guy you can't find is somewhere planning something terrible he won't reveal.* It feels like something inside me wants to explode. I towel off, throw on jeans and pull on a shirt, and walk back out into the living room. Fiona is sitting in one of the living room chairs, her eyes closed. "You getting some rest?"

She opens her eyes. "I was praying."

"Does that help?"

She smiles softly. "At the moment, it's all I've got. You feel better?"

"Yeah. I don't know. Cleaner, anyway."

She hands the phone to me. "Did you eat?"

"No."

"Is there anything in the kitchen?"

"Last time I looked, just eggs."

"Stay here." She walks past me, and in a few moments I hear her pulling out a pan from underneath the counter. *She's this big feminist, activist, liberal. And then she goes to make me eggs.*

I don't have the energy to analyze it. I'm wiped, caught between exhaustion and the nervousness of waiting on Bridges. I wander into the kitchen, set the phone on the breakfast table, and sit. Fiona goes to the refrigerator and pulls out eggs, milk, cheese, a green pepper, and a red onion. "I can do that myself, you know," I say. "I just did, the other night."

"Olive oil?"

"Under the counter."

Within a couple of minutes she has the eggs on the gas range. "Where's the coffee?"

I stand. "You're in luck, Towns. I make the greatest coffee

on Earth." I go through my coffee ritual, grateful for something to do. It feels normal, as though we weren't a phone
call away from having the world turn upside down. When
I've finished, she's got the eggs on plates. I hand her a cup,
and she takes a sip.

"Good grief, Dennehy."

"Yeah, I know."

We sit across from each other at the table, the phone between us. I don't say much, but I'm glad she's there. However
bad this is, it would be worse alone. "They're good," I say.

"Thanks. There wasn't much to work with." She picks at
her food, lost in thought. After a couple of minutes she walks
over to the sink and starts cleaning up.

"Just leave it," I say, over my shoulder. "It doesn't matter." She doesn't answer. I turn and look, and see her staring
into the sink, her hands clenched along its rim. "Hey, you
OK?" I walk up behind her and put my hand on her shoulder.
She turns, and I see she's crying.

"I'm sorry," she says. "I should have seen this. I should
have done something to prevent it."

"It's OK."

She turns and puts her arms around me, pulling me
against her. Her face is in my neck. "Your friend is dead."

I press my hand behind her neck, and her hair falls down
over my fingers. "You drive me nuts, Towns. You know that,
don't you?"

"Yes."

"You also have more real courage than anybody I've met
in a long time."

She pulls back far enough to look up at me. "I'm so sorry,
Thomas."

"It's weird, but Carl would have liked you. He would have

said you were wrong about everything. But he would have liked you anyway. He was that kind of man."

She smiles softly. "I'm sorry I never met him."

"You two would have had a hell of a debate." I kiss her cheek and walk back to the breakfast table. The phone sits silent and dangerous, like an armed explosive. "I can't stand here and watch it all day." I fall back against the chair, letting her fingers knead my shoulders. She moves up against me, and my head leans against her stomach. I close my eyes and let myself drift away a little. She moves her fingers down my spine, then presses her palms outward, pushing tension out with the movement.

"Put your head down."

I lean forward, and she moves her hands down to my belt and begins tracing them slowly upward. She presses her hands back down, and I give in to her completely, letting her work the fatigue out of the muscles. She massages me for ten minutes or so, then bends down to kiss my neck. I turn to face her. "When I saw you in court, that first day, I thought we'd be enemies."

"Me, too."

"Maybe when this is all over."

"Maybe."

I stand, pull her to me, and breathe her in. The scent I noticed before is on her, and on me, now, as well. I pull her closer and move to kiss her. She opens her lips slightly, and I feel her hips press against me. I kiss her, and she opens her mouth and presses her tongue into mine. I pull her hard against me, and we exchange another long, deep kiss. I step back, exhaling. "I'm sorry. I just . . ."

"It's OK," she says. "I wanted to."

Ten minutes later, my home line rings. Even though it's

not my cell, my heart jumps into my mouth. The caller ID shows it's Bec. I answer, and she says, "Thomas? It's me." A pause. "Listen, I just wanted to make sure you were okay."

I exhale, letting my heart rate settle. "I'm fine. Is Jazz all right?"

"She's in her room, playing." Another pause. "All this talk about taking care of Jazz. It's you who's in danger, isn't it?"

"I can take care of myself, Bec."

"It's just that I got another one of my bad feelings. Like something terrible was going to happen." More silence. "Tell me the truth, Thomas. Is this going to be OK?"

"Michael's there, right?"

"We're all here. Michael, Maria, and me."

"Then don't worry."

"I just had such a chill inside. A feeling of dread." A final pause. "Don't take any crazy risks today, OK, Thomas?"

"Try not to worry, Bec. Give Jazz a kiss for me, and tell her I love her."

I hang up, then punch in the numbers for the South station of the police. I ask for the desk sergeant and get a woman named Welch. "Listen, this is Thomas Dennehy, assistant district attorney. I was wondering if I could get a favor from you."

"Anything, Mr. Dennehy. Mr. Becker had friends here."

"Carl's killer is still at large, and I'm concerned about my daughter as a possible target."

"You want an officer?"

"Yes."

"Well, I can't pull an officer off a route to do it. But I can cover it from second shift on."

"That would be great."

"What's the address?"

"Twenty-two Wentworth Place, over in President's Club."

"I'll make this work, but if you want it to go on past to-night, I'm going to need paperwork."

"Thanks, Sergeant. I owe you."

"We'll handle it."

I click off the phone. "So Jazz is OK."

"You're daughter's going to be fine, Thomas. It sounds like *you* somebody was worried about."

I nod. "Before? That was my ex-wife. She's concerned our daughter still has a father when this is over."

"Sounds reasonable."

I walk into the living room, and collapse on the couch. "If I could bring Bridges to me, I would. But he's not playing it that way. He's checking off a list of things I care about."

She sits next to me. "What's left?"

I shake my head. "Lots of things. The whole staff at the DA's office. A good steak. The Atlanta Braves." I pause. "And you."

She smiles. "Yeah, but I'm here with you."

"I'm just saying, if it goes down, I'm not letting you do something stupid and heroic."

"You know something, Dennehy? I'm not the kind of woman who takes orders very well."

"So I noticed." With that, it's over; I pull her against me and kiss her as hard as I can. My hands are trembling. Hell, my whole body is trembling. It's Carl and Indy and the truck and shit-faced, grinding fear over what Bridges is going to do next, wrapped up with eighteen months of untapped lust, and it breaks like a dam over the Reverend Towns. She answers it hungrily, kissing me back so ferociously that I wonder what anguish and frustrations she's been keeping behind her own dam. Whatever they are, it's enough to unravel her as completely as I come apart, and we wrap around each other until I can barely breathe. I can feel how strong she is;

her strength ignites me, and I push back against her, reveling in her strength. "Jesus," I say. "Get this—"

"It's in the back."

"My God." Her hands unbuckle my belt; she pushes her fingers down into my open fly, and I moan, pressing my hips forward. Somehow, her shirt is pulled over her head, her bra undone. What happens next is a pressing, flexing blur, part release, part aggression. It's sex and abyss, blended into one. My pants are stuck on my left ankle, hers are draped over the back of the couch. Her teeth are in my shoulder, her fingernails in my back. We move together, naked, until she opens her eyes wide, her breath coming in great gasps. Her hand comes up behind my head, and she pulls my face down into her neck. For a long time, nothing exists but us.

When it's over, neither of us moves. I breathe in her scent and feel her skin against me the length of my body. I'm crying a little—I don't know when it started—but I know it's over Carl, not what just happened. I haven't wept for him, and I have to, just a little, or I'll go nuts. I roll over on my side and kiss her. "You're staying alive," I whisper. "No matter what."

"People staying alive is what I'm all about, Dennehy."

For a moment—a few seconds—I get it; for Fiona, there's life, and then there's everything else. As long as we're alive, there's the chance for a moment like what just happened, and it's so healthy and affirming and fucking gorgeous that for a few seconds, I don't want to deny it to anyone, no matter who they are or what they've done. Maybe it even has the power to heal a monster. I kiss Fiona on the mouth, still getting used to how she tastes, still alive to the nuance of the shape of her lips. "The Reverend Fiona Towns," I whisper, and I kiss her again. There's something holy about her, even when she's naked, or maybe especially when she's naked; I've seen how it works for her, how even a damaged life can be sacred. But in the same moment, I know it doesn't work that way for me. When I think about the photograph of Carl, I lose my mercy. I know that in the right circumstances, I am fully capable of killing Charles Bridges, and that if that moment comes, something in me will feel profoundly grateful for the chance to do it. I pull her against me and whisper in her ear again: "The Reverend Fiona Towns."

The afternoon passes with agonizing slowness. Against the euphoria and comfort of each other's presence is the torture of the silent phone. Every hour is both a relief and an increase in tension; we've survived, but we know Bridges's end game has moved toward us, too. When, at nearly 5:00 p.m., nothing has happened, Fiona makes an announcement. "He could do this to us for days, Thomas. This is exactly what he wants."

I drag my eyes off the phone. "I know that. It doesn't change anything."

"I'm going to the store. We have to eat."

"You can't go alone, and I'm not leaving."

"It's a cell phone, Thomas. It travels."

"We'll order pizza."

She walks to me. She has on one of my T-shirts, tucked into her black jeans. "There's a sandwich place right up the road. We could order out and bring it home."

I nod. "All right. But we go together."

It's only five minutes to the restaurant, and I go in with Fiona while she orders. Fifteen minutes later we're back in the house, devouring the meal. I haven't eaten properly for a couple of days, and it's catching up with me. But there's still no call. At 7:30, I use my home phone to ring my cell, just to make sure it's working. The cell phone rings, and I hang it up.

"Maybe it's a bluff," Fiona says. "He just wants you to look over your shoulder for the rest of your life."

"Maybe," I say, but I don't believe it.

At 8:45, I force myself to stop pacing; at 9:30, I'm ready to throw the phone out the window. Stress, combined with lack of sleep, are wearing me down; I catch a glimpse of myself in the mirror and realize the man looking back isn't capable of denying himself sleep another night. My body is going to demand its due.

At 10:45, I can't fight it anymore. "I've got to sleep," I say.

Fiona nods. "Me, too."

"Look, I can take the couch."

"If that's what you want."

"What I want is you six inches away from me. I just didn't want to presume."

She smiles, and I know we're past that. I take her hand and lead her into the bedroom. I plug the cell phone into the charger and strip down to my shorts. I flick off the light and climb in bed. Fiona pulls off her jeans and T-shirt, and climbs naked into bed next to me. I lie on my back, Fiona on her side beside me, facing me. "Nobody's spent the night with me in this bed since my ex-wife."

"How long ago was that?"

I smile. "God, I don't know. Three years."

She takes my hand and lifts it to her lips. "Get some sleep, Dennehy. You need rest."

She flicks off the light, and I close my eyes. The last sound I hear before I fall asleep is the sound of Fiona's voice, whispering into the heavens.

* * *

Sometime in the night, I open my eyes. I'm breathing heavily, lying in my bed. I realize I have the sheets in a vise grip, and I let my hands relax. I look over at Fiona and see her watching me in the dim light. She's up on one elbow, her hair falling down below her head. Her body is in shadow, but I can see the contours of her arm, her flat stomach, the rise of her breasts. She reaches over and lets her fingers stroke my chest. "You were dreaming."

"Yeah."

She lifts my arm and climbs inside it, laying her head on my shoulder. I sigh and let myself relax back into the bed. The clock says 1:15. "It's OK now," she says. "Go back to sleep." Her breathing is steady and deep. I close my eyes, feeling her weight, letting her presence calm me. In a few minutes, I follow her back down into the dark. There are nearly two hours of peace. A little after 3:00 a.m., the phone rings. Charles Bridges has set my world on fire.

CHAPTER
TWENTY-THREE

MY HAND IS ON the cell phone before I'm fully awake. By the time I flip it open, every synapse of my mind is on alert. It's Sarandokos's number, and Rebecca is on the line. She's hysterical. I can't understand her because she's not using complete words, much less complete sentences.

"Calm down, Bec. Tell me what's happened."

"It's Jazz. She's not in her bed."

My body turns to ice. "What do you mean? Did you search the house?"

"We've searched every inch. The policeman is looking outside. It's like she just vanished out of thin air."

"I don't understand. The policeman was there all night, right?"

"Yes. I sent her to bed at nine o'clock. Michael and I sleep just down the hall. The alarm was on. There's no way anyone could have come in the house without our knowing."

"Stay there. I'm coming to you."

"What's happened to our daughter, Thomas?"

"I'm coming. Stay together."

I hit the lights and see Fiona is already pulling on her clothes. "Not you," I say. "You stay here."

She pushes her feet into shoes. "I can help."

"I don't have time to argue, Fiona. You're not coming."

"I can talk to him. You can't."

I pull on pants and a shirt and head for the doorway. "If you're not near him, he can't hurt you."

She grabs my arm and pulls me around. "It's your daughter, Thomas. Are you willing to let something happen with me here doing nothing?"

There's no time to think. All I want is to get Jazz away from the monster. "I could lose you both. That isn't going to happen." I see her bend over to pick up shoes, and I use the moment to grab the gun off the nightstand and push it behind my back. Fiona straightens up and stands in the doorway to the bedroom, resolute. I walk up to her and take her face in my hands. "Help me, Fiona. Help me by staying here and letting me do what I have to do."

"You mean that if I'm there, it might be harder to kill him."

"I mean that if I'm lucky enough to find him, there won't be time to have a discussion about it." I step past her, leaving her in the doorway. "Don't open the door to anyone. I'll be back as soon as I can."

I move through the house, jump in the truck, and hit the ignition. The truck roars to life, and I pull out of the garage, barely missing the rising garage door. I slam the truck into drive and lay a strip of rubber as I head toward President's Club and Sarandokos's house. I punch "911" into the phone, and dispatch answers. "This is Thomas Dennehy, with the

DA's office. My daughter, Jasmine, has just been kidnapped.
I need the Tennessee Bureau of Investigation notified immediately. The address is twenty-two Wentworth Place, in President's Club. You got that?"

"I'm not sure . . ."

"You *got* it?"

"How long has your daughter been missing, sir?"

"She's been *kidnapped*. Are you following me here?"

"Sir, if you'll just calm down . . ."

I hang up and call Rayburn at home. He answers, bleary
and fatigued. "David, it's Thomas."

"Thomas. Where have you been? Paul showed me the
photograph."

"Did you get the trap-and-trace?"

"Ginder signed the court order at one-thirty. We faxed it
to Sprint from his office."

"Jazz has been kidnapped, David. Bridges has her."

"My God. Where are you now?"

"On my way to Sarandokos's house in President's Club. I
need you to wake up somebody over at TBI, David. The best
they have."

"Done. Listen, Thomas, how did—"

"Hang up and call, David." I slap shut the phone.

I brush a hundred miles an hour as I haul down a nearly
empty I-65. In less than fifteen minutes I pull into President's Club and squeal to a stop at the gate. I punch in the
entrance code, and the gates slowly grind open. I squeeze
through with inches to spare, turn left a few blocks up on
Wentworth Place, and see Sarandokos's house at the end.
The front door is open, and the yard is lit up with floodlights.
A single police car is parked out front; the officer stands beside the vehicle, talking into his radio.

I screech to a halt, and the cop gives me a warning look.

"The girl's my daughter," I say, showing him my ID. "Tell me what you know."

The officer—a young kid, low on the seniority totem pole—nods. "The lady came outside about forty minutes ago. She was real upset, kinda hysterical."

"You were out front the entire night?"

"From seven-ten on. The lady says she put the girl to bed at nine, so whatever happened was after I got here. I didn't see anything."

"Any vehicles in or out?"

He pulls out a small notebook. "A black Mercedes came into sixteen Carmel Lane at nine-twenty. That's it. I even cataloged the cars on the street, just to note any changes."

"And?"

"There's a red Porsche in a driveway at thirty-one Crooked Stick, a Lincoln Town Car at twelve Sunset Road, and a Hertz panel truck just around the corner."

I look up. "Panel truck?"

The officer shrugs. "It's legit. There's a for-sale sign on the house where it's parked. I asked a neighbor, and he told me the people are moving."

I look up at the house and see Rebecca standing in the doorway, silhouetted by light. She comes down the stairs, but she's no longer sobbing. She's cold, like she's made of metal. She walks toward me like an ice sculpture, so brittle a tap in the wrong place will shatter her into pieces.

"Who has our baby, Thomas?"

"His name is Charles Bridges. I sent him to jail seven years ago."

"To jail."

"Yes. For negligent homicide."

A tremble escapes the stony stillness of her face. "Then he's a killer," she whispers.

"He killed Carl."

She wobbles, but when I reach out to steady her, she slaps my hand away.

"Find the most recent photograph of Jazz that you have," I say. "Do you have any of her hair?"

"Her hair? No."

"Then get her toothbrush. We need her DNA, Bec."

Her eyes glisten with angry tears. "Michael is inside."

I sweep past her up the limestone stairs and see Sarandokos in the doorway, dressed in a thousand dollars' worth of casual clothes. "What the hell has happened to Jasmine, Dennehy?"

"Tell me about the alarm, Michael."

"You'd damn well better get her back."

"The *alarm,* Michael. Tell me how it works."

"All the windows and doors on the first floor are armed."

"How about inside motion detectors?"

"We have them but don't turn them on. Maria sleeps downstairs." He lifts his chin. "I'm going to offer a million-dollar reward for Jasmine's return, Dennehy. I've already called Channel Four. It'll be on the TV this morning."

"The man who took Jazz isn't going to be impressed by money, Michael."

"Everyone is impressed with a million dollars, Dennehy. But if it will help, I'm willing to make it two."

"I need to see her room."

Michael swivels and leads me through the foyer and up the marble staircase to the second floor. He opens the fourth door on the right, and we step into Oz: to the left is a wall of carefully stacked toys; to the right, a collection of porcelain, miniature horses; ahead, a pink iMac sits on an antique desk. The bed is unmade, but otherwise, the room is so immaculate, it's hard to imagine an eleven-year-old girl living there.

I walk to a large window; it's locked from the inside. I slide open the lock and reach down to pull it open, but it doesn't budge. I put my weight into it, but the window only slides upward a couple of inches with a pronounced squeak.

I turn to Michael. "Let's go over this again. The ground-level doors and windows have an alarm."

He nods.

"This window is locked from the inside, and there's a cop sitting in a car out front."

"Yes."

I turn back to the window and stare out. Lights are coming on across President's Club, as the residents become aware that there's a disturbance. I hear Bec come in the room behind me and turn to see her standing in the doorway, holding a framed picture of our daughter and a toothbrush. Anger and grief wash over me, and I force my eyes away in an attempt to keep my mind clear. *Hang on, baby. I'm trying to get to you.*

"Did Jazz know how to turn off the alarm?" I ask.

"Of course," Sarandokos says. "She's seen us do it a thousand times."

"When did you turn it on?"

"As soon as you called. Right after I hung up."

My God. Bridges was already in the house when he called me. Slowly, I turn back to them and look at Bec. "He was here, Bec. Bridges was already inside the house when you turned on the alarm."

Bec's face crumples into revulsion. "What?"

"It's a big house, Bec. You have three outside doors on the back side alone."

"Four," Sarandokos says.

"He could have been somewhere in the house most of the day. A closet. Anywhere."

Bec stares at her husband. "He was in our house, Michael."

"Sometime last night he must have pulled Jazz out of her bedroom, frightened her into silence, and forced her to leave with him." I look at the bed and imagine Bridges leaning over my daughter, forcing a knife to her throat, telling her he'll kill her if she makes a sound.

Sarandokos points to the window. "A car's pulling up. Someone's coming."

We go downstairs and see an unmarked Ford parking in front of the patrol car. Two men in street clothes get out. One, a short, bookish-looking man with mussed, brown hair and glasses, goes to the trunk. The other, a tall man with a narrow face and jet-black hair combed back, walks directly up the entryway and shakes my hand. "Agent Myers," he says. "You're Dennehy, correct?"

"You're TBI?"

He shakes his head. "FBI. Kidnapping the daughter of a government official warrants federal attention." The other man comes up behind, carrying two aluminum cases. "This is Newton. He's our bloodhound." Myers steps past me and introduces himself to Sarandokos and Rebecca, who are just behind us in the foyer. "We need a table, chairs, good lighting," he says. "Do you have any coffee?"

Michael nods. "I heard Maria making some already. This way."

Sarandokos leads us through the house to the dining room, located just off the kitchen. We take places around a large circular mahogany table. Newton sets the aluminum cases on the floor and starts setting up a laptop computer on the table.

"The DA filled me in where he could, but there were a lot of holes," Myers says. "Tell me about this guy Bridges."

"Intelligent, with a medical background," I say. "He's highly organized, plans several steps ahead. He very nearly brought down the entire DA's office. He also managed to commit two murders with virtually no physical evidence linking him to the crimes."

"Where was the girl seen last?"

"Her room," Bec says. "I put her to bed at nine."

"I saw an alarm panel near the front door," Myers says. "Was it armed?"

"Yes," I answer. "There was also a policeman outside all night. And the second floor is too high to scale."

"From which you conclude?"

I pause, considering. "Realistically? There are two possibilities. One is that she walked out on her own. That would take a strong lure."

"You don't look convinced."

"Jazz is smart, and she's had the 'don't talk to strangers' lecture a thousand times. Plus Bridges has until recently been impersonating a homeless man, complete with lack of shower, full beard, and tattered clothes. Jazz wouldn't get within a mile of him."

"And the other possibility?"

"That Bridges was already in the house when the alarm was turned on. He forced Jazz out one of the back doors and left the subdivision via another street. The cop out front wouldn't have seen anything."

Myers nods thoughtfully. "First things first. The DA said you expect Bridges to call again."

I lay my cell phone on the table. "He's been calling this number using stolen cell phones."

"I've already talked to Sprint," Newton says. "They're waiting to hear back from us." He picks up my phone. "Nokia 475. That's good."

"So what's the plan?"

Newton looks up from plugging in cables. "If Bridges is stupid, he'll call us from a GPS-equipped phone, and the Sprint tech will tell us exactly where to find him."

"Bridges isn't stupid."

"We still have a good chance to locate him with cell towers."

"How good?"

"We triangulate his position by measuring the difference in the time it takes for his signal to reach the three closest cell towers. A little calculus, and we have him to within fourteen hundred feet." He plugs in a cable to the base of my phone. "With more towers, I can get it down to nine hundred." He grins. "Once, I got the actual house."

"Trust me," Myers says, "if Bridges calls, Newton will find him. Meanwhile, I want to see all the exits to the house. Let's go."

Sarandokos leads Myers and me through the extensive home. Each door is an alarm point, with a keypad. Myers stops at a door leading from a sunroom out onto the back patio. "So these can be disarmed individually?" he asks.

Michael nods. "You punch star, the alarm code, and the entry number. You get fifteen seconds to open and close the door. It resets after that time."

Myers looks out into the backyard. "What's behind that line of trees?"

"Another house," Sarandokos says. "The street it's on dumps into the main road to the gate, just like ours."

"Any reason to believe Bridges is an alarm expert?" Myers asks.

"No," I answer. "People pick stuff up in prison, but I don't see him taking this on. Anyway, it's not his style. He uses his brains, not a lot of sophisticated equipment."

Myers looks out into the backyard. "Once you get off the patio, it's dark back here." He leads us back to the dining room, where Newton is plugging his own phone into the system. Newton looks up and says, "You ready for me to call Sprint?" Myers nods, and Newton dials a number. We hear it ring over the computer's speakers. On the third ring, a surprisingly young, female voice answers.

"This is Blair Kipling, Sprint technical officer. I'm here to assist you."

Myers and Newton exchange looks. "Agent Myers here," Myers says. "With me is Agent Newton and Thomas Dennehy."

"I have Mr. Dennehy's phone on my screen now."

Myers reaches over and mutes the microphone. "She sounds sixteen, Newt."

Newton nods. "We're probably only gonna get one shot on this. You want to go over her head?"

Myers turns the mic back on. "Listen, Ms. . . . Kipling, was it?"

"That's right, sir. Blair Kipling."

"Can I ask how long you've held this position, Ms. Kipling?"

"Two months, sir." There's a pause. "This is my first actual law enforcement call."

Myers winces. "Is anybody there who might have had a little more experience at this kind of thing?"

"I'm fully qualified for this position, sir."

"That wasn't the question, Kipling."

"I'm the only law enforcement–certified technician available at the moment, sir."

Myers gives Newton another look, and Newton shrugs. "Glad to have you on the team, Ms. Kipling," Myers says.

"Thank you, sir. I'm monitoring Mr. Dennehy's phone

now. The manual suggests we keep this line open while we wait."

"The manual."

"Yes, sir."

"Well, then, Ms. Kipling, that's what we'll do."

"Very good, sir."

Myers shakes his head. "Where's that coffee?"

"Excuse me, sir?"

"I'm talking to somebody here, Kipling. I'll let you know when we need you." He reaches over and mutes the microphone. "Beautiful. She just graduated from third grade."

The waiting begins. Myers sits up straight, eyes clear, his mind clearly working even when no one talks. Newton is less patient; he fiddles with his equipment, drums his fingers, fidgets. Bec can't stand staring at the phone any longer; sometime deep in the night she goes upstairs, although I know she's not sleeping. At 5:30, a thin line of yellow breaks outside, signaling another day is beginning. Maria comes in with more coffee and goes to make breakfast.

Myers pulls his gaze off the phone and looks at me. "This fucker Bridges has got to be loving this," he says.

"Yeah."

"We can't do shit here."

Newton grumbles in his chair and pushes a button on his computer. "You still there, Kipling?"

"Yes, sir. Still here."

"Just checking."

Newton grumbles something unintelligible and slumps down in his chair.

I'm past exhaustion, into something like a dull, horrible buzzing state. My eyes are burning, and I close them.

My phone rings.

"Fuck," Newton says, jerking upright. "You on this, Kipling?"

"Yes, sir," the voice says. "Just a moment."

"Fuck, fuck, fuck," Newton whispers. "Come on baby, talk to me."

"Do I answer it?" I ask.

"Does he answer it, Kipling?"

"Yes, sir. Answer the phone."

I press "talk." "Bridges? Is that you, Bridges?"

"I have it, sir," Kipling says. "It's not a voice call. You're receiving an SMS signal. It might be a picture."

"What's the ID number, Kipling?" Newton says.

A pause. "It's 477911009CDMA."

Newton is typing while she talks. "Come on, come on, come on." We sit, tense, while the picture downloads. When it pops onto the screen, it's fairly dark, and the picture isn't clear. I stare, just to be sure, stand, and walk away from the table.

"What is it?" Myers demands, moving to look. "I can't figure this out."

I look over and see Bec in the doorway. She starts toward the table, and I grab her arm to stop her. She wrenches it away and walks to the table. Slowly, she leans over. A second passes, and she turns toward me, horror in her eyes. "It's a birthmark on my daughter's inner thigh," she says quietly. "Which means she's nude."

"Jesus," Myers says, sitting down. The picture completes, and the call ends. He looks at Newton. "Tell me you have him," he says.

Newton is staring at his computer screen, typing commands. He looks up. "I don't get it. It didn't lock."

Myers stares. "You sure? Was there a good signal?"

"The signal was excellent," Kipling says, over the speaker. "The odds of a successful triangulation were ninety-four percent."

Newton looks up. "It locked on two towers almost instantly. But it never got a third."

Myers stands up, frustrated. "Dammit! There are five towers near here. It should be a piece of cake."

I look at Myers. "You didn't get him."

He shakes his head. "I'm sorry. Look, it's a fluke. He'll call back; we'll nail him."

I nod and walk out of the room. *Always a step ahead. Always smarter than we are.*

I spend an hour alone, trying to exorcize my demons. It's impossible to let myself think about where Jazz is, but great, horrifying chasms of empty time stretch out in front of me, tempting hideous images into my mind. I'm afraid to close my eyes because Bridges waits in the darkness, and Jazz is there with him. Compounding everything is the sense of helplessness. Bridges is in control of everything, reducing us to nothing more than waiting. I don't know why Newton and the FBI can't lock down from where Bridges is calling, but it doesn't surprise me. There was no way in hell he wouldn't have figured that out. This is the culmination of seven years of planning, and we're along for the ride.

I finally wander back into the dining room to see Sarandokos standing in the doorway, wearing a tailored suit. "I'm going to Channel Four," he says.

Myers looks up, surprised. "What's he talking about?"

"He's offering a reward," I say. "A million dollars."

"Why didn't I know anything about this?"

"Because it doesn't concern you," Sarandokos replies.

"I'm offering the money for Jasmine's return, no questions asked."

"Wait a minute; we have to sort this out. We've got to coordinate."

"There's nothing to coordinate," Sarandokos snaps. "Your equipment isn't working, is it?"

"That's not the point."

"And so far you have nothing, correct?"

"Look, you're gonna open a whole can of worms with this."

"I find, Agent Myers, that greed is a great equalizer. Jasmine is going to be dead soon unless something changes. So I will make it change." He walks out. Rebecca waits for him by the door. He hugs her, and she turns and goes back upstairs.

"Great," Myers says. "We're going to have every fruitcake in town sending us on snipe hunts."

"It doesn't matter," I say quietly. "It can't be any worse than sitting here on the end of Bridges's chain."

Newton grumbles and shifts in his chair. "When are those other agents getting here?"

Myers looks at his watch. "By eight," he says. "They're sending Goodman, Jordan, and Chavez. They're going over the house."

"Wonderful. When they finish that, they can sit here and watch this damn phone with us." Newton grunts and settles into his chair. "I'm gonna paint a fucking *S* on this guy's shirt when we find him. How he manages to connect a phone call with that kind of signal strength and it can't be triangulated is beyond me. Maybe we need to get some damn Kryptonite or something."

Myers reaches over and mutes the microphone. "I'll be outside," he says. "I can't take staring at this thing anymore."

The day stretches before us like a festering wound. Every

minute makes it blacker and deeper, and the knowledge that
the waiting gives Bridges pleasure is enough to make me go
mad. Like the horror of the day, my anger deepens, until I
can't see anything but Bridges in my mind, and the thought
of a bullet entering his brain, his face contorted in surprise
and agony.

I don't watch Sarandokos make his pitch on TV, although
Myers and Newton do. When I walk by the dining table afterward, Myers shakes his head and says, "He gave his home
phone number. I'd give it about an hour before the nutcases
start in."

Myers's prediction turns out to be optimistic; it's less
than twenty before the calls start, and Myers is forced to take
the first several, before Sarandokos gets back. When
Michael finally returns, Myers hands him the phone. "Here,"
he says. "This was your idea. You can deal with it."

The agents who were due at 8:00 show up seven minutes
late, earning them a sharp reprimand from Myers. The three
officers—two men and a woman—unload their equipment
and start through the house, examining it room by room. At
least it's something to watch. But I don't care what they find,
since they'll never find it in time to help Jazz.

Myers lets the agents work on the dining room first, then
banishes them to keep them out of our hair. It's necessary,
but it means that staying out of their way relegates us to two
rooms of the house for the duration. Myers, Newton, and I
gather once again around the table, exhausted and tense.

"This could go on for a while, you know?" Newton says.
"I mean, think about it."

Myers nods. "The cops are out looking for him, though.
There's risk in stretching it out too long."

"How long has it been since the last call? Maybe he's setting up a pattern."

Myers looks at his watch. "A little more than three hours," he says.

"It feels like ten," Newton says, leaning back in his chair.

By the time Maria brings in sandwiches at 11:00, we're crawling in our skins. "Eat, Señor Dennehy," she says. "You must keep up your strength." Her eyes are swollen with crying; she loves Jazz like her own daughter, and even though she's staying out of the way, I know what's happened is hard on her.

Myers and Newton dig in hungrily, but I ignore the food. I catch myself falling asleep, blanking out for minutes at a time. It's becoming clear I can't go on like this much longer. At some point, I'm going to have to get some actual rest.

I drift out for long enough that when the phone jerks me back awake, I have no idea how long I've been out. I stare over at Newton, who is punching keys on his computer. "We're on, man," he says. "You getting this, Kipling?"

"Yes, sir. He's changed phones. Give me a moment, please."

Newton is staring at the signal strength on his computer screen, eyes wide. "Jesus Christ, he's pegging the meters. We're gonna get him. I'm telling you, he's toast."

"I have him, sir," Kipling says. "It's a Motorola V600. Just give me a second, please."

Newton looks over at me. "They're easier to track."

"That's correct, sir. Just a second . . . 44386508GSM1. Do you have it?"

Newton types. "Come on, you lousy son of a bitch. I know you're out there somewhere. Come to Papa."

"It's another picture," I say, filling with dread. I look and turn away in horror. The picture shows the same part of Jasmine's upper leg, but now the birthmark has been removed.

Whatever he used to slice off the birthmark, it was razor sharp and wielded with precision. Tiny droplets of blood ooze from the wound. I stand and walk to the wall, holding my sides. Like before, Bec appears in the doorway. She sees me, and I shake my head. "Don't," I whisper.

She slumps, holding herself up by the door. Maria comes in, and I motion her toward Bec. She gets Bec turned around, and they vanish back upstairs.

I turn to Newton. "Did you get it?"

Newton is pounding away, his expression confused. "Dammit! Come on, you son of a bitch!"

"Are you getting it, sir?" Kipling asks. "The signal is excellent."

Newton types a few more seconds, then looks up, the color drained from his face. "I can't explain it," he says, slumping down in his chair. "The fucking *CIA* can't defeat this thing. It's physics, man."

Myers strides to Newton's computer. "What the hell's going on, Newt?"

"I don't know. I've got a rock-solid signal, and I simply can't triangulate it. Dammit!"

I didn't know exactly when my point of collapse would come, but this is it. I walk to the wall, turn, and slide on my back down to the floor. I close my eyes. I know that I'm going away now, and I don't care. I'll be back, although I'm not sure in what condition. But it is simply no longer possible for me to count second after second with Jazz in the clutches of a man I now understand is a complete monster.

"Sir?" Blair Kipling's voice comes over the speaker, but I barely notice.

"Not now, Kipling." Myers walks over and puts his hand on my shoulder. "I'm sorry," he says. "We did our best. He's just . . . I don't know. We just can't crack the thing, that's all."

"Sir?"

Myers turns, his expression irritated. "What is it, Kipling?"

"I was just going to say, sir. The Nokia 475 is a GSM-1 compatible phone."

"Thanks for the information."

"That particular model receives SMS text messages, even when the phone is turned off." Myers motions to Newton to mute. "What I'm saying, sir, is that I can turn on the GPS feature inside that phone remotely."

Newton's finger freezes an inch above the mute button. I look up, not breathing. "What did you say?" Myers asks.

"I can turn the GPS in the phone on from here, sir. It gives an exact—"

"*Do* it, Kipling! For the love of God, just do it!"

"I just did, sir."

Myers sprints to the speakerphone. "Are you saying you have him?"

"Yes, sir. The phone is at the intersection of Avondale and Middleton, moving north."

The three of us stare at each other an electric second; the next we're heading to the door. "Call me on my cell line, Kipling," Myers yells into the speakerphone. "We're moving."

"Yes, sir."

Newton, Myers, and I sprint down the stairs and pile into Myers's car. Myers spins a one-eighty and hauls out of President's Club. His phone rings at the gate, and he answers on speaker. "It's Blair Kipling, Agent Myers. I have you on GPS. You're about six miles from the target."

"You're a damn genius, Kipling. Did anybody ever tell you that?"

"Thank you, sir. We pride ourselves on our service."

Myers looks over at me and grins. "We're gonna get this bastard. He finally fucked up."

"How about a roadblock?" Newton says from the backseat.

"No," I answer. "I don't want him to panic while Jazz is still alive. We have the advantage as long as he doesn't know we're in pursuit."

We pull onto Concord Road and head west toward I-65.

"Talk to me, Kipling," Myers says. "Where is he now?"

"The phone has stopped, sir. It's at the intersection of Avondale and Walnut Grove."

"Jesus," Newton says, "we're less than four miles away."

Myers rockets the Ford onto the highway toward the Moore's Lane exit. We screech down the exit ramp, blow through the stop sign, and turn left. Forty seconds later, Kipling's voice comes on the speaker phone. "It's moving again, sir. It's pulled onto Carothers Parkway and is proceeding south at thirty-eight miles per hour."

"What's this guy doing?" Newton growls. "You think he's having car trouble? Maybe he's breaking down."

I pull out my gun from my belt and check the safety. Myers glances over but says nothing. I stare out the window, counting the seconds before I get to Jazz. Three minutes later we turn onto Carothers, a commercial street which fortunately has light traffic; we scream unimpeded toward Cool Springs Boulevard. There are only five vehicles in sight, and one is some kind of delivery van.

"Three hundred yards straight ahead," Kipling says. "But we're getting down to where I can't be sure about the accuracy of the readings."

"Just tell me if we pass the guy," Myers says. We drive up about sixty miles per hour, passing cars. I look up ahead and see a four-door Chevrolet, and although it's not tan, it's about the right year. There's a single figure in the driver's seat. He looks to be about Bridges's size. "Up there," I say. "That Chevy."

Myers floors it, and in a few seconds we're directly behind the car.

My heart is pounding. The figure might be Bridges—it's
impossible to be sure—but I don't see anyone else. *Where is
Jazz? Down in the floorboards? Stuffed in the trunk?* I grip
the pistol. "Pull up, on the right rear quarter panel. Let me
get a look."

Myers creeps up beside the Chevy. I lean forward, peering through the other car's rear window. "*Fuck.* It's not him."

"What?" Myers says. "You sure?"

"Yeah. It's not him."

"The phone just turned west, Agent Myers," the voice
says. "It's moving at fifteen miles an hour."

"Where, dammit?" Myers yells.

I crane my neck around, and I see the delivery van heading west down a side street. "It's the van! Turn around!"

"You sure?" I ask.

"West, right? You said west?"

"That's right," Kipling says. "Moving about fifteen miles
an hour."

Myers whips across oncoming traffic, narrowly missing a
car. "It's the only vehicle that turned," Myers says. "Hang
on, little girl. We're almost there."

We're fifty yards behind the van now, with a white Toyota
between us. My hand is sweating on the gun. "Come up slow,
so he doesn't panic," I say. *Hang on, Jazz. Just a little longer.*

Myers nods. "Next stop sign that comes, I'm giving him a
California stop."

"If she's in the back, she might get hurt," I say. "Isn't
there another way?"

Myers shakes his head. "If I get in front of that thing,
he'll just drive straight through us. Then we've got a chase,
and that's worse." He looks over at me. "Agreed?"

I nod. "OK." *Hold on, sweetie. It's going to be bumpy.*

"Newton and I will handle the driver," Myers says. "You go to the back and get your daughter away from the van." I nod. "Everybody ready?"

"Yeah."

"Hell, yeah," Newton says from the back. A hundred yards later, the little convoy approaches a stop sign. The van's brake lights come on, and all three vehicles begin to slow. "Hang on," Myers says, and he floors the throttle. He snaps around the Toyota, expertly puts his left bumper just behind the van's right rear tire, and steers left. The van spins halfway around on a tight axis, tires squealing. It lurches to a stop, sliding left on all four tires as its wheels lock up. Our car doors open simultaneously as we sprint toward it. I run to the rear door to try to get the passenger compartment open. Myers has the driver's-side door open, and he's got his gun pointed at the driver. He screams, "Don't you fucking move!"

The rear door is locked, and I pound on the door. "Jazz! I'm here, baby! We're gonna get you out!" I run around to the side, where Myers and Newton have the driver on the street, lying on his stomach. Newton reaches down, cuffs him with plastic strips, and kicks him over on his side. Myers drops to a knee and puts his gun to the man's chin. "Where's the girl, you fucking asshole?"

I take a step toward them and stop cold. *It's not him. Jesus, it's not Bridges.* I look back at the van, then back at the man. "What the fuck? Is he inside or something?"

Myers looks up. "This isn't the guy?"

"No. It's not him."

Myers waves his gun toward the van, and Newton and I advance slowly toward the driver's door, weapons raised. I step inside and peer into the back. It's nearly empty; there's nothing more than a handful of packages in a jumble, toppled after the spin. "She's not here. It's just boxes."

Myers looks down at the driver. "Then what the fuck is he doing with Bridges's phone?" The driver, a skinny kid about twenty years old, is trembling, panicked out of his mind. "Jesus," Myers says. "He wet himself."

A wet spot spreads down the driver's leg.

I turn away. "He doesn't know anything," I say. "Dammit!"

Myers reaches down and picks the man up off the street a few inches by his jacket. "Where's the fucking phone?"

"What phone? I don't have any phone. I don't know what you're talking about." The driver breaks into tears. "I didn't do anything!"

Myers stares at him a second, then releases him in disgust. "Shit! What's going on?"

Exhausted and frustrated, I drop to my knees. I suck in some air, trying to get control of myself. I turn my head to the left. "My God."

Myers walks over. "What?"

I point. "That."

Myers walks to the van and drops down to see. "Son of a bitch." He reaches under the bumper of the van and rips off a strip of duct tape. He pulls a cell phone from underneath the van. "The motherfucker set us up."

I see black and cough up something from deep in my throat. I lean forward until I'm on all fours, and I think I might throw up. *I'm trying, Jazz. Hang on.* Myers stands up and lets out a long string of expletives.

"The driver doesn't know anything," Newton says, walking over. "He was on his regular route. Bridges must have waited for him to come by, pushed "send," and taped the phone while the guy was inside a building making a delivery."

Myers nods. "So wherever the truck was fifteen minutes ago, that's where Bridges was."

"Which means he could be twenty miles away by now."

I pull myself to my feet. "You're missing the point."

Myers looks at me. "What?"

"This means Bridges and Jazz probably aren't even in the same location anymore." I look away. "He could have taken all these pictures hours ago, and he's just letting them out as a game. She could already be dead."

The agents stand silently. Myers looks west, toward Franklin. "We're gonna get this guy. I swear to God, we're gonna get him."

Newton and I walk over to the driver of the truck. He's on his back, sniffling. Newton gets him on his feet, and the man stands helplessly, a dark, wet stain covering his left leg. "I'm sorry," I say. "I thought you were the man who kidnapped my daughter."

The man stares back at me. "I didn't do anything. I don't have anybody's phone."

I nod and walk off. "Let's get back," I say, heading toward the car. "Apparently, the bastard isn't done yet."

Myers calls his dispatcher, and when a couple of agents arrive to make sure the driver is OK, we pull back into traffic. A dozen agents and police swarm the area where the delivery van was when the call was placed, but nobody in our car thinks for a moment that Bridges would be stupid enough to hang around.

"You know how much evidence there is linking Bridges to any of these crimes?" I say.

Myers looks over. "How much?"

"None. None to his parole officer. None to Carl. And so far, none to Jazz. Stolen cell phone calls. Digital photographs. None of it physically connects to him."

Myers grips the steering wheel. "Yeah. I know."

"I'm saying that even if we somehow caught him, with the right lawyer, it's not inconceivable he would walk." I stare out the window. "The ultimate irony."

"It ain't over," Myers says. "You got to hang in there as long as there's hope."

Ten minutes later we're back at Sarandokos's subdivision, but when we drive in, there are police at the gate. Myers rolls down his window and shows his ID. "What's going on?"

The cop looks in the car and nods. "A couple of news vans slipped in behind cars when the gates were up," he says. "We got called to control access."

Myers looks at me. "I told you Sarandokos going on TV was gonna make trouble for us," he says, gritting his teeth. "A bunch of reporters is the last thing we need."

We drive down Wentworth Place and park in front of Sarandokos's house. Bec is waiting in the doorway. She finds my eyes, and I shake my head. *I'm sorry, baby.* She looks at me silently a moment, then disappears back into the fortress of her grief. I drag myself up the stairs and go after her. Not that I have any idea what to say. The adrenaline rush pulled me out of my blackness for a moment, but now I'm drowning inside again. I find her in the master bedroom, alone, sitting on the edge of the bed. The room is large—at least twenty by twenty—with a fireplace and sitting room at one end. She looks up when I enter, then stares back down at her hands. It's so quiet I can hear a clock ticking on the nightstand beside her. I walk slowly up to her and sit down on the bed a foot away. "I'm sorry," I say, quietly. "I thought we had him. He's had a long time to plan this out."

"I can't cry anymore," she says, her voice distant. "It's like I'm already dead. Even if we get her back, I won't be the same." In spite of her words, a single tear falls to her hand, and it sits glistening on her beautiful, slender finger. Without looking up, she says, "You'll kill him if you can, won't you, Thomas? If you get the chance?" The clock ticks away seconds. *Five. Ten. Fifteen.*

"Yes," I whisper. "I'll kill him if I can."

"Swear it, Thomas. Swear to me you'll kill him."

"I swear."

She reaches her hand across the space between us and takes my fingers in her own. Her hand is warm and soft, and the feel of it brings a rush of memories flooding back through me. "I don't want him to go to jail, Thomas. I want him to die."

Myers reconnects with Kipling at Sprint, but the waiting is different now. It's different because we know the pictures Bridges sends may be hours old, and because we know that he and Jazz may be separated by miles. Newton's studious expression has grown detached, like he's already preparing himself for defeat; even Myers's slick, professional demeanor has grown edgier. Sarandokos, who stands fifteen feet or so apart in the living room, has finally given up answering the freak phone calls and stares absently out of a window. Every one of us is a man of action at our core; even Sarandokos, with his slicing off of extraneous fat and wife stealing, isn't a man to stand around and watch. And every one of us is being forced to wait on a brilliant psychopath who, unable to cope with his own failed life, has decided to extract his revenge with grand strokes of cruel irony.

At 6:00 p.m., Maria brings in dinner. *The meals mark time,* I think. *Breakfast. Lunch. Dinner. Sooner or later, days will pass.* I catch myself wondering if we'll ever find Jazz, and even—self-revulsion filling me—hoping we don't, if what he's done to her is too despicable. I try to eat but give up and walk into Sarandokos's sunroom. The agents have finished examining it, and in its emptiness it seems almost innocent, as though nothing were different about this horror of a day. Light streams in through a north-facing wall of glass, and the brilliant light reflects off a floor of spotless Mexican tile. Plants grow in hanging pots and stately, over-sized urns. A fountain sends water down a geometric gathering of stones until it gathers a few feet away from me in a clear, spreading pool. Large, orange fish move serenely through the pool, endlessly circling their small environs. I lean back into a flowered, upholstered chair and close my eyes. *I understand Bec leaving me. It's not just the money, although God knows she loved that. It's this—this hermetically sealed life, protected by wealth—that she really wanted. No mess. No criminals climbing into her backyard. No death threats. But my past caught up with her, and she couldn't make her escape.* Exhaustion creeps over me, now plainly impossible to forestall. The fountain sends its soothing song across to me, and the hazy, dimming light from outside bathes the room. I settle into the chair and feel my breathing slow. My eyes get heavy. *Just a minute. I have to check out for just a minute.*

I sleep, and from out of the darkness grows another dream. Rebecca and I are back in Florida, and like last time, Jazz is with us. Jazz is running on the beach in her little bathing suit, excited to feel the warm sand on her feet. She and her mother are tanned dark by the sun, and, like her mother's, Jazz's black hair is long and beautiful.

Nothing bad happens. There is no drowning surf, no dangerous undertow. I sit in a beach chair in the sand, the sun glinting so brightly off the water I have to raise my hand to shield my eyes. We're a family. We're happy, and it's beautiful.

"Thomas."

I breathe deeply, turn my head, and open my eyes. Agent Myers is standing in the doorway. He looks at me, and I know that my enemy is back. "Tell me."

"He's taken it to another level."

"What do you mean?"

"It looks like he's finally ready to end this thing."

CHAPTER TWENTY-FOUR

WHEN I KILLED WILSON OWENS, he died according to the strict precepts of law. Records indicate he requested a meal of spaghetti and meatballs, a cheeseburger, grits, blackeyed peas, and a beer. I have it from the warden that the beer was supplied, even though it was against regulations. Owens was provided with the services of a minister, which he refused. He was then restrained and walked to the Brushy Mountain execution chamber, where, because the prison is soon to be torn down, he most likely became the last person executed there.

That night, I walked in my mind down the hallway with Owens to his death. I watched him stretched in the death chair, and I saw him struggling to escape as the doctor inserted an IV into his forearm. I watched as the plastic bottles containing the lethal mixture of chemicals were carefully checked. I saw—my own heart pounding—as the doctor turned on the fatal drip, sending the drugs that would paralyze Bridges's heart and lungs. In my mind, I watched—

sitting alone in my office, even though it was 11:35 p.m.—a doctor pronounce Wilson Owens dead.

This is the history I share with Wilson Owens, and it is this history that means I understand the dark irony of the photograph that Bridges now sends to my phone. All of us see that my daughter is naked, blindfolded, and strapped to a chair. And all can see that behind her hangs a large white sheet, eliminating any possible clue to her location. Beside her is a portable camping stove, and on the stove is an open-mouthed beaker. But Charles Bridges is sending his message to me, and I instantly comprehend it. "He's making phosphine," I whisper.

Myers snaps his head toward me. "What?"

"Phosphine gas. It's produced by overcooking methamphetamine."

"What about it?"

"It's the same gas used in a death chamber."

Myers stares at the photograph. "Are you saying . . ."

"This is an execution. He's creating his own lethal gas, just like a prison. She'll die like a common criminal." Jazz is faced toward the camera, her face tilted upward, as if she's listening to the darkness in terror. In her protected, little-girl world, the mind of Charles Bridges has not existed. What he is doing is a violation of everything good in the world. It is a stain on the whole earth. "He's using the red phosphorus method of meth production," I say. My voice is cracking, but I push the words out. "He would normally remove the heat after a couple of hours. But he's not going to remove it from the heat this time. He's just going to let it stay there. Once the mixture reaches the proper temperature, the gas will be released." I look away. "Death will come almost instantly."

"How long does the process take?" Myers asks, in a whisper.

"Five to six hours."

Newton looks up. "There's no way that burner has enough fuel to burn that long. It'll run out of fuel."

"It doesn't matter. Burning phosphorous becomes exothermic after a couple of hours. After that, it will generate its own heat until it's completely turned to gas."

"There's no way to know how long ago this picture was taken," Myers says. "It could have just started. It could already be over."

I hear crying, but I can't place it; then I realize it's coming from the speaker phone. Myers hasn't muted the microphone, and Kipling is weeping into her headset. "Take it easy, Kipling," Myers says. "Take it easy."

"I'm sorry, sir. I just thought we would be able to find him somehow."

"You did your best, Kipling. Just stay on the line. We can't give up now."

We sit around the table, bonded by our helplessness. The background behind Jazz—a nondescript white sheet—could be anywhere in the city. There's nowhere to look. There's nothing to do. Newton looks at his watch and quietly says, "It's three o'clock."

Three o'clock. So no matter when this picture was taken, Jazz will be dead by eight. I stand and step away from the table, stumbling on the chair. I fall forward, dropping to a knee. Myers reaches out to help, but I wave him off. "I'm OK," I lie. "I just need to be alone."

Summer has relented for a time, and it's almost brisk in Sarandokos's backyard. The temperature peaked today at about seventy-five, and great smothering clouds of gray sit immobile in the sky. *She won't feel any pain,* I think. *She'll just breathe in one last time, hating the smell of the room she's in, and the terror and nightmare will be over.* I walk out into the yard, looking at the green, manicured lawn. A rock garden has flowers interspersed through it, but they're summer annuals, and their season is ending. I stand outside a long time. My mind doesn't race to think of any last-minute move to save my daughter because I have ceased to believe that such a move exists. Charles Bridges has applied his warped mind to the destruction of my world. Unrestricted by morality or law, fueled by hate, he accomplished his task.

Since every second that passes brings home my daughter's death, I feel myself detaching from time completely. I can't bear to watch a minute or a second. I numb myself. At some point, I find myself sitting in an outdoor chair. I may have been there fifteen minutes. It may have been an hour.

The sun begins to lower past me, and I become aware that the afternoon is soon ending. I rise and look at my watch. It's 6:35. *It's probably over.* I walk back inside the house and go to the table. Myers and Newton are still sitting there, turning the problem over in their minds. But in another hour, even they will have to admit defeat. They will pack up their equipment and get on with their lives. The futile, grisly search for Jasmine's body will be the task of others.

"Hey," Myers says, seeing me come in the room.

Newton rubs his temples. "What I don't get is how we never triangulated the call. I mean, the signal on Thomas's phone was strong. The connection never wavered. There's a ninety-four percent chance of triangulation to within nine hundred feet on any call with this setup, and he called more than once. *Nobody* is that lucky."

Myers pushes back in his seat. "So you've said, ten times in the last hour."

I pull out a chair and fall into it. *Triangulation.* I picture the process in my mind: the signal from Bridges's phone hitting three towers fractions of a second apart, the difference in time equating to only one possible location for the source. *Triangulation.* A thought is pushing through the fog of fatigue, and I can't quite grasp it. *Triangulation. Three towers.* I look at Newton. "You said it takes *three* towers."

He looks at me, exhaustion etched on his face. "Yeah. But everywhere in Nashville is in reach of three." He points at his monitor. "I'm seeing five from where we sit."

"And when this thing works, you have a circumference of nine hundred feet, right?"

"Right."

I look over at Myers. "What if the other phone is *inside* that radius?"

Myers looks up cautiously. "What?"

"It's a nine-hundred-foot range. So if his phone is somewhere inside that radius, it would be impossible to triangulate. His phone would be indistinguishable from your phone."

Myers looks at Newton. "Is that right?"

Newton's eyes are wide as he works through the statement. "I don't know. Hell, it never even occurred to me."

"What about it, Kipling?" Myers barks. "You getting this?"

"Yes, sir," the voice answers. "I need just a—"

"Come on, Kipling! Is Dennehy right on this thing?" There's a long, agonizing pause. "*Talk* to me, Kipling."

"I believe Mr. Dennehy is correct, sir. But to be certain to work, the other phone would have to be very close. Within yards."

"Move your asses!" Myers shouts, coming to his feet. "Get the cops outside searching the area. Every house. Break down a door if you have to. Nine hundred feet; that can't be more than a couple of blocks. Move!"

I hit the front door in a dead run. A cop outside starts toward me to find out what's going on, and I wave him off. "Get everybody in these houses out into the street." The cop gives me a confused look, which Myers settles with a barked command: "Hit the siren, officer. Search every house, door to door. Every room, I don't care what the objection. Start next door and move outward, one door at a time. And get some help over here!"

The officer stares a second, then moves to his car. A moment later, the air is filled with the searing whine of his siren. Myers is pounding on the front door to the left, and a cop is hammering away on the door to the right. I run past him, mentally calculating: *nine hundred feet. The lots are large, so that's a circle of only five or six possibilities.* Cops are spreading out to the houses nearby, but I grind to a halt. *A house for sale, around the corner.* I sprint down the side fence of Sarandokos's house, running alongside the backyard. At the end of Sarandokos's property, I scale a fence and drop down in the property that backs to it. The house I was staring at from the sunroom is before me. I pull the .45 out of my belt without breaking stride. The yard is a little overgrown, and there's no furniture on the large patio. *This is it. There's no one living here.* I jog up to the patio, slowing down to figure out the best way inside. There are heavy wooden blinds on each window, obscuring the interior. *Fuck it. Blow off the lock.* I empty two rounds into the back door lock, and it explodes with impact, the .45 cutting a swath through the metal and wood. The door swings open. I take a step toward it and stop cold. *If it's already over, the room she's in is my death, too.* I shake my head and plunge into the house.

The back door leads into a breakfast room that widens out into an open floor plan. The light is dim, and I can't see very far across the house. I sprint through the kitchen, calling out. "Jazz! Are you in here? It's Daddy!"

No one answers. I sniff the air but smell nothing except the musty air of a closed-up house. *He could have sealed the door with towels. It would make the death chamber more efficient.* I move through the main floor, opening door after door. Finally, I stand in the entry foyer. Steps lead both up and down. "Jazz!" Nothing. I head upward, taking the steps three at a time. *Fuck, there's a lot of rooms.* Door after door opens, each revealing nothing but a cold, empty space. I work my way down a hallway until I reach the last door. I turn the handle, and it doesn't move. *Locked.* I sniff the air; nothing. I look down at the floor; the hall is carpeted, and there's no visible room between the bottom of the door and the floor. I take a set and kick the lock with everything I have. The doorjamb cracks but holds together; I kick again, and the door swings open.

I walk in, turning left and right wildly. "Goddamn it! There's nothing here!" I run to the window to see if there are any police working the street yet. I look down at the street. *The van.*

The steps downstairs are a blur. I lose my feet halfway down, falling the last half. The gun clatters to the ground but doesn't fire. I pick it up—I've twisted my ankle, but I ignore it—and run to the front door. It's locked with twin deadbolts. I step to the side and fire off three bullets into the locks. The knob now hangs uselessly from the door, and I yank open the door. I sprint down the driveway to the panel van. There are no windows in the storage compartment. "Jazz! Can you hear me?" I bang on the side of the van, but there's no response. I get to the back, find the rear door locked, and realize I have one bullet left for the lock. If I use it on the door and Bridges is inside, I have nothing left. I press the barrel against the lock and squeeze the trigger. I pull open the door. Light floods the cargo compartment. Simultaneously, a horrible, acrid smell floods outward, covering me. There, at the far end, is Jazz. She's still alive, thrashing her head back and forth in terror.

"Don't hurt me! Don't hurt me!"

"It's me, baby! It's Daddy!" I leap into the cargo hold, pick up Jazz and her chair in one motion, and pull her out of the van. The chair topples over onto the street, but I don't stop to help her yet; instead, I rush back to the van and slam the door shut.

"Daddy? Is it you, Daddy?"

I crawl over to her and put my arms around her. "It's me, baby. It's Daddy."

"I'm scared, Daddy. I'm so scared." She's coughing, trying to get the horrible smell out of her lungs.

"It's OK, baby. I'm here, now." I pull off the blindfold. Her eyes are red and swollen. "I'm here, baby. I'm here."

She looks at me a second, then bursts into tears. I rip off my shirt and wrap her in it. When she's covered, I hold her gently, letting the sweet, safe air around us saturate her lungs. I hear voices and look up; Myers and a cop are running toward us. I close my eyes. *I found her. Thank God, I found her.*

CHAPTER
TWENTY-FIVE

WE CLING TO EACH OTHER, waiting for the ambulance. Jazz is coughing between great gulps of air. Her little hands are dug into me, her arms straining to hold me closer. I see nothing. I only know I have Jazz, and that she's alive. The ambulance pulls up, and I hear the back door of the Emergency Response Vehicle open. But before the EMT gets his oxygen unloaded, I hear Rebecca screaming Jazz's name. I look up and see her running down the street as hard as she can, her black hair streaming behind her. She bolts past the EMT and collapses beside us. "My baby. Oh God, my baby."

I release Jazz into her mother's arms. She cradles her gently, rocking back and forth. Bec's face is stained with tears. The EMT comes up from behind and puts his hand on her shoulder. Bec looks up, but she can't let go. The EMT kneels down and covers Jazz's face with an oxygen mask. Jazz looks frightened, but I squeeze her hand and nod. She relaxes, and the EMT listens to her heart and lungs, takes her blood pressure, and shines a stream of light into her eyes. He snaps a blood oxygenation sensor onto her right index finger. After a couple of minutes, he looks up. "She's at ninety-seven percent. It's normal."

I lower myself down onto the pavement. "She's OK," I say. "She's OK."

The sky above me is darkened by the shape of Agent Myers, his head haloed by the sun. I look up at him. "Thank you," I say quietly. "For everything."

"There's somebody who wants to talk to you," he says, holding down a phone. I reach up for it and hear Kipling's voice on the other end, sobbing like a baby.

"I'm very happy for you, sir," she says. "It was an honor to serve you."

I hold the phone, feeling my consciousness slip away. "You did good, Kipling. You did good."

Kipling sobs again. "Thank you, sir."

I hand the phone up to Myers. "Keep people away from the van," I say, and I close my eyes.

Two hours later, Newton, Myers, and I walk down the antiseptically clean corridors of St. Thomas Hospital, looking for Jazz's room. Sarandokos, who performs about half of his surgeries at the hospital, uses his clout to get Jazz in a special, secure area with no other patients nearby. When we finally find the room, two policemen stand guard outside the door. About ten feet away, Sarandokos is conferring with a doctor. He sees us coming and walks over. "Physically, she's fine," he says. "There wasn't any kind of—"

"I understand," I say. "Thank God."

He nods. "At least he didn't do that, the bastard." He shakes hands with Myers and Newton. "I want to thank you gentlemen."

"We're just glad she's OK," Myers says.

"We still didn't get the guy," Newton grumbles.

"That ain't over," Myers says. "Sooner or later, he'll slip up." He looks at me. "When he does, we'll be there, waiting for him."

"I'd like to see Jazz," I say. "Is she asleep?"

Sarandokos nods. "I gave her a mild sedative." He pauses. "But she was asking for you earlier."

I turn to Newton and Myers. "I can't thank you guys enough," I say. "You realize that, I hope."

Myers laughs. "I just want to see the girl I spent eighteen hours of my life trying to find. Any objection, Doc?"

Sarandokos nods. "Go ahead, gentlemen. Just keep it down."

The three of us walk into the room. Jazz is in bed, propped up, but her eyes are closed. Bec sits in a chair beside her, her hand on Jazz's arm. Newton and Myers stand a ways apart, looking at my daughter. "She's beautiful," Newton says. "Like an angel."

Myers nods. "It was a good case," he says, shaking my hand. "You really saved our asses."

Bec looks over at them and says, "Thank you so much. More than I can say."

"Thank him," Myers says, pointing to me. "He saved your daughter." He grabs Newton by the shoulder. "Let's go, Newt. I'm starving." They back out of the door, and they're gone.

"Michael says she's OK," I say quietly.

She nods. "They're running some tests on her lungs, but it looks like she got out before any damage was done." She looks up at me. "You got her out, I mean." I walk up beside her, and she takes my hand, physically connecting the three of us; for these few moments, we're a family again. I look down at Jazz; thanks to the sedative, her face is as untroubled as if she were home, in her own bed, and the last day had never happened.

Bec lets go of my hand and stands. "We should let her sleep," she says quietly. I follow her back out into the hall, and she comes in under Sarandokos's arm. "We're going away for a while, Thomas," she says. "Maybe it will help get this memory out of Jasmine's mind."

"Greece," Sarandokos says. "Jasmine's never seen it. I want her to meet my family there." He kisses the top of Bec's head. "We're fine here, Dennehy. You should get home, get some sleep. You look like you're going to fall down where you stand."

I nod. "Yeah."

Bec looks at me a second, then opens her arms and pulls me against her. We hold each other a long, unembarrassed moment, Sarandokos be damned. I feel her mouth press against my ear. "I wish you could have killed him," she whispers. She lets me go and turns back to Sarandokos. Somehow, she's still regal, even after so much. She takes Sarandokos's hand, and they turn and walk back into their lives.

The Ford's v-8 rumbles sweetly down I-65. Jazz is safe. And the moment in her hospital room means that sooner or later, her mother will forgive me for this intrusion into her perfect life. I will not be banished. What I want is home and great chunks of silence. And, when the time is right—days, weeks, or months from now—time with Fiona. I cover the last four or five miles to Clovercroft, pull into my subdivision, and drive down Springhouse Circle to my house. The garage door opens, and I pull the truck inside, home at last. *Jesus. I could sleep for a week.*

I walk into the kitchen and set my keys and the .45 down on the table. "Fiona? We got her. She's gonna be OK." Silence. "Fiona? You here?" I walk into the living room. There's no sign of her. After the crush of activity, the house feels empty and lonely.

I kick off my shoes and walk through the house, unbuttoning my shirt as I go. *Shower. Sleep.* I push open the door to my bedroom and turn on the light.

"Well, Skippy," a voice says. "Welcome home."

CHAPTER TWENTY-SIX

BRIDGES AND FIONA sit at the opposite end of the bedroom. Bridges is beside her, with a knife—*the* knife, the one he used to kill his parole officer and Carl—pressed against her neck. The point is pressing gently against her skin, causing an indentation. She stares at me, her eyes wide. *The gun. It's back on the table, all the way across the house.* I start to move backward, and Bridges presses the knife harder, causing Fiona to gasp out in pain. "Stay where I can see you, Skippy. We've got things to discuss."

I stare at the man who tried to kill my daughter. He's unnerved, edgy. Things haven't gone as planned. He looks like the slightest provocation will send the blade in his hand through Fiona's neck. "What do you want?" I whisper.

"Justice. You made a mistake. You have to pay."

"The gun Hale led us to at the park was moved," I say quietly. "It was a setup."

"That doesn't prove anything!" Bridges screams. Fiona crumples in fear, and he jerks her back upright. "You fucked up! You sent the wrong man to the death chamber!" He puts his face next to Fiona's. "Do you know what pretrial diversion is, my sweet?" He squeezes her arm with his free hand until she winces. "Tell her, Skippy. Tell her how you fucked me over."

"Take it easy, Bridges." I scan the room for anything to use as a weapon, but come up empty.

"Pretrial diversion, my sweet, is when the accused serves whatever time he's done before trial, and once his parole is over, the record is expunged. I asked you for that, didn't I, Skippy?"

"Yes."

He puts his mouth on Fiona's ear. "He denied me. He said in matters like this . . ." He stops and looks up at me. "Tell her what you said, Skippy."

The words are poison in my mouth. "I said no mistakes could be tolerated."

Bridges's face is red with rabid anger. "No mistakes!" he snarls. "Skippy here sent me to Brushy Mountain, where I was traded between gangs like a deck of cards. And every time they bent me over, I always remembered that this was my fate because, according to the great Thomas Dennehy, *no mistakes could be tolerated.*"

I move a step toward him, and Bridges presses the point into Fiona's skin until she cries out in pain. "Don't," I say, pulling up. "This is between us. Let her go."

He smiles. "You like her, Skippy. That means she's . . . what's the legal term? She's *relevant.*"

"I'll do whatever you want, Bridges. Just let her go."

Bridges smiles. "You got that backward, Skippy. It's as long as I have her you'll do what I want. If I let her go, you'll get other plans."

"So what is it, then? What's this revenge you want,

dammit? You've killed Carl, and you've nearly killed my daughter. What is it going to take to satisfy you?"

"I want you to say you were wrong," he snarls, his face turning red. "I want a fucking *apology*!"

Holy shit. He's out of his mind. "That's what this is about?" I say. "You want me to say I'm sorry?"

His eyes turn to slits, and his voice crawls out of his mouth like spreading gravel. "*Say* it."

"I'm sorry, Bridges. You're right. I fucked up. I never should have charged you. And I never should have charged Wilson Owens."

Bridges stares at me a second, then slumps forward, exhaling. The knife moves off Fiona a half inch.

Silently, I move another step toward him; we're now five feet apart. "I gave you what you wanted, Bridges. Now let her go." He seems tired, like whatever energy was driving him has suddenly dissipated. "I'm sorry, Bridges," I say quietly. "You were right. Let her go now." Fiona looks up at me, but I shake my head for her not to move. "Put down the knife, Bridges. Let her go."

Bridges loosens his grip on Fiona's arm, until his fingers are barely touching her. I nod, and she slowly rises, until she's standing beside him.

"I'm sorry, Bridges," I say. "I was wrong."

Bridges looks up at me and nods, his eyes half open. His fingers are still lightly wrapped around her arm. "I don't want to go back to jail," he says, his voice listless. "I don't want to be traded like a deck of cards."

Looking down on him, I can just make out the slits of his eyes. "Let her go, Bridges. Then it's you and me. We'll talk this out."

"Talk," Bridges whispers. "We'll talk it out."

Fiona inches her arm upward, gradually pulling it from his grasp. *It's OK. She's going to get away.* But out of the corner of my eye, I see the handle of the knife slowly turning in his fingers. It's spinning so slowly, it takes me an instant to understand. *He's turning the blade sideways to slip between the ribs. It's how he kills.* "Move!" I yell, pushing Fiona away as hard as I can. She stumbles backward and falls to the floor; I reach for Bridges's wrist, but he's too quick and comes in under my arm. He lunges forward, and I feel an agonizing pain as the blade plunges into my gut. Before I have a chance to react he's on top of me, withdrawing the blade for the finishing blow. He raises it to my chest, and we lock into an embrace, with the knife point a few inches away from my shirt. Fiona is getting to her feet, and I yell to her. "Get the gun! It's by the door!"

She stares at me a second, then runs to the doorway. She comes back around with the gun, holding it uncertainly. I feel myself weakening; Bridges is grinning at me, his foul breath in my face. I'm bleeding heavily, and in another few moments, I won't be strong enough to resist. Fiona drops the gun on the floor. "Shoot him!" I yell. "For God's sake, shoot him!"

"No!" Fiona hurls herself onto Bridges, wrenching back his arm. She locks onto his wrist with both hands, trying to twist the knife free. Bridges screams out in pain but deftly moves so that he's facing Fiona. She still has control of the arm with the knife, but Bridges is now free to pound on her with his other fist mercilessly.

I rush to my feet, but dizziness is taking me over. *Too weak to fight him. Get the gun.* I stumble toward the pistol, which is lying on the floor about eight feet away.

Bridges is kicking Fiona and giving her sharp blows to her body. She's hanging on, but she won't be able to take that kind of attack indefinitely.

I crawl to the gun, get to a knee, and laboriously make it to my feet. Mustering my strength, I scream, "Let her go, Bridges!"

The room falls silent as Bridges turns his head and sees me.

I know I won't have long before I lose consciousness; I'm seeing double, and my hearing is getting tinny. "Let her go, Bridges. I swear to God, I'll kill you."

Bridges watches me, calculating his situation.

A wave of dizziness comes over me, and I put out a hand to steady myself. *It's now or never.* I raise the gun, trying to fix Bridges in my vision.

"No!" Fiona yells. She makes a last attempt to get the knife free, but Bridges is slowly spinning her back to me to use her as a shield. Suddenly, he cries out in anger and wrenches free his arm. She steps back on her heel, and there's a moment of daylight between them. He brings the blade down to thrust it forward.

I squeeze the trigger. I'm weak enough now that I don't know what I hit, and the recoil nearly rips the gun out of my hand. I see Bridges look over in confusion, then drop to a knee. *I hit him. Dear God, I hit him.* Fiona pulls away in horror; blood is seeping through Bridges's shirt in waves. With my last strength, I stumble toward him and put my foot in his shoulder, crushing him backward and away from her. The knife clatters away as Bridges falls onto his back; with his body's impact on the floor, blood spurts from his mouth. I stand over him, the gun pointed at his chest. I can't stand very well; I come down to one knee, my finger an eighth of an inch from squeezing off the finishing round. I know I can end him with the slightest movement of my finger.

Bridges looks up at me, blood seeping into his teeth. His eyes are wide with fear and hate. He reaches up a trembling hand, grips the barrel of the pistol, and pulls it down to his heart. The room is getting dark; another wave of dizziness crashes over me. "You're under arrest," I whisper, but the words seem fuzzy, distant. I feel one of Bridges's fingers trace up along my hand. Before I realize what he's doing, he presses my index finger backwards.

The bullet rips through his chest, separating flesh from bone. The force lifts his body off the floor several inches, then flops him back down like a rag doll. I fall to the floor beside him, my shirt covered with his blood. I close my eyes and fall into blackness.

CHAPTER TWENTY-SEVEN

THE SCAR, SARANDOKOS ASSURES ME, is something he can make nearly invisible. He says he can use inside sutures to bring the fresh skin together in a thin line, and he's willing to do this for me gratis. He says I should think about how I'll look with my shirt off, like at a swimming pool. He believes that kind of thing is pretty much life and death, especially for single guys like me. I turn him down politely. I have nothing against an exterior scar generally, and this one is only an inch and a half long. It's the interior scars that concern me, both physical and otherwise.

It's two weeks before I can bend over without a sharp pang shooting through my side, and two more before I can put my weight into anything. But I'm lucky in that what Bridges did to me was reparable. His blade nicked my splenic vein, but a piece of synthetic fiber patched it up, good as new. I was unconscious for the irony when my life was saved by a quick-thinking EMT—a man with the same occupation as the one who tried to kill me—who recognized my internal bleeding and pumped fluid into me with three IVs, but I appreciated it after the fact.

Meanwhile, I have spent quiet weeks healing. September has almost passed, and October is preparing to land gracefully in the Cumberland Valley with orange, yellow, and gold on its wings. The poplar and birch trees in my backyard have turned, and the rains have come back at last. The evenings have cooled into jacket weather, and I take long walks.

Fiona has taken a small apartment in west Nashville, near Tennessee Village. She ministers now on her own, because the Tennessee Synod of the Presbyterian Church in America finally had enough of her. In the end, it wasn't her stand on Moses Bol that caused her to be cast out. It was the discovery that having already turned most of the church's failing assets into food and shelter for the city's poorest citizens, there was no longer enough left to pay the church's many creditors. The slow-moving gears of bankruptcy law finally caught up with her, and the Synod sent a representative to try to salvage what was left. At Fiona's last service she preached, unbowed and unrepentant, for nearly an hour. Eleven people attended.

Sarandokos made good on his promise to take his family to Greece, and after more than a month, they will return in another week. In the meantime, I drive to Fiona's small apartment a few nights a week, usually to find it filled with Kurds or Laotians or, as ever, her beloved lost boys. When I see the light in her eyes with them, I know she doesn't need any official permission from a church to know what her life is about.

It's early on the morning of September 29 that the doorbell rings and I see a young woman standing in the rain outside the house. The woman is a short-haired brunette. She's not wearing the short-shorts and bra-less T-shirt she did the first time I saw her, when she answered the door at Jason Hodges's house. Now she's wrapped up in a dark, plastic raincoat, her bare legs sticking out below. The soft tissues around her left eye are puffy and purple, the aftereffects of what looks like a serious shot to the face by a fist. There's another bruise on her left jaw, and her upper lip is swollen.

I push open the glass storm door; she steps inside and stands in the entryway. She peels off the raincoat, revealing a short, garish nightgown of pink Lycra. Both her arms are covered in dark bruises. The thigh of her right leg has a welt on it, like it's been struck with a belt. "J and me had a fight," she says. Water drips off her onto the floor.

"Stay here. I'll get you something to put on." I go to the bedroom and pull out a pair of gray sweatpants and matching sweatshirt. She stands waiting in the entryway, shivering a little. I point to one of the two back bedrooms. "You can change in there. Do you drink coffee?"

"Um hmm."

"Cream and sugar?"

"Sugar. Lots."

I go to make coffee. By the time I come back, she's in my clothes, standing in the living room, looking around. "This is nice," she says.

I give her the coffee, and she pulls out four packets of sugar from my hand. She tears off the tops with her teeth and pours them into the coffee. I hand her a bottle of aspirin. "You look like you could use a couple of these." She drops five tablets out of the bottle and washes them down in a gulp.

"Damn, that's hot," she says. "Thanks."

"What are you doing here?"

"I snuck out early. J's still asleep. I didn't put on clothes or nothing. I just went for the door in a run. I called my girl-friend. She dropped me off."

"Jason Hodges did this to you?"

"J can be mean. But he went off this time real bad."

"What happened?"

"He caught me with another man." She pauses. "Not a customer." She sits down on the sofa. "J's psycho. He's got a real sweet side to him, but when he goes off, you got to watch it. He went too far this time, though. I thought he was gonna kill me." She looks up at me. "What I'm sayin' is that I can't go back there."

"Why did you come here?"

"I seen you that day with J on the porch. That's the only time I seen him back down. He hit me after you left, just to make himself feel better."

"I'm sorry."

She shrugs. "Some a that, it's the business. But I decided right then, if J got outta control on me, I'd come to you."

"I'll call social services for you. They can get you in a halfway house."

She shakes her head. "I ain't goin' to no halfway house. Anyway, it's the first place J'll look." She glances around the living room. "I could stay here," she says, her voice low. "With you."

"We'll find you something. But I can help you with Jason if you're willing to testify he beat you."

"And six months later, he gets out and kills me. No, thanks."

"You have to make a stand for yourself sooner or later, Tiffany."

She looks up, surprised. "You remember my name."

"I'm good with names."

She looks down. "That's nice." She sips the coffee. "Of course," she says quietly, "if he went away for fifteen years or so, that'd be different."

"I can't get him fifteen years for assault and battery, Tiffany."

"How much for murder?"

"Excuse me?"

She looks at me sweetly. "J killed Tamra Hartlett. I can prove it."

Four hours later, Tiffany Murphy, aka Tiffany Amber, aka Amber Murphy, sits opposite me at a large, metal table in the New Justice Building. I had Fiona pick her up a modest dress at T. J. Maxx and some matching flats, paying for them out of my own pocket. She had a shower, and she put makeup on her bruises, but she still looks like hell. With us at the table are two senior homicide detectives. A legal transcriptionist sits separately, her hands folded demurely in her lap.

"Can I get a Coke or something?" Tiffany asks. "My mouth's real dry." I nod, and one of the detectives slips out. He comes back with a can, which she pops open and downs a quarter of in a gulp. "I can't smoke in here, right?"

"No."

"Not that I have any cigarettes." She looks at the detectives. "You got any cigarettes, baby?" One of the detectives pulls out a pack and hands it to her. "Thanks," she says, palming the pack. "You all are real sweet."

"So," the detective says. "You ready to get started?"

"Umm hmm."

She's sworn in and answers questions in a detached voice, as though violence has been a part of her life since before she can remember, which, I have no doubt, is true. She has lost her capacity to be shocked by human behavior, sexual or otherwise. "J killed Tamra," she begins. There's no particular inflection in the statement. She might have been talking about the weather. "He said he'd do the same with me if I ever crossed him."

"Did he tell you how it happened?" the detective asks.

"Um humm. He caught Moses and her together that night." She shrugs. "Moses hadn't paid. Tamra liked Moses."

"Liked him?"

Her eyes darken. "She said he was special. There was somethin' about him. I ain't sayin' she loved him. But maybe she did. Anyway, he was crazy about her."

"So they had a relationship."

"Um hmm. There wasn't no way she could admit that anywhere around the Nation. But she took to him real good."

"But they were arguing before she died."

She nods. "He was against what she was doin'. He didn't like to see her workin' like that. He said it was a shame to her." She looks away. "Which it was, I guess."

"So Jason was telling the truth when he said Bol was angry because Bol didn't want to share her," I say.

She shrugs. "That's J's way to put it. But J didn't give a shit about Tamra, one way or the other. He sure as hell hated Moses, though."

"Because?" I ask.

"Because Moses finally talked Tamra into quitting the business. She told J, and he blew a fuse."

"What happened?"

She shakes her head. "Tamra was real scared. She called Moses that night. Said she was leavin' J for good. Moses was real happy. He came right over. They was gonna make some plans. But J watches out for what's his. He busted in on them, found them together. He told me exactly how he did it. He knocked out Bol." She touches her head, right where we found the bruise on Bol. "Tamra was in the bathroom, takin' a bath. They'd been . . . you know, *intimate*."

"I understand."

"J had a key to Tamra's place. He came in, busted up Bol, and went after Tamra. She locked the bathroom door, but J broke it down. He killed her with the pedestal. Dropped her right back down into the bathtub. Then he fixed things to look like Moses did it."

I sit back, fitting together the details. *The phone call. The sexual evidence. No forced entry to the apartment. The broken-down door to the bathroom. The bruise on Bol's head. It was all there.* "Why didn't he kill Bol?"

"Because he needed him to take the rap for Tamra. He knew the cops always look at the boyfriend first on that kind of thing."

I nod. "Why didn't Bol tell the police what happened?"

"J got to him first. J said he and his crew would pick off them lost boys one by one if Moses told. That's why he fucked up that friend of Bol's the day before the trial. J wanted to make sure Moses knew he was dead serious."

I glance at the detectives. "The timeline's correct. Bol confessed the next morning." *So Bol went to prison to protect the others. The* Benywal *to the end.*

Tiffany nods. "J got a real mean streak. He don't like people to mess with what's his." She sits still, her expression hard. "I tried to leave a couple a times, myself. But he made me pay." She looks up at me. "So you all gonna get him now, right? I mean, he can't do nothin' to me anymore?"

The detective looks at me. "Gentlemen, I believe it's time to swear out a warrant for the arrest of Jason Hodges."

Tiffany smiles and relaxes back into her chair. "Good," she says quietly. "That's real good."

I shake the detective's hand, but my thoughts are already with Fiona. *Moses Bol is coming home.*

CHAPTER TWENTY-EIGHT

THE THIRTY-SIX-FOOT BOAT cuts a clear path through the water, the frothy wake trailing off behind it like twin, billowing clouds. The twin diesels thrum away belowdecks, pushing the vessel through the brine with ease. The boat is used but clean, maintained by a conscientious captain who moved up to a bigger vessel. It's more than I can afford, but for the time being, my credit is good. I see a marker ahead and sight it with binoculars. *R39. That's the one. The snook are supposed to run around here this time of day, at least according to the guy who sold me this boat.* I ease back the throttles, and the boat gently settles down off plane, lowering itself down into the water like a body onto an air-filled mattress. There's a gentle bobbing, and she comes to rest, her bow pointed slightly to the east. I shut down the motors and stand in the small pilothouse, a smile on my face. I pull a rod and bait it up with a one-and-a-half-inch lure, a slippery, silver thing with wicked hooks in three places. I walk out to the back of the boat and hop up onto the fishing chair.

The water is azure, clear as glass. It laps against the side of the boat, gentle and peaceful. The sky above Key Largo rises blue from the horizon, dotted with pale, high clouds. There's a breeze, warm and inviting, like a caress. I lift the rod and flick it back and forth, getting the feel of its heft. I tilt up my face into the sun, feeling its cleansing heat. I whip the rod hard, releasing the line into a long, sweet arc across the water. The lure plops into the ocean thirty yards away.

I look behind me, at the empty chair beside the helm. I've imagined her there, many times, over the last few days. Her hair is tied back, the ponytail falling between her tanned shoulder blades. She's wearing shorts, a bikini top, and the little circlets of color on her wrist that she never takes off. But there are no refugees here to help, no causes to give a life to, except to watch the weather and to find the rhythm of how the fish run. In the end, only one of us knew who he or she was, and it wasn't me. But I'm happy, somehow secure that I am finding myself at last. I call her sometimes, and we have good talks. She's taken a job with the Nashville Peace and Justice Association, and she sounds excited about her work. I tell her about the snook, and about how my first paying customer, who brought home a nice-size tarpon six miles off the coast of Key Largo, tipped me a hundred bucks. She gets a week off for Christmas since the government agencies she deals with pretty much shut down then. I tell her it's warm down here that time of year, and she says that's definitely something to think about. If she comes, I'll have to juggle it with time with Jazz, who comes first.

I fish for a while, but the snook are elusive this day, refusing the temptations of my bait. It doesn't matter. I'm learning, discovering a new life. I don't know how long it will last. Maybe a year, maybe ten. The boat shifts with the wind, gently turning with the tide. I put away my tackle and fire back up the sweet-running diesels. I push the throttles forward, steering the boat until the stern faces west and the sun glints off the boat's sleek bustle, illuminating her name: *Becker's Way.*

AUTHOR'S NOTE

THE DOWNTOWN PRESBYTERIAN CHURCH in Nashville is architecturally largely as described. Its mysterious and extraordinary Egyptian revival sanctuary can be seen at http://www.dpchurch.com/dpctour.htm. As stated in the book, it served as a Union hospital during the Civil War (designated Hospital 8). Today, its small but ardent congregation stands steadfast with the poor and oppressed of Nashville.

The Nation, where much of the book occurs, is based on the west Nashville neighborhood known to locals as the Nations. It borders Tennessee Village, a large complex which is home to many refugees from around the world. The stories that occur inside these locations would fill many books.

The pub Seanachie's has long been closed, but it has been lovingly reopened for the purposes of this book.

((((Listen to))))

🏛 HarperAudio

REED ARVIN

"Arvin writes smart and exciting legal thrillers as well as anyone now working." —*Chicago Tribune*

Blood of Angels
Read by Michael Tucker
Abridged CD 0-06-083148-0
6 Hours/5 CD
$16.95/$22.95 Can.

"An exceptionally clever mystery. Anyone with a taste for sultry, devious, adrenaline-boosting suspense stories may want to cancel a few appointments before opening this one."
—Janet Maslin, *New York Times*

"Breathlessly entertaining…as irresistible as a call from the grave for revenge." —*Kirkus Reviews*

The Last Goodbye
Read by Dylan Baker
Cassette 0-06-059053-X
6 Hours/4 Cassettes
$25.95/$39.95 Can.

Available wherever books are sold or please call 1-800-331-3761 to order.

www.reedarvin.com

🏛 **HarperAudio**
An Imprint of HarperCollinsPublishers
www.harperaudio.com

ALSO AVAILABLE
Harper
LARGE
PRINT
Edition

Look for audiobooks by **Reed Arvin** in digital downloadable versions available wherever downloadable audio is sold.

RAA 0606